whispers from the cotton tree root

caribbean fabulist fiction

Edited by
NALO HOPKINSON

Invisible Cities Press
Montpelier, Vermont

Invisible Cities Press
50 State Street
Montpelier, VT 05602
www.invisiblecitiespress.com

Library of Congress Cataloging-in-Publication Data

Whispers from the cotton tree root : Caribbean
fabulist fiction / edited by Nalo Hopkinson.
p.   cm.
ISBN 0-9679683-1-3 cloth (alk. paper)
ISBN 0-9679683-2-1 paperback (alk. paper)
Caribbean fiction (English) 2. Caribbean
Area—Fiction. 3. Supernatural—Fiction.
I. Hopkinson, Nalo.

PR9205.8 .W47 2000
813'.01089729—dc21   00-057250

PRINTED IN THE UNITED STATES OF AMERICA

Book Design by Tim Jones
for Sterling Hill Productions

FIRST EDITION

Contents

BLOOD THICKER MORE THAN WATER

THE BROAD DUTTY WATER

CRICK CRACK

DOWN INSIDE THE CHUTE

DREAM

Introduction

I LOOK OVER THE STORIES I've chosen for this anthology and realize that although all twenty of the writers are of Caribbean background, most of them currently live outside the Caribbean. That's no surprise from a region where many have found it necessary to leave in order to pursue their goals.

The bulk of the stories are from people from Jamaica, Trinidad, and Guyana. I guess that's to be expected, too. Those are the countries with whose writers I'm most familiar; a different anthologist would have produced a different collection. I hope there will be more anthologies of this type, bringing together works of these and other writers in other combinations.

The cotton tree, or silk cotton tree, is also called the *ceiba;* it's a tall tree with thick roots around which pits and caves form. Spirits are supposed to live in these places, and people will be cautioned to avoid the roots of the ceiba tree. The invitation that I sent out soliciting stories for *Whispers from the Cotton Tree Root: Caribbean Fabulist Fiction* read:

> Bring out your duppie and jumbie tales; skin-folk flights of
> fancy; rapsofuturist fables; your most dread of dread talks.
> *Whispers from the Cotton Tree Root: Caribbean Fabulist Fiction*
> is to be an anthology of fantastical fiction in Caribbean tra-
> ditions. Seeking fiction written from within a Caribbean or
> Caribbean diasporic context. Fabulist, unreal, or speculative
> elements such as magic realism, fantasy, folklore, fable, hor-
> ror, or science fiction must be an integral part of the story.

Very quickly the stories started to show up in my mailbox, and the
process of mutual education began. I am the daughter of a Caribbean
writer; I grew up in a milieu of Caribbean writers and writing. I bring
that sensibility to my own work, but I write within a particularly
northern tradition of speculative and fantastical fiction. There, plot
and content are equally important and the speculative or fantastical
elements of a story must be "real": Duppies and jumbies must exist
outside the imaginations of the characters; any scientific extrapolation
should seem convincingly based in the possible. It's an approach
designed to ease or force the suspension of disbelief, to block flight
back into the familiar world, to shake up the reader into thinking in
new tracks.

But for this anthology I was hearing from experienced writers who
were telling me they really didn't understand what I was looking for,
but here's a story, hope it suits. I was getting stories that were dreams
(a no-no in the science fiction world) and stories that seemed to be
poems and surreal stories that seemed to have nothing fantastical
about them at all, though they were highly improbable.

The thing is, many of those pieces did capture some of the feel I
wanted. I had to come up with the words to explain why. Finally I came
to the conclusion that *fabulist* was exactly the right word to describe
the anthology. The stories invoke a sense of fable. Sometimes they are
fantastical, sometimes absurd, satirical, magical, or allegorical. Northern science fiction and fantasy come out of a rational and skeptical
approach to the world: That which cannot be explained must be

proven to exist, either through scientific method or independent corroboration. But the Caribbean, much like the rest of the world, tends to have a different worldview: The irrational, the inexplicable, and the mysterious exist side by each with the daily events of life. Questioning the irrational overmuch is unlikely to yield a rational answer, and may prove dangerous. Best instead to find ways to incorporate both the logical and the illogical into one's approach to the world, because you never know when life will just drop you down in that hole, into a ceiba space where none of the rules you know operate. Read work from that tradition and you might expect plot to be less important than effect, language to be privileged over exact meaning, and story to be one of the strongest flavors in the mix.

I realized that in compiling this anthology I was essentially trying to marry two traditions of writing that have different priorities and protocols. It's been difficult to find stories that express what I'm looking for, but eventually I did gather a body of work that I think conveys, from a Caribbean worldview, that disorienting sense of when events take you to a place that dips into archetype and otherworldliness.

So here's an uncharted plot, a knotty twisting of sense and un-sense that hopefully will not conform to anyone's expectations. I believe it's the first time an anthology of Caribbean literature has sought to use expressions of the fantastical as its central theme. Read it in the spirit of breaking the rules.

'membah

ONE THREAD OF CARIBBEAN history is of peoples who were forced to chop away their native languages, customs, and beliefs in an attempt to make them into ciphers without memory. But language, custom, and belief are growing things. Chop them up and, like yams, they just sprout whole new plants. To re-member is to reassemble the limbs of a story, to make it whole again. A sense of history gives these next few stories limbs—branches with which to grasp at and weave centuries' worth of dis-membered deeds.

Marcia Douglas's novel Madam Fate *tells the mystical story of Bella, a kin-owl, a shape-shifter. Sometimes the kin-folk are called skin-folk, because they remove their skins to take on their other shape. Under her skin Bella may be strange, or may be kin. What follows is an excerpt from* Madam Fate.

What the Periwinkle Remember

MARCIA DOUGLAS

In the Beginning: Xaymaca—Jamaica

In THE BEGINNING, there was laughter. God was lying down at the bottom of the sea, taking an afternoon nap—her plaits set in motion by the rhythm of warm water, seaweed brushing against her skin. She was minding her own business as God often does; her arms circled her stomach and she dreamed of giving birth to a child who would be born laughing. In this dream, the baby gasped for air and then burst into laughter so loud and so long that the midwife had to slap its little bottom to make it stop. The baby stopped for a while, then took one look at the midwife and began laughing again. Its laughter was so contagious that soon everyone was doubling over and wiping tears from their eyes.

This is a story my Mama, Anna, used to tell. Mama said a long time ago, before this island even had a name, before it was called Jamaica, and even before it was called Xaymaca, God used to take a nap in the warm waters here.

One day God was in the middle of this favorite dream; she had a little smile on her face as fish nibbled at her navel when suddenly she was interrupted by a vision of the future. Now everyone knows that evil travels in straight lines, so when God saw the future billowing toward her straight as a fleet of ships, she became afraid because she saw that these ships were filled with sorrow. On board there was screaming and moaning, and the sea was thick with blood; God saw and heard it all and anger burned red hot in her womb; she howled and rumbled under the sea but all the oceans put together could not contain her wrath. She opened her mouth and the ocean floor buckled, then shutting her eyes tight, she folded over and heaved. God heaved and heaved, the ocean floor trembled, and she spewed out fire—orange-yellow flames and hot lava everywhere. This, said my Mama, is the story of how our archipelago was born.

My Mama said that suddenly in the middle of all this, God, as if remembering a secret, stopped. She squinted her eyes and looked way past the future billowing toward her, past the sea of blood and its red horizon, to dark figures rising in the distance, walking on the water. What God saw was her daughter and her daughter's daughters, and she threw back her head and laughed right out loud. God's laughter spun around and around; it reverberated over the earth, and under the waters that covered the earth. It spiraled up and down and back again. God laughed such a belly laugh so loud and so long that the laughter seeped into the hot lava, effervescing and churning, cooling to form the land under our feet.

Centuries have passed, ships have come and gone, and to this day, if you put your head to the ground, you can still hear God's laughter. Lizards hear this laughter, and so do dragonflies and butterflies, and my Mama said all the women on this island are connected by the laughter like beads on a string; our laughter makes us unstoppable. Mama gave me two bits of advice. She said: Remember your laughter, and when you eat guava, don't swallow the seeds because they might take root and grow in you. . . .

In the beginning there was laughter, but to hear a woman's laughter one must first hear her sorrow. . . .

Her sorrow/my sorrow, my poison arrow, my heart-pain, my troubled thing, how can I tell it? Let's call me Bella. I am also the woman people call kin-owl, that woman who lives in her flesh by day, then takes off her skin, living in spirit by night. A kin-owl must always keep her true identity secret; she must never reveal who she really is. She could be the woman who sells you the morning paper, or the one you see waiting at the bus stop for a ride into town; she could be your neighbor or your best friend, your very flesh and blood—your mother or sister or firstborn—but you would never know. Let's call me Bella. People fear a woman who shifts shape (how many people would feel comfortable knowing that their neighbor sheds her skin at night?), so a woman like me keeps her secret to protect others. Nevertheless, secrets are difficult to bear—there are moments when the soul longs for exposure. There are words which beg to be expelled from the chest. This is my challenge: how to tell my story while keeping my identity secret. I am young and I am old; I am flesh and I am spirit, the beginning and the never-ending. In the beginning there was laughter but inside the laughter was so much sorrow. Sorrow has bloated and filled me up. My insides are puffy, my tummy swollen like a watermelon. This is an angry sorrow. A sorrow that wants to be free, that demands to be told. But to whom can I tell it?

There is a woman, Ida, whom the spirits love. She once heard God laugh, then men in white jackets came and locked her in a mental institution. Ida is a good listener. Sometimes at night she hears my moaning but even she doesn't know who I really am. She sits out in the asylum sun all day talking to the washerwomen or the food service workers or the young volunteers or the other patients—teaching them to listen, she says.

Perhaps she will teach me to lean closer to the ground, to grow my ears long and remember God's laughter.

IDA

Excerpt from *The Long-Ears Woman's Book of Herbs*

Periwinkle *(Catharanthus roseus)*

Common Names: Old Maid, Ram Goat Roses, Brown
Man's Fancy

Other Names: 'Winkles, Brown Girl's Forget-me-not.
Drunk as a tea, this flowering plant is an excellent
cure for diarrhea, toothache, nerves, and other ailments. When admired as a garden flower, its blossoms become long-lasting, long-remembering,
true-true friends.

ONE

PEOPLE ASK WHY I walk with a limp. Well, from when my eyes was at my knee, somehow I always felt lopside. I was born with nine fingers, you know, the little finger on my right hand missing, and in all the picture them, my left nostril always seem little higher than the other one, like the raise eyebrow on that side lifting it up. Nowadays I carry my rain pan in my right arm and the weight on that side seem to even things out a bit. Then at times I hold my head a certain kinda way just so the place a little tilt and everything seem alright. This, mind you, make some people wonder whether the lopside is really something wrong with my head, but let me leave that for them to figure out. . . . Young Miss? Miss-Hanging-the-Towels, you say you just felt rain?

There is something about rain that soothes me—the sound pitter pat, pat-pat, over and over. Pitter pat, pat-pat. Mmm. This whole rain business is a funny funny thing. You know, there's a woman here in the Garden, Mimi, who they say been drive crazy by the sound of water dripping in her head. One drop, plop, dripping from way up the top of her skull and then all the way down to some deep deep water hole behind her tongue. Sake of this everlasting dripping, she can't even hardly speak, her tongue tie, every time the water make plop, she have to gasp and catch her breath, "Hup." So she always sound like she have hiccups. Lord, you should hear her. She write on a piece of brown paper bag, telling me say the dripping behind her tongue remind her of drought—like when the water barrel run low, and the grass all quail up, and all you can get outta the stand-pipe is just a little drip drip drip, and all you can get outta the green water coconut after it done share around for everybody is just enough to barely wet your tongue. What a thing, eh? Every mawga dog and black puss have her own story, I tell you. So listen to this, I think I can help her—I know how to make it rain, you know.

The other thing I enjoy is the whisper in seashell and dry coconut husk. If you put these to your ear, you hear whoosh, whoosh,

whoosh, like someone calling real soft from way back, or way forward. Whoosh, whoosh, whoosh. I am a listener, you know. I listen to rain; I listen to voices calling and I listen to all these animals and plants you see running around here. But let me tell you this, in all my listening (and I've done quite a bit), the voice that grab my heart-ears the most is the one I found waiting for me right inside of a dry calabash. Put that husk to your ear, and ahh, you will hear some things that will bring you to repentance. I keep my calabash pot in a small basket that I always carry around with me; and let me tell you, this calabash is special-special. I use a penknife to cut out the sides with a lizard smiling from around rocks and leaves and things. People say lizards bring bad luck, but that's only because they fraid that the news the lizard brings might not be what they want hear. I keep the other half of the same calabash tuck up in my brassiere; for one thing it's safe there, close to my heart, and convenient, and for another, I only have one breast and so the half-a-calabash in my bra make me look like I have two. Whoosh, whoosh, whoosh—songs of the forgotten dead, that's what that sound is. But you have to be careful who you tell these things to, sister-chile, because when you is a listener, and you understand these voice, and talk about them, people think you mad, and they put you away in places just like this. You try to explain to them what you hear, but of course they just take you for a fool because they don't really listen you. You know what I mean? Which remind me of another thing: By the time I finish having my say with you (yes, you over there, yes, you with the pink apron), you will know how to listen, and you will be a long-ears woman, just like me. Oh yes, I'll see to it.

That's the problem with young people nowadays, you know, they don't take the time to listen. Just be still. Take your mind in your two hands, and steal away. Listen for the place far-far behind the clanking pots them in the kitchen. Drink a little ceracee tea. Wait for the voices them. Trust me, as God be my judge, they are there. I hear them myself. Shhh. Hush, chile.

I WAS BORN during rainy time. The rain was just carrying on like mad that night, batta-batta, batta-batta, all over the little zinc roof. I could hear it clear clear, beating on the breadfruit tree leaf them, beating gainst the window them, beating on the concrete floor on the verandah, then beating gainst the front door, and I knew it was time for me to just come on out and be born. I was born right inna Mother Duncan two big ole hand. There was a presence in the room, something trying to stop me from breathing—I feel it like a big ole paw trying to crush my lungs, but because I was determine to live and live and live, I open my mouth and I holler with all my might. My mother, she smile like a please puss then, and the rain hold off to a drizzle, and for a while all was peace in the little room till Mother Duncan, with her long trumpet-mouth, announce, "Lord God-a-mighty, the chile only have nine fingers!" This was around 1920 (give or take a little) and I don't know how it is now, but back then, a child with nine fingers was not a good sign. Mother Duncan bathe me in a little lukewarm water, take my navel string, wrap it up in a white cloth, and leave it for my mother to bury under the poinciana tree in the yard. She did want to leave the house quick-quick, a nine-finger child was a bad omen, and she had better be gone. The rain was still falling soft when she leave; I hear the front door swing, bam, and she disappear in the rain drops.

My mother, Selma, did young and feeble, and she sick for seven days; she feed me her little thin milk, but she whoop and she cough, and she whoop and she cough and wasn't able to even step foot outside. Papa help much as he could. He was blind as a rat-bat from birth, you know, but the two of them make a living weaving straw and carving wood spoon for Mama to sell in the market with her sweetie and seasoning and thing. That night, he hobble around trying to draw little ginger tea, changing the diapers Mama make from flour bag, singing a little sing song, and all the while it rain and rain and Mama whoop and cough.

Meanwhile, the navel string stay same place on the windowsill where Mother Duncan leave it, till when it begin to rot and stink, Papa find it and plant it best as he could, the poor soul, under a calabash tree.

Now everybody know that a gourdie tree draw spirit, so when word get around the district that Miss Selma nine-finger baby navel string was bury (*mis*bury, mind you) under a duppie tree, Lord have mercy, tongues start to fly from church pew to chamber pot. Mama and Papa, God bless their souls, try to make light of it, but the story follow me all the way to school, the children laughing after me, mocking me and calling me "nine-finger duppie." School-pickney and wickedness—what a tribulation!

(Speaking of which, this nurse that they have walking around the ward is up to no good, I tell you. Look at her over there by the medicine tray with her two-horn white hat, one end pointing west, the other pointing east. A divided soul, that's what she is. Every time I hear her white-polish shoes squeaking on the concrete, I have to turn my head and listen to something else, the everlasting squeak squeak, enough to put my teeth on edge. You try to tell Nurse Watson the truth of things but she can't hear you—her ears all stop up with only God-knows-what. Plenty times I try to make her understand that I am not mad and I am not fool, but she just look through me like I'm not even here. I make it as far as fifth-book, you know. You see me here in this Garden, but I seen things and been places she don't even know how to dream bout, and when I ready I can speak hoity-toity just like her. These people learn a few fancy words and learn how to speak up in their nose, and straight away they believe they have it over you, but they can't even tell head from tail.)

But, as I was saying, as the nine-finger duppie, it was easy for me to just keep quiet in a corner hoping they would forget me. You know what I mean? And the funny thing is, it was round about that time that I start to listen, and I start to hear things. Now across the hill from where we were living was what they used to call a rolling calf race-course. People used to walk and make a wide circle around this spot so as to avoid meeting up with the rolling calf, and sometime in the dead o' night you could hear his chain dragging, dragging, dragging behind him all restless like on the ground. I did never see or hear the rolling calf myself, but people say he was the duppie of a bloodthirsty murderer, so wicked that not even a good funeral with all the proper sweeping and sprinkling and thing could hold him in the ground. I was determine to hear this rolling calf for myself and use to lay wake at night, my head under the covers, but months pass and I never even as much as hear cow-hoof, so I put it away back of my mind.

One night it was raining, real soft-like on the zinc, pat, and it stop, then pat, and it stop again, then pat, and on like that. It was the kinda rain that sound as if it waiting for an answer, almost like a knocking. The rain bring all kinda story and thing, you know. That's why I like listen to it. I use to sleep on a cot in the front room, and outside I could see a little piece of moon hanging up in the blue-black looking like someone broken thumbnail. Every now and then a drop of rain hit gainst the window, and sparkle, pat, so soon the window glass was scatter all over with the shine rain drops them, just like a piece of star sky come down. Glory. The bed was well sweet that night, and I let my head sink way down inna the pillow, and I close my eyes and listen to the rain calling my name, I-da. I-da. Just like that, over and over, the sound taking me away, joy unspeakable. And then I hear like some thing pulling on the ground, real soft-like and real slow. Dragging dragging dragging through the dry-up leaves in the mango walk. Lord-a-mighty, when the drum in my chest realize what going on, it start batta out a tune, Ba-duup, Ba-duup, like I did never hear it carry on with before. Ba-duup, Ba-duup. Ba-duup, Ba-duup. I put my head under the pillow and cover myself from head to toe because I was sure the rolling calf would hear the drum and come find me. Ba-duup, Ba-duup. Ba-duup, Ba-duup. The drum start to pick up speed, Ba-baBa-ba-duup, Ba-baBa-ba-duup, and Lord, I was flat on my back with nothing to do but wait and listen. Then when it seem like the night did stretch itself out pass where it should already end, it come clear that the rolling calf was walking around in circles but he wasn't coming any nearer to the yard, and I start to realize something: The sound this chain making, dragging through the mango walk, did have a kinda sadness to it—a loneliness, you know what I mean? And after I calm down and listen good, is as if something grab at my heart-ears and a feeling overtake me in the bed, and I knew this calf was not a wicked calf at all, not at all.

So, what to do? Next morning, I tell my mother everything. Mama was frying fritters on the coal stove, and she listen to me all quiet-quiet without even as much as saying a word. When I finish, Mama still don't say nothing. She put the fritters in a plate. She cover the plate with a pot cover. She wrap the plate and the pot cover with a dish cloth. She tie the dish cloth in a knot. And stare at it. Then, she turn and look at me all stern-like (but I could tell there was fright standing up in her two eye them), and she say, "Ida, don't lemme hear one more word from you bout any duppie foolishness. People around here already mark you as a bad luck, someting-gone-wrong chile. Don't let dem goat mouth catch up with you." Mama turn her back to me. She put on some water to boil. She start grating a little cocoa. And I knew that was the end of that.

Anyway, next night I was right back there on the cot ready to listen out again, but not a sound. Third night, same thing. Fourth night, still the same thing—not even as much as a mongoose dragging fowl feathers through the yard. On the fifth night it start to rain, this time the drops knocking up gainst one another and howling, Lord, what a howling all the way till daylight. Sixth night, more wailing and howling, all hell let loose on the red clay yard. Seventh night I lay there listen to the batta-batta and the knock-knock on the little piece o' zinc roof, trying to make sense of the drops them, till gradual things settle down to just a whimper and a mild spit spit gainst the window glass. The clouds start to move from across the moon, just like someone parting a piece o' gauze curtain, slow and sneakified, to peep out at things. I watch, and as I watch the moon become more and more brazen and bareface so that soon the clouds them all drawn apart and resting to one side. Shh.

The breadfruit leaves stop swaying. There was a hush. A kinda waiting. Me and the house and the moon and the trees inna the yard and all the little grass-quit line up on the branches—just waiting. In the moonshine I could see a little lizard on the windowsill, her pointy head raise up and tilt to one side, and she listen along with the rest of we. They say moonshine is poor woman jewels, you know. And is true. That night I woulda never give it up for all the treasure in the world. Light glistening on the wet leaves and grass—just like diamonds, just like silver, just like crystal. And the little moonshine lizard! Glass beads line up all along her backbone, a true-true queen.

When the dragging come it was soft and timid-like, coming up all slow through the bush, then stopping. Coming, then stopping again. I hold my breath, and the corner of my mind which keep the deep-and-wide eyes see the calf stopping to look out through the mango leaf at the asleep house, then moving on again, and all the time he hold his head to the ground like this, you know, sniffing for the barefoot, wide toe tracks of the living. The drum was beating steady in my chest and I slip on my dress and tiptoe to the front door. But stick a pin, sister-chile—

Here comes Nurse Watson and I have to pretend to take my medicine. All these little yellow pills. Pro zag-zig zac and what-not, what-have-you. When she leave the room, I'll just slip it from under my tongue and pick up with you again. In the meantime, put the calabash to your ear and listen. In the beginning it won't sound like anything special, and then it will sound like tongues, but keep listening long enough and your heart-ears will begin to understand. Go on. Whether you do or you don't, they'll still think you mad, so you might as well go ahead and try. Don't pay the medicine tray any mind; we don't really need it—is just their trick to keep us fool. Close your eyes. Breathe, long-ears woman, breathe. That's right; whoosh, whoosh, hear it?

TWO

Come, take a break. Let's walk out in the yard, away from this urine stench. That old woman over there, Mrs. Johnskin, always wetting herself, the poor thing, and they wouldn't even change her sheets. One ole woman knows another, and trust me, she don't belong in here any more than you or me or the ole Queen of What-not. You know, this Nurse Watson walk with her toes pointed out, one foot going left, the other going right, just like a woman we had in our district years ago. What was her name again? . . . I just had it at the tip of my tongue. . . .

Come anyway, at least outside here in the yard we can feel a little breeze on our face and admire the periwinkle. These little flowers just about the only bright thing around this place, you know. Every now and then, when I stand middle-day with the sun right over my head, it seem to me like one of them wink at me, real quick, as if they don't want anyone else to notice. Because of this I call them my 'winkles. People don't like to let anybody know they glimpse little things like that, you know, that's why they rub their eye and walk away and miss the rest of it.

. . . Can't remember her name for the life of me. . . . She used to have a hook nose like a parrot . . . and she was a deaconess in the church . . . and she did have a pair of eye's glasses. Ahh, Miles, that's it, Sister Miles. Sister Miles did have a kind of half-laugh with a crack in it, and when I was a child she have a way of laughing the laugh and patting her lap for me to come sit with her. Then she fix her eye's glass on her nose (she was the only one in the district who have eye's glasses and she did well proud of it) and search my face, righteous you know like this, then she ask me if I know, hallelujah, that there's ten, blessed-be-the-Lord commandments, not seven, not eight, praise him, not even nine, halleloo, but ten, oh yes, and all the while she squeezing my fingers between her two tablet of stone. Afterward, she take a paradise plum from outta her purse and put it in my hand-middle and smile at me all nice, but I could smell a foulness coming from outta the pit in her throat and I never trust her, so every time I see her I start catch fraid that more of my fingers or even my toes them would start fall off. And I begin to wonder, why always so much hair in my comb? Is it because I steal two of Marse Thomas bombay mango? And why my finger nails always tearing and breaking so? Is it because I spit in Teacher Brown tea when she wasn't looking? The hog, she deserved it, she rough me up in front the whole class for reciting that poem (the one with all the nice behaving flowers) by that Wordswool or Wool-words (I can't remember which) wrong. Tribulation. This worrying went on and on, till when I grow little more big and my teeth begin fall, I fret so till I decide to tell Mama. Mama listen all quiet and say not to mind Sister Miles for Sister Miles is a busy-body. It wasn't until years later, when I reach third-book, that I come to understand that Sister Miles and the other bad-minded brethren wasn't talking bout my sin them at all, but Mama own, for it was believe, you know, that Mama must be partake of, or watch, or listen to some evil someting herself in order to end up with a nine-finger baby.

Anyway, I say all this to say that by the time I was around twelve and listening out for the rolling calf, I make up my mind that I wasn't going married and I wasn't going have children—no, Ma'am, no way—because I, Ida, did not want them born with any missing limbs. As much badness as I use to carry on with, I was sure-sure they would be lame and bed-strick. But this thing had a turn side you know, for it leave me free to carry on with as much badness as I like without worrying about what going happen to my picknie them. So there I was tip-toeing through the front door on my way to meet the rolling calf.

Now use the deep-and-wide eye that keep inna the corner of your mind and picture this: me, stealing out cross the guinea grass in my ragga-ragga dress (I was a mawga thing then, no bigger than a mus-mus), the moonshine following me, lighting up my bare foot bottom them, quick light like this, flash flash flash, every time I lift up one foot and put the other one down. Everything quiet. Everything still. Just the sound of my bare foot on the wet grass. Shomp. Shomp. Now hush up and try to listen me, a dragging, dragging, dragging something, all soft like, all slow.

That night, the closer I come to the mango walk, the more my heart-ears let me know that this calf was not a calf that come to bother me. This calf was not a wicked calf. This calf was not after blood. By the time I get to the edge of the trees, I hear the dragging clear clear, and I hear another sound—the cow-foot stepping in and out of the wet leaf them. Something switch on inside o' me then, and it come to me that there was a kind of fraidiness in the way the calf walking. Same time as this come to me, I see like a shadow or something cross through the trees. The drum in my chest start to carry on, and I stand still and I watch and I listen, the moon waiting right there with me. At first I couldn't see nothing, only tree bark and branch, but after my eyes settle, I make out the little calf between two stringy mango tree, such a young thing with him chain around him neck. I edge a little closer and I see the eyes, all big and frighten in the moonshine, the skin on him neck trembling. I step closer again, but the calf step back from me, his chain dragging and making a little noise on the ground. So we stand there, the two of us eyes making four, quiet and still, watching one another, wondering what going to happen next.

There we was for I don't know how long—time did on a different track. Then perhaps because it come clear that I didn't mean no harm, or perhaps because I was, after all, just a knotty-hair young girl in a ragga-ragga dress with bare foot, to this day I still not sure why, but the calf step forward, about a distance of two yards from me, sniffing out a circle round my feet, his chain marking out a trail that circle me in the dirt and the leaf. Two time the calf walk around me, and two time I hold my breath; my foot root in the ground and I couldn't move it. My body stiff, like my neck have gum in it, so that even though the calf sniffing his way around me, I couldn't even turn my head to watch him. Each time I wait for him to come from behind me, and each time he come around, still sniffing, watching the ground, you know, his little ears all prick up just like this. By now, the drum in my chest beating out all kinda beat, and then, on the third time a funny thing happen: I make out the sound of another drum, answering mine, Ba-duup, Ba-duup. Beat for beat, drum for drum. Ba-duup, Ba-duup, coming from outta the calf. Ba-duup, Ba-duup, I take in a deep breath and wait for him to make his circle, but this time, what come walking from behind me was not the little calf at all.

People say that if trees could talk, they would have so many story to tell that everyone ears would grow way down to their shoulders. Well, let me tell you: Trees talk, we just don't listen. Where you think this cal-abash come from? A tree, of course. (But we'll get to that in a minute.)

That night as I stand in the moonshine circle at the edge of the mango grove, what come walking from behind me was not a little calf at all. Not at all. I could hear his step with the same fraidiness, and the same sadness, so soft and careful. And I still hear his chain, dragging, dragging on the ground. His drum keep up the batta-batta with mine, beat for beat. Ba-duup, Ba-duup. But what come and stand before me was not the little calf, uh-uh, not the little brown calf. Not the little brown calf with the teeny-tiny horns. What come and stand before me was a young boy, about fourteen or so, naked from the waist on up, an iron collar round his neck, and a chain that dangle all the way to the ground.

The periwinkle have a story they like to ponder. It is the story of a girl who was put up for sale on the auction block down by the bay. This was many, many years ago, when guns at the fort were still used to fire salutes to admirals and lords on holidays and anniversaries, or sometimes, it seemed, for no reason at all. The guns sent a shiver through the stems of the peri-winkles, the soft soil shifting around their roots, ants losing their grip.

The periwinkle say, the girl on the auction block was young and brown. She had been washed down and oiled so that her skin shone in the sun-light; an iron chain was attached to her leg and hooked to a post nearby. When the auctioneer stepped forward, his voice boomed, ONE STRONG MANDINGO WENCH, ONE-EYED, BUT SOUND AS A POUND, and the crowd pressed closer, but the periwinkle remember that the girl appeared dis-tracted, seeming not even to notice the growing throng, much less hear the voice of the auctioneer. With her one good eye, she was looking way past them—past the tops of their plumed hats, past the hill and the fort of a hundred guns, her eye was focused someplace beyond the sugarcane fields and dirt roads, and even past where the land again met the sea on the other side of the island. A man with a wooden cane stepped forward. He examined her teeth, looked into her eyes, but still the girl looked right through him. He tapped her lightly with his cane on each shoulder, on each buttock, on each leg; then smiling, he held her breasts in the palms of his hands. GOING AT EIGHT, GOING . . .

This is what the periwinkle remember: the girl, suddenly bursting into uncontrollable laughter, her head flung back, one arm raised, a long dark finger pointing at something in the distance that only she could see. They all followed her finger—the auctioneer, the man with the cane, and all the plumed hats—turning in unison, peering across their shoulders, trying to make out the object of her delight. But because the heart-eye sees differently, and because their own hearts were without eye, they saw nothing. . . . Mad wench! Their heads spun forward now, annoyed. This is what the auctioneer saw, what the man with the cane saw, what the plumed hats saw: the platform empty; the wench gone. Disappeared—her chain still hooked to its post.

Look. Look. Look. This is what the periwinkle see: a small brown lizard crawling leisurely across the stones, and away from the crowd.

THREE

I TELL YOU this story because I think you need to hear it, and because I want you to know that there is more to this world than what you think you see floating on top the pot. See that sea out there cross the bay? That sea have many stories to tell. There are things bury at the bottom of that sea that woulda make you break out in cold sweat if you ever find it all out.

Speaking of which, the other day me and Mrs. Johnskin sit in the ward just laughing at ourselves. Talking bout how neither of us ever did learn how to swim, or drive car, or even ride bicycle. Mrs. Johnskin say she spen three months over in foreign, and the white people she work for just couldn't believe she live in Jamaica all her life and never swim in the Caribbean. Lord help us, but you know what? And this is the part I want you to understand: Some of us ole people don't know swims, but plenty of us can walk on water.

Listen good. I wasn't always an ole woman. I use to be a mawga girl, with a ragga-ragga dress and bare foot. But is a funny thing, ever since that night in the moonshine when I see that boy with the iron collar around him neck, I been feeling like an ole ole woman. I looked at that collar, and is as if from the moment I set my eyes on it, I start to pick up years. To this day, I hate to have anything dangling around my neck. Because of that, even if you give me a dainty little gold chain string with this and that queen's jewels, I just couldn't wear it. I just can't stand the feel of it.

Anyway, there I was standing before this young man with his chain dangling from him neck. He was a bit taller than me, his face all dirty and scratch-up; his eyes big and sad, just like the little calf own. He did look tired, as if he did traveling from a long way, and I could tell he need food and water and a place to sleep, but my tongue was gum to my mouth-top, and I just couldn't speak. All this time, his drum still beat with strength, answering mine. Ba-duup, Ba-duup, back and forth. He stretch his arms, Ba-ba-duup-duup, and put something round and smooth in my two hands—Ba-duup. Heh, I was frighten, I tell you, because all this time I didn't know he did carry as much as a nutmeg. I hold the thing up to the moonlight, and see that it was a calabash. My arms them feel weak, and I almost drop it, even as light as it was. His eyes smile a bit then, and he just turn and walk away in the trees. I did want to say something, but I just stand there, a mawga ole woman with a ragga-ragga dress and bare foot.

But come with me, step this way. Here come that volunteer lady and is time for us to go inside for crafts. She don't come by often, maybe once a week or so, but when she come, she give bits of this and that to make whatever we want. A nice lady, I think. Sometimes she act sort of fraidy-fraidy, but I think she have a good heart. Last month, I ask her to bring us some straw and I teach some of the women here how to make baskets. My Mama and Papa was good with straw, you know, and don't let anybody tell you that basket weaving is only fool-fool people work because is not true. Most of who you see out there criticizing, well, ask them to weave you a basket and see if they would know how. Oh, I so glad she here today! She promise to bring me some clay and I think I going to mold a little lizard to decorate the floor beside my bed. If you going to be lock up in a place like this, you might as well do whatever it take to keep you busy. There's a little brown polly lizard that I keep see wiggling around outside in the yard, and I think I going make one just like that. If it was left to Nurse Watson, we wouldn't do any crafts here at all, you know. She see us sitting here happy, making our little this and making our little that, and she seem to think we up to tricks instead of crafts. I can't wait to see the expression on her big pumpkin face when she see my lizard.

I NEVER did see the rolling calf after that night. Perhaps he accomplish whatever he did come for and gone at last, to rest. But with my heart-ears, I still hear him: the chain, dragging dragging, the heart, beating, beating . . .

FOUR

LISTEN. Pitter-pat, pat-pat. Is raining again, and your ears already growing longer, I can tell. I can tell. Perhaps I should ask the volunteer lady to bring us few gourds for crafts next month! We could all make little pots and bowls and cut out nice marks around the sides. Pitter-pat, pat-pat.

THIS IS what I like about polly lizards: If you cut off their tails, they grow another one right back. Now that's what you call a back-answer polly.

It's Easter Sunday, a day that Christian Guyanese traditionally spend flying kites to symbolize the risen Christ. Easter kites come in all kinds of fantastical shapes and colors. On a reservation, a young Carib boy flying a kite asks about the stories that say that his people are cannibals. Wilson Harris creates unusual linkages between images and then uses those linkages to build an architecture of dream. In a dreamtime of its own, "the imagination of a continent" tells the tale of its first people.

Yurokon

.

WILSON HARRIS

THE INDIAN RESERVATION of the valley of sleep
lay in an open savannah of the Interior. Stunted bush and occasional
trees dotted this savannah—miles long and wide—between the mountains where a great forest began and rolled endlessly to the sea. From
this naked distance—in the middle of the valley—these forests
appeared like black surf of painted cloud. Yurokon had once or twice
crossed them to come to the sea. It was a far way off but his memories
were intimate and vivid like newly minted letters of space, a harmony
of perspectives.

The sun was up when he succeeded in raising his kite. Soon—by
judicious tugs—pulling in and paying out of twine—the kite caught a
current of air and rose steadily and swiftly into the sky.

He was around fourteen (so the records said); his sister, who had
accompanied him, about ten. They were both small of stature, frail of
limb, reputed to be among the last survivors of an ancient tribe now
called *huntsmen of bone*. They possessed a curious air, devoid of age it
seemed—animated matchsticks, smoldering a little, quiescent a little. It
was the rapidity of their gestures accompanied by an inherent stillness,

a silent relationship. And yet it was as if volumes of time existed between them and words of music fell ceaselessly from their lips. They appeared now half-asleep on earth as the match of space began to slumber. And when their uncle appeared through one of the trees they were glad to relinquish the kite to him, which he secured to the branch of a tree. Yurokon slid to the ground and watched uncle and sister vanish through a hump of land into the houses of the reservation.

They would return, he knew, with food and drink. He lay against the trunk of a tree and could not bear to leave his kite, which he glimpsed through the leaves as it slept on a cloud—and bore him up into a skeleton of light through the valley of sleep.

"Are we really huntsmen of bone?" Yurokon asked, looking down at his uncle and through the sky as he sailed in space. For it was as if the blue trunk of the ocean stood there whittled down to a cross, coral and bone, octopus in whose blood ran tin, sponge in whose crevices ran gold.

"We became huntsmen of bone when we ate our first Spanish sailor," his uncle replied to the intricate sticks of the sky. "For that reason we are sometimes called cannibals." He looked sardonic, his left eyebrow cocked in quizzical fashion, pointing still to the kite, paper of heaven nailed to wood.

"Cannibals," said the boy, startled. "I don't see why anyone should call us that."

It was Easter in the Indian reservation of the twentieth century and Yurokon had been given a kite by a visiting missionary, which sailed through the book of space and continued in his sleep in pages of psyche; coral and gold.

"For that reason we are sometimes called cannibals," the man repeated, pursuing his own thread of thought backwards into time. "We ate a Spanish sailor. . . ." He was jealous of the missionary and wished to distract his nephew, glued to space.

"How can you say such a thing?" Yurokon cried, descending from kite to earth in a flash and stopping dead, riveted now to the ancient trunk of man, the lines and brow, the anchor of subsistence.

They stood under a small tree in the valley of sleep and Yurokon observed a spectral nest hanging from one of its branches; to that bough also he saw had been tied the thread of his kite, which he had ascended and descended on scales of light. "It's chained there," he cried as if he had forgotten whether it was the missionary or his uncle who had done it, "chained to nest and branch."

His uncle nodded to a silent tune and, reaching up into the nest, drew forth a thin bone or flute. He passed it over his lips without making a sound, polished it between the palms of his hands, and after this palaver with the dead gave it to Yurokon, who blew, in his turn, a sad yet vibrating melody of space. All at once he could hear and feel running through his hands the giant tremor of that bird, the ladder of the pilot, as it flew soundlessly through the sky chained to the earth.

He could hear also an unwritten symphony: the dark roots in the past of that tree—a strange huddle of ancestral faces attuned to quivering wings that they plucked with their fingers like teeth. And then silently, as if for the first bitter time, tasted the fear of the strings; ascent and descent; transubstantiation of species: half-tender, half-cruel, like a feast.

They read it, in their mouths, on the craft of Spain—the curious cross of a bird that flew toward them across the sea: crane or pelican or flag. It might even have been their first fleshless pirate, skull and crossbones of the fleet, harp of flesh.

"Do you mean," said Yurokon as the first wave of magical numbers struck him, "that it was a game to make them think they had been eaten . . . ?" He stopped, aware of a waking plight in the valley of sleep, the plight of feeling akin to non-feeling, flesh akin to spirit.

"In a manner of speaking, yes," said his uncle approvingly. *"Make them think they had been eaten.* Make them into a song of spirit: a morsel in our mouths, nothing more, the morsel of the flute, that was all." He waved his hand nonchalantly.

Yurokon nearly spat the flute from his mouth as though suddenly it burned his tongue like fire, immortal burn, immortal skin, immortal native, immortal cannibal. He began to age into the ancient Child of

Legend. It was a story he had been told from the beginning—that he was the last Carib and the first native. . . .

2

YUROKON appeared centuries ago in the valley of dreams as the native heaven of tears and laughter, of carnival and guilt when the revolution of conquest was over.

His uncle was expecting him and though he barely discerned the spiral of smokelike twine coming up out of the pot on the fire, he felt the sting of fire—tears of a match.

It was here in this sky of election—bastard soil—cannibal legend—that the song of the kite was born.

"Make them think it was a marriage of spirits, laughter of the feast," his uncle said languidly, with the glaze of the pot in his eye.

"I am your brother's spirit," said Yurokon and there was a responsive glaze in his mood or brow, a godlike rebellious look.

"Which one?" his uncle said flippantly to the devil of the fire. "Brother oh brother."

Yurokon bowed his head to conceal the ash of many a war feast, sculpture of blood. His uncle had many brothers—some had eaten the symbol of deity. "How can we," he said to his uncle, and the words bit his tongue, "be the first natives when they were here before us—I mean your brothers' Arawak wives—my mother's people . . . ?"

"They're our base of time in the light of Spain," his uncle said secretively as though he reasoned with insurrection in his ranks. "No one before us has made this claim—don't you see?—this black morsel. . . ." He stirred industriously over the cooking pot and gave a sardonic shrug. "It's our last weapon, our first election. In future, come who or what may, this distinction will stand. It will swallow us all for we, too, will succumb."

"Succumb," said Yurokon and he almost laughed at his fate. "Yet here am I," he cried accusingly, "no one and nothing, yet here I stand. Whose fault is it? Whose spirit is it that will not—*cannot*—die?"

"Child," said his uncle with a gleam that might have been fear, "it is true that the revolution of conquest is over but *you*—your rebellious feud of spirit goes on." He turned away from the glaze of the pot; the hunger of kinship was opening at his feet, twine of blood, twine of water, twine of guilt ascending and descending: flint of savage: skeleton of light.

Yurokon held the twine in his hands as if with a snap, a single fierce pull, he would break it *now* at last. Break the land. Break the sea. Break the savannah. Break the forest. Break the twig. Break the bough. The unwritten symphony of the wind, unwritten spark of the wind, made him bark—a sudden bark. His uncle stared at the bristling dog of the fire, fire break, fire bark, delicacy, magic; he smacked his lips and the roast of Yurokon's bark subsided into the silent bay of conscience like an invocation at the heart of the feast: man's best enemy or friend.

Was it the immortal dog of war and peace that sang in the break of the fire, shadowy tail or bone?

Its voice could be heard in the lull of the wind across the valley of sleep. First the subtlest crash of a symphony, staccato fire, forest tail or bay of the moon in the sky.

Second a hoarse thump that came from a falling tree, surf or tail of the moon.

It was the music of ignominy, ignominious conceit, or so it seemed to Yurokon (his own desire to break everything) on his long march across time into the rebellion of eternity. A long march in which the tail of his kite drew a line across the ash of the sky, camp fire or ghost settlement. A line of demarcation, the frontier of sleep, huntsmen of bone, the song of silence.

It was equally the music of origins upon a trail that lay in all the wild warring elements. First, *broken water.* His uncle possessed an enormous cauldron, which he filled with water and set on the fire. Yurokon beheld the dog, his skin soon bubbling there like a cataract of eternity: boiling water that had been innocent before—innocent, that is, as one's own sovereign blood, but now had become the executioner at the feast, native to blood.

Second, *broken fire.* His uncle possessed an enormous spit, a cauldron of fire: as though the sun stood over the valley on a misty morning and began to break its own vessel of intensity through an autumn sunset turning into a tropical, ritual sunrise. So that the steam of the valley appeared to infuse the light, and water boiled fire rather than fire boiling water.

Yurokon saw himself aloft in this cauldron of fire as a dog-kite, the twine connecting him to earth—kite to earth—had been cut by scissors of mist. He stood, therefore, high up as if without anchor or support save that the nape of his neck had been caught by fingers of fire: fingers of a god that had been innocent before—innocent as one's sovereign flesh, but now had become an executioner at the feast, native to flesh.

At this moment on the trail beholding water and broken fire, he looked backward and forward at the combat of heaven: immortal outcast, outcast of participation, innocence and guilt. Heaven lay both within and without the things and the people he had taken for granted, and the kite of deity had, on one hand, consolidated—as uncle hinted—a base of time, an election of time to swallow all ages and men, but, on the other, had equally inspired a curious break within the anatomy of the feast—a spiritual hunger and rebellion whose consequences would reveal the inmost vessel or nativity of fate, song of fate. He had passed through broken voices of water and fire. Now broken atmosphere lay before him like the breath on his lips fried thin as a wafer, flat as a leaf. And so when he moved he began to fly with the feud of air into broken distances: broken water and fire cooked into walls of space by leaves of wood as though water and fire were cold and wood and leaf were hot: wood and leaf that had been innocent before—innocent as nature, but now had become the kite of distance, native to sovereign execution, death-in-life, life-in-death.

Fire. Water. Air. They were all, in a sense, the weapons of a savage dreaming time on a trail where *once upon a child* everything had slumbered on a leash like a victorious shroud but now had become the cauldron of heaven that the huntsmen of bone had not foreseen when they appointed themselves the cannibal or ogre of place to fashion both their Catholic native and repulsive sack of the seasons.

That the leash would become the Easter twine of endless participation through an immortal outcast, and that the repulsive stocking or sack of the seasons would invoke stomach upon stomach of consumption whose hideousness would be reflected in a deeper and deeper child-like pool of innocence (ogre of water, boiling fire)—raw material of the elements—none had foreseen as the undying birth of freedom. . . .

For it was as if—just as angelic blood was consumed by cannibal water—fire by an atrocity of wood—broken savage time lay, too, within its native soil eternity.

Yurokon was approaching a bend in the trail and he saw both the shroud and sack of the seasons before him. The shroud may well have been a caul such as certain children are born with. The sack or stocking may well have been the pillow of conquest, Eiger in Roraima, snow of the Alps in the Andes in the Amazon. He could now hear the gift of a symphony in the silent bed of earth—black-out shroud of vision, white-out stocking of translation. He had heard the missionary on the reservation speak of the Polar North as an organ of fire it was so cold. Yurokon believed and accepted this paradoxical truth as much as he trusted the song of himself in the sorrow of the bone and the flute—the ages of man—valley of desolation.

"Once upon a child," the shroud said to him advancing along the trail like the dance of the black keys of earth. "Once upon a time," the sack said to him advancing along the trail like the dance of the white bones of earth. Yurokon hopped to the white bone and the black flute. He could see clearly now, with the eye of his kite, the ballet of the Caribs as they stubbornly withdrew within the music of the centuries upon the skull-and-crossbones piano of age. At each campfire they grew extinct in the ash of reflection, but were born again within involuntary pillow or shroud, caul of vision.

Yurokon stepped upon these keys of birth-in-death—broken water and broken fire—black-out . . . white-out . . . ash of earth that he rode like a ladder into the sky.

3

THE LADDER of the trail ran up into the mountains. And each day as the Caribs withdrew into the clock of the centuries they painted the blue sea falling away beneath them in an underworld picture, an underworld kite that flew in the broken sky of conquest. Flew under their feet upon a rope of ash that descended through knotted stations of fire where the burnt relic of each day's march was buried. It burned itself there—imagination of a continent—rope and kite—ladder of ascent, and they threw the sea upon their pots and vessels—something fantastically small (a drop of ocean)—something immensely wide that began to consume them at the grassroots of innocence like a cauldron of fury.

The sea-kite possessed many shapes and colors, some gay, some somber. Some—like the octopus—amused the huntsmen. It made them almost enjoy the innocent malady of the gods since unholy, holy evil was reputed to have a stomach of mail that drank tin.

"Once upon a child," said the stomach of mail to the conscience of the tribe, namely Yurokon, "you ate me," and it tangled its tail and rope around him on the ladder. His uncle laughed, and his sister, taking pity on him, grabbed the octopus by the bones of the kite and ran a little way off across a wave of land to give him room to coax it back into the air.

Another kite, which rose in the underworld sky at his feet, resembled a sponge and this, too, was an endless model of diversion. When the battle of conscience drew it, infinite drops of gold splashed on the ground from the heart of the pelican.

"Once upon a time," said the sponge to the pelican, "I flew in the sea with wings of bone."

In addition to the kite of the octopus and the kite of the sponge there flew a kite of coral, a submerged reef crossed with ritual cousins, related to the sponge, calendrical mosaic, music. It curved and dwindled in shallows and deeps, skeleton of the sea, harp of the feast from which a stringed sound issued, fossil of cloud.

Far beneath the ladder of the mountains the ocean crawled within itself, ribs of bone splashed by huntsmen of shadow. Yurokon observed in the middle of that kite of ocean a loop of burning paint. This was the cauldron of the kite within which octopus and coral and sponge, innocent evil and maleficent good, were living morsels of divinity in their native organ. The laughter dried on his lips—flute of bone—and he tasted instead plankton or euphausiid harnessed to blood: harnessed to the urchin of the sea, spiked hedgehog or jealous god of the ocean. This spiky pattern upon the cauldron of the kite reflected the jealous sky of the sea—the brittle constellations and stars, prickly sea-lilies, sea cucumbers set in a mosaic of fossil and keyboard of ancestors. As though the spiky music of the urchin of stars, the election of the first native of earth, drew one deeper and deeper into a furnace of innocence, consumption of guilt.

Yurokon was the hedgehog of the land, Carib land-urchin to Spanish sea-urchin. He could bark and bristle on the land as if fire were his natural element, sea-dog of night, and with the fall of darkness he no longer flew the sea-kite under him, but rather the land-kite over him.

He imagined himself standing upon the shore of the sea with a new boatload of arrivals, looking up with their eyes at a distant campfire of Caribs. The ground was strewn with the dead of battle, but the bone of the kite blazing on the mountains spoke volumes of the savage character of the land, dancing around its flute. It was as if the dance of the bone wished to declare itself after a day of battle—to all who had newly arrived—by a music of silence, spirit of absorption, gaol of flesh.

That absorption reflected the many shapeless kites of Yurokon in the heart of the invader as well as invaded. There was the night octopus of the land whose dance differed from the tail of the sea in that the daytime octopus was a morsel of divinity, morsel of the sea, but the nighttime octopus, as it blazed its points far up on the ladder of the land, seemed the very antithesis of the gods: land-urchin's shroud or sack: campfire of bone: trunk or tree on which Yurokon laid his head in the valley of sleep. Each splinter of the dance, seen from the foot of the cross, ladder of the mountains, flared in the match of a dream, matchstick limbs, twine and distance: glimmer of the pointed hedgehog.

4

YUROKON'S field was the grain of the land and sea whose seed-time was conscience, battle of eternity.

As the Caribs withdrew across the ridge of the land and began to descend into a continent of shadow, each knot of ash linked them to the enemy. And Yurokon was the scarred urchin of dreams, victor-in-victim; over the centuries he remained unaging (ageless) as a legend, a curious symptom or holocaust of memory, whose burned-out stations were equally embryonic as a cradle, fugue of man, unchained chain of fires. It was this that drew the Caribs to the end of their age. They ceased to fret about names since namelessness was a sea of names. They ceased, too, to care about dwindling numbers since numberlessness was native to heaven, stars beyond reckoning. The tree, in fact, against which Yurokon slept was known as the tree of name and number. And there were two paths that led to it from the mountains around the valley. The first was called *the ladder of the geese*. It was a game Yurokon had designed in which he dreamed it was all happening the other way around. The mountains were paper—flat as a map. The valley was above, sailing kite, and the barnacle geese that flew toward him rose from paper to kite: hatched not from eggs like other birds but from sea-shell into land-fish, orphans of the globe. For they, too, like Yurokon, were an ageless omen, Good Friday's meat, fish rather than fowl. None grieved for them save Yurokon who accounted himself sibling to a shell—sibling to a fast—as Uncle accounted himself guardian to a morsel.

It was the true name of the geese, the true number of the fast, that baffled all men. Yurokon drew the flight of the geese as currents or arrows gainst the shadow of continents—gulf stream or orphan of masses, equatorial current or orphan of hemispheres.

"Barnacle currents," he thought. Wing by fin the land-fish flew—the souls of a drought, the fast of the drowned—waters under the earth.

> *The valley of sleep had been taken by assault—the fiercest savan-*
> *nah fire of living memory; so swift had it been, all were killed who*
> *were taken unawares. Stunted trees remained—bones of grass.*
> *Uncle had died, as had Yurokon, in the glare of battle. And now—*
> *after three or four years—the scene was revisited by the Catholic*
> *Missionary of the Interior, Father Gabriel. It was he who encircled*
> *on a map the charred tree of Yurokon as a new root or mission of*
> *psyche, spectral nest, bone and flute: it was Eastertide again.*

HE HAD visited the mission and given Yurokon a kite two days before
the blaze—had he remained he, too, might have been killed. Now here
he was again to make a new start, both defend and attack from within
and without. An unorthodox priest he was of Spanish and Indian
blood, and a composer of music. He dreamed of a native symphony
that would reflect a new organ of capacity, a primitive flowering of
faith. It was not inconsistent with the last dream of the Caribs, the
dream of Yurokon, which haunted him, as it haunted them—annunciation of music at the beginning of the end of an age.

"Sailor," said Yurokon to Gabriel. The priest began to protest. But
his voice was muffled in his cloth of vocation. He wanted to say—"I
am not your mask or morsel." But instead—like curtain and theater—
he let the faceless robe of God descend; Yurokon set aside the flute
from his lips and placed collar or shell to his ear.

There were two ladders (Yurokon remembered) leading to the robe
of name and number. The first was called tree of the barnacle goose,
the second simply *hemispheres: shell of the spheres.*

Yurokon kept the shell to his ear until arrows of rain evoked an
abstract pitch, volume within line. The music he now heard was both
hollow and full, sea-fast, land-fast. When the sea fasted, it still climbed
into the rain of the land: land-fish, Good Friday's arrow.

Yurokon could hear her sing—his sister who ran before him now
through the day of the battle of the savannah—arrow of fire—when
mail or flame swept on. As though in the singing theater of God, history reenacted itself. . . .

The fire voices came from everywhere and Yurokon woke to the voice of the tree in which he slept.

He was rooted, in that moment, in fire—as his sister ran before him with the singing kite of the savannah—fiery attack, fiery defense.

In the grain of that field of battle—open to conscience—open to sun—an omen resided, multiplications of grace, zero as well as fulfillment. This was the logic of Father Gabriel—the open book of the centuries: annunciation of the native of the globe.

And now—as his sister ran before him—Yurokon saw a chain of fires (formerly ash, unchained chain of divinity) but linked or aligned to him now beneath his robe. He recalled the naked campfires of his forebears whose arrows swarmed on the brink of a continent like currents of ocean barnacled to land. They were lit, he remembered, as the first grim tide of welcome to the flag of the pelican. They were equally an offensive/defensive swarm, blazing at the door of the land—sponge of the sea—blood of gold: blazing ribbon of coastline, legend or sponge. He recalled the fierce battles that raged day after day; the retreat that followed night after night, the fatalistic withdrawal into hedgehog and mountain.

The chain of fires along the roof of the coast was the first curiously horizontal phase, therefore, in a vertical war—a vertical cloak or retreat that Yurokon encompassed at this stage as the shroud of the land-urchin over the sea-urchin, land-kite over the sea-kite, night over day.

It was a slow and long pull, he recalled, from the sea to the crest of the land, but they drew their train after them up the mountains, braced themselves in the current of the wind, wing to fin, bone to sack, goose to hemisphere—fast of name and number, tree of camouflage, feast of camouflage, trail of campfires in a single line or uninterrupted break of terror.

One last crackling glance back at the sea-kite from the sky-ridge of the mountains where they stood; he could see them again as they leaned forward, reluctant, sad, and drank a toast (farewell to namesake sea) lip to bowl, lip to the engraving of Spain (and all who came after, bowl of England, saucer of France, vessel of Holland): they engraved it on their lips—primitive fire or callous—like an animal's protuberance, mouth of the sun whose tongue ran with them as they descended the other flank of the mountains—away from the sea—into the lap of the land.

Halfway down they looked back with Yurokon's eyes and saw her standing there—Sister Fire—Viking Amazon. Her eyes met theirs as she turned from the flank of the sea to the cloth of land. And this time Yurokon felt the parenthesis of the orphan, sea-shell into robe.

Every protection, nevertheless, seemed precarious to him now as the battle of ridge and flank, forest and savannah rolled on: as though his own sister possessed a chain of ambivalences—a menacing outwardness as well as inwardness, unearthly stillness chained to storm, locked propensity, locked voices of fury.

He could see them—his forebears of bone—with their chain of flesh and spirit across the land. They had crossed the naked flank of the sea into the vessel of the forest and now—as they descended into species of Bush and Savannah—Yurokon was aware of the intensity of the flame they drew with them, which, like vase or pottery in a rage of color, signified an acute vice in themselves, blaze or furnace.

He had never been aware of it quite so strangely before—the flimsy scaffold of the robe, shroud of name and number, urchin of the stars, caul of birth, which—like ash—night-kite over day-kite, could mercifully fall to release the chain; or like earth, in the hands of a wise potter, could unlock the vice; but which (in the fold of that vice, color of fire) broke, for no other clear reason but to instill terror: as if—in breaking—it had not broken at all, save to clinch an outer flesh to an inner mold, an outer fire to an inner blow.

It was this inner blow that, despite the appearances of hell, drew Yurokon back to prize the ash—not as the holocaust it seemed to be, but as the robe of mercy it originally was, parenthesis of the orphan.

Nevertheless, in withdrawing there, he could still see—within his own glimmering shadow—that the chain of the battle rolled on; the fire voice of the savannah sang close at hand of the flesh and spirit of the tiger that had been joined to withstand (within and without) forces and enemies.

And the voice of the tiger, fire voice, fire vase—in line with sea-flame, mountain flesh, muse of the ridge, toast of ancestors, penetration of flank—instilled terror. And like an apparition of ancient campfire, it disported its robe of ash, bars of shadow through which its naked sides shone: insane factory of war: jointed engine of battles upon which the cloth of the priest precariously stood—not as the sport of unfreedom, but as a necessary condition, leash of grace.

It was curious (half-comic perhaps, half-tragic perhaps) that in a sense, this ash (this prison) was the flimsy sponge of nature that alone drank volumes of need; the ill-protected, the ill-served—true voice of the tiger.

True voice of the tiger. It began to sing with rage and scorn: rage at the conversion of prison: scorn at the factory of grace. And as it sang—in repudiation of the ash of truth—its rage and its scorn were joined to flesh and spirit.

This was the last chain, last repulse of the Caribs in that battle of the savannah, whose commemoration rose in a vase of flame: such music of color it embroiled the savannah in the sea, the mountain in the valley, forest in scrub: bowl of earth, pottery of earth, toast of the valley by the huntsmen of bone who had drunk before from the bowl of the sea.

Such commemoration of color—such a draft of sensation—such a feast of sensibility—embroiled all things and species in a breakwater of reflection, stretching from the harp of the sea to the kite of the valley.

That music of paradox began with a bar of shadow—unchained fire—*hiatus* of ordeal as the robe of God, the need of man; followed, however, by the wildest repudiation of that need in the sack of truth: though this very sack or body of rage began to point again, back to itself as to an ironical witness, an unremembered, unacknowledged sibling of truth on both sides of the veil.

For if, in fact, the inner tiger of war repudiated its veil or shadow, there were other species whose storm or sack drew them back without protest to the spirit of placelessness, as to the salt of the sea. The eel of fire, for example, as it ran into battle, coiled into an eye of relief that could have been a needle of snow. For eye of snow, like barnacle of fire, legendary feather, had been spawned on a distant scaffold—

desert or Pole—where it grew like an arrow from a subtle hand mapping the globe.

The bird of species as well, as it flew into battle, spun the feather or the thread in the needle in the very eye of snow. For the thread of the needle (eye of snow) had its loom on an indifferent scaffold—North or South—whose seamless fire was a *different* shadow, cloth over the Pole.

Yurokon spied that cloth—East, West—as it sailed on high beneath and above Sister and Uncle. Sailed on high, composite bird, flower, tailed beast; sailed in the spiral of the winds as he tugged gently, pulling in, paying out his twine with masterly skill. He was the child of legend and the lord of creation and his paper or map, kite or globe, was a magical witness of curious survival, the terrifying innocent play of a timeless element in all places and things. In all its manifestations it seemed to Yurokon to spell relief at the summit of his need. His small sister, running before him, began to sing to the kite with joy.

"Eastertide again," Father Gabriel said to himself, "annunciation of music."

The history of the Caribbean forced or brought together people of a number of races. It's left a legacy of descendants whose relationship to identity must always be complex. Tobias S. Buckell's story asks, Which history is history? Where is home?

Spurn Babylon

TOBIAS S. BUCKELL

Easing back on the throttle of the company's yellow Scarab powerboat, just clearing the rocky point of Hassel Island, I found myself stunned by the lack of yachts. Usually St. Thomas's Charlotte Amalie harbor was a forest of masts and a rainbow of hull colors. Now only two ships sat at anchor, looking lonely and out of place. The recent hurricane that had closed down the island's airport, forcing my company to send me here by boat rather than plane, had swept this anchorage clean.

Even more incredibly, a three-masted square-rigger lay lopsided on the waterfront's concrete shoreline.

"Where'd that come from," I wondered aloud.

I shook my head, wishing I had a camera.

It didn't seem like things were all that bad, I thought later, sipping a Red Stripe and relaxing underneath the flapping awning of the Greenhouse Restaurant. Even only two weeks after the worst hurricane in

Virgin Islands' recorded history, things looked okay. Maybe even "irie," as my supervisor seemed to glory in saying, trying to imitate local dialect. I distantly understood that half the houses on the island were uninhabitable, and I could smell seaweed no matter where I walked. But these islands were well-known for recovering quickly.

I let the condensation roll off the side of the brown bottle and down the back of my hand, a cold contrast to the heat shimmering off the concrete all around me. In the distance a generator hummed, keeping even more beer cold. Life went on.

"Evening," someone said.

J. Ottley sat down onto the seat across from me. The plastic hinges squeaked. He removed a well-worn straw hat and set it on the table. His long-sleeved shirt was soaked under the armpits. He ran the St. Thomas cell of B. E. Aerospace, one of three sections.

"Evening to you," I replied, handing Ottley the keys to the Scarab. Sombrero Island held our main launchpad complex, weathering the storm with minimal damage. St. Croix supported additional docking and shipping facilities for our sea-launch sections and shipping for the launch complex. St. Thomas housed even more shipping facilities. I'd spent the past week running around St. Croix helping rebuild the damaged sterile clean rooms that prepared satellites for launch. Cutting edge. Now it was time to check in and make sure our warehouses here in St. Thomas were okay. "Ottley, what is that?" I pointed at the ship across the street from us. Now I could see a thick patina of silt clinging to its sides.

Two brown-skinned men with dreadlocks and baggy gray trousers stood around, poking at the hull. A few uniformed students in red trousers and white shirts from the local public school had climbed aboard. They hung from the long wooden pole that stuck out of the front of the boat. The bowsprit, I think it would be called. The topsides seemed about seventy feet long. It looked just like my mental image of a traditional old wooden ship.

"An old ship," Ottley said. "Very old. From under the sea."

And that was all he would say. He gave me folders with pictures of the damage to our warehouses. Roofs ripped off, boosters inside damaged. There was water damage to a few satellites.

Yet my eye kept wandering from the pictures of fractured composites to the silhouette just on the edge of my vision.

A waterspout spawned by the recent hurricane must have sucked the ancient wooden ship up from the silted bottom of Charlotte Amalie Harbor. And then set it next to the asphalt road in a pool of stagnant seawater and gray harbor mud. But even as I tried to envision that I struggled. There should be more damage. What strange force had preserved it from decay?

I SPENT the next day busy coordinating the recovery efforts. We had a warehouse near the airport, more or less on the west side of St. Thomas; one in Red Hook, the east end; and an office in town. I tackled Red Hook first. Later, as the sun began to shimmer and kiss the distant salty horizon, I sat down exhausted on a lounge chair next to the pool and bar of the Marriott Hotel; Frenchman's Reef. From the pool I could see the entire curve of the harbor and the whole waterfront skyline.

Charlotte Amalie is a beautiful little Caribbean town. Its Dutch architecture is mostly symmetrical, and the facades of the stocky two-story buildings reflect that with arches and squared windows in even numbers. The colors of the walls are vibrant bright yellows, pinks, clean whites, contrasted with red shingled roofs. Similarly colored tiny houses cluster all over the steep mountainside.

And sitting there I realized a familiar wooden shape was still up on the waterfront.

I took out my surveyor's monocle and zoomed in. The dark-skinned crowd still surrounded the ship, and they had tools. I could see them hacking away at the hull. It seemed an inefficient way to move the ship.

Another sip of Margarita later I left to find my room.

I HIRED a taxi to take me out to the warehouse near the airport. It was a blue Toyota pickup with bench seats and a large canopy strapped onto the bed. "Safari bus." I sat in front with the driver, who had what sounded like reggae thumping away in the cab. A harsh scratchy voice in a strong accent swore and belted out angry lyrics.

"Buju Banton," he said, turning it down.

"Sorry?" I didn't understand. He pointed at the tape and I understood; the name of the singer. "Airport."

"Right."

New York taxi drivers had nothing on island driving. We took off out the driveway and onto the road. Every corner seemed the last, with the pickup leaning, the contraption on the back shifting as we turned. Particularly since I couldn't shake the conviction that we were driving on the wrong side of the road, the left. The driver honked and waved at every other car or pickup going the other way, and at the pedestrians alongside the street.

The road took us down gently into town, and there we slowed down to a crawl with all the other cars. Finally I could get a close look at the ship. Crowds still surrounded it, but I didn't think they were government workers. Children, old women, a Rastafarian with long dreadlocks and tattered jeans; some of them wielded tools, scraping away at the ship. Others stood around, singing hymns, or just watching. Many had tears in their eyes.

Some of the wet planks were pulled away to expose ribs. I could see the dim gleam of white inside. Skeletons? It suddenly dawned on me that this was an old slave ship. Horrible. I shivered. St. Thomas had been one of the central points of the trade, being one of the best natural harbors in the Caribbean. Had a pirate ship fired and sunk this slaver in the harbor? Divers often searched the bottom after large cruise ships stirred up the silt, looking for history. But here it had been brought straight to land.

I leaned over and tapped the driver, who was just as fascinated as I was.

"What are they doing?" I asked.

"Taking care of it," he said. He had a strong accent: "Tekkin' cyare af it."

"What is it?" I whispered.

"It old," he told me. "Very old."

I HAD LUNCH again with Ottley. It was nice to relax and talk business with the skinny round-faced local. We reviewed plans for fixing the warehouses. Afterwards I walked out onto the concrete walkway that extended across the bay, following the old shoreline.

"You goin' ah see it?" a passerby asked me. I nodded.

I left my beer on the table, feeling that standing there and looking at the ship with a beer in hand would be sacrilegious. I felt this strange, deep tugging that called me closer.

The crowd around the ship parted and let me through. I could see a full range of color. From the darkest black man to the pale and grizzled yachtsmen, they all stood around watching me. Work paused. The wind kicked up a haze of dust that brushed past, tugging up my shirt and cooling the sweat on the small of my back. Someone coughed.

Placing the tips of my fingers on a plank I looked at my tan hand and wondered how I fit in. I pressed against the wood, and it gave slightly, soft with age. Beyond that I could feel something else beneath the surface. A sense of history, the past talking directly to me. It was a knot in my stomach.

And yet, I still remained distant. Maybe because my ancestors were mixed, and I could never bring myself to identify with either side. It was the same struggle I had with deciding what race box to check off on paperwork, or applications. Black? Definitely some; there's my unnaturally easy tan. White? During winter I would blend in with the average mall crowd, an easy anonymous decision.

Or maybe even a little Latino, and some Oriental thrown in for good measure. I was trapped in dispassion. In the end, I always chose "other."

I pulled away, and an old graying Rasta next to me nodded.

"Hear it call," he said in a deep voice. His muscles stood out as he grasped and ripped a plank away. I looked into the heart of the ship. Sometime during the night the bleached remains of the scattered skeletons had been removed, but the chains and manacles still hung from the bulkheads and partitions, the iron blacker than the skin of the man standing next to me. They should have had barnacles on them, or been rusted, yet they gleamed at me as new as the day they were made. What force was at work here?

Then the moment passed, and the crowd began to attack the hull of the ship again. I wandered off and found a stand selling Johnny Cakes, fried dough of some sort. Pates were a rolled-up pastry with meat inside. One of each and a Coke made for a good lunch.

EARLY THE next morning I went through the motions of moving our office to a building in better shape. But even in the back streets of town I was near enough the ship that it dominated my thoughts. At lunch I wandered through the alleys with small shops and cool shade until I ended up back at the ship.

"Eh, whitey-man. Hyere."

The same old Rasta greeted me. He'd been waiting. He handed me a pick and I joined him at the hull, pulling off the old planks. We spent a sweaty hour ripping off old wood and stacking it up near the sidewalk. After that we took a lunch break, eating pates, squatting on pieces of wood. Two skinny old fellows slapped dominoes on a table, and Soca music drifted over from a small tinny speaker.

Eventually three other men joined us. The Rasta passed around a joint, and the five of us sat in silence for fifteen minutes, seeking enlightenment, drifting to the warbling in the air.

"Come." The old Rasta got up, and I followed him around to the other side.

Here I found my surprise. They weren't just taking the ship apart; they were rebuilding it. New waterproofed lengths of wood replaced the old. I hadn't paid attention before, but the sound of sawing I'd heard while pulling planks off was not that of the old planks being broken apart.

"Why are you rebuilding it?" I asked. "Will you make it a museum?" I was trying to understand. The Rasta shook his locks.

"The whore of Babylon fall soon. We have ah be ready."

"The whore of Babylon?"

"Babylon America," he told me, shaking his locks. "Jus' like in Revelations." Revvy-lay-shons. "U. S. Virgin Islands part of Babylon, is time for we to spurn Babylon."

My head spun from the sweet smoke in the air, and I blinked. The ship hummed.

IT SCARED ME. The wooden planks, the manacles, the calm intensity of the people working at restoration. Yet they didn't plan to restore it. I would have understood restoration. I wanted to help with that, to rediscover a hidden part of myself, make peace with myself. Just like the Jewish I read about who returned to Auschwitz.

These people were planning something different though. I didn't understand what. So I drank alcoholic drinks with umbrellas back at the hotel. Every time I visited the bar at the pool I could see the waterfront, and I couldn't push the ship out of my mind. It was a relic, a reminder, and a key, and I didn't understand how to use it.

I wandered through the silent corridors looking for anyone, until I found a single busboy. He sold me a packet of his best red. I lit up on the porch of my roof and smoked until I fell asleep on the cold tile.

I dreamed of naked and emaciated black specters rising out of the muddy waters of Charlotte Amalie Harbor, thousands of them, marching in force up through town, and then swinging out towards the point that the hotel sat on. They picked me up and carried me back down into the sea with them.

THERE WERE lines up and down the waterfront. Islanders lined up and waiting to see the restored product, I thought. The taxi driver dropped me off, and I found the Rasta.

"'Ere we ah go," he said smiling.

I noticed someone had painted a name on the rear: *Marcus Garvey*. One of the founders of the back-to-Africa movement a long time ago. I paced the length of the ship, trying to figure out what exactly it was they were doing.

"This is insane," I protested. The Rasta nodded again.

"Massive insanity," he agreed. I briskly walked back away to get a better view of the deck.

An old woman in a green shawl stood just under the forecastle. A young boy in a green and white uniform from the school just up the street stepped to the front of the deck. Her old withered hands reached out to give him a sip from the green gourd she held. He shivered and fainted, crumpling in on himself, then rolling onto the deck. I could see the tiny chest rise with a slowing rhythm of breath, until the child fell still. My stomach flip-flopped with memories of stories of mass suicides.

The woman next in line, maybe his mother, took the liquid just as calmly. Behind her a policeman waited his turn.

As soon as they lay limp on the deck two men would bear the unconscious down into the ship's holds.

The silent ritual repeated itself. I whirled upon the Rasta by my side.

"What is this? What are you doing?" I demanded, heart pounding.

"They sleep zombie-style 'till we ah come there."

"Where?" I asked.

"Land of milk an' honey." He shrugged. "Or anywhere else. A new place. They will wake in Zion."

"But why this ship?" I wanted to know.

"We ah bring we history with we. We face it, not run from it."

I made my way to the hull and touched it. It sang now, full of energy. It sounded like a temple of Buddhist monks, an *ooom* sound that hinted at deep power.

My dispassion faltered for a moment. I was trying to think about work, rational facts, anything but what was happening around me.

"I have to go," I said. I was expected to return soon back at Sombrero Island; I had to leave tomorrow. What could I do here, when even the police were lined up?

"You missin' it," the Rastaman said. He looked disappointed.

I turned away and walked back to the taxi. My hand trembled as I opened the door.

A slave ship could hold maybe four hundred bodies stacked in the worst imaginable manner. Yet it seemed that most of the population of the island stood waiting their turn to be led into the hold.

Impossible.

I SLEPT fitfully that night until the deep *ooom* called me. I sat up, stood, and walked to the pool. The night was deathly quiet, and the clouds twisted in long strands above. The moon shone full on the shimmering harbor water, and lights blazed across the massive natural amphitheater of the harbor and curving backbone of the island's mountains.

Anchored in the air above the town was the ship. As I watched it cast itself free and floated up over the hill. The long streamers of cloud that usually just scraped the tip of Crown Mountain, the highest point on the island, seemed to reach down and take the boat up into their depths and out of sight.

It's a dream, I told myself, grabbing the railing. The cold metal railing told me different.

I WOKE UP the next morning nervous. Today I was to take the water taxi from the hotel's dock into town where Ottley was to be waiting with the powerboat's keys. From there I'd go back to St. Croix. Then fly to Florida.

Now, waiting by the dock, the taxi already late, I knew I hadn't been dreaming. I couldn't see the slave ship way off in the distance on the waterfront. Only bare concrete. No cars moved through the street.

Hours later, after wandering throughout the deserted hotel to find something to eat, I walked down to the waterfront. The entire island had gotten into the boat yesterday and left. I understood that. Where they were going I still was not sure. I sat on the concrete rim of the waterfront, trying to explain to the wind why methane booster rockets were more efficient than kerosene, but I couldn't remember, and it didn't matter really. The entire waterfront, loud and bustling, lay dead quiet. I remembered other busy cities I'd lived in. I remembered production deadlines and dirt-free clean-suits, laptops and cellular modems, and being asked to have the numbers on the desk by the next morning.

A tiny wooden skiff bumped up against the large truck tires hung off the edge of the concrete to protect the ferries. I looked down. The green, red, and yellow letters read *Little Garvey.* My hand started to tremble again, and I wished I still had another joint with me.

The skiff had a bench in the middle, two pegs on either side to put the oars between. It bobbed and hit the tire in rhythm with the swell. I carefully clambered in, untying the hemp rope, and pushed off from the waterfront. Somehow they had all managed to subvert that horrible legacy, the slave ship and what it represented, from the past and take it with them proudly into a new future.

How?

I wanted to try.

I set the oars between the two pegs, closed my eyes, and leaned back. The oars bit into the water, the small boat began to move. Trust, I figured, was important. And belief.

I began to row.

science

SOME AFRICANS brought their herbal lore with them over the water. In plantation society, slave doctors did as much business as the European men of science, and likely as much good. African medicine included philters and rituals for the mind as well as the body, although slaves were forbidden to follow their own spiritual beliefs. The old people used to call African herbal lore "science." The beliefs went underground for a few hundred years, but they've never gone away. Sometimes its practitioners are feared and their rituals poorly understood. Sometimes they can move with authority in their lands.

Inspired by the story of the Morant Bay Rebellion (Jamaica, 1865), Roger McTair has written this story with more than a nod to H. P. Lovecraft.

Just a Lark

(or The Crypt of Matthew Ashdown)

ROGER MCTAIR

T HE LATE AUTHOR of the manuscript was a friend and colleague of mine. He frequently published papers in the journal I edit. His specialty was Mercantilism and the Triangular Trade; mine was Newfoundland fisheries. These specialties may seem disparate but they are not. In fact, we once collaborated on a monograph: The Effect of The Antillean Plot Farming on the Newfoundland Economy 1834–1875.

He sent me this manuscript a few months before he died. His notes indicate it was not a final draft, but obviously it was close to completion. I have to decide on publishing it. Is it fact or fiction? Is it a fitting last testament from an outstanding scholar? Is it one of those junctures where history meets with the monstrous and the results should be quietly interred? Or can understanding—even self-awareness—be gained from examination? Because you have had a more than serious interest in the sources of men like Poe, Lovecraft, and Stoker, I would like you to have a look at, and advise me on, this manuscript in the context of your interests and his, and purely as a historian, of mine.

R. M. T.

P.S.: His text begins with this epigraph:

But enough of these horrors: They can no longer be perpe-
trated. But they must not be forgotten in an attempt to
form a judgment of the present.

The West Indies/Underhill/1862

I T IS NOT FASHIONABLE to believe in the superstitions of yesteryear. In my youth a pervasive Christian environment,
and total acceptance of superficial colonial mores, which we reverently
proclaimed as civilization, debunked any validity of the supernatural.

It is probably still so on the island, but I do not know for sure.
Sadly, I have not visited my birthplace since 1962, and now may never
visit it again.

In these times, however, I am sure superior communications, access
to literacy, the placing of street lights on major thoroughfares, an
awareness of science, and the power of radio and television have kept
superstition and interest in the supernatural at the very perimeters of
consciousness.

All this is for the good.

In Canada, where I have lived and worked for years, I have given
much thought to these things. I have read the Victorian literature of
the genre. I have said that my interest in ghosts, goblins, and duppies
of various sorts was recreational and literary, and that belief in polter-
geists has been the province of the unlettered.

That has been my public stance.

In my youth, however, I was a player in a set of circumstances that
led to tragedy. It radically altered my perceptions and my life. The facts
have never been told. Now, before I pass away, I intend to place the
truth as I saw it on the record. I refuse to offer any explanation that is
not rooted in the world as we know it and can ask the reader only to
draw his own conclusions.

As a young man, in my early twenties, just after the war, I belonged to
a group of men-about-town, as men-about-town as we could have been

in a colonial Caribbean island. We were the scions of well-to-do families, by caste and color, children of privilege. There was little to do, except supervise clerks at our import-export offices and search diligently for fun.

None of us had managed to get to the war.

The hostilities were over. Churchill nattered on about not presiding over the dissolution of the British Empire. The island's elite and middle classes concurred fervently and waited for the island to return to the placidity of the early thirties: cricket on the greens, the governor's garden party, horse racing, *Tom Brown's Schooldays, Wisden,* and *London Illustrated* on the side table, servants who knew their place, and workers who wouldn't join unions or riot in the streets.

The late thirties had been quite explosive but a Royal Commission and the distraction of the war had shelved the disturbances.

Regardless of Churchill's warnings, my friends and I didn't mind a little dissolution, if it involved alcoholic beverages and intrigue with the ladies. The former was quite easily had (I can, I venture to say, still mix an agonizingly perfect cocktail); the latter, I have to admit, was much more difficult.

Like any other coterie of young men, we held socials, had picnics, played tennis and cricket, went to the beach, and exerted ourselves only in pursuit of a delightful rum punch or a comely lady. Ardent pursuit of cricket or tennis didn't count.

We were living as our fathers lived, or so we thought, but you must remember it has been a space of 45-odd years; the intensity of my dissoluteness may be unjustly amplified by memory.

What I am sure of, in retrospect, was the effect of William Gordon on our group. He had come from a suburb of the capital, Cherry Lane or Cherry Heights or Cherry Gap, I forget the exact name. He had gone to one of those private secondary schools that "externally" educated teachers created to bilk the poor out of their earnings in exchange for an education for their children. Of course that was before the extended secondary education franchise.

I have heard that some of those schools were quite good. They turned out graduates who went far. But in my youth they had a bad reputation. Frankly, in our set you were boarding school or you were nothing.

I do not know why William Gordon was accepted in our circle. He was very articulate and quite polite, but he wasn't one of us. He was a friend of Billy Hill's who, could we have imagined it at the time, turned out to be a flaming radical and union lawyer.

In those days Billy Hill was quite the swank; suits made in London and all those Liberty of London ties. He introduced William Gordon to the group.

Gordon was formal, as so many of that aspiring class tended to be. We could never call him Gordie or Willie. It was either Mr. Gordon or William.

I'm afraid Mr. Gordon introduced rather solemn ideas into our group, and caused a bit of a rift among chaps who had been friends since childhood. He was very much an advocate of self-government and, "as soon as the people were ready," independence. Among radicals these ideas were quite the thing at the time. He wasn't a fanatic, but these ideas couched in emotional language, or at an inauspicious time, would have been seditious.

Gordon and Hill's ideas publicly expressed during the troubles of '38 would have certainly landed them in the dock. They frequently espoused these ideas at our get-togethers, and the rift in the clique began. There were those for no social or political change and those for radical change. I was horrified at the chaps who suddenly took politics seriously. It broke my heart to see the lads who had worked hard to perfect the fox-trot doing a number with economics and political science. It got worse and worse.

Sammy Ronay named the factions swankers and swotters. I drifted between both. Billy Hill had become a swotter of the worst sort. His family had a history of social criticism and I supposed it erupted in his blood. Gordon was the voice of exhaustive research and unrelenting reason. The man was a political information machine, polite but implacable.

The swankers were led by Jamie Pearnell and Eddie Shears, both absolutely dapper and à la mode. Eddie was the smoothest dancer I have ever seen. His trouser seams were so sharp they could cut butter. Only Sammy Ronay's trousers had sharper seams than his.

Neither swankers nor swotters were happy with me. The swankers were upset because I had developed a bit of political vocabulary; the swotters, because I never participated in a really informed manner in discussions, and I still got my neckties from London.

We were beyond our parents' influence, although we lived at home. The parents were none too happy with the direction of the group. Nationalist politics were taboo in most respectable homes.

Johnny Eyre's father packed him off to Australia where he had relatives, and "Batty" Eyre, Johnny's younger brother, was sent upcountry to the Eyre estate to learn to grow sugarcane. "Tippy" Somers, another equivocator like myself, hung around both factions until he slunk off to Britain after the tragedy.

Within three months of Gordon's arrival, my clique was disintegrating. This made me very unhappy. I decided to take action. I gave a big party and invited them all. Jamie Pearnell made the rum punch. Mummy (dear departed Mummy) organized the cooking, she even brought in an extra cook and maids to help. Dadoo (dear Daddy, may he rest in peace) imported the latest dance records from Miami. The scene was set for a pleasant evening.

Mummy decorated the living room with red and white hibiscus blossoms. There were tables in the garden under a tarpaulin tent. The cassia tree was in bloom, if I remember, and Mummy hung a large hurricane lantern next to golden blooms. There were many positive remarks about that touch. But our preparations were in vain.

That week a reformer in the representative assembly made the statement that the new constitution was too little of one thing and not enough of the next; it was defective and needed change. The *Island Gazette* denounced the speech, letters to the editor poured in. The reformer was accused of precipitating anarchy, of advocating treason, of wanting to sacrifice the island on the altar of Haytiism.

The invitees to my party seemed intent only on discussing the statement. Hill and Gordon were drafting a reply to the editorial. People who preferred dancing tried to get on with it, but only looked forlorn in their attempts. An argumentative crowd gathered around Gordon and Hill.

While this party-pooping spread insidiously over my party, Jackie Arvel came to me with a suggestion. He thought the party could hardly get worse (unless Gordon and Hill declared Independence), but that a midnight excursion to Bristoltown near Morante might salvage the evening.

"Why," I asked, "why Bristoltown?" I had never heard of the village.

"It's lonely and dark and isolated. It'll be a lark."

"But why?" I asked.

"There's an old graveyard there, more than a hundred years old. We could take some rum punch and have a midnight party."

I didn't like this game, not that I was superstitious. I never liked Jackie Arvel. He often disappeared for weeks to his father's lands in Palgrave. He was reputed to have a peasant mistress there. The family had been landowners for generations. His father was a mathematician and folklorist. It was whispered the senior Mr. Arvel had gone native, dabbling in obeah. Other whispers said he was a graduate of Miskatonic Institute situated quite close to Salem and the ancient legend-haunted city of Arkham. He had been in class, it was said, with H. P. Lovecraft, the celebrated chronicler of tales of the fantastic.

Jackie often hinted his father possessed the only copies on the island of the rare and dreaded Necronomicon; the 3-volume canon of the Meditations of Albertus Magnus; and the fragmentary but ineffable Book of Eibon; as well as a threadbare mysteriously lambent swatch of the ceremonial purple cowl of Abdul Alhazred, whose name still evokes reverence and dread from those who know.

Jackie was too much associated with the superstitions of the time. We called them Black Arts then; given the island's sensitivity, who would call them Black Arts now? He never said he believed, only that he knew.

Jackie was not to be denied. He arranged it all, the wrapping up of the party, the people, and the cars. Hill, Gordon, and most of their faction did not come. Others, frankly, were scared. All the ladies refused to go. I went because I was never a party pooper and was game but grave.

You must imagine the state of the country roads at that hour, dense, bleak and rare of humanity. It was a major excursion, thirty miles or more on poorly constructed roads and in almost impenetrable darkness. After about two hours we arrived at Bristoltown. It was deserted. Every hut, shop, and shelter was closed. Only a few dogs prowled the streets. Even in the darkness I could see it was a poor, old, forlorn little village.

We stopped about a mile outside the village. The road had ended abruptly. It was awfully dark. We were surrounded by a dense undergrowth of trees. Fireflies and glowworms darted in the darkness. The sky was a dense opaque bowl. Arvel said we had to walk from there, for some distance; but before we left he had to arrange his "substances."

We were beginning to be disturbed. Our laughter on the drive to Bristoltown had changed to nervous silence. Arvel asked to be left alone and I could just barely see him peering deeply into a bag he had taken from his pocket. I thought I saw a strange glow emitting from the bag.

Something brushed my face. It made a fluttering sound, unseen wings oscillating somewhere around our heads, then suddenly fading in the denseness.

"No need to worry," Arvel said when the echo died away. "Just a fruit bat."

"Look here, Arvel," Eddie said, "is this necessary? I mean, we have proven the point, old chap, we have come! Why can't we just call it a night and go home?"

"Call it midnight, you mean," Tippy Somers said nervously, "Midnight . . ."

Jackie Arvel's eyes seemed to gleam in the dark. Then he said, "It's just a lark. I thought we were all men here." Tippy Somers laughed, a little hollowly I thought, and afterward we agreed that the echo of his laughter seemed to linger just too long over the trees.

"At one time, all this was cultivated land," Arvel said when the echo reluctantly faded away. "It was a slave plantation, quite prosperous too.

The last owner was brutally murdered. People have tried to grow provisions and cultivate food here since, but they never seem to succeed. Only goats roam now, and even they don't seem to thrive."

"Are we going?" Eddie Shears said.

"Well, yes, if we're all ready," Arvel said. "Follow me."

And he headed into the bush. Later Eddie Shears swore he meant were we going back. But afraid to look like fools, we all plunged into the undergrowth after Jackie.

It was not a pleasant jaunt. The rutted track was barely visible in the gloom. Branches of undergrowth encroached on it, poked our ribs, tore our shirts, and whipped our faces. Tippy Somers turned his ankle in a rut and said a mild "damn," one of the few times I heard Tippy swear.

Some time later we stumbled into a small clearing. There was no need for Jackie Arvel to declare, "We're here," but he did. There was a knife edge of a moon. From where we stood we could see the hard shadows of gravestones, crosses, and commemorative stelae. The silhouette of a huge tree dominated the furthermost extremity of the burial ground. And dead in the center was a dark and looming edifice.

"The crypt," Arvel said in the dark, pointing at the overwhelming structure. "The crypt of Matthew Ashdown."

"Why," said Eddie Shears with his teeth knocking, "why are we standing around? We've seen the place. We've had our fun. Let's go back."

For some reason I was no longer scared. I was itchy and sweaty and bored. A branch had slashed my face and a trickle of blood congealed on my cheek. Since we had come this far, I wanted to see what would happen. I suspected nothing would.

Jackie Arvel ignored us all. He held his bag in his hand and was muttering strange words. I didn't think he was aware of us at all.

Sammy Ronay had said little all evening. He was always game for anything; now he lit a cigarette and said, "Well, Jackie, what's next on the agenda, a little spirit-calling?" The flame of his match showed his smile of unbelief. "What are you going to do now, Jackie?" he continued. "This isn't exactly the Savoy you know. I've been in jauntier places."

Jackie's voice sounded ethereal in the darkness. "This is no joke, chaps."

"What are you doing?" Tippy asked, his teeth audibly knocking.

"I am going to raise Matthew Ashdown from the grave."

Tippy breathed so heavily in the darkness I could feel my mustache move.

"Let's get on with it," Sammy Ronay said. "Maybe only the dead can revive this party." He laughed out loud, long and sarcastically, and the echo of his laughter came back at us long and loud and hollow.

Jackie Arvel placed us all at a point equidistant from the crypt and the giant silk cotton tree. He stood in the middle, facing the tomb. He had warned us, regardless of what happened, of whatever we saw, to hold fast and remain silent.

"Shall we pray?" Tippy Somers asked, his voice cracking with fright.

"Prayers can't help you if this does not go to plan, or if the substances do not have their potency. Only maintaining the configuration can."

"Get on with it, Jackie," Sammy said, sounding quite languid in the darkness.

"Yes, quite, get on with it," Eddie Shears said, imitating Sammy's tone, though not at all convincingly.

"The show begins," Jackie said.

We couldn't see his eyes or mouth, just a silhouette in the darkness. He was muttering the incantations he had muttered at the edge of the clearing, but with urgency as if commanding something to obey him. Nothing out of the ordinary stirred.

We were being eaten by mosquitoes. Jackie's silhouette twisted and turned on his chosen spot, the fists on his outstretched arms clenched and moving in irregular patterns. The whole scene began to smack of an elaborate charade. On the other hand, although I was not superstitious, I didn't want to disregard the possibility of Matthew Ashdown popping out of his crypt.

The group was getting restless. Even Tippy Somers was shaking his head. We were about to break the configuration when we heard an agonizing wrenching sound. Our gasps were almost unanimous. A sudden breeze shook the trees and even above that we could hear our breaths rushing. Even Jackie stood still, his arms frozen in the middle of some esoteric movement.

The breeze came up and the wrenching groan erupted again, grinding across the darkness, riveting us to our spots.

"Well, hallo," Sammy Ronay said, his voice light and cheerful in the dark. "It's your friendly man-eating silk cotton tree trying to bring us back from the dead."

We broke out laughing. The silk cotton tree had been swaying in the breeze, and the groans had come from its trunk and branches twisting in the wind.

"What's up, Jackie?" Sammy said.

Jackie laughed too. "I suppose," he said, "the wraith of Matthew Ashdown will have to wait for another midnight. The damn fool won't respond."

Our laughter was loud and various in the darkness. The adventure was over.

Word of our nocturnal adventure spread very fast. We were instantly notorious.

The *Island Gazette* carried a stern editorial against flirting with the forces of evil. We were thunderously denounced from the nonconformist pulpits. The Anglican Church ignored our little jaunt, but we heard there was much criticism in the vestry. Mummy walked around for days with the air of a wronged woman, and Daddy called me to the library to say I was too old to be still frivolous. It was the first time since I left boarding school that I had had a serious chat with my father. After the paternal reprimands, he asked if I had thought seriously of my future. I hadn't.

He said the new constitution was an intermediate but irreversible step toward political independence and more changes would come. He suggested I study law in preparation for a career in politics; there would be great opportunities for local men. I was very surprised. Mummy and Dadoo were great wavers of the Union Jack; photographs of the Royal Family hung over the mantelpiece. Daddy had studied law in Britain. He never gave any indication he foresaw changes in the status quo. Mummy could never imagine a day when we could separate from England.

I said if he thought politics was a good idea, I would certainly consider it for the good of the island and all that, and wandered off to find Eddie.

Eddie was reveling in the notoriety. He had become very popular with the ladies. He had convinced them all that he had led us to the brink of the flaming abyss of hell itself. With delightful shudders, some of the ladies demanded to be taken out to Bristoltown at midnight. Eddie demurred, hinting that only the initiated could withstand the insidious attraction that emanated from the crumbling crypt of Matthew Ashdown.

Since that night Jackie Arvel had disappeared. Sammy Ronay said old Mr. Arvel had heard of Jackie's escapade, was appalled that Jackie risked incurring forces that, once evoked, he could never control, and had ordered him to remain on their estate where our apprentice necromancer was supervising the reaping of a pimento crop.

We were terribly upset about this. Jackie's presence would have been great for a giggle. Tippy Somers only had to twist, stretch his arms, and enchant the "secret" words for the company to double with laughter. Tippy was so good we howled every time.

William Gordon didn't find this funny at all. He still visited with Billy Hill. Both men were very critical of our midnight revel. Billy Hill thought we were being uncivilized by even joking about the possibility of the supernatural. Gordon's disapproval took the form of a glacial silence on the topic.

It was only when Eddie Shears announced a "cryptic picnic," on purple invitations with silver polyhedronic figures deeply recessed on the borders, that William Gordon urgently sought my ear. He waited until we were alone and warned that we were foolish to encourage superstition or seek thrills in the repressed historical memory of the island. If I could not convince Eddie to cancel the picnic at Bristoltown, he would only ask me to talk to a man whose knowing might make me change my mind.

By now I supposed I liked Gordon. He was grim but I recognized if I followed Dad's advice and got into politics people like Gordon and many of his class would be useful to me. Besides, they were the wave of the future. Dad was right, reform couldn't be stopped; I could see that now. Nehru was insisting on independence for India. The Gold Coast was negotiating for a new constitution. Every African colony, Tanganyika, Northern Rhodesia, and Nyasaland, was demanding self-government and self-rule.

The *Island Gazette* was none too happy about this. They ran fierce editorials about the all-encompassing benefits of being under the English heaven. They published articles on British scientists who could find no biological ability for self-government in non-European races, and they supplemented these articles with photographs and cartoons that were insulting even for those times.

I made my choice. I told Gordon I would go with him to meet his friend. I drove, he pointed the way. I was very surprised to find we were headed toward Morante but I said nothing. The journey was much easier by day. The road was busy with people, peasants and laborers, mules, donkey carts, bicycles, hand carts, the occasional car. Many of the women and carts were loaded with produce, the women carrying huge bundles and baskets on their heads. We passed crowded village markets on the way.

It was a beautiful morning. After all these years I can think of no landscape as engrossing as an island in the morning; so many shades of green, such varieties of vegetation, sunlight that shimmers and plays on leaves, on fruit, on birds; the sudden glimpses of startling blue sea, subjects for a Monet or a Siseley; rudimentary huts and homes of country folk, spare unyielding church facades, quaint villages, and field workers. Emotionally I still respond to these remembered images.

We bypassed Morante for some miles. Gordon then directed a turn down a country road. Further along the main road lay the town of Amity Hall, which, I had heard, had borne witness to brutal events in our island's history. We drove down a track that grew worse as we went on; on both sides were citrus fields. We saw a few peasants who stood on the sides to let us through. After some time we came to a fork in the road. We turned left and drove to a small settlement surrounded by fields of corn, bananas, and provisions.

"This is Pinnacle," Gordon said. We were expected, although the people showed no excessive curiosity. An older boy asked if we were looking for Teacha Paul and escorted us to the end of the settlement. There were houses along the way and we could see men and women attending garden plots or doing domestic duties. The boy, who looked seventeen, brought us to a wooden house. The house was fronted by a well-kept garden.

My mother was a member of the Garden Society. From being the patient buttress against her horticultural anxieties I had learned about flowers. This garden would have impressed her. There were beds of purple gloxinias, more purple indeed than the artificial color of Eddie Shears's sinister invitation. Between the gloxinias were clusters of red marigolds, African violets, and morning glory. A bougainvillea bush of lush and proud magenta stood in glorious isolation at one corner of the house.

A voice from the doorway welcomed us. Gordon embraced the man. He was an average-sized black man. I shook his hand. His gaze was notably frank and direct.

We sat at the back of the house on a small veranda. There were hoes, forks, and other gardening implements stacked in a corner. The backyard was bare and surrounded by a stockade. This surprised me. The ground was flat and packed as if it had been stamped into evenness. It looked like a ceremonial space of some sort.

I looked at Gordon. His eyes were fixed on our host, who sat in a wicker chair next to the hoes and forks. He gazed over his backyard. His eyes seemed to inspect every inch of the packed dirt. I wondered why Gordon didn't initiate some discussion. I felt uncomfortable.

Without taking his eyes from the backyard, our host spoke to me. "All I tell you is what you know."

Well, I didn't come here for hocus-pocus, I thought, already regretting being convinced by Gordon to make the trip.

The man turned his eye on me. I knew he knew what had passed through my mind. A shiver of annoyance brought me back to my senses. He can't know what I'm thinking, I thought, I'm succumbing to Gordon's fears and this rural atmosphere.

Our host kept talking to me, his head turned again in the direction of the yard, yet I had the unsettling sensation that I knew what he would reply before his mouth uttered words.

"The sea not touch a shore on which there is no dead. The sun shine on no tree on which rope or gibbet not hang. No field, no gully without a bed of bones. Evil and vile; evil Eyre, evil Ashdown, evil Milner, evil Niembhard, evil Jonas, evil Edward, evil Riland . . ." He said the names in a quiet measured way, so that the names were blended in emphasis and just the stressed "evil" punctuated the montage.

To my horror I recognized many of the names of prominent families on the island, some of the namesake families were our friends, families like ours. To staunch the roll of names I quickly asked, "Were the Ashdowns really that evil?"

He replied, "Evil Ashdowns. One of many."

"Is that their graveyard and crypt around Bristoltown?" I asked rhetorically.

"Yes! The last Ashdowns lie there. More evil than most, no less than any!"

"Can't you see, Gordon, this whole picnic thing is a joke?" I was exasperated.

"Matthew Ashdown was no joke," Teacha Paul said. "The evil Ashdowns were no joke."

Gordon leaped to his feet and said seriously, "In 1865 there was a revolt. Ex-slaves and apprentices rose up in arms. It started here, in this parish. The revolt was crushed. The government couldn't afford another Hayti. It was legal slaughter."

"What does that have to do with Matthew Ashdown, or me, or Jackie Arvel or the picnic, or with . . . ?" I was agitated.

Gordon gave our host a patient look. "Matthew Ashdown, his wife, his mulatto mistresses, and all their children were put to the torch during the rebellion in that parish. Some were thrown into vats of boiling sealing wax. They were techniques learned from the masters of the Ashdown Plantation themselves."

"But that's one hundred years ago, that's history!" I said.

"At rebellion time," our host said, his eyes still on the yard, "at rebellion time my Pappa was twenty years old. I was his seventh son in his fortieth year. He saw the troubles—blood, bayonet, gibbet, and fire. His brother was hanged, my uncle. I tell you as my father tell me."

"Don't you see," Gordon said tersely, "in this political climate you don't want to remind people they were once chattel, not in that way. If you have that picnic, if you begin evoking the memories of that time, do you know what you can let loose in this colony? There's enough unrest and bitterness as it is. We're going to have reform and it's going to be fast—but it must be fast and orderly."

I could see his point. Although I didn't see why the issues of yesteryear would be of such importance now. The peasants were happy, their provision plots and five-acre farms seemed to keep them healthy. They were certainly breeding abundantly. Only in the cities were the workers disgruntled, stirred up by agitators, as they had been stirred up in '38, causing unnecessary trouble. I was sure it would blow over.

"Eddie is going to have his fun," I said. "I can't stop him."

We sat in silence for some time. Then putting into words thoughts that had been haunting me for some time, I said, "Is there any chance that Jackie could have called up something from that crypt?" With that question I felt there was genuine communication for the first time. God knows the question was unplanned.

"Why you ask?" our host said, turning to look at me. "You don't believe shadow-catcher hocus-pocus!"

"I don't know what to believe, seems like a joke to think some, some . . . thing can come floating out of a grave. It's preposterous in these times!"

"You sure?" our host said. He asked it very intimately, as if we were old friends. I felt a shiver go through me. In that bright country morning, I became terribly afraid.

"What are we going to do?" I asked lamely, looking from our host's impassive mien to Gordon.

"Stop this foolish, boarding school game; all this mumbo-jumbo, ju-ju foolishness. Purple invitations and cabalistic signs, good God, how can you fool around with all that, how can you fritter away your youth with Eddie Shears and Jackie Arvel? Get this devilish picnic thing canceled and get down to work."

"How?" I said. I was taken aback by his vehemence and couldn't meet his gaze. I was to blame as much as Eddie or Jackie or Tippy or Sammy Ronay. I had gone along, even encouraged the cryptic picnic, but now I felt an intense sense of impending disaster. Deep in my mind I believed the unspoken communication Teacha Paul was relaying to me. Some dreadful tragedy awaited us in the graveyard on the ruined plantation near Bristoltown and unless I submitted to processes, everything my upbringing, my family, and my parents taught me to denigrate, there was nothing I could do to prevent it.

Gordon argued that if we couldn't convince Eddie to cancel the picnic, we should petition someone in authority to advise Eddie to halt and desist. I didn't like the idea of getting authority involved, it would only get back to my father. Besides, I thought I could make reason prevail. I would talk to Eddie and Jackie.

Gordon wasn't so sure. Strong immediate remedial action was needed. Teacha Paul kept his counsel while we argued the matter. I knew I could not stop Eddie from taking a party to the graveyard, but I was sure I could convince Jackie not to repeat his foolish experiment. Gordon disagreed, he had no faith in my friends' judgment.

I turned to our host and asked, "Teacha Paul, wha' fe do?"

Gordon stared at me like a man gone mad. He had brought me to be made aware of the secreted truths of the island, and rather than react like an educated man, a young man of station, I had succumbed to the man's power. I wondered if Gordon felt it too. They had embraced, they had to be intimate. But Gordon seemed distanced. Was it that Teacha Paul's power, his followers, or his settlement in the bush was only the realization of one of Gordon's political principles?

Merely a free village that Gordon approved of, a manifestation of peasant competence and self-sufficiency? Was that all?

If that was the essential of politics, I wouldn't be good at it. I already
had a bond with Teacha Paul; I had an emotional investment in his
powers but it wasn't political.

Teacha Paul signaled us inside the house to his inner retreat. Outside
the door Gordon demurred, Teacha Paul held his eye but Gordon violently shook his head. He backed away and sat at the living room table,
looking taut and tense.

The Teacha's retreat was not the kind of room you would find in
any peasant's house. Books lay everywhere, on shelves, on the floor. I
noticed Tacitus, Agricola; a history of Ethiopia; *Ancient Records of
Egypt;* Scipio Africanus, *History and Description of Africa,* and at least a
score more. There was even a bible.

In the center of the room on a table lay a soiled manuscript in progress,
an ink-stand and an ink-stained steel-nibbed pen, and some bound volumes. I took a quick glance. There were two dictionaries and old histo-
ries of the islands. Some of the titles were familiar, but I had not read any.

In one darkened corner were clustered four Congo drums made
from tree trunks covered with goatskin and secured with taut rope.
Next to these was a carved mahogany chest. On the chest was a box of
long blue candles and a huge brass bell. On the walls were secured clip-
pings of Abyssinian soldiers paying homage to their king; a framed
photograph of Selassie enthroned and a group of robed Tuareg horse-
men charging across a desert landscape. In shadow on the wall opposite the desk was pinned a magazine illustration of a town, labeled
"Stony Gut Rebuilt"; and next to it a photograph of a striking young
black man dressed in an old-fashioned suit, whom I took to be Teacha
Paul's younger relative, or his son.

Gordon knew I had entered Teacha Paul's private retreat for "protection." He had refused to be party to it. Doubtless he considered it a
reversion to primitive superstition and his skeptical rational self couldn't
accept it. I could scarcely believe I was accepting it myself. Our family
were High Church Anglicans; my mother and father would be shocked

I could acknowledge the potency of the supernatural. Even as I accepted the pouch of calabar beans, garlic, herbs, and granules he would not name, I asked myself why I had accepted counsel and fetishes from someone to whom I was educationally and socially superior. Teacha Paul smiled to himself as I took the pouch of "protection" and placed it in my pocket.

We heard Gordon stirring in the living room outside. Teacha Paul held me by the arm and whispered instructions into my ear.

Gordon said little to me in the week after we returned from Pinnacle and Teacha Paul's. I think he was disappointed with me. I had let down the side. I had strayed from the high road.

Arvel returned from upcountry with the news that he had found the solution to the problem of the Ashdown crypt in the Necronomicon's penultimate acronym. He was very excited. The code had been broken by matching the acronym's abstruse cues with obscure passages he had unearthed in the esoteric writings of Albertus Magnus, the medieval alchemist. The solution was simple, he said, just a matter of arranging some select everyday words in a certain construct like a narrative or tale. Once the form of the construct was known and set, arbitrary or specific variations using correspondences of sounds to unify and verify the form would evoke any number of unreal or not-real situations. The formula was unpredictable only if a sequence of arbitrary variations within the known form was pursued; then there was the possibility of an abject failure or an unexpected result.

Gordon was furious when he heard Arvel had returned in time for the picnic and was planning to descant his arcane passages at the Ashdown graveyard.

I managed to placate him but even then he insisted on taking time off from his schedule to come with us. I wasn't happy about this. I supposed I had reverted to being a swanker. I was terribly embarrassed by that whole episode with Teacha Paul at Pinnacle. I had told no one. I kept the pouch of preparations hidden in my room and decided the Teacha's power was self-delusion on my part, and a hoax on his.

On the Saturday morning we gathered at Eddie Shears's house and drove to Bristoltown. Eddie had made all the arrangements. We had reserved a suite of rooms at the decrepit old inn at the edge of the village. From there we would set out for the cryptic picnic at the Ashdown graveyard in the early afternoon. We would return to the inn after sundown and rest and recuperate with dinner and drinks. We had agreed not to go to the crypt at midnight. The next morning we would go back to the capital.

Eddie had hired a young man and his brother from the village to clear the brush that encroached on the path to the graveyard. The young men would also meet us at the inn to help with the picnic baskets. They knew the area well.

We had expected a party of eighteen. Only thirteen, including Gordon, showed up. He alone was not in a festive mood. His face was set and cheerless. Tippy Somers said Gordon looked as happy as a man to be hanged in an hour.

That afternoon, Deacon and Moses, the young men of the village, led the way to our sepulchral destination. They had done a fine job of clearing away the brush, so good a job, in fact, I noticed the path was recently used by some large animal; hooves of a goat from some villager's pen, I supposed.

In my picnic basket I carried fruit, light delicacies prepared by my mother, and a bottle of champagne. I also carried Teacha Paul's pouch. I had debated whether to take the preparation I had accepted at Pinnacle, and decided yes, it could do no harm. But I felt quite foolish knowing it was there.

The cemetery in the daytime was an ordinary sight, broken headstones, crosses, leaning stelae, urns, broken marble slabs, and the huge crypt of Matthew Ashdown standing in stained silence close to the gnarled bark of the silk cotton tree. I noticed one small difference from the excursion of the night of my party. The huge seal, the ornate A, surrounded by the polyhedronic figures, that was encrusted on the facade over the iron gates of the crypt, leaked some noxious liquid that formed a pool in the dirt to the entrance of the tomb.

We hung our baskets on the branches of misshapen trees, and watched Eddie rush about trying to conjure up some fun.

It wasn't a very bright day, and it was sweltering, a clammy unhealthy kind of heat. A viscous humidity made us irritable. The sky hung low. Even the vegetation seemed stricken in the leaden air. Occasionally we got relief when a reluctant wind would blow, evoking groans and moans from the barely swaying silk cotton tree.

Jackie sat under the tree for most of the afternoon. He was uncharacteristically morose. Sammy Ronay said a cryptic picnic should ideally take place on the midnight of the witches' sabbath, not on a Saturday afternoon. Tippy Somers still looked nervous.

The afternoon dragged on. We tried to make the best of it. Madeline Thomas was especially nice trying to cheer us all up. There was an overabundance of food, which nobody ate except Moses, Deacon's brother. Eddie arranged silly games with the young ladies. They tried to be frightened but even they were bored.

Gordon tried to get some political opinions out of me. I told him I agreed there was a need for political reform and manfully tried to change the conversation. Mainly it was too hot to think and the champagne didn't help.

Gordon was relieved at how innocuous the day turned out and spent most of his time discussing the economic situation in the parish with Deacon and Moses.

Jackie sat under the silk cotton tree thinking seriously. Sammy looked cool but disappointed.

Then Eddie, ever irrepressible, devised a game whose penalty for losing was incarceration for five minutes just inside the iron gates of the Ashdown crypt. No one wanted to play for that penalty, although Sammy said he would do it, if he were playing the game—which he was not.

Gordon got very tight-lipped.

Unable to get participants in his game, Eddie walked alone to the crumbling sepulchre. He made esoteric signs to the four corners of the earth, touched his forehead with the oozing ichor that formed a small puddle in front of the tomb, and pushed the iron gates. They opened easily to Eddie's push, like the door to his own bedroom.

"Haven't you gone far enough?" Gordon snapped. Instead of answering, Eddie stepped inside. No one followed, and I thrust my hand into the picnic basket and scuttled my fingers among the receptacles searching for the pouch of Teacha Paul's protection.

The iron gates swung shut with a decisive clatter, but not before we saw the sudden detritus and damp walls of the antechamber; and beyond—steps that led down into the depths of a lower chamber.

Gordon rushed to the gates and stepped into the antechamber. Eddie leaped out in a white sheet roughly stained with red polyhedronic designs. Gordon was startled, even frightened, and Eddie hooted with laughter at his discomfort. He had set up the joke the day before, oiling the gates' hinges and hiding the sheet inside. Jackie Arvel did not laugh.

The sun turned a purple-red in the sky and slunk behind the far horizon. The picnic was over. Gordon's fears were unnecessary, and my ambivalence, my fear and skepticism, had been in vain. It had been an idle afternoon.

A pleasant evening at the inn awaited us. I was looking forward to it. I hoped dinner would be adequate. I was in need of diversion. I had no intention of ever returning to that cemetery. The day had hardly been a lark, nothing at all like the frolic Eddie had touted.

Sadly I realized I had outgrown my friends. But what was I going to do with my life? I had no real skills, no real passions. I couldn't pretend to be moved by great issues. Gordon's style and concerns weren't my own. I suppose the island had to have self-rule, even independence, one day; I felt no urge to help precipitate it. Colonial rule was what I knew, there had been some reform and much resistance to it, I had no quarrel with either side.

I had to tell my father the idea of law didn't excite me and that ruled out politics. I didn't have it in me to be a politician.

The village inn wasn't the Savoy, to quote Sammy. We were billeted two to a room. Our room had three: Gordon, a friend of Tippy's called

Burke, and myself. The facilities were primitive; just having a bath took major negotiations among us.

Gordon seemed animated by the pervading gloominess and at dinner talked at length about the history of the parish. It seems during the insurrection of '65 Mad Ramsay the militia leader had billeted troops at this inn, strategic meetings with planters from surrounding estates took place in the dining room, officers slept upstairs, the stables, now broken and unused, housed men, horses, and small cannons.

One rebel leader captured in a nearby gully was chained in the cellar until his summary execution on the courthouse gallows. As the militia crushed the revolt of freed slaves and apprentices in outlying areas, a festive caravan of planters, officials, wives, and retainers gathered in the front courtyard of our hotel and set out to see a score of blacks hanged. Appreciative planters watched as the corpses were thrown in a trench outside the town.

I saw no reason why Gordon should tell that abominable tale, it quite spoiled my dinner. Someone suggested a stroll in the village and we set out, glad to be rid of the bleak mood in the dining room. Deacon and Moses came with us. Gordon had our hostess, Mrs. Parbodie, fetch them from the kitchen where they had had their meal.

The night was cool, a pleasant difference from the afternoon's heat. Gordon and Deacon walked ahead talking politics, Deacon enumerating the pitiful wages and iniquitous conditions in the area.

There was nothing to do in the village. At a brisk walk you could span its length in five minutes. The police station showed a solitary window light but that was all. Apart from the roaming mongrels and the occasional lonely howl, the historic country village was dead to all but ourselves.

Gordon turned from his companions and said to us generally that we had wasted twenty-four hours. Rachel Mannheim mimicked his words, ". . . wasted twenty-four hours . . ." in a whining voice. We all laughed.

The laughter echoed and re-echoed through the night.

We hurried back and sat drinking around the dining room table. The ladies went to bed, they slept in one room. After the disappointment of the day, they had been prepared for a benign evening. But Gordon's depressing talk and the echoes of our demonic laughter in the village had unnerved them.

Jackie and Eddie had also rushed off to bed. Sammy Ronay fell asleep in an armchair. Tippy and his friend Burke kept on drinking.

Gordon explained that the laughter had probably come from some house we couldn't see, and continued discussing politics with Deacon.

Mrs. Parbodie closed the window and stale air accumulated in the room. It was as if the odor of centuries was secreting from the walls. I felt stuffed and choked.

Gordon suggested we call it a night and Deacon bade us goodnight. He was affected by Gordon's talk, I could see. He was intent when they spoke of politics. I thought Gordon had made a staunch friend and had enlisted a believer in his ideas.

He was to sleep on some blankets on a cot in the dining room. Mrs. Parbodie made him get the cot from the cellar. I was glad the day was over. In the morning I would resume my life.

The stairs complained as we tramped upstairs. Gordon's history lesson came back to mind and I shuddered at the event he said had happened in this house, in this cellar, in this front courtyard. I intended to ask him why he thought it necessary to excavate the charnel pit of yesteryear.

As we were preparing for bed, Tippy knocked urgently on our door. Jackie and Eddie were not in their rooms. Earlier they had suggested a midnight foray. No one had responded, now they were gone. Outside their door he had found a luminescent bit of cloth. I knew what it was at once. It was the threadbare mysteriously lambent swatch of the ceremonial purple cowl of Abdul Alhazred, whose name still evokes reverence and terror from those who know.

They must have dropped it while sneaking out, anxious to evade detection.

"The fools," Gordon said, "they have gone to the tomb. We must go now!" He flung on his shirt and scrambled for his boots. Tippy uttered a little sob. Burke stood watching.

"Let's go," Gordon said.

"I can't," Tippy replied. "Don't you see, I'm frightened." He turned pale, put his face in his hands, and whimpered. "I'm sorry, Gordie, I'm awfully sorry; I'm letting down the side, aren't I?" Burke quickly said he would stay and take care of his friend.

"Get Sammy," Gordon ordered. "Get Sammy now."

Sammy was dressed in blue silk pajamas. He refused to budge. Not even the devil could get him out of bed, he said, lighting a cigarette. I hurried back to Gordon.

"We go alone then," he said to me.

"Deacon! Deacon can go with us," I said. The more the better, I thought. I didn't want to go back to the graveyard, but my memories of Jackie's previous failure, Eddie's clowning with the white sheet that afternoon, and my lifelong reluctance to appear weak-kneed made me follow Gordon as if there was no danger.

We dragged Deacon out of bed and told him what we feared. "Are you afraid?" Gordon asked. "No, sir," the young man said proudly, "I have Jehovah on my side and evil cannot conquer good."

"I hope so," Gordon muttered. To this day I have never forgotten young Deacon's face. He was confident. He reminded me strongly of the framed photograph of the young man that hung next to the reproduction of "Stony Gut Rebuilt" at Teacha Paul's house at Pinnacle.

I wished Moses was here. Moses had the fine physique of a warrior, a Coromantie, unlike Deacon's less substantial frame.

We charged outside, Deacon at the head. He shouted, "Wait!" and ran inside and returned with a machete. Its keen edge glinted in the dark.

I had no time to think as we ran down the path. Had I been thinking, I might have turned back. But everything was pure sensation, tangible and yet unreal. Even now as I try to reconstruct the events, I have intense impressions that are difficult to arrange into words.

Except for a pale grim scimitar of a moon partially obliterated by churning clouds, the night was frightfully dark. Since the afternoon fresh brush seemed to have sprung up along the path, whipping our faces as we rushed past. Trees loomed toward us, menacing in their configurations. Our feet fit into imprints in the rutted track, as if something had prepared a way for us.

I heard nothing but the crack of underbrush, my hard breath, and the dull thud of my heart in my chest, until we paused at the edge of the clearing. Out of breath, we peered into the ruined graveyard. The night breathed heavily with us.

From where we stood we could see the gates of the crypt swung wide and a strange purple glow emitting from its depths.

"They've got a lantern," Deacon said.

I fumbled for the pouch Teacha Paul had given me, rubbed some of the contents on my brow, placed a little under my tongue, and held the rest in readiness in my hand just as he had instructed me. As we made our way to the tomb, I heard the first faint but still terrible cries. Then they were loud; a grunting effort, a whistling crack, then whimpering punctuated by more grunts and cracks. And all the while the distinct noises of chains. A smell arose from the pit, like that of burning flesh.

The skin on my body was clammy with fear.

Gordon stopped at the entrance to the crypt, just outside the sepulchral glow. He was flabbergasted. My impulse was to break and run. But the entire landscape heaved with unspeakable terror. Cries and shrieks reverberated in the air. Somewhere in the treetops I could hear frantic fluttering, as if some large winged thing's passage had been disturbed. The vile effluent of the tomb rolled up and out into the graveyard. It hung under the silk cotton tree and climbed and caressed its trunk. I swear I heard that tree grunt and groan in venereal response.

Gordon's uncertainty lasted only seconds.

He shouted to me, "There may be a chance to save them!" There was no need to shout. I was as physically close to my companions as I could get. Screams, grunts, and whimpering enfolded us. I needed the meager compensation of bodily touch.

Gripping the machete at the ready, Deacon wanted to rush into the tomb. Gordon said, "Hold!" and with deftness and urgency created a makeshift chain with their belts. He strapped one end to his wrist; Deacon did the same with the other. So shackled they plunged into the purplish phosphorescent ooze. Gaseous clouds now hung calf-deep everywhere, the fluttering had died down, and the tree no longer made its suggestive noises.

I was left alone.

I heard Gordon and Deacon calling instructions to each other, coughing, stumbling. My eyes were riveted on that necrophagus abyss.

Then I heard screams so intense it is forever indented on my brain, and no day passes, still, when I do not shudder as I think of it. I tried to call out to Gordon but the words gibbered on my lips. Stinking vapors erupted from the crypt again. From deep within the distinct beating of wings grew loud and ominous and throaty, fiendish chuckling resounded from its depths.

I dared not move and was willing, begging my feet to take me away from that reach of corruption when I saw rising with the vapors a pair of corneas gleaming in that foul glow, directed with malevolent intent at the very spot on which I stood. My eyes made four with those evil orbs. I was staring into my doom.

From what inspiration I found the presence of mind to force my hand up and fling the remaining contents of Teacha Paul's shamanistic preparation into the face of inhuman sight I do not know. All I do know is my action precipitated an eruption of darting embers and an unearthly prolonged scream, as if some tortured energy was resisting subjection. The screaming was accompanied by a rumbling that seemed to generate from the depths and rim of the earth. Trees, tombs, and darkness writhed and trembled with unwholesome passion in the heaving shadows and before my very eyes the time-stained monument to Matthew Ashdown shuddered, sundered, and collapsed into a reeking crater of loathsome rotted stone.

There was a pause; and as a last lurid action, as if my shattered nerves could withstand more, a sigh of deep release came from the new-formed chasm and a column of glowing crimson vapor defiled the air in great diffusive swirls.

I had lost all feeling. It was as if all my tendons had been removed. I sank to the ground and stared impotently at the scene. Nothing passed through my mind. I just sat and watched the smoldering ruins.

It was in that position that I was found the next morning speechless and vacant. I was of no use to my questioners, who, little by little, deduced the facts.

I was taken to the inn. The disinterrment party, armed with shovels, picks, and forks, were assembled in the front courtyard. They were the men of Bristoltown. I saw terror and pity in their eyes.

The facts of the escapade were officially hushed up. The *Island Gazette* reported Arvel and Shears had fallen down an unusually steep gully and Gordon and Deacon had died trying to save them. I knew better.

The coffins were sealed for the funerals and rumors abounded. I could not attend. I was under medical supervision.

Shears's and Arvel's funerals were exhaustively reported and extensively photographed for the *Island Gazette*. They got the front page. The list of mourners read like a listing in the Island's Who's Who. Like a powerful clan they had come from all over the island to mourn their young—matriarchs, patriarchs, elders and aunts, brothers, sisters, cousins, distant relations, many from overseas—a congregation of kinship and power. I have often imagined the gathering at those funerals with a shudder.

Gordon's funeral got moderate coverage. Deacon's was hardly mentioned at all. My father attended both and reported the mourners were many and the grief intense. I wished I could have been there, but I was in no condition for stress.

Weeks later, a man who was present at the postmortems told me this story; I present it to you as he related it to me:

The bodies were in terrible shape. The collapse of the tomb or being buried under marble couldn't account for the injuries.

Arvel's and Shears's eyes bulged in rank terror when the bodies were exhumed. Whatever they had seen in the crypt's lower chamber had solidified their organs of sight. Repeated attempts by the surgeon could not close them, and they went to their graves staring at infinity.

Jackie Arvel's back was lacerated as if from a long and brutal flogging. Eddie Shears's bore similar marks, and terrible burns from a substance identified as boiling sealing wax.

Both Gordon's and Deacon's necks were broken in a manner corresponding to the effects of hanging. Deacon's neck was imprinted with the marks of a rope, as was Gordon's. On the upper right shoulder of each man was cauterized the seal of the Ashdowns. The ornate A with figures of polyhedronic design encircling.

What did it all mean, my informant wanted to know; by then I knew.

The historical account Gordon had related at the inn hours before his death had driven me to examine the early records of the island. These archives were restricted but it is who you know and not the law that determines these things in our islands. I arranged access through my father's influence. He was reluctant. I insisted. He didn't want me to know the island's true history. He knew much about its past and he had left me in ignorance of it. He had kept it to himself. Finally, and with great sorrow, he agreed. A letter of introduction from my father to the right authority gave me access to the island's archives and the island's secrets were opened to me.

The accumulated material is sad and terrible. It is an encyclopedia of horrors. The Ashdown legacy was only one narrative—there were hundreds more.

The Ashdown plantation was founded in 1795 when it was a grant from the English crown for service in the Seven Years' War. It went to ruin because of the intractability of Matthew Ashdown, the last of the Antillean branch of the family. He had refused to accept the realities of abolition and with the support of his fellow planters and local magistrates, and the island assembly, had instituted a system of coercion almost as brutal as slavery itself. He was intensely hated by the people of the parish. The grievances of generations erupted again in 1865 when Matthew Ashdown and his kith and kin died in the blazing plantation house. They were a greedy, cruel strain even in a plantocracy noted for its brutality.

The seal of the Ashdowns was branded into all their property: coaches, cattle, tableware, doors, linens, clothes, machinery, and slaves.

It was this seal that was found in the flesh of our dead acquaintances. The wildest conjecture cannot say how that infamous insignia scarred my friends' bodies that night; nor can reason explain all I saw in the country graveyard.

My knowledge of these islands, this lake of misery, was based on schoolboy notions: Columbus discovering an idyllic New World, friendly gentle Arawaks, dashing buccaneers and privateers, pieces of eight, doubloons and legends of the Spanish Main, the master narrative of these islands. I sat in the Island Institute perusing old journals, looking at old maps and naïve engravings, scanning the dishonorable annals of the past, and recognized my life's work would be to place this evaded history in the records. I would trace the continuum of past to present. I have not strayed from that vow.

I never saw Teacha Paul again. While still recuperating I read in the *Island Gazette* the settlement of Pinnacle had been raided by the island constabulary; its leaders arrested, its followers dispersed. The official reasons given for the raid were sedition and blasphemy, and cultivation of dangerous substances.

The editors of the *Island Gazette* took time off from denouncing "reformers and agitators" to give full coverage and approval to the raid. Most of the Letters To The Editor concurred fervently. My father, who knew of my trip with Gordon to the settlement, did not; my mother, who was ignorant of the truth of the midnight picnic and my visit to Pinnacle, did.

Three months later no longer an innocent, and without announcement, I boarded a freighter bound for Liverpool. I would enter an English Academy to read for a degree in the wellsprings of Antillean history.

Haitian science fiction writer Claude-Michel Prévost, who lives in Vancouver, recently completed a screenwriting workshop. This excerpt from the script shows Voudun, that much-maligned spiritual practice, in a different light than the Hollywood notion of "voodoo" with its hordes of undead black zombies and its evil "witch doctors" with rolling eyes. Come as it has through the crucible of a holocaust, Voudun can be a frightening religion for frightening times, but Prévost also clearly shows the bond of healing and care that the practitioner feels for her patient. Prévost begins the excerpt with a small taste of how his fellow classmates in a workshop in Canada reacted to work as fierce and politicized as this.

Tears for Érsulie Frèda: Men without Shadow

CLAUDE-MICHEL PRÉVOST

THEY'VE BEEN WANTING to talk out loud for years and years. I knew the Black one's voice would be louder, angrier. I had him beat the White priest senseless, THUD, CRACK, first time they ever met on paper. The rest of the class was silent for a moment; nobody looked at me. My teacher tried to uncross his hands over his stomach. Someone suggested a cigarette break.

I let the Voodoo shaman dance around the body of the Catholic priest for another month. I turned Glen into a noisy stupid punching ball for the entire first draft of "Please, Do Not Feed the Gods."

Turns out, Glen was nasty himself, too. He had been trained in another kind of war. He had as much rage and detached coldness, calmly walking in the cafeteria, switching the normal pop concentrate bottle with another one loaded with Ecstasy. He even watched the beefy Vancouver cop gulp down his second cup of root beer. Both men exchanged eye contact; Glen never blinked. He, too, wanted to be right.

In the second draft, my little White Man—along with almost everybody else—had grown a spine and a soul. He carried his own cross since the drug-induced slaughter that followed his spiking trick; he was homesick and without wife, hiding as a fake priest in a forgotten slum nestled like a smelly armpit against the mountains and the sea, smoking weed alone without his drum. He had seen a mermaid and he was about to meet with the meanest Hougan this side of the south of Haiti.

Ladies and Gentlemen, Men without Shadow: a priest, a shaman, a mermaid, and a hurricane. Excerpt, where priest, shaman, mermaid, and Mother Earth meet.

EXT. CONTINUOUS. CHURCH. — MORNING

Glen limps toward the back of the church. He carries his backpack. He picks a doobie, stops, intrigued.

FX: Roosters call; dogs bark; donkeys bray. Nonstop.

EXT. CONTINUOUS. CHURCH BACKYARD.—MORNING

A young tree feeds itself from a broken grave.

Glen searches for a light, surprised at how much he shakes.

FX: Deep low rumble. The earth shakes. Tree branches shiver. Fruits and leaves fall.

Glen hesitates. Stumbles for cover. Finds a nearby tree.

EXT. CONTINUOUS. TREE.—MORNING

Slow-mo heavy thuds. Coconuts hit the ground around Glen.
He watches, guts clenched. Suddenly realizes this is not a safe spot. Starts moving away from the tree. Too late.
A coconut lands straight on his coconut. Lights out.

INT. KACHOU'S TREATMENT ROOM.—AFTERNOON

Rudimentary skylight. Small trees. Shelves. Planters. Elixirs. Shells. Crystals. A jar shelters a carp.

The rain drums softly on the skylight. Voodoo flags. Poster of a mermaid. Massage table.

Glen lies on his stomach, naked, unconscious. The top of his head is bandaged. He looks like a fakir apprentice.

Kachou rubs a salve on his neck and back. She stops and examines him, proud, amused, slightly aroused by his youth.

Kachou pinches his calf, caresses his thigh. Glen reawakens.

KACHOU
Father Fontaine, this is not how we
open coconuts, around here. You
know you split your head in three?

Kachou's hand climbs up his leg.

GLEN
I don't use it much anyway.

Kachou pushes on two pressure points.

KACHOU
Feel something, here?

Glen belches. She tries a third pressure point.

GLEN
Uh oh! I can't feel a thing.

KACHOU
Can you move your right leg?

Glen relaxes. His leg barely twitches.

GLEN
Is this when I am supposed to panic?

KACHOU
Now, move your left arm.

Glen concentrates. His arm barely moves.

GLEN
Should I start panicking now?

Glen focuses forcefully. His arm barely moves.

GLEN
One, two, three, four, five . . .

KACHOU
You need to rest. I am disconnecting
you for a few hours. How do you
feel now?

Glen can barely twitch his eyebrows.

GLEN
I am very afraid. More. Please.

Kachou presses on another meridian near Glen's neck.

KACHOU
I am unplugging your vocal cords.

Glen's eyes are two big saucers. His mouth grimaces. His throat is
frozen. He finally relaxes.

KACHOU
Good, good. Close your eyes and
sleep. Hear me? Sleep.

Glen's eyes are peaceful. They blink twice, with trust.

KACHOU

Sweet dreams.

Footsteps approach, coming from the front room.

JACQUAREL (O.S.)
Yo! Kachou? You Okay?

Kachou heads for the curtain. Jacquarel is already in.

JACQUAREL
Whose white ass is that?

KACHOU
Out. Get. Out. Now.

Kachou rushes to Glen's side.

KACHOU
He's having a heart attack. Get out
of here. Hear me? Out! Now!

Jacquarel reaches Glen. Forces open one eyelid.

JACQUAREL
Bouh!

Glen is dying to move. Jacquarel studies and enjoys.

KACHOU
Father Fontaine. This is Kachou.
Please, listen to me. This is Kachou.
Open your eyes. Open. Your. Eyes.

Glen emerges from his trance. Blinks twice. Drowns under another
wave. He realizes he will not resurface.

KACHOU

Father Fontaine, listen to me: there
will be four mountains, four
mountains, on your left, tall like
needles, covered with snow, head for
them, go, Father Fontaine, go.

Jacquarel watches Kachou, impressed, envious, respectful.

KACHOU

Don't stop, there is a lake in the
middle, yes, yes, a soft green lake,
follow the sun across the lake, go,
Father Fontaine, don't land yet,
don't stop, Father Fontaine, go . . .

Jacquarel nods to Glen's learning how to die with dignity.

KACHOU

This is Kachou, Father Fontaine. I
am right along with you, look for
the cluster of lily pads, on your
right, below, seven o'clock.

Glen rides his last spasms, detached, almost peaceful.

KACHOU

You can rest now, see the turtle, on
the lily pad? Her name is Bertha,
Father Fontaine, say hello to Bertha.

Glen's body convulses one last time. His glaze fades.

> KACHOU
>
> Yes, I see her too. Thank you,
> Bertha. Wait for me right there,
> Father Fontaine. I know, the light
> is so pure, but don't leave yet,
> wait for me. I will be back soon.
> Wait for me.

Glen relaxes in his peace and death.

> KACHOU
> See you later, Father Fontaine.

Kachou leaves the room. Jacquarel gently applauds. He checks Glen's dead eyes. Slaps him hard.

> JACQUAREL
> I was first, hear me, Shithead? I
> was first.

He keeps examining Glen, resentful, jealous.

> JACQUAREL
> She loves me more than you. Get
> used to it.

Kachou reenters. She has a splendid machete in her hand.

> KACHOU
> You're not amusing anymore.

> JACQUAREL
> Interesting. Go on. Surprise me.

Kachou cuts his head off. His blood sprays a spiral. Kachou grabs his head before it falls, dances with it.

> KACHOU
> You're fucking up, Boy! We got better
> things to do.

Nonchalantly, Jacquarel's body gets on all fours. Still spurting blood, it starts looking for its head.

Kachou masterfully kicks Jacquarel in the ass. His body rolls under the table.

> KACHOU (O.S.)
> Even I didn't see the earthquake
> coming. I heard my doves calling
> for help and the next second, there was
> the ugliest vibration I ever felt.

Kachou places Jacquarel's head on the bed, gently closes Glen's eyes, and goes looking for her elixirs.

> KACHOU (O.S.)
> Like an enraged, poisoned whale . . .

Both heads rest beside each other.

> JACQUAREL
> Bouh!

> KACHOU (O.S.)
> I heard that! You're so plugged up
> with your own shit you can't even
> listen. Many will die, Jacquarel!

> JACQUAREL
> Black or White?

> KACHOU (O.S.)
> Oh, grow up will you?

Kachou returns shaking a bottle. She holds Jacquarel's head by the hair, rubs a bloody paste around the cut of his neck.

JACQUAREL
Phew!

KACHOU
Would you rather do it yourself?

Jacquarel smiles. They kiss. Again. Deeply.

His hands reach under Kachou's dress. Caress her heels. Define her calves. She enjoys, shrugs, kicks him away.

She passes him his head. With a bit of difficulty, Jacquarel adjusts it back onto his neck. He bangs himself against the table.

JACQUAREL
Ouch! That hurts!

He gets up. No blood or marks. He cracks his neck.

JACQUAREL
That was fun.

Both circle Glen, touching him along veins and meridians.

KACHOU
Back to business, motherfucker: Where
is your code of honor?

Jacquarel still wants to fight, but finally acquiesces.

JACQUAREL
Never engage in battle with weaker
opponents.

They stop at Glen's feet and head, inhale fast and sharp.

KACHOU

Ready?

JACQUAREL

Ready.

Both grunt and howl. Shiver and shake. Move one step back.
On the walls, the ground, Jacquarel's blood fades away.
Glen doesn't move. Jacquarel plays with his thumbs.

KACHOU

Hold on, Baby, don't leave, don't
leave.

Glen's chest starts moving. He opens his eyes, scans around.
Jacquarel is gone.

KACHOU

It's okay, it's okay. Trust me.

Glen starts shaking violently. Kachou strongly massages him. She
reaches for a stone, forces it into his hand.
Glen finally grasps the stone. Kachou braces herself.

KACHOU

Let it go, Father Fontaine. Let.
It. Go.

Glen's screams spurt out. He bolts. Kachou holds on tight against
him. Glen hits her on the mouth, draws blood.
Kachou hangs on and dances with him, half singing, half sighing,
until, finally, his visceral tears soften.
The stone has crumbled in his fist.
Glen catches his breath. He has the tired eyes of an old man. The
scared eyes of a betrayed child.
Kachou undoes her blouse. She opens her bra. Cuddles him.
Glen explodes in tears. The rain drums on the window.

blood thicker more than water

Sometimes the whispers from the cavelike places are in voices we know, voices of our own kin. . . .

The echoes of history affect race, class, and behavior. The villagers have their own explanations for why Ataviso treats his family the way he does, but no one will intervene. It's family business, and they leave it up to family to deal with.

The Village Cock

H. NIGEL THOMAS

THE STRAIGHT ROAD that curved exactly where the village began was now paved; the dirt road that powdered everyone golden during dry spells was now trapped under tar. As he looked at the new stream of black tar—for that was how the road appeared—and the telephone poles and hi-tension wires, he knew that there had been dramatic change. The old wooden houses had for the most part been torn down and replaced with larger concrete structures. He gasped. "Sorry for poor"—that huge breadfruit tree that his grandmother said had been there when she had been an infant, which had got its name because during a terrible drought when every green thing turned brown and died, the breadfruit tree that had been a pelican and had adopted the villagers as its young had kept on wrenching fruit from its entrails—had been cut down; and to David, that was sacrilege.

And so it was that he was surprised to hear a woman, her head tied, as he remembered his grandmother's, in a plaid rag, saying, "If you do good, good going follow you. Take care; if you plant dumb cane, you will never reap tannia." She said it much as his grandmother, he was sure, had said it to his mother, as his mother had said it to him; and

David wondered whether he too would say it to his children. At least that had not changed. The little boy she spoke to was about four and clothed only in a shirt, leaving his mud-marked extremities and genitalia unprotected. He eyed the pea switch in the woman's hand. She pleaded with him to advance but the youngster stood rooted, his gaze fixed on the pea switch that moved ever so slightly in the woman's fleshy arms.

David moved on, trying to remember who had lived in the wooden shacks where these spacious cement houses now stood, too spacious for the little land whose soul they were crushing. But one spot had not changed. There, marring the symmetry of generous porches encircled by potted palms, flowering gerberas, and geraniums, was Ataviso's shack, listing heavily toward the valley decline. Huge beams were angled at the side—massive stilts transversely rooted in the earth came to the aid of the shack, hindering it from gaining whatever it hankered after down the valley slope. Not unlike the clothing of Ataviso's wife, which had placed a barrier between him and her tormenting spirit. David wondered whether Ataviso was still alive. If he were, he would have to be in his sixties. He had been Ataviso's neighbor.

In his heyday Ataviso was called the Village Cock. He boasted five mistresses and fifteen children. In fact, one night when one mistress sent for Ataviso at his wife's home to go fetch the midwife, who lived three villages away, he had met another of his sons bearing a similar message. So he had fetched the midwife, who delivered him two more sons that night.

The following Wednesday when Ataviso stopped off at the rum shop, where every impoverished rum drinker was habitually waiting, they had another detail to add to the repertory of his fine feathers, his castle-like comb, and his ever-flowing sperm jug; now his hens had had simultaneous hatchings. A marvelous rooster was Ataviso, and Ataviso was pleased, and the fat wad of dollar bills the hundreds of bunches of bananas had been exchanged for earlier that day was in turn exchanged for the rum that kept the compliments coming. And Ataviso was pleased. Later that night he got home staggering and saw only the

blurred outline of the expectant faces of his wife and the three children, who fearfully wondered whether they'd manage to sleep there
that night or have to run—at first it had been in their pajamas, their
mother in her nightgown; now they kept their street clothes handy, to
grab whenever they had to run—for Ataviso knew that on banana-selling day his wife expected money, and with none to give, he would beat
her, and the children too, should they cry over their mother's pain.

At that time, Ataviso's oldest son was fourteen, and David remembered—the words had a way of gripping his intestines—"Big man like
you still pissing yo' bed!" And Ataviso would throw the barfleur mattress out in the yard; there would be explosive sounds against the roadside wall of the house; and the lanky youngster, who looked more like
ten, would emerge, his right hand cupping the side of his head that
Ataviso had used to resonate the walls, smiling broadly no doubt as he
did so. That smile always accompanied Ataviso's infliction of pain.
Derivo (his real name was Alfred; Ataviso's was Percy; they were
renamed by David's brother, who had a passion for foreign languages;
eventually the names gained currency in Hillsdale) would drag the
mattress to the back of the house, more out of sight, while Ataviso
looked on chuckling.

"Yo' want yo' bladder sew up! And I will sew it up fo' yo'! Be Christ,
I will!"

He would then look around him, at his wife and the other children,
for signs of defiance. (He always boasted that he was not like other
men, who had lost their pants. For if a man did not beat his wife and
women, it meant that he was wearing their bloomers and they his
trousers. "Go from me!" he would tell his drinking buddies; "I bet yo'
wife got on yo' trousers and you wearing her bloomers.") Derivo
would remain behind the house and would slip his forefinger and its
neighbor into his mouth; the habit had bleached the lower half of
those fingers white and the sucking left a constant flow of saliva down
his chin and neck. The blows did not cure the bladder weakness, and
so Ataviso found a novel idea, borrowed no doubt from the tar-and-
feather practices of earlier times. He got a twenty-five-pound empty

Palm Tree butter tin, still colored in saffron yellow, and two drumsticks. He attached a string to the tin. He stuck some feathers to an old sheet. The children and neighbors looked on at the activities in the open yard.

Around 4 P.M., the following Sunday, when all the Methodists who attended church had already returned and dined and the children who attended Sunday school were emerging from the church, they heard a few unwilling drum sounds and saw a strange apparition followed by a small procession descending the hill. The villagers came onto the side of the road, and children on their way home stopped. It was Derivo, draped in his pee-stained sheets, the feathered sheet thrown on top of these. Ataviso walked behind him, from time to time hitting him with a piece of rope. Derivo knocked the drum (the butter tin) languidly, a little faster each time he was hit by the rope. At times he staggered. A procession of gazing children followed. Some parents ran toward the procession, pulled their children away, and took them home.

When Derivo passed the church, those at the front of the procession smelled feces and saw it falling in liquid drops from beneath the feathers and the sheets. Ataviso laughed. The children looked on, frightened.

About three houses below the church, Beulah Abbot stood up watching the procession. When it got to her gate she approached Derivo and shook her head. She pulled off the feathered sheet and pee-stained rags and threw them on Ataviso. Her right hand firmly clasped around Derivo, she said to Ataviso, "You're not fit to take care o' jackasses, let alone children. I hope you die without anybody there to give you a drink of water. Watch out, 'What you sow is what you going reap.'" She pulled Derivo into her yard, where, away from his father, Derivo spurted a blood-streaked, sour-smelling vomit.

Ataviso's children always trembled. And if a teacher asked them a question it increased the trembling to the point where it resembled an ague. Therefore, the following Tuesday, when Derivo was seen trembling, no one paid any attention. The trembling increased, and Derivo blacked out. A message was sent home and his mother came. He was taken to the hospital in the capital, where it was found that he had a bleeding intestinal ulcer. From his father, David learned that the next night the rum drinkers changed their tune about Ataviso.

"Phoo, man! What smell like that!"

"Did you see the blood in the vomit?"

"Some men love their children to beat them, all the way in the gut, until they shit theyselves."

Ataviso had remained quiet through all this but had continued to pay for the rum just the same.

Derivo was released from the hospital on a Thursday. David had gone to see him and was still standing at the gate when Ataviso arrived from his lands.

He entered the yard and screamed at his wife, "Yo' ain't finish cooking yet? What the fuck you been doing home all day?" This was followed by the sounds of iron crashing on stones and his wife's, "Lord Jesus, hear my cry!" The neighbors gathered to watch the steam rising from the food and the pieces of broken cast-iron pot on the bleaching stones. Gradually the fowls began to gather, waiting for the heat to subside. Mrs. Jones (Jones was her maiden name—they called her that in defiance of Ataviso, whose surname was Sweet—long changed to Sinistro by David's brother) had run to sit squat in the middle of the yard. With her eyes turned to the sky and her body shrouded by the rays of the setting sun, she clutched her two-year-old quite tightly. The child had begun to wail.

At home David told his mother what he had seen. His father too had witnessed it and instructed his mother to prepare enough food so that there would be a meal for Mrs. Jones and her children. She made oatmeal with milk for Derivo. She sent David to sit on the porch to watch for Ataviso's departure. Around 6:30 she and David took the food. There were a few neighbors there. Each of them had brought some of what they had cooked. Mrs. Jones was sitting on the floor of the living room, wearing a dress that had been bleached colorless from countless washings. The infant was asleep on her lap. Some of the women sat on the floor with her. They coaxed her to eat, telling her she had to keep her strength to defend her children against

Ataviso. One of the women pushed back the loose strands of her hair and started to hum, "What a friend we have in Jesus, all our sins and grief to bear . . ."

Worst of all was the evening when Ataviso arrived home, walked into the house, and dragged (Egado) Maurice into the open yard. His hand tightened Egado's shirt collar, choking him, and he shook him so violently that sometimes he lifted him completely off the ground.

"Yo' is a man?" he asked Egado. Egado did not answer (he could not answer).

With his free hand Ataviso slapped him. "Answer me! How you could order Lisa off the land?" (Lisa was one of Ataviso's mistresses.) He choked Egado some more. The neighbors looked on. The shirt collar deeply indented Egado's neck and his eyes bulged. Finally Ataviso let him go long enough to give him a knock-down blow. "Yo' is a man, yo' must take man blows." Egado fell to the ground. Ataviso placed his right foot on his neck. From the pocket of his overalls he produced a coil of mahoe, which he unraveled and began raining down blows on Egado. It seemed as if he had lost all awareness of what he was doing. David's father and another neighbor, Mr. Burch, had had to restrain Ataviso and literally box him back into reality. Mrs. Jones had collapsed at the sight of her husband's actions. The women came with buckets of water and revived Egado. Ataviso remained long enough to see Egado revived and then walked away. For a long time the neighbors debated what to do with Ataviso. Some said he should be sent to the insane asylum. Some said he needed a dose of his own medicine. Some said it was because the law never did anything to people like Ataviso that they went on as they did.

That night David asked his father why Ataviso treated Mrs. Jones and his children like that.

"He's an estate nigger, that's why. He's not from this village. Ataviso is the crudest estate nigger I know of. They're not much different from animals.

"You see, son, Ataviso comes from people who treat their children exactly the way white people used to treat their slaves. They use whips and their fists to get obedience. It's as if that is how they were trained to bring up children. I bet you Ataviso doesn't know the difference between how to treat his jackass and his children."

"But why did Mrs. Jones marry him?"

"That's a difficult question. I could easier tell you why he married her."

Mrs. Jones was a mulatto woman, the daughter of a white father and a black mother. She was ten years older than Ataviso and was already in her mid-thirties when she married him. Her mother had already been dead, but her father opposed the marriage, even though Mrs. Jones was pregnant. "Anything," he told her, "but an estate nigger."

But she married Ataviso. At the beginning he was a model husband. So Mr. Jones let him have the use of most of his unrented land. He also gave his daughter the money that bought the plot and built the house they lived in. For three years Ataviso lived like this. Eventually Mr. Jones made him manager over his entire two-hundred-acre farm. A year after this Mr. Jones suffered a stroke and died. Gradually Ataviso became involved with other women and began having outside children, and when his wife protested he began to beat her. She saw less and less of the money that came from rents, from nutmegs, cocoa, coconuts—all of which had been planted before Ataviso had married her. It got to the point where Ataviso forbade her from going to the farm on the pain of being beaten. When the last child was born and Mrs. Jones complained that she was destitute, Ataviso suggested that she consider whoring. David remembered hearing his parents and the neighbors discussing this. This was hard for them to accept, considering that Mr. Jones had been a university graduate and his wife an elementary school principal. They could not understand why she remained with him. Except maybe it was because Ataviso was a handsome man—very slim with a glistening black skin, strong jaws, an angular face, and dancing eyes that blazed when he was bestial.

The years passed and the situation in Ataviso's family remained much the same, except when Robert, the youngest child, was five, one of Mrs. Jones's sisters, who was a university lecturer in Jamaica, came home to Isabella Island for a visit. She could not persuade her sister to leave Ataviso, but she convinced Mrs. Jones to let her take Robert to Jamaica with her. Mrs. Jones consented.

Four nights after her departure it occurred to Ataviso that he had not seen Robert. He inquired but got no answer from his wife. He began to beat her and vowed he would not stop until she told him what had become of his son. Egado rushed outside and returned with a machete with which he proceeded to chop his father as if his intention were to retail him by the pound. His mother screamed. Derivo screamed. The neighbors came and took the blood-effusing Ataviso to the hospital. The doctors saved his life with transfusions of Derivo's and Egado's blood.

The community was divided in its feelings. There was the belief that a child who hit his parents would be cursed for life and that the curse would devolve on his offspring. But some, mostly women, thought it was a token righting of wrongs. They also noted that Ataviso did not seek revenge. The left arm never completely stretched out after the wound on it had healed. It remained at an angle of 110 degrees; and scars, a shade lighter than the rest of his skin, on his neck, both of his upper arms, his back, and even on his left buttock, formed ridges of proud flesh rising from the skin's surface like termite tunnels. After that day he never beat his wife or her children. Some people remarked that the cutting up should have come sooner. But Ataviso turned to beating his mistresses and their children.

During the dry season a year later, Mrs. Jones grew paler and more gaunt. Her jaws were now sunken and the skin on them lay in parallel folds; her bluish grey eyes had less blue in them and sank deeper into their sockets, and her shinbones were blade-edged. She had a wracking cough that was obviously getting worse. When evening chills and fever and a damp brow began to accompany it, everyone knew. By the time the rainy season arrived she had to be taken to the TB sanitarium. Within a month she died.

When Ataviso heard the news he got drunk. But even in his drunken stupor, he was able to purchase the lumber for the village carpenters, who built the coffin cost-free. The village grocer, out of kindness to the memory of Ataviso's father-in-law, brought the body back to the village in his grocery van. She was interred in the Jones's burial plot.

The Third Night arrived, the night when his wife's spirit was deemed to visit. A huge tarpaulin tent was set up in the yard, for it had been raining constantly. The Spiritual Baptists came to sing the eulogy to the dead and to pray for the living and whatever it was that they did as part of their secret code, until midnight, when the spirit arrived.

As the magic hour drew near, Ataviso began to tremble. At midnight everyone jumped when he shouted, "There she is!" and fainted (of course, no one saw her). The women applied ammonia salts to his nostrils and rubbed his neck muscles with Limacol. When he recovered he began to run and shout and later sob, "Tell her to leave me alone. Tell—her—to—leave—me—a—lone." His head bobbed up and down uncontrollably. "She is cha-cha-cha-s-ing me." His teeth chattered. With his arms held out before him and his palms upheld in a defensive gesture, as if fending off something, and without once turning his head to see the road, he backed into it, tripped on something, fell, got up, and continued down the road. He did not sleep in his house that night, nor did he ever return there. A few days later he moved into the shack at which David was now looking, and in which he still lived when David left the village for England eighteen years before.

Ataviso had frequent and prolonged visits from his wife. When he was lucid he told how she hugged him and pressed her lips onto his, while the flames leaped from her eyes. And perhaps it was true, for everyone had at one time or other heard his shouting.

One night he moved through the street, his arms stiffly stretched out before him, his shoulders hunched forward, his head thrown back, and his feet dragging as though someone were pulling him. People shouted at him, but it was clear that he heard nothing; he merely moved along, like a calf roped for the first time refuses to walk and is pulled along. The people followed at a distance. Eventually someone had the insight to dash a bucket of cold water on him, the impact of which shocked him into reality. After a few minutes he spoke: "My wife was leading me—Leave me alone!—have mercy, leave me alone—she had a rope around my neck—leave me alone! . . ."

The villagers led him back to his house, and two men watched over him that night.

The next day the villagers exchanged ideas about what needed to be done. The Spiritual Baptist leader rounded up his flock and they assembled in the yard of Ataviso's shack that evening. They sang and prayed, invoked the ancestral spirits, performed ecstatic rites, and with long, flaying brooms and branches they flogged the ground and the sides of the shack inside and outside. Then they marched around the shack seven times uttering an incomprehensible chant.

For two weeks following this Ataviso had no visitations. He believed the cure had worked and so decided to pay a visit to one of his mistresses. But he never quite got to her house. A month after that Ataviso was reduced to two-thirds his former size. He exhaled an odor of apples in their earliest phase of rot. His eyes rolled constantly in their deepening sockets. It was as if some string beneath the skin was tying back his facial muscles. His blue dungarees, which now he did not change, looked as if they were hung on a six-foot mobile cross to form an animate scarecrow. The mud that splotched the dungarees brown in some places mixed with his sweat and fermented and dried, coating him with an odor that the wind blowing by his shack took away in varying amounts. The smell became known as Ataviso's cologne. At this stage Egado trudged to the estate ten miles away, where his grandmother squatted and still worked as a day laborer, to ask her to come and look after Ataviso. Mrs. Sweet came, an overpowering, strapping woman with thick braids, a commanding voice, and a penetrating stare. She remained watching him at nights for about three weeks.

David liked her and thought that what his father had told him about "estate niggers" did not apply to Mrs. Sweet. He had heard her talking and giving advice on various occasions.

"How your son doing?" a woman asked her.

"As best he can."

"But I hear you good at medicine yourself; how's it you can't help him?"

Mrs. Sweet looked at the woman intensely and then away before saying, "They got some people medicine can't help. Some people can only cure theyselves. If you know any bush that good for a bad conscience you must let me know."

"What you mean, a bad conscience?"

"I mean it ain't nothing but his conscience creating them things he seeing. You know how he treat his wife."

David heard his father reporting another story about her. "That woman is special," his father said to David's mother. "I heard she met Clarissa on the road taking her baby to the doctor, and she asked Clarissa what wrong. Clarissa told her the baby pining away because her milk dry up. She told Clarissa to forget about the doctor and find somebody with a goat that giving milk or else a cow, but better a goat. 'Buy at least three cups for the child. Instead of giving the child plain water to drink, give it a mixture of three leaves of cudjoe root, two leaves of man peaba, two leaves of woman peaba, and two leaves of grannyhaulback boiled in two cups of water. Squeeze the juice of a' orange and give that to the child. No doctor medicine better than that.' Sure enough the child's eyes not turning inwards anymore."

His mother had been standing at the sink drying dishes while David washed them.

"How can an 'estate nigger' know such things?"

For a while she seemed lost in her thoughts, and David, who had had many arguments with her on her class views, knew that she was searching for some platitude to disparage Mrs. Sweet. Finally she said, "Well I guess there are exceptions. She's the exception."

Eventually Mrs. Sweet returned to her village. Her husband was bedridden and she depended on neighbors to look after him while she was taking care of Ataviso. She told the villagers that how a person made up his bed was exactly how he would have to lie on it. This was not how she had brought up Ataviso. She went on to say that her husband had never hit her and she had rarely ever beaten her children, so

Ataviso did not learn his behavior from her. The dead would have to bury their dead. After she left, people began suggesting all sorts of solutions to Ataviso. Someone suggested he roll on his wife's grave at midnight for forty nights; he rejected that. One woman brought him a pail of dirt from his wife's grave and told him to mix a little of it in the water he drank. This brought him a little relief.

One night he appeared on the street naked and completely incoherent. The men physically carried him to the shack and had to tie him up to get him to stay still. One of the rum drinkers whom Ataviso used to entertain remembered the "bloomers" story and told his buddies of a little trick they might play on Ataviso. Eventually they told Ataviso that one of them had had a dream in which Ataviso's wife told him that if Ataviso wore one of her dresses and a pair of her bloomers, she would no longer torture him. Ataviso balked at first. Later he sent a message to Egado and arranged to have his wife's clothes brought to his shack. He later told anyone wanting to hear how his knees had buckled at the thought of putting on his wife's clothing. He said she had waved a forefinger at him and ordered him to put them on.

Within a few days the entire village knew of the joke the men had planned. They intended to have him appear in public dressed in his wife's clothing.

For the four days he wore her clothes her ghost did not trouble him. He would wait until around 3 A.M., when everyone was asleep, to empty his chamber pot and to bring water from the standpipe. Now that he was free from torture his appetite had returned. He had eaten up all the crackers his mother had left and finished the sugar, too, drinking sweet water. How would he go to the shop?

The villagers intervened. "Ataviso, it's days we ain't see yo'; answer us if yo' still living."

He said he looked down at the skirt he was wearing and clamped his teeth. He made an attempt to change it, but his wife's ghost appeared and his hands froze.

"Ataviso, we's coming in."

The men entered and began laughing. And the crowd outside began laughing too. Without realizing it, he got up and walked out into the yard. First came the chuckles of children, then scattered guffaws, followed by laughter like a convectional downpour. When one of the men lifted up the skirt and showed the panties, some of the crowd embraced the nearest partner. The laughter kept dying down and rekindling for some ten minutes as more and more people came to see what was going on.

Later that day, when the crowd had left, Ataviso went to the shop and bought what he needed, and people lined the street to look at him. He later said that it was the first time in years that he had felt at peace with himself.

He reported seeing his wife's ghost twice after that. Once after Derivo's death. He died two days before the second anniversary of his mother's death. His health had declined considerably. Egado and the neighbors had helped care for him. Egado even provided his father with money to look after his needs. Derivo developed a fever one night and his abdomen became as hard as stone. He died just before daybreak, in the ambulance transporting him to the hospital. Mrs. Jones returned to tell Ataviso he could wear a suit to the funeral. The second occasion was a month later. Ataviso's in-laws had come home to settle their father's estate. Forty acres had been willed to Mrs. Jones. Legally it now belonged to Ataviso. When he attempted to visit it, she appeared in front of him in her vengeful form. So he never went back or attempted to claim ownership.

It was obvious that Ataviso as well as the villagers became accustomed to his dress. His major concern was what would happen after the clothes were worn out. One of the Spiritual Baptists returning from a two-week sojourn in the spirit world reported, among her other encounters, one with Ataviso's wife, who she said looked happy and well, and who wished to inform Ataviso that he could have new female garments made, only he had to have a piece of her original garments sewn into the new ones. She promised to release him after fifteen years.

David's thoughts returned to the present. He wondered why the villagers had never thought of Ataviso's suffering while he was abusing his wife. He beat them to make himself feel important; those he couldn't beat he bribed. Was he so different from kings and politicians? For the villagers, Ataviso had represented the bottom where the dregs sank and stayed, what they conveniently called "estate nigger," where the distinctions between man and beast were blurred, where the "better class"—for so they considered themselves—dared not descend. Only when those dregs that would not sink floated on the surface with disturbing visibility did they become bothered. And if they had heard of Jack the Ripper and his sons and grandsons—not to mention his ancestors—their need to feel superior made them forget. Ataviso's problems probably would not have occurred had he let his wife wear his trousers, even if he had not worn her "bloomers." Even that, too. Oh David, what does mankind know?

He got up from the stone he had been sitting on and resumed his walk through the village. All his school friends had emigrated. His own parents and brother lived in New York. But there were still a few people he'd remember and who'd remember him. They would tell him what had become of Ataviso.

Sookoo is a proud man. He speaks his mind, he follows up his words with action, and once he's taken a position, he never backs down from it. He believes that the way to fight power is with greater power. Sookoo knows another man like him, and sometimes he tells that man's story.

Shadows Move in the Britannia Bar

ISMITH KHAN

T HE BRITANNIA IS OLD. It is hard to say which is older, the city of Port of Spain or the rum-shop. No one alive today can say which one gave birth to the other, the rum-shop to the city, or the city to the rum-shop. It stands at the corner of Frederick Street and the South Quay, facing the old railway station, the customs house, and the sea. It was located there for convenience, for a past that is dead, for travelers who no longer ride the railroad, for a lighthouse whose beacon is lost, and a customs house without traffic.

In an odd way, the Britannia is the womb of the past. It is the only museum that Trinidad has to offer, for the island's history is written on the rum casks, the walls, the floors, the brass spittoons, and, most of all, the men who gather there, held and drawn like puppets by thin threads of time and memory. There are those who swear by its rum, by its ancient wooden kegs whose staves and worn-down rusted hoops are held together by innumerable coats of paint. Others swear by the shadows they may hide themselves between, and still another group will tell you that the place has a strange magic, an ether that draws men out and wraps about them a warm and immediate camaraderie.

And they come, all manners of men, in search of its ether. They gather in small cliques, just large enough to house the warmth of chat and chatter. Five men, six men, one more would drown out the magic. Instinct and the essence of their topic alone will determine the size of the clique.

This was Sookoo's clique. He was perhaps just a boy when he first came in to the Britannia Bar. Today he is old. The hair on his face is thick, like grey steel wires, his crown bald, with the soft fuzz of baby's hair, and his eyes are constantly searching.

Each time the swinging half-doors of the rum-shop fly open, he looks up as though he's awaiting someone. But his movements, his expressions, are from his eyes alone. They circle, they dance, they draw tightly together, and sometimes they flash. The old man had his clique about him, about five or six other habitués of the Britannia, and he was talking in his usual rolling, lilting, sometimes angry and abusive way.

"The time dat I talkin bout, all yuh fellars didn't dream to born yet. Dem was the old time days. People uses to have a kind of belief in dem days, a respec' for all what they see happen with they own two eye. What I mean to say is dat tings still happen, but is people like all yuh young fellars, is people what blind, they eye shut, it half-close. But it have something. Where? Up in the sky! Inside your belly! A man! God! It have something!

"In dem days it didn't have so much motor-car to jam up the road; Port of Spain wasn't pack-up with so much people. Trinidad? Hm! Dis island uses to be different in dem days, boy . . . different. People uses to work hard hard hard! Not like nowadays, all you hear is 'Independence,' 'Federation,' 'Hilton Hotel.' People askin me if I ent see how the town change up. 'But look how we have six-storey sky-scraper . . . look how we have elevator in the department store . . . look how we have Woolworth and five and ten.' I have to laugh because I ent see nothing change. People in Trinidad stop the same way . . . chupid! It have something, and I know because I see it with my own two eye.

"One o'clock, two o'clock we leavin dem far far places in the bush to reach Port of Spain before dayclean. Nobody on the road. And dark?

Pitch black! All you have is your lil hurricane lantern prop up on top your cart, and it loaded down with coals. But what good dat lamp is? Is for police nuh . . . for dem not to give you a case, lock you up for driving without light. But where you do find police at dat hour? Dem rascals gone to catch a sleep somewhere too.

"O-ho! So you think dat is thief I talkin 'bout? Boy what thief want to hold-up coal-man? Is joke you makin. Everybody know dat a coal-man ent have a cent with he when he goin in town. Not thief man . . . not livin' people. Dem is not what I talkin 'bout—something else. It have people who could do something to you, and all-yuh young fellars can't see because you ent believe. Dat is why you ent have the respec' what we old time people have for dem tings. It have to have something. Dis world ent make out from nothing. *Somebody . . . something* does make it turn 'round. And I see tings dat make me know dat. And if I ent see dem, my name ent Sookoo, and I-is-a-blasted-liar-so-help-me-God. I say my name ent Sookoo and God lick me down with a big-stone if I lie! I know what I talkin 'bout and if I lie I die. I see 'nuff ting to make your blood crawl and dat ent all.

"You remember it have a fellar name Mahal? 'Member how he uses to walk miles doin up he hand and foot like if he drivin motor-car? The man uses to walk *quite* from Tunapuna. All the way through Curepe and St. Joseph and San Juan he shiftin' gear and blowin horn. . . . You tink is mad he mad? He family the same way too you know. Is somebody who make him get so. He had a sister who uses to crawl on she hand and foot like a dog, and she uses to bark like a dog too. I tellin you is something bad dat family gone and do, and somebody make dem come so. You living in Trinidad so long and you never hear about obeah? You say you *hear* but you ent *see*. Well you ent see because you ent believe, and is your own bad luck if you ent want to listen to peo-ple what see for theyself. But I know dat it have something outside there, boys, something big and strong, and I see it already.

"What I see? You ever hear about La Diablesse? Well comin in to town one night, you know when you pass police station in St. Joseph it have a small cemetery bout quarter mile down the road? I turn up the hurricane lamp bright bright bright when I passin the police station because I don't want no trouble from dem scamps. Soon as I pass dem a lil way, I turn the lamp down. The pitch-oil was low nuh . . . and I was tryin to make it last till I get in to town. The cart going crick-crack, the donkey going clip-clop clip-clop. Now I say to myself, now is the time to get a lil rest . . . for the eyes you know. I hear they say after you do this coal work for years your eyes does get weak, so I say let me give dem a lil rest.

"Bam . . . I start to hear a funny kind of noise. I say, what happen at all? The donkey limpin or what? It sound like if he walkin on three foot, then it sound like he walkin on five foot. I say, man, I dreaming or what? I put my hand on the donkey back . . . to feel he nuh, to feel if he walkin even even. The donkey have he head down like he ent hear nutting. You know how animal have more sense than people? Soon as something bad come near, is dem who smell it first? Anyway, the funny noise stop and the donkey sound like if he have all he four foot an dem on the ground.

"We go a lil way, and just before we get close to the gate yard to the cemetery I see it. It look like a ball of fire what pitch-out from behind the train line and it explode! In my half-sleep I say, well it must be another cart or a car or some vehicle. But the ting remain stand-up by the gate . . . shining like a bright piece of galvanise in the moonlight. I look up to the sky, man. I say, but this is dark-dark tonight, it ent have no moon. And soon as we come up longside the cemetery gate yard, the donkey begin to bawl. I jerk the rein hard in he mouth, and the animal begin to *trimble! Trimblin* like if he have the fo-day-fever. And the cart? Well it jerk to a stop like if it have a *brakes* in the wheel.

"I keepin my head on all the time you know. After you travel the Eastern Main Road like a coal man for thirty years, you bound to see a lot-o-tings. But in all my days I never bounce up with anything like this. *One nice woman!* She-pretty-for-so! And she dress up in a yellow sateen dress. Dat is what I see shinin in the dark you know, she dress. And when the cart come up close-close-close, I begin to smell dis sweet ting. You know how fainty dem dadmin flowers does smell when you mash up one of the plants in the bush? Well, is just so I smellin dis fainty smell. Well I thought it was comin from the cemetery, you know how a lot of people like to carry a wreath make up from dem flowers when they bury they dead.

"My friend . . . when I come up close-close-close, I hear she say, 'Good night, mister. You so hurry to go to town, you ent have time to stop and talk.' All this time so she stand up in front the gate yard to the cemetery. The only movement you could see is when she take a breath, she belly and she tot-tots, shining like silver under dat dress, and she have a cigarette in she hand, an she only puffin an smokin. Was a big woman you know! Is not fat she was fat . . . *nice.*

"I get down from the cart. I look below one wheel, I look below the other wheel, it ent have nuttin. But the donkey still cryin. Not a kind of loud bawlin like they does make when they hungry, but a quiet quiet kind . . . like a chile when he just wake up. And then I hear the woman, say, 'Have a cigarette with me nuh. . . . You does smoke?'

"Boy my head have so much worries bout the coals and what time I go reach town, I just say no without even lookin at she. I come round to the front of the cart and start liftin up the donkey foot one by one to see if he have a nail or a stone dat make he walk so chupid. I look and look. I take down the hurricane lamp and start to look with dat too . . . I can't find nuttin. I was still stoopin down on the ground, and when I lift up my head, *what* I see from between the donkey foot! The woman comin cross the road to my cart. And dat is when I hear the same clip-clop clip-clop that I hearin up the road. Good ting I was stoopin down low otherwise I never see it with my own two eye . . . she have one foot like a woman, and the other like a horse.

"I say 'Oh God! Is not a woman . . . is a La Diablesse!' And with that I run round and pick up the rein in my hand and jump up on my seat. I have a big-stick right under my seat you know, but I realize dat it wouldn't do me no good . . . not with a La Diablesse. But I ent no fool. I know I have something *better* than any big-stick. 'I don't take no cigarette from no La Diablesse!' I bawl out to she. I hear she foot you know. She make she mistake when she begin to cross the Main Road, and is then I know why I did hear dat funny sound before, like if the donkey have three foot one minute, then five foot later. But she still comin, clip-clop clip-clop, and she hips twistin up nice when she movin from one foot to the next one.

"The woman still smilin smilin and comin closer to me with the pack of cigarette open and one or two sticken out. You know how dem La Diablesse like to give a man all kind-o-ting to eat and drink and smoke? And then after the man take them and they go to a quiet lonely place together she make him lose his senses and he wake up naked next mornin in a bush full of stingin nettle? Well boy, I start to loosen-up the button of my sleeve, I ent fraid you know. I say let she come real, real close . . . then I go give it to she. So I wait till she come right close to my shoulder and I *pull up* my sleeve, and I show she *this!*

"You see it . . . you watchin it good? What the hell all-yuh pissin-tail boys from nowadays know at all? This lil box you see I have tie on to my arm make from pure silver . . . solid solid silver. Any of you know what kind of obeah it have inside dat? Hai-aye-aye, boy! Is obeah man *poopah* what make this for me. Nuttin in the whole world could touch me.

"I hear one loud scream from she voice and I see she turn to one ball of fire right before me eye and it gone peltin down the road. And then I hear this ugly nasty laugh pitch up high like a fowl . . . a chicken, comin from far far down by the police station. And I could still hear it ringin in my ear up till today: 'Soooookoooo . . . Soooookoooo . . . Soooookoooo, you get away this time, boy.' And then dat laughin what I tellin you bout like a fowl what have a sore throat and he tryin to crow fo-day mornin.

"Oh-ho . . . so you ent want to believe me? Look how I go say it again. If I lie . . . God lick me down with a big-stone! You see? You see I still here and nuttin ent happen to me? Now you go believe? Listen! Li-sun! Li-sun nuh man. I ent drunk you know. I ent gettin light-headed like some of dem rum-suckers who can't hold they liquor. It take mo than a nip o' Black Cat Rum to make my tongue heavy; I know what I talkin bout. And you know why? Because I ent only see . . . but I *believe*. I believe dat it have something . . . something stronger than *even* this rum. Let me tell you something else. I ent see this with my own two eye; it happen to somebody else, not me, a fellar who name . . . em . . . what the hell the man name now? Look at how I does forget tings? . . . Oho, Rajan. Dat is what he name. He uses to be a coal man too, but you know how everybody gettin lectric and gas stove and nobody usin coal-pot these days? Well this man can't make a livin at the trade no mo. Soon as he stop work, he gone by he son and he say, 'Well boy, I get old now, and I take care of you all your life, now is your turn to take care of me.' Dat worthless son, he have kick him out the yard and they begin to fight . . . *right there!* All the neighbors comin to watch the bacchanal. Nobody put hand, nobody interfere. Is not like long-time you know. A boy never kick out he poopah in dem days. And what else? Nobody want to break the fight, all the neighbors only come to watch . . . to enjoy theyself. Anyway the old man was a powerful fellar still. You know you does work hard when you do this coal work, liftin up them heavy heavy bag on the cart, hoisting them down to show a customer for them to inspec'? The man was powerful! He still have big big muscles all about in he arm and he shoulder. He chest was still big in dem days. He tumble dat boy on the ground and he beat him like a old snake, then he get up and he left he. But the boy only *playin* like a snake. He well coil-up when the old man bustin licks on he, and soon as he father turn he head, the boy get up and snatch a big stick and he give he father *one lick* on the head. I was right there, man. I hear the blow, the crack what the stick make when it hit the man head. And then on top of dat, the stick break . . . right in the boy hand. Must-be it was an old dry-stick . . . I would lie?

"The old man turn round and he begin to rain mo blows on he son. He say, 'You want to kill me here today with big-stick? I go show you who is man . . . I go show you who is man here . . . today today!' And with every word the old man say, he give the boy another blow. And when he ask the boy if he had enough, you know what dat rascal say to he poopah? He say, 'You go dead bad!' The old man hit him again . . . hard. 'Dat is the thanks you get in dis world for makin children!' And when he hit dat boy again, he ask he, 'Dat satisfy you? You gett nuff licks? It have plenty mo where dat come from.' The boy say three-four-five time, 'I go work a obeah on you . . . you go dead bad!' And the old man standing up with one foot pon he chest all dis time so . . . watchin to see dat he don't make another move. 'It ent have nuttin like obeah, you fool. What you think, is fraid I fraid? If you want to play *man* you want to fight like *man,* get up and let we see who is *man . . . today today!'* But the boy look like he get nuff blows. He fraid the old man. He wouldn't get up from off the ground. All he could say is dat he go work a bad obeah on he poopah. By this time so the father get vex because all kind o' people gang up to watch the fireworks, and it look as if he shame to make people see how he well beat he son, and he ent have no feelin's for he own chile . . . he own flesh-an-blood. So now he change he tune. He say to the boy nice nice nice, 'Tell me you sorry you did lift you hand to hit your poopah what bring you in the world.' You know what dat boy do? He spit on the ground an he cuss again . . . bad bad words! The old man temper *really* get hot now, but, it look like he still feeling sorry for the boy too. He take the boy hand and he twis-it behind he back. 'Tell me you sorry now . . . let all these people hear you sorry dat you hit you poopah.' The boy twis-up he mouth like a dry-up hibiscus flower . . . like if he tastin' something sour, and he suck he teeth makin a nasty noise. The old man twis' harder. 'Say you sorry! You worthless scamp!' The boy coil round on the ground till he couldn't bear no more pain, and then he say, 'Oh God . . . Oh God—oye . . . Oh God I sorry.' And then he father tell he, 'Say you sorry, PA . . . PA. I want to hear you say you sorry, PA, befo I loosen you.' And the boy say again, 'I sorry, Pa!' *Then* the old man loosen he.

"Eh-eh! Soon as he loosen him, the boy fly pon he father . . . just like snake. And he put *one bite* on the man chest, and it begin to bleed right-there-and-then. The old man catch him by he hand again and every-body swear dat the old man go kill him dead dis time. What? No police around him! Where you could find a police? Where dem scamps hear it have a fight somewhere, they run like hell befo they get lick down too.

"The old man have the boy hand twis' . . . and it look like if the boy hand lose all the strength it have in it. But the boy ent cryin you know.

He face like Mad Adam stone . . . like if he ent have no feelin's at-all, at-all. 'Kiss me!' the father order he. And the boy was still layin down on the ground. 'Kiss me and tell me you sorry,' he poopah tell he. And when the father twis' the boy hand nuff, he well crawl up like a animal and he kiss he poopah foot. 'You go work a bad obeah on me, eh? Well kiss me other foot and tell me you sorry.' The boy say quiet quiet that he was sorry. 'Louder! Louder! So dat dese people here could hear what the hell you sayin.' The boy say he sorry again, and this time the old man drag he up by the collar, and make he stand up. 'Kiss me right here where you bite me like a dog and tell me dat you sorry.' But the boy hold he face bout four-five inches from the bite and he wouldn't do it. 'Kiss me right here, you damn rogue. Right here where you make the blood come out. . . . You did want my blood? Well taste it! You taste it befo when you did bite me, taste it again! I is you father and you want to kill me? . . . You want to work bad obeah on me . . . come on now and kiss me on my chest, otherwise I break you hand like a dry-stick.' And the old man did mean it. He did mean every word he say. He pinch the boy hand hard . . . HARD. And then the worthless scamp kiss he poopah chest and tell he that he sorry. But when he poopah loose he, he run from the yard like a mongoose peltin down in the bush bawlin out to he poopah, 'You go dead bad, I goin bus' a bad obeah on you, you go dead bad!'

"Well . . . nobody see that boy face from that day, but he old man begin to take in more and more sick, and it look like if he fraid what the boy tell he. At first he didn't believe, but later people say he uses to hang around in all kind of rum-shop talkin to people like if he fraid to go home in the night.

"Another time I hear somebody say that the old man heself begin to believe the boy work a strong obeah on he so he gone to a *more* strong obeah man to break the spell, but it look like he ent believe in the obeah man at first, so the obeah man can't do too much for him.

"And you know what the obeah man tell he? He say that if that boy really mean in he heart of hearts what he say, and he go to a obeah man, that it bound to come true, that the old man go dead bad one day.

The man still strong, you know. I does still see him. He lef' the coal work, he had a few shilling save up here and there, and all he could do is spend all he money on one obeah man after another. All a dem make him bring chicken, dey make him bring rum, dey make him bring goat brains, the obeah man he go to . . . they tell he the same-same thing. They will take the money first you know, then they say they can't help he because he ent believe.

"Well boys . . . I ent know what to tell you myself. But the man look like if he possess! Like if he haunted! Some people say dat he waitin . . . waitin for the day when he so go *do* for he. He turn frighten! The man turn *coward-coward!* And all the time he lookin round to see if some-body followin he. Sometimes he think dat he believe in one obeah man and he say dat things does happen . . . next day he have a lil doubt, and he start to trimble . . . trimblin like if he have the fo-day-fever, and all he could do to ease he mind is to get a nip-o' Black Cat.

"What you say there, boy? You closin shop? Alright, just let me fin-ish tellin these boys an-dem something. Alright-alright, man! I know police go lock you up for sellin liquor after hours. You think I born yes-terday? Ah me . . . is just a lil pain dat I have here in my chest. Give me a lil glass of water to drink, and I go clear out.

"Listen, boys, this man have to close up the rum-shop. He have the law to respec'! Otherwise he get in bad trouble. You can't blame a man for dat; everybody have to have something dat they must respec'! Gim-mie a lil hand and let me go outside and sit down on the pavement where I could catch the sea-breeze in my lungs. That's it . . . that's it . . . easy now . . . thank you . . . thank you. Just put me down here and let me stretch out on the pavement a lil bit. I know how dis pain does come and go. I go feel better just-now . . . j-u-s-t—n-o-w."

Sookoo was breathing heavily, with short gasps between each breath, and one of the men from the clique banged on the door of the Britannia to get some more water for him. The old man lay prone on the pavement of Frederick Street trying to reach up to rub his chest. One of the younger men helped his shaky hand to loosen the buttons of his shirt and began massaging the spot where the old man complained of feeling a burning pain. The door of the Britannia opened a crack and the other man came out with pitcher of water and a light. And when the beam of the torch fell on the old man's chest, they all withdrew with a little gasp as he said his last words.

"Oh God, boy . . . you come at last? You come at last? Been waitin for you so long."

He turned up his eyes in their sockets, and his breathing halted as he lay on the dark pavement outside the Britannia Bar. On his chest, close to the nipple of his right breast, was the scar of teeth marks, an upper and a lower semicircle of small dark indentations punctured in his dark brown skin.

Some say that mother and daughter is the closest bond there is. . . .

My Mother

JAMAICA KINCAID

IMMEDIATELY ON WISHING my mother dead and seeing the pain it caused her, I was sorry and cried so many tears that all the earth around me was drenched. Standing before my mother, I begged her forgiveness, and I begged so earnestly that she took pity on me, kissing my face and placing my head on her bosom to rest. Placing her arms around me, she drew my head closer and closer to her bosom, until finally I suffocated. I lay on her bosom, breathless, for a time uncountable, until one day, for a reason she has kept to herself, she shook me out and stood me under a tree and I started to breathe again. I cast a sharp glance at her and said to myself, "So." Instantly I grew my own bosoms, small mounds at first, leaving a small, soft place between them, where, if ever necessary, I could rest my own head. Between my mother and me now were the tears I had cried, and I gathered up some stones and banked them in so that they formed a small pond. The water in the pond was thick and black and poisonous, so that only unnameable invertebrates could live in it. My mother and I now watched each other carefully, always making sure to shower the other with words and deeds of love and affection.

I WAS SITTING on my mother's bed trying to get a good look at myself. It was a large bed and it stood in the middle of a large, completely dark room. The room was completely dark because all the windows had been boarded up and all the crevices stuffed with black cloth. My mother lit some candles and the room burst into a pinklike, yellowlike glow. Looming over us, much larger than ourselves, were our shadows. We sat mesmerized because our shadows had made a place between themselves, as if they were making room for someone else. Nothing filled up the space between them, and the shadow of my mother sighed. The shadow of my mother danced around the room to a tune that my own shadow sang, and then they stopped. All along, our shadows had grown thick and thin, long and short, had fallen at every angle, as if they were controlled by the light of day. Suddenly my mother got up and blew out the candles and our shadows vanished. I continued to sit on the bed, trying to get a good look at myself.

MY MOTHER removed her clothes and covered thoroughly her skin with a thick gold-colored oil, which had recently been rendered in a hot pan from the livers of reptiles with pouched throats. She grew plates of metal-colored scales on her back, and light, when it collided with this surface, would shatter and collapse into tiny points. Her teeth now arranged themselves into rows that reached all the way back to her long white throat. She uncoiled her hair from her head and then removed her hair altogether. Taking her head into her large palms, she flattened it so that her eyes, which were by now ablaze, sat on top of her head and spun like two revolving balls. Then, making two lines on the soles of each foot, she divided her feet into crossroads. Silently, she had instructed me to follow her example, and now I too traveled along on my white underbelly, my tongue darting and flickering in the hot air. "Look," said my mother.

My mother and I were standing on the seabed side by side, my arms laced loosely around her waist, my head resting securely on her shoulder, as if I needed the support. To make sure she believed in my frailness, I sighed occasionally—long, soft sighs, the kind of sigh she had long ago taught me could evoke sympathy. In fact, how I really felt was invincible. I was no longer a child but I was not yet a woman. My skin had just blackened and cracked and fallen away and my new impregnable carapace had taken full hold. My nose had flattened; my hair curled in and stood out straight from my head simultaneously; my many rows of teeth in their retractable trays were in place. My mother and I wordlessly made an arrangement—I sent out my beautiful sighs, she received them; I leaned ever more heavily on her for support, she offered her shoulder, which shortly grew to the size of a thick plank. A long time passed, at the end of which I had hoped to see my mother permanently cemented to the seabed. My mother reached out to pass a hand over my head, a pacifying gesture, but I laughed and, with great agility, stepped aside. I let out a horrible roar, then a self-pitying whine. I had grown big, but my mother was bigger, and that would always be so. We walked to the Garden of Fruits and there ate to our hearts' satisfaction. We departed through the southwesterly gate, leaving as always, in our trail, small colonies of worms.

With my mother, I crossed, unwillingly, the valley. We saw a lamb grazing and when it heard our footsteps it paused and looked up at us. The lamb looked cross and miserable. I said to my mother, "The lamb is cross and miserable. So would I be, too, if I had to live in a climate not suited to my nature." My mother and I now entered the cave. It was the dark and cold cave. I felt something growing under my feet and I bent down to eat it. I stayed that way for years, bent over eating whatever I found growing under my feet. Eventually, I grew a special lens that would allow me to see in the darkest of darkness; eventually, I grew a special coat that kept me warm in the coldest of coldness. One day I saw my mother sitting on a rock. She said, "What a strange expression you have on your face. So cross, so miserable, as if you were living in a climate not suited to your nature." Laughing, she vanished. I dug a deep, deep hole. I built a beautiful house, a floorless house, over the deep, deep hole. I put in lattice windows, most favored of windows by my mother, so perfect for looking out at people passing by without her being observed. I painted the house itself yellow, the windows green, colors I knew would please her. Standing just outside the door, I asked her to inspect the house. I said, "Take a look. Tell me if it's to your satisfaction." Laughing out of the corner of a mouth I could not see, she stepped inside. I stood just outside the door, listening carefully, hoping to hear her land with a thud at the bottom of the deep, deep hole. Instead, she walked up and down in every direction, even pounding her heel on the air. Coming outside to greet me, she said, "It is an excellent house. I would be honored to live in it," and then vanished. I filled up the hole and burned the house to the ground.

MY MOTHER has grown to an enormous height. I have grown to an enormous height also, but my mother's height is three times mine. Sometimes I cannot see from her breasts on up, so lost is she in the atmosphere. One day, seeing her sitting on the seashore, her hand reaching out in the deep to caress the belly of a striped fish as he swam through a place where two seas met, I glowed red with anger. For a while then I lived alone on the island where there were eight full moons and I adorned the face of each moon with expressions I had seen on my mother's face. All the expressions favored me. I soon grew tired of living in this way and returned to my mother's side. I remained, though glowing red with anger, and my mother and I built houses on opposite banks of the dead pond. The dead pond lay between us; in it, only small invertebrates with poisonous lances lived. My mother behaved toward them as if she had suddenly found herself in the same room with relatives we had long since risen above. I cherished their presence and gave them names. Still I missed my mother's close company and cried constantly for her, but at the end of each day when I saw her return to her house, incredible and great deeds in her wake, each of them singing loudly her praises, I glowed and glowed again, red with anger. Eventually, I wore myself out and sank into a deep, deep sleep, the only dreamless sleep I have ever had.

ONE DAY my mother packed my things in a grip and, taking me by the hand, walked me to the jetty, and placed me on board a boat, in care of the captain. My mother, while caressing my chin and cheeks, said some words of comfort to me because we had never been apart before. She kissed me on the forehead and turned and walked away. I cried so much my chest heaved up and down, my whole body shook at the sight of her back turned toward me, as if I had never seen her back turned toward me before. I started to make plans to get off the boat, but when I saw that the boat was encased in a large green bottle, as if it were about to decorate a mantelpiece, I fell asleep, until I reached my destination, the new island. When the boat stopped, I got off and I saw a woman with feet exactly like mine, especially around the arch of the instep. Even though the face was completely different from what I was used to, I recognized this woman as my mother. We greeted each other at first with great caution and politeness, but as we walked along, our steps became one, and as we talked, our voices became one voice, and we were in complete union in every other way. What peace came over me then, for I could not see where she left off and I began, or where I left off and she began.

MY MOTHER and I walk through the rooms of her house. Every crack in the floor holds a significant event: here, an apparently healthy young man suddenly dropped dead; here a young woman defied her father and, while riding her bicycle to the forbidden lovers' meeting place, fell down a precipice, remaining a cripple for the rest of a very long life. My mother and I find this a beautiful house. The rooms are large and empty, opening onto each other, waiting for people and things to fill them up. Our white muslin skirts billow up around our ankles, our hair hangs straight down our backs as our arms hang straight at our sides. I fit perfectly in the crook of my mother's arm, on the curve of her back, in the hollow of her stomach. We eat from the same bowl, drink from the same cup; when we sleep, our heads rest on the same pillow. As we walk through the rooms, we merge and separate, merge and separate; soon we shall enter the final stage of our evolution.

THE FISHERMEN are coming in from sea; their catch is bountiful, my mother has seen to that. As the waves plop, plop against each other the fishermen are happy that the sea is calm. My mother points out the fishermen to me, their contentment is a source of my contentment. I am sitting in my mother's enormous lap. Sometimes I sit on a mat she has made for me from her hair. The lime trees are weighed down with limes—I have already perfumed myself with their blossoms. A hummingbird has nested on my stomach, a sign of my fertileness. My mother and I live in a bower made from flowers whose petals are imperishable. There is the silvery blue of the sea, crisscrossed with sharp darts of light, there is the warm rain falling on the clumps of castor bush, there is the small lamb bounding across the pasture, there is the soft ground welcoming the soles of my pink feet. It is in this way my mother and I have lived for a long time now.

the broad dutty water

THE SONG WARNS, "Wai-oh, wai-oh, wai-oh, the broad dutty water." The rivers and seas that give sustenance, that are places to bathe and play, are also sources of danger and death when their banks swell or storms whip the water to frenzy. Broad waters with their capricious power to bring life or disaster figure large in the next three stories.

Language is a constant site of battle in the Caribbean. Speech is one of the easiest ways to mark class differences, and educators can spend a lot of time trying to take "bad" vernacular speech from people's mouths and replace it with "good" speech. The tale-teller in Olive Senior's story "Mad Fish" is easily placed by her relative wealth and her high-handed use of language and attitude. Even when her messenger Radio does finally find the words with which to communicate, she takes those words out of his mouth, and belittles and modifies them when she tells the tale in turn.

Mad Fish

OLIVE SENIOR

THIS REALLY HAPPENED, I swear. I was right there when Radio came rushing up the hill from the fishing beach all out of breath. Radio is our messenger and he likes to be first with the news. But everyone called him Radio not for that reason but because of his serious speech defect, which made it difficult to understand him at the best of times, almost impossible when he was excited, which was when he had fresh news to tell. This caused him endless frustration for by the time he'd calmed down enough to make sense to Jeremy, who was one of the few persons who could understand him, someone with a more agile tongue would have arrived to reel off a version of the story and cheat him out of the novelty of telling. Not this time though. Jeremy and I were about to have our first cup of coffee when Radio burst into the dining room, so excited he couldn't even get out words that sounded like language, just strange inhuman water-filled noises that were wheezing out of him like a drowning accordion. The only word we could make out sounded like "fish." He said that word over and over, and he wanted us to come, pointing to the beach. Why should a fish on a fishing beach cause excitement? But Radio was so urgent and insistent that we left our coffee untouched and followed him down the hill and across the road.

As we approached, everything on the beach looked so normal, I started to mentally curse Radio for pulling one of his jokes on us, as he liked to do from time to time, for Radio is sort of simple, or so I used to think, though Jeremy never agreed and now I'm not so sure. We could see the fishermen and the higglers standing about in little groups. There were the usual idlers and mangy dogs lurking and the old men sitting under the Sea Almond where they played dominoes all day. But as we got closer we realized something was not right. The whole scene was like a stage set with knots of people standing around in tableaux, waiting for the curtain to go up. Nobody was making a sound and those who moved did so in slow-motion as if in a dream. It was as if each one had just received news that a beloved person had died and was still too shocked to take it in. Jeremy and I walked up to the largest group, which was by the boats, and nobody paid us the slightest attention, amazingly, since Jeremy is sort of the village squire and people are always quick to greet him. Now they were behaving as if we weren't there, but not in a rude way; it was as if they were too preoccupied with more important business. But something made us bite our tongues and say nothing too, as if we had also fallen under a spell that had gripped the entire beach, for even the sky, which hadn't shown a cloud in nearly a year of drought, was suddenly turning black and shadows were beginning to fall on the white sand. I actually shivered. Without exchanging a word between us or with anyone else, Jeremy and I turned and went home without a clue as to what had happened. Once inside our house, everything seemed so normal we went back to having our breakfast, each of us confident that others would arrive with the tale before long.

But amazingly, no one came forward to speak of what happened, that day or any other. And when fragments of the story did surface to corroborate what Radio eventually told us, it was not at all like the stories these people liked to tell, augmented and ornamented and embellished, built up of versions over time. This was utterly downplayed, individual elements singled out and spoken about only in terms of "signs," "tokens," and "miracles" as if people were not so much interested in the story as narrative as in teasing out all the possible permutations of meaning.

Still, those who were there might eventually have come around to talking and laughing about the episode, as these people tend to do with everything else, except for one or two elements. From our fishing beach that day, four men in a car with a fantastic fish had disappeared not only around the bend in the road but totally off the face of the earth. From the minute they drove off, nothing was ever seen or heard of them again. We know this for a fact, for Jeremy's police friends had also heard the story and could verify that a lot of people had come looking for the men, including their relatives. The police would have been happy to find them too, for other reasons, and set out to do so. But all investigations had proven fruitless. As soon as they drove off, the men, the car, and the fish had simply vanished.

There were other repercussions. Big Jake, our most popular fisherman, never went to sea again and spent his days playing dominoes and drinking himself into idiocy. Some said he had lost his nerve, afraid of what he might catch. Others said that from the day he raised his hand against his brothers, they had taken over the boat and banished him from it. It is also a fact that it was on the day of the so-called Mad Fish that the year-long drought broke, though the day had dawned with a cloudless sky and—so people said, for I wasn't keeping count I was so sick of it after a while—rain fell for forty days and forty nights.

But the most miraculous thing of all is that after we returned home that day, ate our breakfast, fed Radio, and calmed him down to that point where his speech, though rough, would begin to make sense, to our astonishment and without any warning, he began to speak beautifully and clearly, as if he had swallowed mercury, and he has continued to speak so ever since.

You won't believe what a change these things have wrought around here, everyone suddenly so sober and serious. People have put all these happenings together and taken them for signs and wonders—"tokens" they call them—of the end of the world and such Millenarian rubbish. Radio is giving himself airs, refusing to answer to "Radio" and insisting on being called by his rightful name of Joshua. He's been given a message, he says, a big announcement to make, but he's being coy; he won't tell us what it is until the time is ripe. A lot of people are taking him seriously, too. Now instead of running our errands and helping around the yard, he spends his time riding his bicycle up and down and ringing his bell, making himself all Biblical and apocalyptic, condescending to pop in from time to time to regale us with the latest news interspersed with wild talk about Leviathans and fishing for souls.

I keep telling Jeremy it's time to get rid of him, he's got perfectly useless, but of course Jeremy won't hear of it. He and Radio have been together since they were boys, and Jeremy, I suspect, has always found him kind of amusing, as if he provides the yeast for Jeremy's rather dull soul. Plus, Jeremy is ever faithful and loyal. That's the trouble with this country, people ignore the big things and make such a fuss over the little. I don't want to think this, but I believe even Jeremy in his heart of hearts is beginning to believe that something world-shattering happened that day. I keep my mouth shut, for whenever I say anything, he rubs it in that I'm not from here so I can't understand the culture. What culture? I keep asking myself. After fifteen years I should have seen signs of it by now. I certainly don't see any of it in Jeremy's other planter friends and policeman drinking buddies or the fishermen and higglers down on the beach. Well, you can judge, for here's the story as told by our little silver-tongued Radio, a.k.a. Joshua, all acted out, with many dramatic flourishes, if you please (though for your sake I have taken some care to render it into a closer approximation of the English language than Radio so far uses. I've also taken some liberties to explain certain things in a more sophisticated way than he did. But I've tried to retain some of the color and flavor of how he told it, for that you'll find amusing).

PICTURE THIS, says he. The fishing boat is pulling up on the beach. Big Jake and his brothers and all the little hangers-on hauling on the net, fish spilling out like quicksilver, leaping and spinning, one last jerk and they are lying unconscious and silent, as fish suppose to be. But what's this commotion over here? Something jumping and moving as if a big animal just leap off the boat. The first person to get a good look scream and the next one too, and after that, everybody dashing around like mad-ants shrieking and pointing. First the boys helping to pull in the net, then the higglers waiting for the catch. What a commotion! Big Jake and the crew haul in this huge fish that is like nothing nobody ever seen before. Gold on top, silver on the bottom, and all the colors of the rainbow in-between.

Big Jake and the other fishermen stop what they doing to get a good look at the fish, which by this time launch itself out of the net and dancing around on the ground. Everybody waiting to hear the fishermen pronounce the name of this fish, for they suppose to know every creature in the sea. But when Big Jake and the rest stand there for a long time just scratching their heads and looking like they lost, and people figure out that even they don't know, the wailing and the shrieking break out fresh again. You have to understand, is not just the looks of the fish for is not a bad-looking fish at that. The problem is that the fish is not behaving like how fish out of water should behave. This fish not just moving, it dancing. A-wiggling and a-moving its tail and spinning and turning and wining, its big body glistening and flashing in the sun.

After a while, everybody quieten down, we just standing there watching this fish. Is like everybody suddenly feeling fraid in the presence of this mysterious creature that land up on our beach. For who can tell if is call somebody call it up, for it have people in these parts can do them kind of thing. Then a man in the crowd call out:

"Wait! Is a Dance Hall Queen this."

Everybody laugh, like we get relief, for that's just how the fish stay, like a dance hall girl in her fancy dress and her tight fish-tail sequins like scales, moving her body to the latest wine. So little by little people stop feeling frighten and start making joke.

"Well," one man proclaim, "the only fish I ever see live this long out of water is Mud Fish."

"Is not Mud Fish this," another one shout. "Is Mad Fish!"

And is true, the fish acting like it crazy; not like a lunatic but happy and don't care mad, like it drunk. And somebody actually say the word "drunk"—"the fish look like it drunk"—and is like the word set off something running through people mind, for suddenly, everything change, is like a cloud passing over the sun, for somebody, I don't know who, whisper the word, "cocaine." And the word pass from mouth to ear until everybody taking it up like a chorus. "The fish drunk with the coke." Everybody know what that mean.

"Coke!" Quick as a flash, the word like a sword slashing at all of us. That word making people jumpy for the whole coast awash with story bout small plane a drop parcel into sea so boat can pick it up. That is okay—people don't business with that. Is just that sometime the parcel fall into the wrong place—and end up in the wrong hand and this is what everybody getting excited bout. For it come like a lottery now. Everybody dreaming bout finding parcel and getting rich overnight. Everybody know is dead them dead if certain people find out. Up and down the coast they hanging out all kind of rumor on their clothesline. Which fisherman can suddenly buy new boat. Which boat disappear after the crew pick up something. Which old lady find parcel wash up on a beach and hide it in her three-foot iron pot, till her house suddenly burn down with her and her three grandchildren lock up inside and no sign of the iron pot in the ashes. Suddenly, fishing taking on a whole new meaning; fisherman dreaming of a different catch.

Well, Big Jake is one of them alright for though up to now he in the middle of the crowd laughing and joking bout the fish (that still dancing like crazy), the minute he hear the word "coke," is like he turn into a different man. Quick as a snake Big Jake reach into the boat and haul out him machete and start to lash out with it, as if he suddenly gone crazier than the fish.

"Stan back, all a unno from mi fish. Stan back," he start shout.

But people already backing away for his two eye looking wild and he leaping about and swinging his machete left and right. Everybody looking at him in shock for never mind his size, Big Jake is normally the most peaceful man around.

By now, is like Big Jake and the fish together in a ring, surrounded by the crowd, with all eyes on Big Jake. But is like I can't take my eyes off the fish, for I seeing it quietly moving round in the circle till it come right to where I standing and it stop, just like that, and it lift up its head and it look straight at me. I swear. I can see that it not looking too well just now, tired like, as if the life draining out of it, the colors fading away. And is like the fish calling to me, calling me without voice as if is the two of us alone in the whole wide world. Like it pulling me down towards it. And I can't help myself, I feeling sorrowful for the fish that just sitting there on the sand for I feeling the life going out of it as if is a part of myself leaving me. I bend down and reach out my hand to touch the scales and as I bending down, a drop of my sweat fall right on top of the fish and I swear, is like electricity, the fish jump as if it suddenly get life all over again and it look at me, directly at me, and is like it sucking me in—I swear I black-out for a minute there for I don't remember nothing more. When I come back to myself I see the fish reach clear to the other side of the circle, leaping and jumping and dancing, its colors bright and dazzling like it just come out of the water.

All this happen so fast that nobody notice; everybody still watching Big Jake. But I feel my finger tingling and when I look I see a little drop of blood, as if I prick myself on the fish, and I don't even think, I put the finger in my mouth. I don't have time to worry about doing something like that after I touch the Mad Fish, for Big Jake brethren Ernie and Ray take up their machete too and the three of them circling one another with their weapon now, arguing over is who own the fish. You see my trial? The three of them fishing together from the same boat from them born, it belong to their father before he die, and never an argument about who own what fish till somebody mention coke. This is where it reach: the three of them circling one other, getting more and more rile up, and people just watching and nobody doing or saying nothing. The whole thing looking so serious to me, that is when I decide to come and get you, Mass Jeremy, to see if you can talk sense into these people, otherwise is wholesale murder going to happen right here in Whitesands Bay.

So I start push my way out of the circle of people to reach the road and by now, the crowd so big those at the back don't even know what causing the commotion up front, though plenty rumor flying. You know how people like to go on? One lot of people saying: "Three fisherman drown." A woman swearing: "Is whale them catch." Another one say that fishing boat come back with one missing at sea. A set of little children jumping up and down saying is a Mermaid. One boy telling his friend them that they catch a big fish that vomit up dead body that starting to come back to life and another saying no, what they bring back is a fish that join together like is Siamese twin. But all the way too, like is a snake sliding underneath the joking and the laughing, you could hear the buzz, "Them catch the fish that swallow the coke."

And just as I manage to reach the road, laughing to myself at all the foolishness people talking, this big black car flash by with all the windows dark and roll up so you can't see who inside. Then, as the driver see the crowd, him draw brake and stop, and back back right down to where I standing. Ehh-he now, I say to myself. Every window roll down same time. Four of them in the car. Black dark glasses. Nobody smiling. The people standing by the road who see the play pretend they don't see nothing but same time you see them start to move, away from the road and back to the sea, and you can tell the word traveling. The driver come out of the car and he slam the door so he can lean against it and fold him two arm across him chest. "What a gwan?" he ask and you can see him scanning everything with him eyes. But everybody suddenly tun dumb. Not a soul saying nothing till the silence getting dangerous. "Is something them catch, sar," one little boy finally squeeze out, and you can hear the shaking in him voice. Him mother cuff him same time she drag him in to hold him close to her body. One of the men in the backseat of the car lean out the window and take him finger call to a young girl who standing with a set of young girls who can't stop look at the car.

"Nice Queen, what a go on?" he ask her in this sweet-sweet voice. Well, this little piknie so thrill to have a Don calling to her she just forget herself and make her mouth run weh. "Dem find a fish that swallow coke. It don't stop dance yet. Dem seh is Dance Hall Queen."

Poppyshow! Is how this piknie stay clear back here and know all that? By this time she dying with laugh and trying to step boldy to the car while her friend them holding on to her skirt to drag her back.

Well! You'd think these fellows drill like soldier every day. For is like with one movement, the three in the car come out and slam the doors with one slam: "Blam." The driver fall in beside them. Four of them dress in black from head to toe. Then like they practice every move, the four of them straighten them black suit and them gold chain and them shades, then line up two by two and step off down the beach. The crowd part in front of them like the Red Sea part before Moses. People didn't even turn to look, they just sense a deadly force rolling towards them and they move out of the way. I couldn't let this pass, so I fall in behind the men to see the moves.

They look neither to the right nor to the left; they just march forward through the parting crowd till they reach the circle round the fishermen who still quarreling and making pass with their machete. The four men just stand there, arm fold across them chest, just taking in the scene, not saying a word. It take a little while for the brothers to realize something happening, and as each one of them turn and see the men in black, his face change as if he seeing duppie and everything just drain out of him. Big Jake and his brothers just drop their machete and freeze. Nobody move. People look as if they not even breathing as they watch the four men turn to study the fish. They stand there looking at it for a good long while, then they turn to look at the one that is the big Don and he give a little nod and the four of them bend down one time to take hold of the fish.

Well, me not lying, is like the fish that never stop moving from it come off the boat been waiting for something like this, for the four men don't have to struggle with it too hard, is like the fish allowing them to pick it up, for they manage to hold on to it and lift it without any trouble; the fish keeping suddenly quiet except for a little trembling that running through its body now and then.

Still without saying one word, the four men carrying the fish march back the way they come, straight to their car, the silent crowd parting to let them through, everybody pretending like they not seeing nothing. I still following right behind them, so I see when one of them drop his side of the fish long enough to open the trunk, and then the four of them struggle to lift up the fish and throw it in. Then they slam the trunk shut, dust off their hands, straighten their clothes, get into the car, and drive away.

This is the end of Radio's narrative and that is the last anyone ever saw of the car, the men, or the fish, though people swear that even before they moved off, the car had started rocking from some mighty power like thunder rolling around inside the trunk.

Well, there you have it. Make of it what you will. Maybe you can even find some Culture in it. All I know is, from the day the Mad Fish came, Radio got voice and attitude and it rained for a long, long time.

One of the West African deities that traveled across the sea is the persona of the sea herself: Yemaya, Yemanja, Yemoja; one of the African Powers. Her colors are the blue and white of the waves and she is as beautiful and unyielding as oceans.

In a hardscrabble community such as a fishing village, where the sea has a god's power over fate and existence, someone who laughs a lot may be cautioned not to "give away laughs for pea soup"—not to be too ready with her joy, lest she also leave herself open to too much sorrow. June-Plum is having a very personal battle with the Power who controls her happiness.

Widows' Walk

OPAL PALMER ADISA

SHE GOES LOOKING for Neville. This is obvious to all. Many times she has to blink her eyes, which keep fooling her into believing that she sees his boat out at sea. It is only a mirage. Another wave swells up before breaking on the shore.

June-Plum was tense all week, even before Neville left, but she never articulated her fears. Then, just before he left Sunday morning, she broke a saucer—a sure sign of unpleasant news. She didn't know then that it was connected to Neville, but she should have. Several times within the last couple of weeks she was visited in her dreams by a beautiful chocolate-colored woman with thick, wild hair piled upon her head like a straw basket. This shapely chocolate goddess with inviting hips and thighs wore a cloud-white dress with several ruffles of blue cotton that flounced with her every move. She taunted June-Plum that she was the more desirable of the two, but June-Plum did not heed. She stubbornly refused to believe that her dreams or the broken saucer might have anything to do with the very contented life she led with Neville. How foolish could she be? June-Plum bursts out with a big laugh of astonishment at her own foolishness.

June-Plum's deep belly laughter, so big that it scared people off because they couldn't imagine a pleasure as enormous as the one her voice suggested, used to delight her mother. "Yuh gi weh laugh fi pea-soup," she would say. June-Plum recalls that her laughter was like pea soup in those days, in neverending supply. Happy memories of her mother heighten June-Plum's sadness and she fixes her face like a funeral mask. She lingers on the boardwalk long after all the other women have turned into their houses and closed their windows to bar the mosquitoes entrance. A handful of stars shines through the purple sky. To block out the wind, June-Plum folds her hands over her belly swollen with child. The waves are just ripples gliding calmly, and, at each fold, they glitter. There is almost no flow, only motion going nowhere. The effect is inviting, yet disturbing.

Neville should have returned yesterday. The smell of smoke and burning bush (to keep the mosquitoes at bay) swirls through the air like perfume—no more like the pungent smell of the flamboyant tree's blossoms. June-Plum sighs and hugs herself more tightly, hearing the waves beginning to grumble.

She searches the expanse of water while waves splash against the boards, sending salty foam rising up like vapor into the night. Each time she thinks she sees something, someone. Who is this goddess Yemoja? As ruler of the sea and children, she is as generous in her gifts of children as she is ruthless in taking men. But June-Plum is not her enemy. She, too, is woman and mother, and she wants her man. This one Yemoja cannot have, and June-Plum means for her to know this, means to challenge and fight her if need be. As her thoughts take form, June-Plum takes in a deep breath and lets it out with a sigh. She takes several abortive steps before throwing off her slippers and descending into the water to wet her feet.

The waves rush in as if to meet her challenge. They chase her and she runs to and fro before standing her ground, lifting her dress until her thighs are bared, confronting her competitor with knowledge that she too has thighs, almond-stained and diaper-soft, which wrap them-selves around her man's back when he enters her deeply, pleasing her to tears. But soon June-Plum is disarmed by the comforting touches of this woman. She eases in completely, and the salty water, cool, bathes her aching heart and massages her weary limbs so that she forgets herself and simply imagines Neville's hands about her body as the waves continue to recede.

Gasping for breath and swallowing water, June-Plum treads until her fingers touch the sandy bottom. She wipes salty water from her eyes, shakes her head, and drags her drenched body to the shore, sighing and laughing. This woman is mistress indeed, and more powerful than she, June-Plum, could ever hope to be. Flopping on the damp sand, she wonders where the sea ends and the sky begins, as it all just seems a mass of blue and white foam. But it doesn't matter; she likes the unity of blues—only how can she and Neville become melted in unity like that? Then she remembers that Neville is already part of that unity. The woman has already taken him. He might be that very wave, which is the same as the one before and no different from the one that follows it. June-Plum knows that she could not win if she fought Yemoja, so that all that is left is pleading, hoping that as a woman Yemoja will understand her need and give her back her man. "De sea so pretty; yuh so free and easy. Ah ave fi gi Neville time wid yuh, but memba dat me need im."

June-Plum comes to the quay and strolls along the boardwalk, the sea mewling beneath. Her sense of destiny tells her nothing. What is today, anyway—Wednesday? Thursday? Friday? Yes, it's Thursday—Thursday is the only day the fishermen sell their fish to whoever comes to buy, not putting aside any for the higglers, the small vendors. Neville left early Sunday morning, when the sky was ashen white and the wind oblique.

"Im been gwane longer dan tree days before. Why me mus worry meself wid bad expectations?"

"Nite, Miss June-Plum, yuh out ere late by yuhself."

"Bertram, ah didn't even ear yuh approach."

"Yuh nuh fi worry yuhself. Ah confident widin me body Neville gwane return safe."

June-Plum allows herself to hear what Bertram has said. He is confident Neville is safe and will return. She doesn't know if she should laugh at such consolation. She is doubtful . . . afraid . . . not able to eat anything. Not sure of what to say, she looks up at the sky. "De nite so pretty. Not often de sky so purple wid stars. De sea calm. Look how de waves hardly move. De book people dem seh de world round, den somewhe at de hedge de sea and de sky lock fingers."

She looks out at the sea, forgetting that Bertram is with her. Her mind cannot hold any one image; it flits from Neville to the children, to last Sunday's sermon, to all the wash that still has to be done. Why is she here on this walk? Her children are home asleep and she should be in bed. And her husband is at sea or gone. June-Plum rubs her arms where cold-bumps have appeared, then turns, remembering Bertram.

"Bertram, wha yuh doin out ere? De nite wind cold. De sky and eberyone lie wrap warmly in bed. Yuh ave a good nite and seh howdy to Beverly."

She lingers longer on the boardwalk, raises her wet dress and examines her thighs. Then, on impulse, she pulls off her dress and jumps into the sea, floating on her back like a piece of log washed to shore. She probably would have passed the night there, but she is suddenly aroused by a harsh voice and firm hands that drag her out of the water and roughly pull her dress over her head.

"Is fool-fool yuh fool or is nuh sense yuh ave. Ooman, yuh ave picknie in yuh belly and four at yuh house—is mad? Yuh mad? Way afta midnite yuh a wade in de sea. Seems like yuh nuh know de sea bad. She nuh joke; she is a funny ooman. Seems like yuh mus mad." And so Miss Country, the old woman who sells fried fish, roast fish, and bammy from a little shack by the seashore, reprimands June-Plum as if she were a disobedient child. At this, June-Plum laughs and allows herself to be pulled along and fussed over by Miss Country, who walks her directly to her house and makes sure she is safely inside.

At home, June-Plum makes herself a cup of cocoa and the radio provides company while she rambles around the kitchen wiping off clean countertops and drying plates that are already stacked in the cabinet. Finally, she sits and folds her hands in her lap. A couple of times she catches herself nodding. . . . "Who on de ladder? Neville, wha yuh doin up dere? Eberytin look so funny. De sea upside down! Whe all dis leaf come from on dis wata-wooden shack? Neville, min yuh drop! De ladder nah lean pan nutten! Wata can't hold yuh. Mek de sea so rough. Neville, come down, come down, de ladder a shake. De waves gwane cova yuh!"

June-Plum focuses her eyes and looks around the kitchen. Her cup is half full of cocoa and the only sound that comes from the radio is hissing. She didn't hear the national anthem but she knows it is after midnight, so she pulls herself up heavily from the chair. Four children have made her stout and motherly, and in another four months, there will be a fifth. She doesn't want any more children as times are too hard, but the Pill is something new, unfamiliar, and Neville never will use rubbers. She sighs. The Bible did say be fruitful and multiply. She hangs her dress on the nail behind the door and opens her Bible:

> Then the Lord said unto Moses, Now shalt thou see what I
> will to Pharaoh: for with a strong hand shall he let them go,
> and with a strong hand shall he drive them out of his land . . .

Something bangs. June-Plum springs out of bed and runs to the back door, thinking Neville has returned. Mist and emptiness greet her. She goes outside into the yard, opens her back gate, and looks down the lane. She sees a figure. A smile rushes to her face, and her voice is a gong in the night: "Neville! Neville, yuh come home." She waits by the gate, suddenly aware that she's barefoot and in her nightie. The figure disappears and only the night remains. Again, her eyes have deceived her. No, she tricked herself—allowed herself to be fooled.

She closes her gate and looks out at the wailing sea that is sending big waves up to the sky. Then she sees her, the woman with whom she shares her man. Yemoja is riding the waves. A lacy turquoise and white turban is wound around her head, ascending to the sky like a cone. She

wears strings of shells around her neck and arms and she is naked
except for a satin blue cloth around her waist. This cloth blows in the
wind like miniature wings. Yemoja's nails are blue on fingers and toes,
and a diamond fills the gap between her front teeth. She is beautiful,
more lovely than the moon, more lovely than an idea. June-Plum bows
to her. Yemoja winks at her, then dives into the roaring waves.

June-Plum is suddenly very cold. Shivering, she runs into the house,
bolting the door behind her. For several minutes she stands by the door
afraid to move, trying desperately not to think of anything, not even
Neville. After several deep breaths, she walks to her children's room and
switches on the light. They are all there—safe. More or less. She shakes
her head. The noise she heard was her youngest son Garfield fallen off
the bed again. She looks at her children—two single beds, four children,
a little dresser, and there is no place to turn in the room. June-Plum
sighs, rubs her stomach, and bends down—bending tears at her back—
and picks up Garfield. She starts putting him back on the bed beside his
brother Floyd, but then she turns and takes him to sleep with her. June-
Plum tosses. Garfield kicks her at every turn. A rooster crows one, two,
three times. The sun rushes through the window like an unwanted fly.
June-Plum pulls her dress over her nightie and heads straight for the
kitchen, where she puts on water to boil. She burns herself.

"Jennifa, get up. Wake up yuh broda dem, an come grate de chocolate fi mek oonuh tea."

"Marnin, Mama, me a fi guh school today? Ah could help yuh wash
and company yuh to de market."

"Jennifa, nuh boda ask stupidness: Yuh know yuh go to school wen
it rain, wen yuh sick, an if school did open pan Saturday and Sunday,
yuh would guh too. If me did only ave fi yuh chance."

"Daddy come home today, Mama?" Jennifer cuts off her mother,
having heard her mother's lament numerous times about how she had
to leave school in the fifth class after her mother took ill to help care
for the house and the other children. June-Plum sizes up Jennifer and
reaches for the bottle of Solomon Gundy (smoked herring with pep-
per and scallion), her craving, along with guavas, since she became

pregnant. She smiles, thinking if it's a boy she will name him Solomon and if it's a girl, Guava. After all, that was how she got her name, June-Plum. Her mother supposedly ate several of the green prickly plums daily during the last two months of her pregnancy.

"Mama!" It's Jennifer, interrupting her memories: "Daddy comin home today?" June-Plum regards her daughter and is angry at her question. She doesn't know when her husband will return, if he ever will. Since she has to make some response, she snaps, "Yes, Jennifa, maybe."

That early hour of the morning, the sun shining through the kitchen windows reminds June-Plum of a pack of fierce, charging dogs. She feels the heat very keenly, and her thighs are beginning to sweat and rub against each other. She raises her dress and examines her thighs, another of her habits since being pregnant, and gradually becomes aware of someone watching her. As she raises her head, her eyes meet Jennifer's, who acknowledges her look before turning to the stove. Jennifer's eyes are so like her missing father's that June-Plum kisses her teeth before emitting one of her deep belly laughs as she leaves the kitchen and walks to her backyard. From there she surveys the sea and the entire community. In another couple of months it would have been ten years since she and Neville began living here where the sea and its smell are always dominant.

Anton Bay is a fishing community. The sea is everywhere. The dock has been christened "Widows' Walk" because many wives, sweet-hearts, and mothers have paced the boardwalk awaiting their men, some of whom have returned from fishing trips while others have not. Women usually gather there in the evenings to exchange gossip, to throw kisses to their men already out at sea, and to stare and marvel at this beautiful / treacherous woman who feeds them, lulls their men and soothes their bodies with her waters. Mostly, though, the women wait. June-Plum feels as if she's been waiting all her life like the rest of them for a man to bring happiness into her life.

This morning, the sea is a smooth blue blanket in sharp contrast to her backyard, which is a mixture of gravel and leaves. The guava tree is in bloom, but birds have picked at the green fleshy fruits. June-Plum runs her hand between her thighs, waves a nonchalant hello to someone passing by her gate, then goes and sits at the open kitchen door where swarms of flies compete, and where a few minutes later her children stumble past her, after kissing her on the cheeks, on their way to school.

June-Plum settles in the doorway, her back partially resting against the door frame. She pulls up her dress and absentmindedly massages her thighs as she again succumbs to her memories.

Ten people were living in four small rooms and she was one of the ten, the older of two girls and the fourth of eight children. When she was eleven, her mother had a stroke, so she had to leave school to wash khaki pants, darn plaid shirts, clean wooden floors using a coconut husk, cook, and on occasions, help dig yams and pick cocoa to sell at the market. The work was not as painful as not being able to go to school, and the Bible was the only book in the house to read. So each day, June-Plum would read to her mother. She began at Genesis: "In the beginning God created the heaven and the earth. And the earth was without form, and void; and darkness . . ."

Halfway through Revelations, her mother died. "And there was given me a reed like unto a rod; and the angel stood, saying, Rise and measure the temple of God . . ."

June-Plum didn't cry at her mother's death. Nor at the funeral, and not even during the Ni-Night celebration, the feast for the dead nine days later. She was happy she didn't have to live each day with the painful look in her mother's eyes and so she grew, keeping things to herself and surviving without friends. She learned to be patient and to cup her sadness in her palms—to guard her feelings.

For ten long years, June-Plum washed clothes, cooked, and cared for the house of her father and brothers, while Jennifer, her sister, had been rescued to live with their maternal aunt and family. Jennifer had not come home to visit, but she always remembered to send June-Plum a card on her birthday. And that was why June-Plum named her first daughter Jennifer—in remembrance of her sister.

June-Plum rouses herself. The children's breakfast dishes are still on the table. She looks at them and frowns, moving off into the room where she and Neville have slept for the last nine years. She sees Neville curled up on the bed, covered from head to foot, regardless of the heat. She tugs at the sheets and he dissolves right in front of her eyes. . . . A wail rocks her body. Her lying eyes.

In a drawer to the back, hidden under some clothes, is a picture of a man and a woman. The woman is slim and tall, wearing a white dress that stops midway between her knees and ankles, a white hat, and white shoes. In her hand is a bunch of hibiscus flowers. The man is tall and muscular, wearing grey baggy pants, a white shirt, and a plaid bow-tie. His face says his shoes are pinching his toes. The woman's smile does not conceal the uncertainty she feels about herself, but they look nice together, standing beside a bicycle that the man holds. June-Plum sees only the bond that exists between the two persons as she recalls how she met Neville.

On her way from the market she had stopped to buy fish, as her father insisted on having fish for dinner every Saturday. Neville had been riding his bicycle, shouting: "Fish! Fish! Fresh fish! Fish nice wid yam, fish nice wid rice, fish an bammy, fish an chocho, fish an pumpkin. Fresh fish! Buy some fish!"

She waved him down and watched as he jumped off his bicycle with ease, reached into his back pocket for a handkerchief, and wiped the sweat from his face before looking at her and flashing her a mischievous smile.

"Wha de lady wan fi buy?"

"Leh me see yuh snapper."

"De finest snapper yuh gwane get, mam, de very finest. Catch dese meself early dis marnin."

"Yuh fisherman, too?"

"Yes, mam. Catch me own fish an do me own sellin."

June-Plum resented him calling her mam, especially since heat was prickling between her thighs. She barked at him, "Gi me five pound snapper."

"Yuh wan me clean dem, mam?"

"Nuh worry, me'll clean dem meself."

"Yuh husban and chilren gwane enjoy dese fish."

"Me nuh ave no husban, nor children sah."

"Such a pretty ooman like yuh."

"Yuh sell fish out ere ebery Saturday?"

"Yes, mam."

"Good. If me like yuh fish, me will look out fi yuh." With that, June-Plum walked off, feeling the fish-vendor's eyes following her. The thought made her stumble, so she was glad when she moved out of his vision and only his voice was heard trailing off in the distance: "Fish! Fish, fish, fresh fish. Fish nice wid yam, fish nice . . ."

June-Plum shakes her head at those memories and goes to sit under the guava tree. From there the sun moves from directly above at noontime to an angular slant indicating that the day is passing, but still June-Plum sits, the memories traveling through her head until she is startled when Blackie her dog barks and runs off to greet the children returning from school.

Floyd is the first to approach: "Mama, is true Daddy lost at sea?"

June-Plum's heart skips a beat and she makes laughter drown her fear. "Floyd, mek yuh mus ask stupidness, go inside and tek off yuh school clothes." The children all go in to be fed.

After dinner, the kitchen clean, June-Plum moves to her veranda to pass the evening in her cane rocker. Every so often, she is interrupted by a good evening or a howdy or by the children's bickering, but for the most part, her mind lingers in the past.

The next week when she went to the market, after she hurriedly bought yams, tomatoes, and other produce, she sought the fisherman. When she heard "fish, fish" behind her, she turned around with delight on her face, but only a toothless man with greying hair hopped off his bicycle, coming to stop in front of her. June-Plum looked at him, kissing her teeth before walking away. She had not run into the young fisherman. Disappointed, she climbed onto the bus and slumped down on the seat. There was no fish in her basket. A woman carrying two large baskets entered the bus and accidentally brushed against her, and June-Plum immediately flew into a rage: "Yuh did gi me dress put-down. Yuh tink me is wall fi push gainst!" All of her pent-up anger and frustration were released. Two older women sitting in the back of the bus commented quietly that John Crow must have spat in June-Plum's eyes, while another woman, looking pleased with herself, declared that all June-Plum needed was a good piece to keep her quiet. At this, the men in the bus chuckled and massaged their crotches, while the bus sped around corners at a dangerous speed, sending goats, chickens, and people scampering onto the bankings.

When June-Plum got home, her father greeted her: "Me did sit ere worry bout yuh. Yuh out late."

"Me a big ooman an can come an go as me please," she retorted.

"Chile, wha troublin yuh? Wha mek yuh vex wid the whole world?"

"Me just tired," complained June-Plum. "Me nuh clean an cook an keep house fi nobody but meself nuh more."

The next day, June-Plum quietly packed an old cardboard suitcase and left home, heading for an unknown destination with very little money. After numerous failed attempts at securing a job in several towns, June-Plum went to a bus stop to rest. The sideman of one of the buses bounced off his bus, picked up her suitcase, and secured it on the top carriage of the bus.

"Come, daughta, jump in; we ave fi keep movin."

She complied and the bus lurched off, sending her stumbling down its aisle. At the next town, Anton Bay thirty-six miles away, she got off. The town was surrounded by the sea. The air smelled salty-sweet. Four fishermen with nets were gathered, talking. June-Plum walked past them, glancing at their faces, hoping to see the young fisherman. They nodded their heads and bid her good evening. Timidly, she reciprocated the head gesture. Her feet were tired, but she must find a job and somewhere to sleep. She came to a small grocery store and entered.

"Mam, could ah trouble yuh fah a little ice-wata?"

The woman behind the counter looked at June-Plum from head to toe before going to the back of the store, from where she returned shortly with a glass of water. June-Plum drank thirstily. Finishing, she wiped her mouth with the back of her hand.

"Tank yuh, mam. Me did well thirsty. God bless yuh." She moved off to go, and still the woman behind the counter had not said a word. June-Plum turned to her: "Excuse me, mam, ah new ere. Know anyone who wan help?"

"Yuh can count money?"

"Count money? Yes, mam."

"Yuh know how fi handle people?"

"Yes, mam, me had to deal wid me eight broda dem."

"Yuh start now?"

"Start, mam?"

"Yuh wan de work or not?"

"Yes, mam, but . . ."

"Yuh a fi live in, keep yuh room clean, help keep de shop clean, an sell behine dis counter ere."

"Yes, mam."

"Yuh in de family way?"

"Oh, no, mam, me nuh sleep wid man yet."

And this was how June-Plum and Neville finally got together. Two weeks after June-Plum began working in the shop, the fish vendor rode up and parked his bicycle in front of the shop. A happy mood came with him.

"Pretty daughta, whe de ooman?"

June-Plum looked at him and was tongue-tied. He did not remember her, at least so she thought.

"Daughta," he began again, his eyes shining, "ah wan yuh fi tell de ooman dat de fishman out here wid her favorite fish."

At that very moment the woman walked in and the fish vendor turned to speak with her, leaving June-Plum to stare at him. The woman and the fishman were on good terms, joking with each other. When the woman took the fish and went to the back of the shop, the fishman turned to speak to June-Plum: "So how yuh like workin wid de old ooman? She nuh talk much, but she is a good soul."

He laughed as he spoke, but June-Plum just stood there. He ordered a soda, which he took his time drinking, relishing each swallow. June-Plum turned her back and began straightening the jars of sweets, sweat forming on her brows and beneath her armpits.

The fishman watched her, remembering the first time he saw her.

June-Plum remained with her back to him, her heart racing.

"Daughta." It was the fishman. "A little youth wan buy sometin."

June-Plum turned and attended to the little boy while the fishman finished his soda. She then took his empty bottle and went to place it in the crate with the other bottles. When she turned back to face the counter, he was already on his bicycle, shouting, "Fish, fresh fish, fish nice wid yam. Fish nice fried, fish nice fi mek soup, fish . . ." His voice trailed away. For the remainder of the day, June-Plum pouted and was short and unfriendly with all the customers.

It was several weeks again before June-Plum saw the fishman and it was only then that she learned his name. He entered the shop and his presence was like a welcome afternoon breeze. "Wha happen, pretty daughta? Long time nuh see. People who know me call me Neville. De old ooman seh yuh call yuhself June-Plum. Me like de fruit well bad and me like the person who guh by de name, too."

Neville reached over as if to tickle her and she drew back, startled. "Who vex yuh suh? From dat first time yuh buy snapper from me, me did wonder who step pan yuh toe. Yuh fi laugh. It will do yuh good. Yuh name suit yuh: yuh fleshy and nice and prickly, too."

So June-Plum smiled because she felt happy and because Neville the fishman was jolly, and yes, her name told of her personality.

They became friends, and each week when he came, she had his favorite soda ready for him and they talked and laughed and he told her when he would be coming again. For four months, Neville and June-Plum saw each other only inside the shop. Then, on one of his visits, he asked her to go to the dance with him.

At the dance, Neville was popular. His friends shouted greetings and June-Plum, shy, did not know how to act. Neville sensed this, so he kept his arms around her. A pretty woman with pearly teeth came up to Neville and stroked his arm, and June-Plum felt her face get hot. She wanted to slap this woman, to stake claim. The music was loud and sensuous, but she did not feel confident enough to dance. Neville insisted, though, so they danced, June-Plum losing herself in the rhythm and heat of the crowd. After a while, Neville took her outside, where it was cool, and kissed her on the mouth. She felt hot and faint. It was her first kiss. She pulled away from him and ran ahead. Neville caught up with her and she abandoned herself to him, resting her head on his shoulder.

Six months later, during the hurricane season and the dark nights, June-Plum, two months pregnant, moved into Neville's one room and two months later one Saturday morning, they dressed up and went and got married. It was the first time June-Plum had had her picture taken.

"Mama, Mama!" It is Floyd, shaking her gently.

June-Plum wonders if she is dreaming. "Neville . . . Neville is yuh? Yuh come home?"

"Mama, is nite and Daddy nuh come yet. Time yuh guh bed." Floyd is embarrassed by his mother's tears. He helps her off the rocker, locks the door behind them, and leads her like a blind person to her room. As he walks back to his room, he mumbles to himself: "Me hope Daddy come tomorrow. Im gwane longa dan im seh."

June-Plum tosses and wakes at every turn. She's afraid to sleep, visualizing herself swallowed up by the sea. She's angry at Neville for not coming home and not sending word to her. She hears her heart racing and tries to drown out the noise by covering her chest with Neville's pillow. This only adds to her agitation, as she smells Neville until his smell fills the room. June-Plum pants for breath. Neville's smell and the sea's—his face and Yemoja's—merge, making her dizzy. The bed spins and June-Plum holds on for dear life. The splashing of the waves rises to a crescendo and all she can do to keep from going mad is to hold her head and plead, "Please, please, leave me alone. Yuh can keep Neville. Keep im." After a while all noises stop and June-Plum dozes, waking at 5 A.M. She gets up and heads for the beach, where the fishermen are drawing in their nets. The early morning air is cool and the gray of the night is almost gone. On the beach, she abandons her slippers and heads toward the group of fishermen. She makes out Tony, Bill, Bigger, and Nobel—no sign of Neville. Still, she approaches the men, whose muscles are taut from hauling in their nets. Bigger is the first to notice her:

"Marnin, June-Plum. Neville still out pan de sea?"

"Seems like it, Bigger. De sea is im true wife."

"Well, yuh know we men ave fi ave more dan one wife."

"Wha mek? Guess we oomen just ave fi catch who catch can."

The men turn back to their fish nets. June-Plum stands looking at the fishermen, a forlorn look in her eyes. As the sun begins to peep over the horizon, she walks further down the beach where the rocks jut out, forming a closure, and there, she undresses and, wading out into the water, submerges her body all the way to her neck. Her teeth chatter and she can feel cold-bumps all over her. By the time she comes out, the fishermen have gone off with their haul and only a tangled net and fish bones are on the beach. June-Plum bends down and scoops up a handful of sand, which she sends swirling through the air, crying out Neville's name at the same time. She does this three times, then scoops up a handful of seawater and drinks it. She is beginning to understand Yemoja, more powerful than any person, including herself. She is a force in nature that prevails. Surrendering to her is not defeat; it's wisdom. June-Plum breathes more easily as she heads home.

Her children are already at the table eating breakfast. She is grateful for her very independent children. She kisses them all on the tops of their heads and sits where a place is already set for her.

"Mama." It is Garfield, her youngest. "Daddy come?"

"No."

"Wen im comin?"

"Soon."

"Mama," cuts in Jennifer, "how Daddy gone so long?"

Floyd comments, "Im seh im would be back Wednesday nite. Today Friday."

"Me know what day it is, Floyd," June-Plum offers weakly.

"So wen Daddy comin?" insists Jennifer.

"Oonuh guh to school an stop de one million question."

"Mama, yuh tired?" As usual, Dawn, her very sensitive daughter, is concerned. June-Plum shakes her head in denial. Four pairs of eyes stare at her; she stares back at them, massages her thighs, sighs, and then declares, "Oonuh Daddy comin soon. Now guh to school fore oonuh late."

The children scramble out and June-Plum follows them outside, stopping by the guava tree, where she squats for an inordinately long time before going back into the kitchen. She turns on the radio just as the announcer is saying, "It's 10:45 this beautiful Friday morning." The morning is passing. June-Plum looks around her kitchen. The dishes are still there from breakfast, there are clothes to be washed, the house has to be cleaned, and there is still much more to be done. She goes to fetch the dirty clothes. At the door, the sun blinds her and she shields her eyes. Blackie, by the fence, sees her and comes and rubs up against her leg. When she bends and pats his head, some of the dirty clothes fall to the ground. June-Plum looks at Blackie and smiles. He is her only company all day and she is in the habit of speaking to him.

"Blackie, whe Neville, deh? Ah time im come home. Me nuh like man who stay out longa dan dem seh."

Blackie whines in response and June-Plum rubs his back. She puts the clothes in the basin to soak and goes inside to wash the dishes and to prepare lunch for Dawn and Garfield, her two younger children. She takes a long time doing everything, and by the time she finishes cleaning the kitchen, Dawn and Garfield are home and she has not made lunch for them. She sends Dawn to the shop to buy four patties and two cocoabread, which they have with mango nectar.

Afterward, she walks her children back to school, all the while looking behind her, craning her neck out to sea, looking for a familiar sight. June-Plum stands by the school fence, watching the children play. In all of their movements, she sees Neville with his strong arms pulling in his net full of fish. After a while, when the bell has rung and all the children have gone to their classes, June-Plum wonders why she is there.

She does not want to go home and wash clothes or finish her cleaning. She resolves to wander until her feet decide where they will lead her. After all, genius is a capacity for withstanding trouble.

Finding herself at the seashore, where some boys about ten years old are swimming and playing naked in the water, she looks at them, examining their small bodies, black and wet, glistening in the sun. She remembers, it seems like for the first time, how she used to swim naked in the river with her sister and friends before her mother died. But that seems like another life. Remembering that scares her. She had forgotten all the good times before her mother died. Could she so easily forget Neville? Since her marriage and four chidren, her body has become stout and, yes, ugly—something to be covered up. She throws off her slippers and pulls up her dress. The water is warm and the sea is very different today—not so blue, and seemingly satiated. The boys see her and cover their privates. June-Plum bursts out laughing and calls to them in a friendly voice.

"Nuh boda cova up. Me ave boys and see tings ebery day."

The boys giggle and continue to splash each other. The water feels so good June-Plum wades in further, wanting to go deeper until it reaches her shoulders and then covers her head. This woman, this Yemoja, is alluring with her blue waters. June-Plum pulls up her dress further, lapping it between her thighs. Two more steps forward and her dress will be up to her panties, but she cannot stop herself. She wades further. Perhaps if she shows Yemoja how capable she is of holding up despite the loss of her man, if she stops competing in a game that she does not understand and therefore must lose, then maybe Yemoja will leave her alone to bring forth another life and to enjoy the four she has already been given. Clearly Neville is out of her hands now, completely in Yemoja's power.

"Sista June-Plum, come si down wid an ole ooman an remine er of tings." It is Miss Country, as old as spit. No one in the community knows Miss Country's age, but she seems older than the trees. Everyone who comes to the village sees her, and she knows everyone: children, cousins, aunts, uncles, and grandparents, and even great-great-grandparents. Miss

Country spanks any children she sees misbehaving and sends them home to their mothers, who come to thank her for caring. Children are almost perfectly behaved when Miss Country is around. She is nutmeg color with a face as lined as the Sahara Desert. Toothless, she seldom smiles. Her arms are strong like a man's and she never wears shoes, her soles rubbery-tough like a tire. She says when she dies they can sell her feet to Bata, the shoe-store chain. "Come, Sista June-Plum, yuh moda neba tell yun fi min old people?" Miss Country walks off, erect, a large basin of fish on her head, her stool in her right hand and a large knife in her left.

June-Plum pulls herself out of the sea and runs to catch up with this living history. Her legs are wet and her dress clings to her thighs, her firm and shapely thighs that she loves. People meeting June-Plum salute her with "Peace" and "God-bless," but no one mentions Neville, though everyone knows. Everyone in the village knows even the most intimate details about everyone else, down to how many times a week a woman "does it" with her man. So June-Plum knows that they know. She feels like a naughty child caught in the act with everyone whispering behind her back.

She sits on an empty crate and helps Miss Country gut her fish and wash them off with lime. Only their eyes and hand movements speak. Two pretty grey-turquoise ground lizards play nearby. Miss Country is smoking a cigarette with the lit part inside her mouth. June-Plum has always wanted to ask Miss Country how she smokes with the fire inside her mouth, but she has never had the nerve. It was the same way she felt around Neville. There was so much she wanted to ask him, especially Sunday morning before he left when they lay awake in each other's arms. She had wanted to ask him how he felt about their having another child, but refrained, fearful of what he might have said. She couldn't bring herself to tell him how much she loved him either, how she wanted then to do something because she didn't want any more children. But her heart was in her mouth and she didn't want to spoil the peace, the beauty of the moment, because she knew—sensed—that Neville would not be returning as he said. How could she have known and not said anything, not done anything, to prevent him from leaving? June-Plum was too accustomed to acquiescing, to wait-ing patiently like a good woman for her man. Well, those days were over with, she decided. From now on, others would wait for her. Neville's going freed her of the cyclic burden handed to her from her mother, who took it from her mother before her. Women forever wait-ing for something to happen. June-Plum sees Miss Country observing her. "Betta late dan neba," she mumbles to herself and pushes out her chest. She will ask Miss Country about the fire inside her mouth.

"Miss Country, yu eat de ashes dat fall from de cigarette inside yuh mout?"

Miss Country looks at June-Plum and frowns. "Wha mek a big ooman like yuh mus guh lif up yuh frock, expose yuhself to boy pick-nie? Neville nuh guh like it wen im come back and people tell im how yuh act foolish."

June-Plum spits. Silence surrounds them like a mosquito net. "Miss Country, yuh tink Neville comin back?"

"Me look like de sea to yuh? Me an dat see-ooman nuh bosom-buddy, she nuh tell me nuttin."

At this, June-Plum knits her brow but says nothing.

"Wen de baby due? Yuh mus tek advantage of some a de new ways. Yuh an Neville a sensible people. Picknie expensive. Galang a yuh yard, guh cook fah yuh picknie dem."

June-Plum wipes her hands and heads home, feeling admonished. She looks back, and Miss Country is still gutting and cleaning fish with smoke coming through her nose and the lit part of the cigarette hid-den inside her mouth. She still does not know how Miss Country is able to smoke without burning her mouth, but she shakes her head and moves on. Just before turning inside her gate, she looks out at the sea and sees Yemoja standing in the center of Neville's boat, combing her hair with a long wooden pick. June-Plum kisses her teeth and turns her back on her rival.

Her children are sitting around the kitchen table, a sad lot, looking like wet puppies. The suhsuh from their friends at school, who, in turn, heard it eavesdropping on their parents, has it that their father is lost at sea. Floyd and Jennifer are upset by this rumor. They remember that last year one friend's father and uncle drowned during the hurricane season when their boat capsized. Their father was a good swimmer, it wasn't hurricane season, and he had painted his boat blue and white in honor of the sea goddess Yemoja, but there were no guarantees. The sad faces of her children assail June-Plum. She silently warms up yesterday's fried fish and rice and puts the food in front of them. Her stern look warns them not to ask any questions. Blackie is fed most of the evening meal. She sends the children to play, but the girls, Jennifer and Dawn, choose to remain with her. They sit on the veranda but all are restless, so June-Plum decides they should go for a walk. They stop every so often to exchange greetings and a few words with people on the street and to clap at the mosquitoes that buzz around them. They end up at Widows' Walk.

June-Plum stops and stares out to sea until the shades of blue make her dizzy. Unsteadily, she holds on to the railing. Miss Country can be seen seated by her tray of fried fish. Jennifer and Dawn are playing closely by the seashore; they have abandoned their shoes and are wetting their feet. June-Plum sees them, but they seem far away. She calls to them, but no sound comes from her mouth. The waves are full. A trail of blackbirds is flying home. The sun is lost in a cloud. She looks at the waves. They dazzle and pull. Her head spins. Her thighs feel like logs. Suddenly she is going down, down. The salty water plays around her face and gets in her ears. She can feel the damp sand beneath her and hears the gentle cry of the waves. This woman means to take her, too, so she succumbs giggling, her mother's words echoing "Yuh gi weh laugh fi peasoup . . ."

June-Plum finds herself lying in bed. Her head swirls like the waves. "Whe Jennifa and Dawn? She tek dem too? Neville seh de sea is im most beautiful ooman; dat why im love er. Im love er more dan me."

Miss Country, hearing June-Plum's chatter, enters the room and proceeds to rub her face and neck with bay rum. June-Plum smiles, still thinking she is a part of the sea, and remembers her earlier jealousy—how she wanted to master this woman, this sea that surrounds their lives and is woven into the beauty of the landscape. She is everywhere one looks and her song is the consistent noise lulling one to sleep. Almost all of the men of the community belong to her, and sometimes, in her greed, she takes one or two of them to live with her permanently.

NEVILLE SPENT two weeks fixing his boat. He painted it dark blue with light blue oars, and he and Bertram and some of the other fishermen bought a large bottle of white rum to offer to the gods for protection and good luck. In addition, he had Basil, the local artist, draw a stately black woman with big legs and nappy hair like a mane surrounded by foliage at the stern. She was as June-Plum had seen her in her dreams—beautiful, enticing. Neville was so proud of himself he invited the entire community out on the beach for a feast and Miss Country prepared the fish and had everyone licking their fingers and smacking their mouths for days after. With this larger boat Neville could get a bigger haul on each trip. June-Plum was happy for him, but she was never able to say this to him, as each time she felt a lump in her throat.

HIS NET is heavy. The waves are furious and sudden. He smiles, his white teeth the only light in the dark night, his laughter drowned by the wailing of the waves. Neville relaxes and surveys the sea. "Ooman, yuh wild tonite. Yuh mus need more rum." For a moment there is calm. Neville reaches out to pull in his net, but just then, a big wave tosses the boat. He lets go, losing his net.

"Wha vex yuh, ooman? Relax—mek we talk nuh." Another wave comes, and still others. Neville wrestles with his boat, but the waves have pushed it into a current and he is unable to take control. "Now look ere, ooman, me ave wife a yard. She nah guh undastan." Neville is pulled along and the waves cave in on him, creating a valley. He sees no way out. He surrenders to his mistress, Yemoja, who leads him further, taking him into her depths until he goes under, smiling. . . .

"Nooooooo!" June-Plum screams, her voice echoing through Miss Country's house and out the window, stopping passersby in their tracks. Miss Country, in her kitchen listening to the news on her transistor radio sent to her by her great-grandson in New York, hears that a fisherman was found at sea.

Miss Country enters the room again and faces June-Plum, who is sitting up straight as a board, perspiration covering her face. Miss Country chews on her gum and shakes her head at June-Plum. "Radio man seh dem fine a fishman. Yuh should kill dat big ole roosta yuh ave an mark yuhself wid de blood."

June-Plum stares at Miss Country, who apologetically mumbles, "Me neba did hear nuh name. De radio man neba seh nuh name," she ends, staring at June-Plum, who slumps back on the pillow, the child kicking in her stomach. After what seems like an eternity, the thought comes to June-Plum like a whisper: "De beautiful ooman tek him!" Tears fill up her eyes, but she quickly wipes them dry, ashamed of her weakness. Miss Country's eyes relate an understanding of her grief as she hands her a cup of tea. June-Plum drinks the pumpkin leaf tea, then slowly gets out of the bed, Neville's words playing in her head, "Bet yuh ah tickle yuh." She hugs herself and bursts into a laugh, an attempt to drown the sob rising in her bosom. The sound is hollow, disconnected, joyless, stopping Miss Country from leaving the room.

Miss Country looks at her: "Chile, yuh a lose yuh head?"

June-Plum shakes her head, her face shining like a full moon. Yemoja was always more woman than her. The sun is bright—splendid, in fact. June-Plum parts the curtains and looks out. Seeing people dressed in their Sunday best, she is confused. It was Friday evening when she went walking with Dawn and Jennifer. Miss Country anticipates her question: "Yes, yuh did sleep an toss an act fool-fool fah a whole day an nite. De picknie dem alrite. Wen yuh faint, Dawn run come get me. Big ooman like yuh should know fi eat wen yuh a carry chile."

Suddenly, there is a great commotion. "Miss Country! June-Plum! June-Plum! Neville alive an comin home, Neville alive!" It is Beverly, Bertram's wife, running and panting with the news. June-Plum sticks her head through the window, her eyes large. Beverly grips her hand. People on their way to church wave to her. June-Plum is immobile for a while. Then, with great haste, she pulls on her dress, leaving her hair wild. Her slippers clap as she hastens to her house, thinking of all she has to do before Neville comes home: wash dishes and clothes, clean, bathe herself, and kill that rooster. Beverly says she will help. Neville is alive after all.

As she hurries along, June-Plum feels young again. She remembers that first evening she and Neville went to the dance, his mouth wet and hot on her neck, his arms firm around her waist. People greet her, but her smile is not for them, it is for Neville.

Claire Marie is worried about her friend Drew. Drew is ill, Drew is in trouble. But Claire Marie is having troubles of her own; her dreams keep telling her so. Pamela Mordecai has done a lot of writing, but until I put the notion in her head, she'd never before written science fiction. "Once on the Shores of the Stream Senegambia" is the result of that planted notion. What visions might knowledge of the past prompt when a Caribbean eye looks through the lens of the future?

Once on the Shores of the Stream Senegambia

PAMELA MORDECAI

for Rosario, Nalo, and my Great-Granny McFarlane

I DON'T KNOW HOW this thing I still calling "my life" come so, for one time it had so many bright things. Even my dreams— long, clear as springwater, down to colors of people clothes, and pictures in corners, and what-you-can-see-through-the-window. Drew always say she don't know nobody dream so. And is true. I spin dreams like embroidery, so fine they return again and again, like they know they weave so well, woof and warp, that they deserve a body to look at them, touch them and feel them, over and over, for they better than the stuff of life.

Take my Drew dream. In it, I see Drew at last, for the first time in how many years. How many years?

Is spring, and I come by bus from Miami to New York. Mrs. Rita Schwimmer get acquainted with my Auntie Vida because the Schwimmers give a chalice in memory of their son Alex, a twenty-year-old white youth that they beat to death in a Florida town because he try to break up a lynch mob. The chalice come by serendipity to my Uncle Roy's church in a bruck-down part of Kingston. None of it exist no more—priest nor church nor Kingston—but that too is a next story.

Auntie and Mrs. Schwimmer stay fast friends long after the three hundred pounds of my uncle fall into heaven one Sunday morning when he vesting for mass.

Is time to sing. Must think hard to dredge up the song. What is here is only patches. Bright, yes; clear, yes; but only patches. Still, I got to sing whatever will come.

> Once on the shores of the stream Senegambia
> something and something gather to dance . . .

I could never tell you how bad I want to sing the whole song. How bad I want to just open my mouth and sing it right out. No chance of that though. So I make do. Turn my hand make fashion. Cut frock to fit cloth. Sing my song out loud inside, the bits and pieces that will come. You know the way. White people say one swallow don't make summer. That always make me laugh. Black people take one mosquito make summer. You just got to have the making spirit, is all.

Help. Something running in my body. Beating in it. Like maybe is a meetinghouse and the cacique talking with the tribe. Like maybe ten, twenty drums, drumming, drumming. Thumping, thumping.

I going to visit 'Merica, so Auntie Vida give me Mrs. Schwimmer phone number. When I call, Matt, who is now Mrs. Schwimmer one-son, he say he can drive me to Mary Ann wedding in Boston, for it just happen he going to be in New York that week and he going home to Boston the very Saturday morning.

So said, so done. We drive four hours straight and reach the reception place and I jump out of Matt car and crash the wedding.

"Oh Claire Marie!" Mary Ann say, "I can't believe you came all that way!"

And the groom kiss me, and all the white Irish women declare they glad to see me, the Neyga-gyal. So they say, anyway, as they smilingly call me "Neyga-gyal," half-bold and half-blushing, like we all gone back to the country day school. And I laugh, cause for sure I still poor as puss, but, as I consider them, I know I look like a million dollars. I look down at my mesh stockings and my brown sack dress and my chocolatey-gold shoes with heels you could spear a fish with. I see the deep brown of me, and the not-quite-so-brown of Drew, who is also, with her little slip of a self, looking mighty fine. I think about it and decide that we two look muy preciosa. Not flashy. Just bright and polished. Mighty fine.

I remember how the reception place light up, as if, between Drew and me, we bring in the sun, its light playing catch on the leaves. As if we-self summon, beyond that great light, the blue, carrying-on-forever sky. As if, according to some invisible webbing, together we are a tiny piece of an everlasting parchment that is fit to write a vow on, or a little portion of a vast brown drumskin waiting for a promise to sound against it. . . .

That is the last time I see Drew.

IS NOT MUCH I can see from here. Of course, if is eyesight you trusting, the place have neither top nor side: it put me in mind of one of them inside-outside room that was a big fashion one time—which time, I not too sure. Inside this big big outside-inside room is a giant sloping grassy field, with deep blue sky up so, and somewhere nearby (for you can hear the water lap-lapping and sometime it splash and the sea spray blow on you), somewhere nearby, a big river, or sea, or ocean.

Tha's what it seem like to me.

And it seem like we lying here in the sunlight (also don't know why I know is *we* for I can't see nobody, but I *know* is we), each one in a hammock maybe, or one of them big porch swings, long enough to lie down in, soft so if you have to, you could sleep. And, just like I hear water, I smell the crisp salt smell of sea. And I sort-of-see trees— coconut, poui, jacaranda. And I smell jasmine when night fall, or more true, when the light fade—whatever light-fade mean. . . .

*Once upon a time, Brer Anansi was hungry bad, more hungry than he
ever hungry before in his life, for a wicked famine was on the land.
Anansi hungry, him wife hungry, and the poor little spider-piknie them
dying of starvation. . . .*

Is only some skemps little bits of song and story come, but I glad for
anything at all. Same like, after and before certain times, only scrapses
of my life float up. I don't think bout it too much, for it well frighten
me, and I know big fraid could kill a body. Is like somebody capture me
one day, and drag me away from home and friends and family, and
places I know and love. Like they take for themselves the one thing
that is truly truly mine: the comfort of my own story, my memory of
days and places, the things I say and promises I make and songs I sing.
Sometime I not even certain if how I speak is mine.

A SMALL WOMAN. Skin very black. Hair very white. Fine, press-hair.
Look like a head of white cotton candy. She eating a mango, laughing
and serious one time. The last of the juice running down her chin and
she still sucking hard on a nearly dry seed with some stringy blonde
hairs hanging off of it. . . .

"So is me them send you to with that kind of question, Alvin? Well, I
know why. Is cause they know Gran going to answer you true-true, never
mind you small. You see that weenie you have in front of you? Someday
it going find a wonderful warm place to put itself, inside of some nice girl
that going to love you with her whole heart. And it going be so excited
and happy it not going to able to contain itself. It going stand up strong
and dance around a while, and then it going to spill some sweet sweet
water. And that's going to make a baby. Your water in her belly going to
make a piknie for you and she. Now what you think about that?"

The boy look down at his small dark brown body. Put his head one-
side to consider. Then he say: "Granny, me going make plenty piknie
like that." And he laugh and run off, head down considering the weenie that is going to do this splendid thing.

And the old sugar-candy-head woman say: "I hopes to God you live so long my baby. Now they harvesting egg and seed. Now they raising human being like pig and chicken. Soon they going to tell we who to breed and who to barren. And I know who belly they going lock down first."

She shake her head and slide the mango seed from her mouth. It is white now and only one-two blondish hairs straggle from it. She dump it in a pile of leaves and trash and put a match to it.

"Burn, baby," she say. "Burn."

> Help. Somebody, help. The thing running in my body
> again. Beating in it. A sweet rhythm but I fraid it too
> bad, for it just drumming on, all by itself, and I don't
> know what cause it nor what it going to bring. For sure,
> it going bring something. Is a noise with a promise.

DON'T RECALL when I first start dreaming Drew. One time, we meet in a cris Paris restaurant. Another time is in a ritzy part of London. All these places dream up—not any place I been. Always I say to Drew how I glad it is real, the *actual meeting*, at last. And Drew is the same: little rat face and pointy nose and small body bending forward a little bit above the waist. Little feet getting smaller toward the toes, receding as they go because they don't rightly belong on the ground and should maybe be touching on some other element—probably fire.

Last century they would say how I love this girl is queer. In Newton, Massachusetts, one of the ten wealthiest cities in the USA, then-time and now-time. In the sixties, beginning of Civil Rights and the one time the great beast Amerique-Nord struggle briefly to its moral feet. In the hoity-toity Country Day École du Sacré Coeur where I was the one so-so little black "scholarship" piknie.

That little brown Drew girl, she got so much money the touch of the tarbrush don't hardly matter—and too besides, is probly true that only we, with our Antillean eye that ferret out misogyny at a glance, never mind how it far back, only we would see that long ago some black warrior or some feisty mama did bless her family. That girl save me. Make me laugh and sing and play in the rain. Make me don't too notice how them white gyal piknie look on me, how them run them finger over my skin like is accident, then gallop round the corner to pretend to blow away the blackness, or take eraser rub it out, or wash it off with a flourish in the goldfish pond. Always always big big laughings round the corner from wherever I be.

Hear Drew: "You too foolish, Clarabella. In this school, only you and I look like we do. You've never heard of scarcity value? That's what we have, querida. Like diamonds. We are exploding prisms of light. Muy preciosa."

I smile—a lopsided monkey-face smile.

Drew say: "Dice: 'Soy preciosa.' Dice: 'Somos preciosos.'"

Was the first Spanish I learn. Here I say it now, every minute, over and over, like a chant. "Soy preciosa. Somos preciosos."

I would give my life for that girl. I love her better than my own self. Nothing to do with anything but the salvation of my very inside-insides, the sanity and right functioning of my black head.

The thing is, this place make me nervous from the beginning, for somewhere in the very pit of my stomach, I know it really don't go so, never mind what I think I seeing, what I imagine I smelling and touching. Somebody someplace some long long time ago tell me to trust that funny feeling you get in your belly-bottom, and my belly-bottom say this not no large space. No way. If it so big, why I feel like I got a big weight top of me, like things pressing me in from the two sides? Why I feel like I in a small tunnel, and it getting smaller every day?

DREW AND ME fight too. We fuss bout all manner of things. Like when spring come and that girl gone way down to the end of the field on the next-door college campus, way down by the Quonset hut where none of we not suppose to go, and she find some little bird that drop out a tree and bruck him foot, or some mangy squirrel that losing it fur, and bring it back up into the day school, into MY room.

"You keep him, Claire Marie," she say. "You know they're really afraid of you. Nobody's going to come in here, into this room, to look for anything. It just needs to stay a day or two, till the bones knit." All this time, she taking a couple matchstick and some string and making splint for the bird foot.

I roll my eyes. I say, "I don't want no bird in my room. Is your bird. You find him. You keep him."

"Is not a him, is a her," Drew say. (How the deuce she could know, I always wonder.) "You don't have any feeling for a wounded member of your own sex?"

"I got plenty feeling for me, myself, and I," I tell her. "Them three wounded takes up all my energy. And doing the work—homework and housework and work-at-the-switchboard work—that I need to do to stay in this place and keep my head up mongst the five hundred likes of you. You think it easy?"

She laugh. "Not the likes of me, for sure," she say. "There ain't no likes of me here—'cept of course for you."

She put the bird down in the cover of my little straw sewing basket.

"I don't business with you rich girl. You okay, I suppose, but I can't afford to business with you. What I have to do is to survive in this place, and I not going able to do that if I providing lodging for your birdies and your squirrels and all the other half-dead things you drag in here from out the bush!"

> Drumming again. And the beat a little faster, like the
> feet trotting. I not sure why I so fraid for it. Maybe
> because is something in my body, and I don't know
> how it come to be there. . . .

Every so often, we "wake up" and find we not rocking in the hammocks or the swings or whatever they be, anymore. We still lying flat, but we in water. Aquamarine, clear, pretty water, with what look like white sand quite near up under us. I think maybe this is exercise time, and, tell the truth, it come easy to float or swim or just splash around, for it is cool and wet—"lucid limpid liquid," as Drew would say when we dancing in the rain. Clever as they be, they would have to come good to make us think we swimming in water if is not so. I don't know bout the white sand, but I pretty sure the water is water, and I think is as clean as it look. And salt, like tears or the sea.

Is always warm and sunny, though we don't actually see no sun. And as usual, I don't see no "we," nor no evidence of "we," but still I know is not me one. This is the one time I feel like somebody again, like a ordinary person in a place doing something Drew would call "quotid-ian"—that girl does love a big word, when she ready! Is the one time I feel like I am real, with a past, and a now, and maybe a time to look for-ward to.

GOING TO do some singing again. I got to smile when I think of me and this singing-singing! When they make me sing at the country day school, I spit out the song. Now I too ready to open my mouth, to hold a melody and hope to hearken to words that I know is there. . . .

> Babymother have a little prince,
> Babymother have a little prince
> Babymother have a little prince
> Something and something Gee-zus.
> His locks is like lamb's wool . . .

IS ONE TIME when I was swimming that I see something. It happen in a flash—ten, fifteen seconds or so—but I own-way enough to be damn sure that I see what I see, for I don't close my eyes for fun when I not asleep in this place. My eyes wide open the whole time, and ears wide open, same way.

So I on my back in the sea one day, and whether eye flicker or no, I won't swear, but suddenly there is no sky no more, no sun and grassy slope and trees. Instead, I am squinting against a blinding light, so I suspect somebody want to dark-eye me, so I struggle to see. And I discern that I am under a very high dome of something transparent like plastic or glass or maybe even ice. In a flash, but clear as day, I see the round icy shell a far way up, and I see that against the sides are wide shelves that extend above one another into the dome-space. And I see layers and more layers of thin, shining threads like very fine wire, worked all the way up the sides of this gigantic upside-down bowl. And the last thing I see, or almost see, for I glimpse it so fast, is bodies, hundreds of dark bodies, like mine, moving close to me in a huge container of water that put me in mind of a fish bowl.

I blink, and when I open my eyes good and wide, I see myself all alone back in the sea, the light of the almost-sun bright around me, the waves lap-lapping in my ears, the salt smell filling up my nostrils till it burning my lungs, and the never-ending blue-blue sky over my head.

I lie in that water like a lump with no life in it; till now I don't know how the heaviness in me never sink me right down to the bottom onto the lovely white believe-it-for-you-see-it sand.

And now, this is the part I really not sure of. Not sure whether I think it up in panic, me-myself, or I really see it happen. I recollect that the outside-inside room flicker another time for just a split second, and I see the pool again with all the bodies in it. I see some pale pale people in white uniform, and they pulling a young woman, black like me, naked as the day she born, from the pool. Her belly is huge, like she been drinking the pool water and it swell her till she going burst. And she is screaming and screaming, like she stark raving mad.

Then it vanish in a flash, and a blast of jasmine scent overpower my nose like chloroform.

So I not sure of it, not sure I see it, like I sure for sure I see the dome. Times after light-fade, though, when I hear that screaming again, I think is no way I could make up that sound.

I KNOW something is missing. Or maybe is that I missing something. So many scraps. The scraps of talking-with-a-shape, like the songs and stories I am trying so hard to remember. The scraps of what I take for my life. Like sharing shoes with my sister (she go to school one day, I go the next) for she is the only blood kin, besides Auntie V and Uncle Roy, that I recall, and Auntie Vida and Uncle Roy long dead. We on a long dry road running north into the city, and it have a open drain all the way down one side, and all of us that go to Alpha school gathering round the drain to launch our paper boats when school over. The drain cover with morass, mostly black but sometimes a deep emerald green, and so pretty, is hard to think that such a color belong to something so nasty.

I GLAD TO see my sister, but I want to see some other body belonging to me. Yes, there is Drew, and Mary Ann, and Matt and Mrs. Schwimmer, and all those, but they not real like my sister. All that time in that cold Massachusetts place wasn't real. For sure I was there. For sure I watch through five summer and five winter, boiling and freezing in turn. For sure I see spring and fall pass like a film over my eyes five times. But all that time, all that growing-up time, don't somehow have the weight of running barefoot down South Camp Road beside that drain, green with morass, rushing to push a little boat over the garbage and muck that blocking the drain, encouraging it past every other little boat till we see it wash triumphant out into Kingston Harbor, and take off bravely into the true indigo waves of the Caribbean Sea.

I NEED TO know. Where I come from. Where me and my sister come from? Who send we to school? What happen to she? Where she be now? Where I be now? How I reach here? How I reach from Kingston to the Massachusetts country day school—and Drew.

Now, IN this place, sleep is not by choice; it come by its own bidding once light fade and the dimness start to creep over. By the time the real darkness set in, all o' we knock out like we dead. If you ask me, it must come through a tube or a wire (though I can't see neither one nor tother coming into me) like food must come, for I can't recall eating no food from I find myself here. And we rise same way, as the light come, like morning glory and buttercup: something poke us, promising that if we open of our eyes, something good going happen to make it worth the effort.

Not up to now, though. Not up to now.

I THINK ONE light-come, something must have misfire, for I wake to find I feeling different. Not good. Not comfortable. I draw breath quick and realize that one of the things my body forget is bad feelings. Discomfort. Is only the drumming that come near bad feeling, and, where the drumming concerned, is not my body that shiver but something else, something deep inside. And, like spite, I give thanks that day for how my belly feel—sick, like everything in it going to come up through my throat and pour over me. And as I gather this discomfort to me, I sort of see a shape that I recall but cannot name: not just bright scraps like Drew, and school, and my sister and me sharing shoes, but a shape like a walking river, like a road hurrying on. I see it only faint, for a brief while, but I know it as my road, my river, and I think, "Something is taking myself from me. Maybe all this good feeling is why I can't find the thread, the story of me—the thing that does make me myself."

I make up my mind to encourage bad feelings, for maybe they help me remember myself. I think to myself that somewhere in my body, in my skin and blood and bone, is the writing of my life. I think if I can get it back, I can figure out this whole thing: what is real and what is not. Why I am here, and how I come to be here. And who is doing all of this. And why.

> *Brer Possum walking down the road one bright morning, chirpy as a John-Twhit, when suddenly he see, right in the middle of the road, Brer Snake with a brick on his back. . . .*

The old black woman lying flat on her back, hands at her side, feet bare. Still, so still, like a dead somebody, except that when I look close, her small chest is rising and falling, rising and falling, like she in deep sleep. Her face is lit, like the black skin is giving off a deep blue light, and the countenance—and her whole self it seem—resting, every muscle in repose. Strange, though, at the very same time, every cell lock onto something. That is very clear. So still, so succumbing. To Something—my mind cannot bend to think what.

On the floor beside her I see some things. Her head-tie—for the cotton candy hair is loose and having its own way, like a tiny white cloud caught on the top of the black head. Her spectacles and her apron. A old leather belt. Her thick pink old-woman stockings. Some shiny things too: a narrow gold ring; a pair of silver bangles.

When I look again I catch my breath. I notice she is not lying on anything: she is floating. Floating maybe a hand's breath off the ground. I stare at this impossible thing and see her very slowly rise, as I watch, rise half a hand's breath, still deep in sleep, still glowing, still resting, still whole-self holding onto some great thing. . . .

I LONG FOR a deep abiding sleep. I long to get rid of the heavy thing that pressing on my head, pushing in on me from two sides, never mind the distant blue-blue sky, and the soothing lap of the waves, and the smells that I trying hard to teach my belly to throw up at. Strange how life go, contrary like. I want to rest, to sleep, and same time I desperate to make myself feel bad, so I can get back the thread of my life.

I SMILE a big smile as I think of days at school with Drew. How she always taking care of things. Specially small things. How she say I am precious; we are precious. How she say me and she is "likes." I don't now have in my head anyone but Drew and my sister that I am "like." Them dark bodies in the pool, if they really there, then I guess me and them is likes. But I not sure. Belly-bottom say likes on the outside don't always mean likes on the inside. I need people likes to me on the inside. Don't even so much need them here, now. Just need to be sure that they be.

DREW SAY something to me one day, just a couple weeks after I come to the country day school. She and me in the dining hall. I eating breakfast late, for I serve that morning and never get to eat till nearly everybody else done eat and gone. Drew here keeping me company.

"You know, I just had a feeling you would come," Drew say out to me, just so.

"Say what?" I ask her.

"I knew someone like you was going to come."

"So you know that from before I get here?"

"I guess so."

"So how you figure that? You must be a prophet. . . ."

"Well," she say, "I'm not too clear about that myself, but I'll try to explain, if you want."

She look around at the nearly empty dining room.

"These girls here are fine, I guess," she say. "Not any worse than any other bunch of white girls in any other country day school on the continent. But they're ignorant, and so their view of the world is small and backwoodsy, never mind they rich. I know they look at me sometimes and wonder how I got here with my little brown self."

I look up at her from down in my cereal bowl.

"So?" I say.

She look at me hard, and I see her think bout whether to go on, but I done decide I not carrying nor bringing her.

"And they wonder how my father got his piles of money—BIG piles," she take up the story. "I don't really mind, but it didn't seem right that it should be me one here with my little brown self that know the world is a big brown world."

She look at me. "There wasn't no way I was gonna turn into them," she say. "I figured if I kept on being me the best I knew how, I would eventually get some company."

I grin, coming up from the cereal for air.

"Girl, you making fun," I say. "No way you and me is company."

And the two of us laugh out a big laugh, and all the eyes left in the dining room reach around and find us.

I think that's what start me singing and telling story and telling about things I remember. What make me think that pain, bad feelings, will bring something back to me that I need to have. Is sake of Drew I trying to make something of the little that I know about myself.

> Once on the shores of the stream Senegambia
> something and something gathered to dance
> And something and brazen and something for picking . . .

Is Mangoes! Mangoes for picking! I gather the one little word, like a blanket, to myself.

I count up what I have: I think my head still working pretty good. And I know I can trust my belly-bottom, for is it make me smell out something funny in the first place. And I have the scraps: the little pieces of song and story, and the bright bits of my life that are so clear, is like I still there living through them. They have stuff in them, bits and pieces that I must try to put together.

Then there's this place that's all around me, here and not here, with sun we can't see, and sea that's not sea, and odors that kick you like drugs when them ready. And the dreams: the Drew dreams. And of a sudden I *realize* for the first time that I been seeing a old black lady, a woman with fine white press-hair on her head. A small old lady, thin, with strength tie up into her like a tough piece of rope. Nobody I know. And one time I see her talking to a little boy, naked as the day he born. . . .

"DON'T FORGET how you feel. . . . Listen to how you feel." It come to me inside my head, a voice clear as a bell. A woman voice. Not old. Not young. Not any voice I know.

> The drumming, again, loud, savage. Got to find some-
> thing to do with it, a place to put it, before it trample
> out my brain.

But I busy now, thinking, and it don't seem to make sense to try to puzzle out who the voice belong to. Not now. I know it talking to me, and my belly-bottom say I can trust it, so, instead, I consider what it say: "Listen to how you feel." How I feel? That could mean more than one thing. Could mean I must consider what is making me feel what I feel . . . and by now I convince that them doing we something to make we sleep, and I thinking more and more that they all the time doing we something to make we feel good.

Could mean, too, I must consider the state my body in—if I feel well or sick. . . . Which is confusion, for I think is not myself that feel well, and so I longing for my body to feel sick, for that would really be myself.

And it could mean the way I feel inside-inside my body: the drumming, and the way it frighten me; the weight pressing on my head, pressing me in on two side.

No way to decide which meaning, so I make up my mind I going consider everything, all of them.

And then there is the dome house, and all the rest of we that I know is there, never mind I can't see them, and the bodies swimming in the pool, and the pale people in white coat, and the screaming woman . . . I decide I got to leave them for the last. Cannot struggle with them big things now.

> **The noise again, the feet galloping now, and still there is nothing, not a thing I can do to stop it: drums—beating, beating—like the pulsing of blood, and feet, running, running, like is to save their very life.**

The running so insistent, so harnessing my body that it leave me no choice. For the first time, I give it no resistance. I let myself go with it, like a tiny boat in a strong current, this noise like a whole bunch of people tumbling toward something, tumbling tumbling and still keeping time. A herd of people-elephants lunging through my belly.

Which is craziness. How I could have a bunch of people in me? People can't have people in them—only if they crazy, and in all of this it don't occur to me once that is mad I mad. 'Cept they making baby of course, and nobody make twenty and thirty baby at a time.

And too besides, if I make a guess and try put two and two together (for my brain crank up now), the candy-head lady did say that is black people body they going lock down when they start to decide who to breed and who not to. So chances are, if is somebody lock me up in here, lock up a whole lot of nigger women in here, is to make sure them don't breed. I think of the screaming woman with the swell-up belly. Maybe they feeding us something in the swimming water, something to make us swell up and burst. . . .

And it come to me that I don't even know who I fighting with. For certain, is not the pale people in the white uniform, for I know them is just orders-takers, people following instructions. Black people can tell that kind. Easy.

"Black people take one mosquito make a summer . . . Black people have a making spirit . . . Black people can tell orders-takers . . . Black people is forever singing, dancing . . ."

I think them get me brain. I don't want to be in this place. Them holding me against my will. AGAINST MY WILL—chain or no chain. I don't take up myself and come here.

I don't think this good before I feel a buzz pass through my body. Run deep into it, and right straight through it. A sweet feel-good ripple that thrill me way inside. "Rawted," I say to myself. "Them brutes is reading my head. They must know I up to something. How the bumbo they could know?" Same time I feel a wetness on my forehead, like a little tear. A little bead of water. And I remember sweat.

"Perspiration," I think. "Them see me sweating."

And I know for certain that all around me, above, at the sides and below, whatever I feel bearing down and pressing in is a thing that is also watching me. A thing that not only watch, but tell somebody what it see. And this somebody that I cannot see can arrange to do things to my body. To reach way inside it, to make it feel good—and so, for sure, make it feel bad, if they want?

I don't know what I can do about that.

Something leaking slow, slow, into my head. It pushing, like a word on the tip of your tongue that you know you going to speak eventually, but it taking it time to let you call it. Then I get it. I can't move. Not foot or hand or trunk-of-my-body. Fingers and toes and the muscles on my face—ears, nose, those I could move—and the ones I use to pee, but nothing more. And I think, "I is one big jackass! Is true. How me never see that before? We only move when we swim. The rest of the time we floating like angel, like we got no limbs, like we handless, footless, trunkless . . ."

And, glory hallelujah, that very minute I feel wetness under me, creeping out from my groin in a big warm patch. Little most I smile, but I remember the eyes-all-around and I let my face be. I only sense it for the tiniest bit of time, but I remember that dampness from way, way back—from another time that I was always on my back, I guess.

Glory hallelujah! I pee up myself. I. My pee. *I wet up myself with my pee.*

I bask in this glorious feeling for a while. I think I earn it. And I am careful to lie still, relaxed, so no sweat will betray me.

But now there is a big problem: how to get things done without they know. It is plain to me that this is something I must do INSIDE, since outside I cannot lift a little finger. And right away I feel really down, and sad, and grieved, for they are outside, and my struggle is against them, and they are all-powerful, and I am therefore defeated before I begin. My battle can come to nothing. I fix my face. I speak to my skin, the little muscles in my neck, my jaw, my teeth, the hair on my head. I tell them to be absolutely quiet, so all this going on inside me will belong only to me. These one-and-two little efforts make me feel better, make me feel I can do something for me, against them.

I decide to rest my brain. To empty it out. Give it a little break, for it don't gallop like this since I come here. I don't hear the drums this long time, but when I stop to consider, it come to me that they now going nonstop, but everything else going so fast, the drumming noise is just part of one big enormous galloping, rushing, thundering ruckus. . . .

> . . . pulse pumping, drums beating, feet running, running, like is for their very life . . .

And the little black lady, floating, floating in the air, just come into my mind, same so. And I think, I going to try to be as cool and resting and relax as she. And I vision again that she head was deep into something. Very deep. And not just the head, but the little black body did follow it to wherever place it was. So it seem I need to be deep into something same time as I resting quiet—which is well enough, but deep into what?

Still and all, I going to try. I going to empty my head right out, and I going to beg whatever is out there that—That what? Well, whatever is out there that is decent, and mean no harm, to let me fix my whole self onto it. Is the best I can do. Can't think of nothing better.

Cannot describe what follow. I going say something about it, but that is far from what happen. Very far.

As I struggle to drop things out of my head—and is a terrible struggle, for suddenly so much things that I don't understand is happening—I hear a singing sound coming from far-far. I think it say something like "mah rah nah tah" and, though it is tuneless, only a drone, I have this sense that I am following it, hearkening to it and it alone, and traveling with it, up and up. My body change gear, as it lift, and things fall away from it, from me. Then somewhere in the warm red blackness behind my closed eyes, I see a point of pulsating blue light—a blue that is not green blue, or yellow blue, or red blue, but the true true blue of maybe the light inside a candle flame, maybe the light of the life inside of things.

Then I am lost in whatever it is that is there. Still as one slain. At rest.

After, long after, I sleep, and in that sleep I dream a terrible dream. It is, again, a dream concerning Drew. I think now she send it to me as a warning. She lying on a gurney, flat down like I lying now, her face wintergreen or deathgreen, take whichever you want. The place tile with shiny blue porcelain tiles that put me in mind of the birthing room in a hospital, though how I know what that look like, I can't tell. It have some people in gown like Ku Klux Klan standing over her, and I know they are doctoring people for they hold shiny instruments. I spot one as the head, for growing from his forehead is a corona of intense white light, and it seem like he holding a sword of light: sometimes long, sometimes short; sometimes bright orange, sometimes pale green so I can barely see it. He use it to cut Drew body, then he get busy like a little ferret. I see him pulling small bloody parcels out of her, delivering them to a endless line of hands that appear to receive them as he pass them over his shoulder.

"Oh blue heaven!" I think to myself. "She sick. She sick unto dying. They cutting, cutting away the sickness, and they can't finish because there is so much of it."

I so frighten that I check to see if is really Drew. I look hard in her face and I know is she, yes. Then I run my eyes down her body and come to her middle. Her belly is a huge bloody empty shell with fif-teen, maybe twenty navel strings hanging from the sides, draining into the wombspace. When I look in her face again, she is weeping, weep-ing, her eyes moving crazy from left to right, then to left again, hunt-ing, hunting after something. . . .

I stumble into wakefulness, like the sight make me buck my toe and so I wake up. And for a moment it is almost clear to me. Almost clear.

There is a blinding light in my eye. I can clearly see the dome, the glass shelves extending out into the dome space, the warren of wires. I am rising rising, like I am on a see-through elevator. I know that them chain me, hand and foot and torso, to a gurney. I see four, maybe five, pale people in white uniform beside me. I cannot see the ones at my feet for my belly is so big that I cannot see beyond it. Then a tide of good-feelings wash me, and my insides quiver, and I am in my ham-mock again, the sun warm, the sea murmuring, the salt smell biting my tongue.

It is the cotton-candy-headed black lady and her two arms is full for she is holding two big baskets, and, when I look inside, they are full of small white bundles, like the way, on ironing day, we first sprinkle the white clothes—after they done wash and bleach in the sun, and we blue them and dry them—and then we wrap them in on themselves and set them to wait their turn for ironing. I am thinking, "Poor lady, so much to iron," when I see at the top of each bundle a pale little head with stringy blonde hairs hanging from it, and wide-open, blue-blue eyes.

It startle me—I tell no lie. And I don't swallow that good before I see Drew running to meet the old lady, and, following behind her like a line of little ducks, more little blonde children, with heads trailing wisps of blonde hair, and eyes blue as the blue-blue far-away sky in this impossible place. As usual, it is bright, clear, just like I am there. And I move to the old lady and speak. I say, "Whose children is these? Why so many? And why they look so?"

But she don't hear me. Drew don't hear me. Them just going on together about their business.

I watch as the old lady take the baskets, and the children follow Drew to a grassy place with a big round flat-top stone in the middle. The old lady set the baskets on the stone, and she take out from deep in her thick layers of skirt—for she look like she wearing clothes on top of clothes—a long shiny thing like a saw. And Drew take out two things from her skirts that look like sticks with something big and round at the top. And I think, "Lawd, no. They is only children. You can't kill them!"

The duckling children form a little circle inside a big circle.

From her skirts, again, the magic black lady produce a thin bit of metal and she take it and start to scratch at the saw. The children in the small circle stamping their feet. The children in the big circle clapping their hands. And Drew shaking the sticks—and I laugh out loud, for I know now they are gourdies, and that this is a dance to the music of saw and maracas, and the little blonde niggers, the duckies and the laundry, blue eyes and all, they is all Drew's babies. And they are not lost, not lost.

I LOOK ON my belly. I see it is higher today than ever before. I study the tight shiny black mound. To date, it don't jump. When it jump, I know I in trouble and I done with trouble one time. I smile. It don't occur to them that my mouth corner and my soul case don't have to be in alignment. . . .

As for me, I work and work to keep my children. I tell them every little thing that happen to me that I remember. I sing them every song. I recite them my dreams. I show them their ancestors. I relate, again and again, every story, all the bits and pieces, that I know.

I swear by the skemps little bits of my life that I will reclaim them, keep them, for I have told them they are precious, and marked them with my words and songs, stories and dreams. I think of Drew and ratchet up my will one notch. I feel them paleface maneuverers start with her. After she, how many of us before they now reach me?

> It is a drum. A pulse of a drum. It is the noise of my
> body. Our bodies. The driving of all of our hearts.

So I lying here, gazing at my tight belly. I sure I see one tiny ripple and I catch my breath. Is time. I am in their birthing room and they will cut me now. And the drumming galloping noise I been hearing in my head will finally go. And maybe I will go with it. Yellow hair, yes, and blue-blue eyes, but they will be my babies, my nigger babies, the mold of my story growing on their bones.

LIGHT-FADE. Time to sleep now. I going "sleep" easy. Going dream the children drumming, dancing, singing a Senegambian song.

crick crack

THE STORYTELLER SPINS her tale, getting ever more outrageous with each weave of the web. Every so often she asks her audience, "Crick?" If they're still with her, still caught up in the threads, they reply, "Crack," and she keeps spinning.

The next four stories use irony, satire, and humor to spin out tall tales that use smiles to help their messages go down smoother.

Lillian Allen is known for her work as a dub poet, a musician, a teacher, and an arts activist. This rare piece of prose fiction from her is a tongue-in-cheek allegory from a woman who's done years on the modern-day battle lines of committees, boards, cooperatives, and focus groups.

In the Beginning

LILLIAN ALLEN

Before there was memory, before "In the Beginning," everything was the same and the same and the same. And we yearned as one for difference. But we were one and the same and everything was just the same.

The same and the same and the same.

"In the Beginning" is how we described it when we first created God. The first time we remembered. The place where memory starts when we relinquished the rigidity of sameness. Memory starts here because the human mind can remember only by the experience of contrast. Before difference, the human kind has no memory.

We created God to ease the monotony. This was our first human act of art. We gave God the ultimate responsibility for creating and for all things. This was how we first gave in to the possibility of difference, of motion, of flow—letting go the rigidity of sameness. This possibility produced free will. And God said this is good. This was God's first action—to speak—to say this is good.

And God felt good.

And these words and God's emotions of feeling good created

motion. And this motion we call time. And we moved for the first time for the sheer effort of imitating God. And God called our motion dance. And our dancing was rhythmic and created the waves on which our voices rode and the movement of our voices on these waves created music. And the first organic life appeared on the downbeat of a song.

We said to each other: "We created God and that gave us possibilities. Possibilities made us move, movement made us dance, our dancing gave us music, and music made new life." For the first time we saw old and we saw new and saw that we were old. So we say to this God, "All things old, make it new."

And God said, "I don't make things new. That's your job. My job is to create difference. That's the job of God."

And we said: "We hate difference!"

And God replied, "Then how about saving yous from yourself?"

And we said, "Tacky, tacky, tacky. Had we known you were bringing your own agenda to the job we would at least have made this a temporary position with a probation period and possible renewal only on mutual agreement of the parties . . . with witness. . . ."

God said, "Too late now. Our job agreement has locked us in forever. We are going to have to tough this one out."

So we said, "Shucks! In this case we'll need to get you a job description quick because the next thing you know you'll be doing anything you darn well please."

And God said, "I feel a little bit of distrust developing here. What you need to understand is that I do what God does. Not what I darn well please."

ON THE way to creating a job description for God, we experienced the first possibility of dissent. At first we formed a committee but everyone now knowing feelings of distrust wanted to ensure that their opinion had the same prominence as any other, so we became a collective. This process went on for millennia. Everyone was giving their input, making sure details and conceivable eventuality were covered. Then there were changes and discussions and debates and arguments and everyone couldn't agree on every single point. People argued over why we even needed God in the first place. Some argued that they could do the job. On their prodding a subcommittee was struck to work out a compromise delineating lines of accountability once the God thing was settled. Sometimes people forget what it was they were trying to do. Some didn't like the way others presented. Some went off and had wars with those who didn't agree with them.

And finally someone said: "God has to serve my individual unique needs or else why would I have a God."

And another said: "Look, we have to get on with it. God needs to get on with the business of being God."

Another said: "I've got my own job description for God. Why don't we all write our own." And so we did, each and every one.

At the end of the process each person had fashioned God's job description to his or her own liking.

And God said, "You can make any kind of job description you want. When it comes down to it, I can only do what God does. Nothing more and nothing less."

And we laughed and said, "We'll see . . . !"

And that was in the beginning.

Uncle Obadiah is a man of strong opinions, and he's making sure to pass them on to his nephew. Nothing much phases Uncle Obadiah. He'll take anything in stride, so long as no one damages the things he cares for most. Geoffrey Philp rings the changes on the space western, the type of story that takes all the trappings of Wild West fiction and transfers them to Alpha Centauri. Uncle Obadiah's alien has swooped a-hootin' and a-hollerin' down from outer space into Uncle Obadiah's field of finest herb with a message from his people, and Mars needs, well . . .

Uncle Obadiah and the Alien

GEOFFREY PHILP

EVERY SUMMER I used to look forward to going down to me Uncle Obadiah farm in Struie. Him had me doing all kinds of things on the farm: tying out the goats, feeding the chickens, and helping with the cows. I enjoy doing the chores, for it help to get me mind off school. Uncle Obadiah make me do all these things because although him did expect me to pass the "O" levels in England, him said a man should always have something to fall back on and farming was the best work a man could do.

So one Saturday evening as I was standing on the barbecue and pulling the tarpaulin over Uncle Obadiah six-foot statue of Haile Selassie, I hear *ching, ching, ching, chingeleng, pang, pengeleleng, peng.* I figure it was the Chinese people down the lane giving a name to they latest baby. Uncle Obadiah said Chinese people name they children by throwing a twenty-five-cent piece through the window and the first sound the coin make, that's what the child name. But this was too loud for a twenty-five-cent piece.

I make sure the tarpaulin was on real tight, for although a Rastaman not supposed to attach to material possessions, I know that if even a speck of dew did settle on Uncle Obadiah statue, there would be hell to pay.

I run down the gully and see this thing that look like a black Volkswagen minibus, but it never have no window. A cloud of smoke trail from the sky down to the back. At first, I think it was a army helicopter, but it didn't have no propeller. It look like a long, black, metal gas tank, like some thing from NASA or a Russian Sputnik. But when the door open, I see something with space suit, laser gun and everything.

Well, the minute me eye clap on this thing, I take off up the hill straight to Uncle Obadiah for him was the only one who would believe me. But when me get to him house, even him didn't believe me.

"After that arse-tearing yu father give yu last week for telling lies, yu still doing it?" him said.

"I not telling lies anymore," I said. And I guess by the look on me face, him decide to believe me.

So him put on him Wellingtons and come down the gully with me. By then, the alien was trying to come out of the spaceship. When Uncle Obadiah see the alien, him spliff drop right out of him mouth, for it was horrible.

It had long, wiry brown hair, big black eyes, and horrible crooked teeth. I was going throw some rock stones at it when Uncle Obadiah discern why the thing look so ugly. It was the dead stamp of Margaret Thatcher. No wonder it looked so evil, and if we did know better, we would have sent it packing right there. Uncle Obadiah stand up on the side of the gully and look down at the alien.

"Wha de raas yu doing in me herb field? Yu killing off all me herb plant," said Uncle Obadiah.

And the alien said, "Terribly sorry, my dear fellow, but I appear to be stuck. But don't worry, I'll have it fixed in a minute."

The alien was trying to get it foot out of the door, and when Uncle Obadiah see that, him do what any Rastaman would do, him go down the gully to help out a fellow being.

The two of them rocked the spaceship, but still the alien couldn't come out, so Uncle Obadiah call me down. At first, I never want to go, but Uncle Obadiah tell me that everything was all right.

Night was coming fast, and we could barely see each other, which was good, because who would want to look at a thing as ugly as that in the dark? We rocked the spaceship again, and the alien pull him foot out the door.

Then the alien turn to Uncle Obadiah to thank him, see him face, and said, "Menelik?" and that's when the friendship start. For Uncle Obadiah realize that this was no ordinary alien. This was a roots alien.

We walk up the gully, lead the alien to our shack, and introduce ourselves. The alien had a funny name that we couldn't say too good, so we decide to call it Maggy.

I said to Maggy, "Everybody on your planet look like you?"

"As a matter of fact, and that's quite intuitive, we do," said Maggy.

"You mean the same, down to yu toenail?"

"The same."

A cold chill go through me body and I begin to tremble when I really think about a whole planet that look like him. Maggy could see that I was worried.

"I know I look awful, but that's why I'm here. We don't like it either, so I've come for the antidote. But don't worry," Maggy said, "my condition is not contagious."

I breathe a sigh of relief.

So I decide to ask Maggy, "If you all look the same, how you tell the male from the female?"

"My dear boy," Maggy said, "haven't you figured that out yet?"

"Watch the boy business," said Uncle Obadiah. "Is me nephew, show some respect."

"Just some man-to-man humor to ease the tension," said Maggy. "I never really meant any harm," and then him went on to explain how him planet fall into such a state.

"After millions of years of in-breeding, our people were dying out from all sorts of genetic defects. We've been studying your planet for centuries, and when we realized that our bodies were almost like yours, we decided to introduce genes from your planet to our planet. The last time I was here, I collected thousands of gene samples from all over Earth, but unfortunately, I crashed when I got back to my planet."

"Yu always crashing like this?" I asked.

"I always get what you would call 'bad vibes' when I enter your solar system. With all the wars, starvation, murder, and suicide in your part of the universe, I've always found it necessary to stop off at a bar just outside your galaxy and order an Arcturus Assassin. It helps to settle my nerves."

This alien, I was beginning to figure out, besides being a great scientist, was an intergalactic drunk driver, and Uncle Obadiah said that maybe we should put a big learner L on him spaceship so that other aliens would know to stay out of him way.

"Only one sample survived from the crash, and it belonged to the sweetest, kindest, gentlest person I met on Earth. She was a young girl when I met her, but when she discovered I was from another planet, I had to erase all memory of myself from her mind with a new drug. It was premature, and no one knew how it would affect humans. We did know, however, that an overdose could have serious side effects. It could reverse positive character traits, and it could even kill certain essential brain cells. Nevertheless, I had to do it. I gave her the drug and then made the fatal mistake of taking the cell samples after she got the drug."

"No wonder that woman so hard!" Uncle Obadiah shouted. "Alien mind drug warp her mind."

"I should look her up, to see how she's doing," suggested Maggy.

"Let sleeping dogs lie," said Uncle Obadiah. "We can never undo the past."

"The sample mixed with the drug saved our people but produced this horrible side effect. It changed everyone's metabolism and now everyone looks like the woman you call Margaret Thatcher. I've come to Earth for the antidote. But again I gave into my single vice. I stopped off at the bar for another Arcturus Assassin and crashed again."

"So why you call I Menelik?" asked Uncle Obadiah.

"On the same visit to Earth, I collected cell samples from the man who was the ruler of Earth. He was a short man, with a trimmed beard, and he wore a ring with two triangles—the seal of royalty throughout the universe."

"Selassie I!" roared Uncle Obadiah.

"Precisely," said Maggy. "And you, Sir, bear a striking resemblance to his father."

"Maggy," said Uncle Obadiah, "yu soun like a real English man. Yu talk English good. For an alien."

Maggy blushed.

"So how yu get to know His Imperial Majesty?" asked Uncle Obadiah.

"Selassie," said Maggy "had the most superior genes of anyone on Earth. He comes, as you may know, from a lineage of a family possessing all the characteristics of what we, as a specie, would have desired to resemble. Instead we are a freakish scientific mutation who look like a German frau who has eaten too many sour limes."

"Doan be so hard on yuself," said Uncle Obadiah. "Just give thanks you never take it from Queen Victoria."

Even Maggy, who had traveled to the ends of the universe and back and had seen so much, was frightened at such a prospect. Obadiah was right. Fate, in all its complexity, was kind. Yet, there was some things that still confused him.

"I'll never understand, though, how the other nations of Earth just stood by and watched Ethiopia being destroyed."

"Is a shame, yes," said Uncle Obadiah.

"From as early as the turn of the century," Maggy said, "we have been watching over Ethiopian affairs. With His Majesty's permission we intervened in the war between Ethiopia and Italy."

That explained it. For how else could a small, ragtag, ill-equipped army have defeated the great war machine of Europe without intergalactic help?

"For each shot an Ethiopian fired," Maggy continued and pulled his laser gun from its holster, "I fired a laser from my spaceship and killed ten people. No one really knew the difference for I was cloaked invisibly behind the clouds. In the end, it looked as if the Ethiopians had done it all alone, but the Ethiopians and Selassie himself knew they had received help from the heavens."

"So wha happen to His Majesty now?" probed Uncle Obadiah.

"Oh, he's fine. He's the king of our planet. That's why I'm here."

"Jah lives!" said Uncle Obadiah and him danced around the room. "Selassie I lives!"

"So what about all them news report dat His Majesty dead?" I asked.

"Don't believe anything that those newspapers and televisions tell you," said Maggy. "It's all a bunch of lies. The same people in Rome who opposed him on Earth now oppose him even after his supposed death. I took His Majesty away during the last months of the coup," said Maggy with a touch of pride, "and substituted a clone of Selassie."

This explained to me why the army said His Imperial Majesty was behaving like a tyrant.

"It wasn't the real King of Kings," said Maggy, "just a lump of protoplasm engineered to look like His Imperial Majesty," and he put the laser gun back in its holster.

"No one ever killed His Majesty. He went with me back to my planet, and we accepted him as our king. There he rules justly and benevolently. We tried to change the results of the experiments, but nothing worked. Then His Majesty, in royal wisdom, decreed that I should go to Earth for the antidote. That's why I tried to land in your marijuana field. Throughout the universe, in all the galaxies, marijuana is used for myriad ailments. We know of its many uses, but never figured it could be used to reverse genetic defects. But as His Imperial Majesty said, 'Herb is for the healing of a nation.'"

Well, from what Maggy said it seems as if Uncle Obadiah's herb could heal the universe.

Now Uncle Obadiah wasn't a drug dealer or anything like that. Him grow only enough for himself and the idren in the village. The police know about it, but them know Uncle Obadiah's herb was for meditation and reasoning, not for getting high like those American tourists do.

"I'd planned to snip a few buds from your crop, but took the last sip of the drink, lost control, and landed in your field. I know I shouldn't be drinking the stuff, for His Majesty said that if I wanted to get high, then I should meditate on Jah."

Just as I was about to ask him if His Majesty and Jah was not the same, Uncle Obadiah uproot a whole plant and pop a spliff in Maggy's mouth.

"Try dis instead of yu Arcturus Assassin. Dis is de Jamaican Jamboree. An it won't give yu no headache or mek yu crash yu spaceship."

Maggy took a draw on the spliff and inhaled. And that was when the bangarang start.

Him head start to grow and him whole body start to shine. Him jump on Uncle Obadiah jackass and start ride through the countryside. All through Struie, Rat Trap, Lamb's River, and Bethel Town. As him was riding the jackass, it look like him head disappear and that is why people down to this day still believe stories about rolling calves, duppies, and headless horseman. All because of Maggy and Uncle Obadiah jackass.

We couldn't calm him down. And then it get worse. Him take out him laser gun and start fire it all over the place. At first, it was great, for it was just disintegrating everything. We never mind. In fact, me think Uncle Obadiah wanted a stray shot to clap the busha up the hill for him grandfather was a slave owner in the old days, and him son was now a politician. But then Maggy fire a shot and disintegrate Uncle Obadiah's statue of Selassie.

That's when Uncle Obadiah wrath, and Maggy sober up same time. You never want to see a Rastaman wrath. Uncle Obadiah tell him right straight that him had to leave.

"Maggy, get off me land, get out of me village, get off me island. In fact, get off me planet. Leave Earth."

Maggy tried to apologize, but Uncle Obadiah wouldn't hear none of it. Uncle Obadiah just keep staring off into space, where him statue was, tarpaulin and all. Maggy gather the samples and put them in him spaceship. Him tell me there had been a systemic failure in him navigational apparatus. Him never know where the hell him was.

"What was that stuff? " Maggy asked me.

"Lamb's breath," I said.

"I'd better dilute it to a thousandth of its strength. This is the best marijuana in this galaxy."

"We know," I said. "So please, Sah, don't start running around and tell everybody in the universe. Make it be our secret. For if you tell everybody, then soon soon we going have spaceship landing in we backyard, blowing their horn, and pulling up to Uncle Obadiah's shack at all kinds of hours in the night, trying to buy herb that not for sale. Besides, me an Uncle Obadiah is the kind of people who like to keep to weself."

"It will be our secret," him said with a smile.

Then him apologize to Uncle Obadiah and said him could rebuild a duplicate from him spaceship.

"What done, done," said Uncle Obadiah and him accept Maggy apology for everything.

"So when yu coming back," I ask Maggy.

"Selassie has decreed," said Maggy, "that no one should return until all Africans have been reunited and all nations of Earth accept His Imperial Majesty as its rightful ruler."

I wave good-bye because I know me wouldn't see him again.

"Jah guide," said Uncle Obadiah.

"Selassie lives," shouted Maggy from inside the spaceship, and blasted out of the universe, off course, but far away from Earth with antidote in tow.

I don't believe him did keep our field a secret though. For on some nights after Uncle Obadiah and me finish reasoning and smoking some herb, I see strange lights and all sort of things down in the gully. That's why Uncle Obadiah say if any alien come up to you house and ask you where Struie is, just point them north and as far away from him shack as possible, for him don't want Maggy coming over to him house, smoking all him herb, and shooting up the place with laser gun anymore.

"My Grandmother's Tale of the Buried Treasure and How She Defeated the King of Chacachacari and the Entire American Army with Her Venus-Flytraps" is the opening piece in Robert Antoni's collection My Grandmother's Erotic Folktales. *Grandmother has a linked and branching sense of story and a bawdiness that could rival that of Scheherazade, that beautiful wordsmith who kept her king from killing her by mesmerizing him with a thousand and one amazing tales.*

My Grandmother's Tale of the Buried Treasure and How She Defeated the King of Chacachacari and the Entire American Army with Her Venus-Flytraps

ROBERT ANTONI

Yes, THAT IS A STORY! It's a very good story that I can tell you if you want, but Johnny, don't tell nobody I told you that thing that is a very bad story, like you mummy and daddy. A very good bad story that is one of my best, and you know that it's a true story, because there you hold the brick in you hand—look, almost all the gold has rubbed off over the years—and it happened right here on this island of Corpus Christi, many many years before you were born. It happened in a place up in the north of the island, at the tip tip of the— how do you call it?—of the peninsula that is on the side of Venezuela, in a place called Chaguarameras. And it was in this place that I had the cocoa estate, that is to say in Spanish, *chagua,* which means "farming-land," *rameras,* which means "prostitutes," the Farmingland of Prosti-tutes that they took away from me to make the American Base during the war.

Because at that time of the war I was already a widow of several years. I was left that cocoa estate by you granddaddy there in the pho-tograph, Bartolomeo Amadao Domingo Domingo—the one they used to call Barto—because he died when you daddy was very young, and I was still a young woman with nine boys and one girl and Yolanda's daughter too. Because when she died of course I had to take back Inestasia, and I took Yolanda's daughter Elvirita on top. So I tried to give away one and I got back two, but don't mind, because at that time I was a young woman, and strong, and beautiful, you hear? Young and beautiful just like you mummy there, with beautiful hair and skin and beautiful tot-tots that didn't used to fall down, and beautiful beautiful teeth I used to have, big and white like pearls!

So it was in this place called Chaguarameras that I had the cocoa estate, and we used to ship cocoa all over the world. Big big estate, you know? So big you could never see from this side to that, and they used to say it was bigger than a hundred acres, but nobody knew for sure. And we used to have bananas, and chickens, and goats and all kinds of things, and we used to export copra from the coconuts, but the main thing was cocoa. We used to have the little house there, and when Barto was still alive we would go for excursions on weekends, and pack up the children and drive to that estate that was only twenty-five miles away, but in those days it was two, three hours driving in a motorcar from St. Maggy where we were living.

We used to like to go especially for the cocoa harvest. That was the time of festival at Chaguarameras they used to call to "Dance the Cocoa." You see, when the pods ripened and turned all purple and rosy, and they picked them to crack them open to take out the beans, the beans would have that white fuzz stuck up all over. So they would spread out the cocoa on the big platforms with wheels to roll them in the sun every day to dry. But before the beans could dry they had to take off that white fuzz. So everybody would pull off the shoes and roll up the pantaloons to go on top the platforms to dance, that the fuzz could stick to they feet and between they toes. But the thing about the fresh-picked cocoa beans, now, was that when you stood up hard and pounded you feet it didn't make no noise a-tall, but only the soft soft little sound that you could hardly hear, like poe poe poe. So when the festival started everybody was drinking rum, and eating roti, and playing music and thing, and Kitchener—not the Lord Kitchener of today, but the father, that was a young boy then—Kitchener even made a calypso of that fete yes, with all of us jumping up first thing to sing and dance like this:

> Mister Barto,
> I'm coming to Chagua-ramo!
> It's there to dance the co-coa,
> and make me feet cry poe . . . poe!
> poe-poe pa-tee poe . . . poe!
> poe-poe pa-tee poe . . . poe!

Sweet heart of Jesus! I can't hardly pick up the old feet again! What a thing eh, when you get old? I'd best sit down quick before the legs break off! Ninety-six years, you know? What a thing! But the head is still good, and the blood is not so yellow, and the wrinkles are not so bad for an oldwoman that has been a widow over sixty years. You see what is life? Ten children and I'm not dead yet, thank the lord. In truth, I don't know what Papa God will give me to kill me yes, because I've never been cut by no doctor—even though I made eight of them myself—and never stitched, that the one time I was chopping patatas and this little piece of the finger went on the ground like that, I just picked it up and pushed it back together and the flesh stuck, that you daddy always says would defy medical science. And I have him to take care of me and bring me here to you house, so I could have my little room with all the grands, and great-grands, and all the great-great-grandchildren coming to visit me and shouting down the place at all hours of the day and night!

So where I was now? Oh yes, so at that time I had this estate that they took away from me to make the American Base. But when Barto was still alive it was still the cocoa. And we used to drive to Chaguarameras almost every weekend to see about the affairs of the cocoa and things, but the main reason was because that was the time when Barto had gone crazy to fight the cocks. Crazy crazy for that cockfighting business, you hear? And we had plenty roosters, and a Venezuelan named Toy Muchu that he brought from Caracas to train the birds. Barto had the best in all Corpus Christi, and the men would come from Venezuela and Colombia and all over the place to Chaguarameras to fight they cocks against Bambolina, that was the best cock Corpus Christi had ever seen. Beautiful beautiful rooster, you hear? With bright bright eyes, and the wrinkles hanging just like this, and the headdress red red, and that was toenails, papa-yo! Because at that time they didn't have so much cockfighting in Corpus Christi again, except what they had in the mountains and in the bush, but Chaguarameras was too far out in the country then to worry the police. They used to say Barto bought that estate only to fight he cocks that was he passion. And something might be true in that, because that was before the time of the prostitutes—Barto liked to play the sagaboy, you know?—and in truth, we didn't used to make so much money from the copra and cocoa.

Because at that time Chaguarameras was still called Chaguaramos, that is to say, the Farmingland of Flowers. You see, when the cocoa made the flowers they would be covered all over with yellow and very pretty, and that was why they called it so to start. And it was just so the estate remained with the flowers and not the prostitutes for several years after Barto died. I had the overseer there that we used to call On-the-Eggs! and he had lived there on that estate all he life. And On-the-Eggs! took care of everything, because who was I at that time but a youngwoman and very beautiful who knew all about cattle from living on the ranch in Venezuela from a little girl, but didn't know a fart about cocoa. So On-the-Eggs! looked after that estate, and he used to send me the little few dollars that came from the cocoa every month to St. Maggy, and it was that money that went to feed the children and send them to school.

So when the war started now the English brought the Americans—because at that time Corpus Christi was still belonging to them—so the English brought the Americans to look for lands. The Americans didn't have no interest in oil that Corpus Christi had plenty, but only looking for lands lands lands to build a Base for they soldiers. And it was the English Lawyer for the Crown that came to me—with the Yankee soldiers standing up behind him listening—and he said that I would have to give up my estate for the efforts of the war. The Lawyer for the Crown said my cocoa estate was the best place for the Americans to build they Base, because it had the deep water right beside to bring in the ships, and for the time of the war the estate would belong to them. But Johnny, the truth that I only found out after was how the English had already exchanged my land for forty-five old broken-down battleships in a kind of agreement they called a "land-lease treaty," so the English could have all those old ships for they famous fleet. But what the Lawer for the Crown told me was that nobody wouldn't have no money until after the war. When that time came the Americans would pay the English for the value of my estate, and then the English would turn around and pay me, but not until the war finished I wouldn't see no money a-tall. The Lawyer said that if I didn't accept this, then the only thing for me to do was to fight the Queen that was Elizabeth the Segunda one, and I said that I have never fought no Queen before in all my life, and I'm not going to start now.

And so it happened that the Americans took away that estate and they knocked down the cocoa and coconut trees and all the rest to make that Base for they soldiers. And then when the Americans arrived the prostitutes only came following behind. Let me tell you every whorewoman in Corpus Christi descended straight away on that place, and so too again half the whores in Venezuela crossed the sea in saltfish-crates, and cigar-boxes, and whatever else they could find to get at those American soldiers fast enough, because it's true what they say that the Yankees would pay any amount of money because they don't have no sex in America, and that is why the Americans only like to fight wars.

So now you have the history of how Chaguaramos came to be called Chaguarameras, The Farmingland of Prostitutes.

WELL THEN, the war had continued so for a good time already that I had long ago forgot all about Chaguarameras. Then one day I was making pastelles in the kitchen and I heard somebody come pounding down the door of the little house I had there on Mucurapo Road that Barto left me with. Amadao came running to the kitchen—he was only a youngboy twelve or thirteen years like you then—Amadao came running to say that it was Ali Baba or some genie so at the door. I told Amadao that I didn't know no genie, and if it was Ali Baba in truth all he had to say was "Open up Sesame!" or some nonsense like that, and those hinges would fall off the door in one. Amadao went and came back again saying that it wasn't Ali Baba, it was the King of Chacachacari that "would wish to speak to the madame of this fine house." I told Amadao I'd never before heard of no Chacachacari, and if the person at the door didn't stop playing the fool, I would mix up the boil coocoo in he panties and wrap up he cojones in a steamed banana leaf to make the next pastelle! So Amadao went and came back again to say the King of Chacachacari would wish to speak to the madame that was "the proprietress of that farmery at Chaguaram-eras"—or something so—"concerning the matter of she duly deserved fortune." Well! by this time I was vex too bad and ready to send Amadao to tell the King how the Yankees took Chaguarameras a long time ago—and the only cocoa that grew there now was cocoplumbs in the shape of bambams!—but then I decided I would go to the door and see who was this person skylarking like that.

When I reached at the door now I found this man dressed up like he was playing mas in Carnival. He had one big set of cloth wrapped up around he head like if somebody started to make a mummy and only reached by the ears. With a big ruby upon the forehead flashing, and earrings dangling, and rings rings rings, each with a jewel—diamonds and rubies and things—but not on the fingers, only on the little fatty toes! And I decided that those rings must have been made special for those dirty toes, because you've never seen such funny little things, only looking like shortie fat blood-puddings struggling to squeeze out the skins! But the strange thing now about this King was that even with all the jewels and paraphernalia he had, the only clothes he was wear-ing were dirty old dungarees, both the pantaloons and the shirt. And even so, the dirty old shirt—with every button gone—was tied up around he midriff with the big stomach spilling out, and a next maco ruby big as you fist like this, pushed up inside he bellyhole! It was like if these people didn't care what kind of clothes they put on once they feet and they belly were shining with jewels, because the King had some little baboo-boys there dressed only in what looked to me like diapers. Four of these little baboos were to carry the King around who was sitting in a kind of pirogue, or canoe, or something so, with the legs hanging down like he was making sure nobody missed the toes. With two more little baboos only to hold a palm leaf over the King's head for the sun not to shine, and five or six more behind with the big grey Samsonite suitcases that I decided must have the rest of the jewels and the dirty old dungarees and diapers.

By now the whole of Mucurapo had reached at my doorstep to see this King that nobody had never seen nothing like this before, not even on Jouvert morning! Then the King gave me that speech again that he gave Amadao about the "proprietress and she duly deserved fortune," and he wanted to come inside, but I said not so a-tall was he bringing the whole of St. Maggy inside my house and the pirogue and suitcases and everything so. The King said that it was only him that needed to come inside, and the one servant that he required for the King to sit on he back. Well! I answered the King that nobody sat on top nobody in my house, and he could come in if he wanted, but he had to behave heself and sit in a chair like he had manners.

So the King came inside, and when I told him that I must go and check on the pastelles I had boiling in the kitchen, he pushed a chups like if he didn't wait on nobody. But when I came back again the King was smiling ear-to-ear like if the chair ain't paining he soft bamsee no more, and now he started off to talk and talk and talk like he just ate parrot.

The King said that he had come from he country across the sea in search of the long-lost treasure of Chacachacari. This treasure was forty-two bars of solid gold that the Spanish had stolen in the year 1776. So I asked the King—because I was a very smart woman, even then—

that first of all, where was this Chacachacari that I had never heard nothing about it before? and what did this treasure have to do with me, a poor widow that didn't have nothing in the world? and then again this story was only smelling like toejam to me yes, because 1776 was the year the English took Corpus Christi and the rest of these islands from Spain, that they weren't worrying about nothing a-tall at that time except how to hold on to these islands that they owned.

"Ah-ha!" said this King now like if somebody was scratching he back. "Precisely!" So I asked the King what did he mean by all these "ah-has" and "preciselies." The King said to me that was precisely how the treasure of Chacachacari came to be buried at Chaguarameras. What the King said was that this Chacachacari island had belonged to Spain at that time too—that was the year of 1776—that Spain was afraid to lose that island like all the rest. And that was how the Spanish ship, the one they called the *Maria Estrella del Mar*—and I remembered hearing about this ship from the history of Corpus Christi—that this *Maria* had stopped at Chacachacari on she way to defend Corpus Christi against the English, that in case they lost that Chacachacari too, at least they would still have the treasure.

So the King stopped now like if he'd aready proven everything clean clean. He was sitting up straight in the chair like he wanted to jook he head through the roof, and he clapped he hands twice—bam bam—and just then one of the little baboo-boys came running with a map. "You see, good madame," said this King, "you know as good as me that the Spanish ship, the *Maria Estrella del Mar,* was sunk by the English off the north coast of Corpus Christi, is that not correct?" And I told him that I thought so. "Ah-ha!" said the King again, smiling. "Here I have a map that shows precisely without any questions the place where the treasure was buried by two Spanish soldiers that escaped that *Maria Estrella* when she was sinking down in the sea. And this map says the treasure was bury precisely on the approximate location of that farmery of which you are the sole proprietress!" So the King made a big show to snap open the map like this and he stretched it out across the table, and when I looked good I saw that in truth, right there where the red X was marked was just where was Chaguarameras!

But as soon as I could catch my breath I told the King straight away—because I didn't want no bub-ball—that it was not me he had to consult with about that treasure, it was the American soldiers who took that estate away a long time ago to build they Base. So the King asked me if the Americans paid me any money for that land, and I said no, that they were waiting for the war to finish. The King went on with some more "ah-has" now, and he said that therefore the Americans owned everything above the ground, but that I was still the rightful owner of everything below, and that was why the treasure still belonged duly to me. But I told the King I was not about to fight no American Army—not even for forty-two gold bricks!—and then again, that map was only saying that the treasure was buried somewhere near Chaguarameras, but it didn't tell me where was the place to dig. "Well," said this King, "it is certainly clear to me that you are a very very intelligent woman and not foolheavy"—and I said yes, that is a fact—"and therefore you will certainly see the wisdom of this proposition that I have for you." Now the King clapped he hands again—bam bam—and a next little baboo-boy came running with a funny machine that looked like the vacuum cleaners they have now of days, except not so fat, and it was only blinking the lights and making funny noises.

Sweet heart of Jesus! When I saw this machine now I quick forgot all the questions I had for this King, because I was only watching at the lights and hearing the machine speak! The King asked me for some few coins, so I took out the little money that I used to keep between my tot-tots tied up in a kerchief, which was several of those big brown English coins that we were still using in Corpus Christi then. The King told me now to go and pitch them out the window as far as I could throw, and he would talk to he machine and find them, every one, but I said not so a-tall was I going to throw good money out the window for those people waiting outside to grab it up and run home before the King even got a chance to stand up out he chair, far less to start to talk to he machine! The King said that in truth he forgot about those people waiting outside, so for me to hide the coins all over the house, and the machine would tell him precisely where to find them. And so I did just that. Now the King started to talk to he machine, and in no time a-tall the King found out where was hidden every one of those coins, even the one I dropped in the chamberpot beneath my bed that still had in a little weewee from last night, that I didn't think nobody would think to look inside there! So when I saw this thing going on now inside my own house, I was ready to do anything the King told me.

What he said was for us to go first to the Americans and explain everything so there wouldn't be no bub-ball, and then we could start to look with he machine, and when we found the treasure divide it in half and take out the twenty-one bars each. But I told the King there wasn't no use for me to go quite to Chaguarameras because I had the children to take care of—and anyway I didn't speak the language of he machine so I wouldn't be no use to nobody a-tall—so for him to go and say to the Yankees that I had given him permission to look for that treasure, and when he found it he could take it out and bring it back here. The King seemed to like this plan good enough, and that was what he said he would do. So he took off one of the rings from he big toe—this was a diamond one—and he gave it to me to have "for a gesture of good faith," as he said, and the King went and climbed back up in he pirogue and took off again down the road with the little baboo-boys toting him, and the whole of Mucurapo following behind like a band of jumbies on Old Year's Eve morning! So I stood up watching at all this commess now for a while, and when they disappeared around the corner I went back in the kitchen to finish seeing about the pastelles.

AND IT WAS almost a month that I didn't hear nothing more about the King—and I didn't think much good things about him neither—because when I took the ring to get the size changed to fit my finger, the man told me that as soon as he went to heat the metal the diamond melted like a jubjub beneath the sun! So after a time I forgot to remember the magic of that machine, and I began to think how that King ain't nothing more than a big pappyshow, and I probably wouldn't see him again if I'm lucky.

But just as I was telling myself this I looked out the window, and of course, here was he coming up the road with Mucurapo still following behind like they'd all walked clear to Chaguarameras and back. So the King came inside again—and he made sure he had he machine next to him blinking the lights and carrying on so—because the King knew good enough that when I started to watch at that machine I couldn't see nothing else, like a person dreaming with they eyes open that somebody has given them separina tea to drink. The King said now that the machine had told him precisely without any questions where was the place the treasure was buried, but of course, when I asked him to see the bars he told me something else.

The King said that just as he was starting to take out the treasure an angel came with big silver wings flapping all about, and the angel took away the shovel and threw him down on the ground, and he showed me the purple blow on he forehead where he got the knock. This angel told the King that he would never be able to take out that treasure until he and the widow made a sacrifice by burning ten thousand dollars first, because you will both be multi-multi-multi-millionaires from all that gold!

But this story was smelling blanchyfoot to me yes, so now I decided to try to catch up this King in a good boldface lie. And as the saying goes, it takes one to grow one, and nobody could bake the cake better than me. So I asked the King how he knew it was an angel that knocked him down with the shovel? The King said because of the wings. Well then, was it a man or a woman angel, I asked. The King said that it was a man angel. But when I questioned him how he knew for sure, he said of course, as you very well know my good madame, angels don't wear no drawers—and I said yes, that was generally true—and the King told me that when the angel bent over he white robe slipped open a moment, and he saw the parts. So I asked for him please to specify, what parts was he talking about? Now the King got vex with he face red like a roukou and he said, "Parts, the parts: two hairy coconuts and a big fat toe-tee hanging down between like a celestial silver sausage!" Now I told the King that was all I wanted to hear—so please to calm down and relax heself—and Johnny, now I knew not to believe nothing this King said, just as I'd already suspected. Because the truth, if you've ever seen an angel—and I have seen plenty in my time—the truth is that they all are smooth. But when I looked at that machine again blinking in the corner and talking like that, now I couldn't help myself from asking the King how was he to get this ten thousand?

The King said that in Chacachacari they didn't have no money except for gold and beads and old teeth, and it was obvious none of those things burn too good—and I said yes, that was obvious enough—so then the only hope was for you to take out that money from the bank. So I asked the King how he knew what money I had, and he said the angel also told him that my husband, the one they used to call Barto, had left me ten thousand dollars to send the boys to study medicine in Canada when they grew up. Well! Right away I started to think, because nobody knew nothing a-tall about that money Barto left me with, nor what he said that I was to do with it. So I asked the King if he knew for sure it was a boy angel? The King said now that come to think about it, the angel did flash a lightning bolt at him, so maybe he couldn't be sure what he saw—if it was a silver sausage or a doubles with golden channa inside or anything else—but he sure did know good enough what the fuck he heard.

So I told the King that I must think over this sacrifice business good, and for him to come back the next day to hear about my answer. The King said certainly, that I was a very intelligent woman and must weigh up all the consequences, and did I mind if he left he machine to stand up there so in the corner because it was very valuable, and sleeping in a tent like he did somebody might come in the night to thief it.

So that afternoon I was trying my best to decide about this sacrifice, and the whole time that machine was only winking and blinking at me and distracting me, that he didn't give me no chance to think. I even sprinkled on him the dust that I scraped off my forehead from Ash Wednesday, that they said would make anybody drop down in a deep sleep, but that machine only went on to talk and talk and talk just like he owner. So I told Amadao and you daddy to carry the thing outside and play with him to see if maybe they could make him find some more treasure, or maybe the instrument would get so tired he would drop asleep. Because in truth the only person of all of us there to understand anything of the language of that machine was you own daddy—that he had only reached to five or six years then, and just beginning to talk heself—with the two of them conversing and discussing very serious together sometimes for three hours at a stretch. Inestasia and Elvirita—they were the oldest of the children, about sixteen and seventeen then—they came in the parlor now to ask me what about this King and the treasure? So I told them the whole story of the sacrifice and everything to see what did they think. Of course, the first thing they said was that I must consult Uncle Olly—he was the brother of Barto's father and a professor of bones and rocks and a very brilliant oldman—and I said of course that I had already sent word to him, and he was coming from San Fernando that evening to discuss all this business, but what did they think?

Well Elvirita didn't say much except to wait for Uncle Olly. But Inestasia now, she'd been holding this grudge against me such a long time, and she only started off straight away about how I was a very ignorant woman to give away every cent Barto left me with only for some cock-and-bull story about buried treasure, and she couldn't believe she had such a foolish and chupidee woman for she own mummy! But Inestasia was only using that King for an excuse to mamaguy me, because she never could understand, even though I explained it to her time and time again.

The Story of How She Gave Away One and Got Back Two

YOU SEE, the story goes that when I was married in January of 1913 I was only seventeen years old, and I had Nevil in November. That was before

I could even reach to eighteen. And Nevil was a beautiful child, you know? With curly curly rings in the hair, and bright eyes just like Barto's own, and good arms and legs running and jumping all about the place! But when he grew to eighteen months he got sick with a thing they had in Venezuela then—because at that time we were living in Venezuela, that Inestasia and Rodolfo and Reggie were all born in Venezuela, and the rest in Corpus Christi—they had this disease in Venezuela then called meningitis. So Barto and me sent to Caracas for the doctor to come as soon as the child grew sick, and this doctor had not observed Nevil five minutes before he called out, "Señor Domingo, ven acqui! Los sesos estrujan a este niño." That is to say, "he brains are squeezing him." Then the doctor looked in the child's ears with he instrument and he saw the brains crawling out like a long worm from each one, and he said Nevil would be dead by next week.

So as soon as the doctor left I shaved off Nevil's hair to take out the pressure, and I pushed plasters made from cottonwool and cornstarch in he ears to try and hold in the brains, and I even pushed he head in boiling water to try to shrink them up, but nothing worked a-tall and the next night the child died. Well, I was feeling so distressed by this thing that when Inestasia was born not long after, they had to take her away from me so I wouldn't throw her out the window. You see, I was desperate for a boy now to replace Nevil, and when I saw this girl I went crazy crazy and said that I wouldn't accept nothing to do with no child that was not a boy. But Papa God made me do enough penance for saying that yes, because he put eight boys on me straight away—bam bam bam—one after the next. That by the time I reached to you daddy I was crazy for a girl now, and I used to dress him up in little dresses and I grew out he hair in long blond curls reaching right down he back, but even that didn't help much and he almost drowned three times when I pitched him in the sea. So they had to look for somebody to take this Inestasia away, just as I was saying, because they knew good enough that I would pelt her through the window if they only gave me half a chance. So Yolanda—she was a Domingo too, and very much in the mind of the family—she said that she would take Inestasia up, so I sat down to write on a piece of paper:

I, Marìa Rosa de la Plancha Domingo, do give to you forever this my daughter, Inestasia Rosa de los Cagones Domingo, that you, Yolanda Domingo Domingo, can have her and do with her whatever the ass you want and I will never take her away again so long as you can live.

Yolanda was just then getting ready to marry sheself to Barto's brother Stefano, so she wrote to him in Corsica to say that she could not marry now that she had to take up Inestasia, but Stefano said yes, that this had convinced him for sure for sure even though he'd never laid eyes on her in he life, and he would give up he fortunes and come to Venezuela to marry her and the child both. But the interesting thing about this story now was that Yolanda—remember I told you how she was very much in the mind of the family? Well listen good—Yolanda's mummy and daddy were both Domingo cousins in the same way. Twice Domingo too. So when Elvirita was born not long after that it made her Domingo Domingo Domingo Domingo. Four times Domingo! What a thing, eh? You ever heard of any family business to go crazy like that? Sweet heart of Jesus!

So Yolanda died when Elvirita was thirteen years old, leaving only her, and I said that nevertheless I had so many children to take care of I would take Elvirita for sure especially as she was four times Domingo, and of course I didn't have no choice but to take Inestasia back on top. But even so Inestasia developed this grudge against me, all these years, and she's probably still carrying it too.

So UNCLE Olly arrived that evening and I related to him the story of the King and the treasure and everything so. Well Uncle Olly was a scientist of bones and rocks and a very brilliant oldman, so the first thing he said to me was "Yes, angels are smooth, but it's also true that devils can disguise theyselves as seraphs and give theyselves whatever kind of parts they want. The point is not what parts the angel has, but whether or not he's an angel a-tall. Because if he's a diab then he has probably taken out that treasure already for heself anyway, and therefore he wants you to burn up all that money only to make you a fool." The thing to do, Uncle Olly decided, was for him to go back to he laboratory and make up ten thousand dollars of fluke money to give the King, that if he was a true angel he would know right away the difference. But I reminded Uncle Olly that the King was coming in the morning, so how would he get a chance to make up all of those ten thousand dollars overnight? He said that the only thing for him to do was go he laboratory right now and start to paint.

So Uncle Olly arrived the next morning with the ten thousand dollars, and I said how that money would fool even St. Peter. Uncle Olly said that, in truth, that money would fool even him—but he was only putting goatmouth loud on heself by saying that, because as the story turned out Uncle Olly was fooled by he own fluke money as you will see—however, as Uncle Olly rightly said, the one person you could never fool was a true angel. The King soon arrived and I gave him the money and begged him please to take away that machine because I didn't sleep one blink last night only for watching and listening to him talking and talking in some language I still couldn't understand. But the King said he would prefer to leave him there with me since he already knew for sure without any questions where the exact location of the treasure was—and the only thing for him to do was to burn up this money quick quick and take it out—and since that instrument was so valuable he would appreciate leaving him there in the corner, but he would explain to him and make sure he machine understood that he must behave heself good and no more noise and winking.

But I don't know what the King said to that thing yes, because as soon as he left now the machine started off to wink and blink and talk at me more than he ever did before, until I thought I was soon to go vie-kee-vie! And I didn't get no more sleep for the next week that I couldn't wait for that King to come back and take him away. Now when he did arrive he was vex vex and bawling like he'd just sat down on a live coalpot, and he showed me the blow he received on the shoulder this time. The King said that the angel had increased the price now to fifteen thousand for the sacrifice, and when I told him that ten thousand was all I had in the world, he told me I should have thought about that before I tried to pass off fluke money on a real angel! He said that I would have to borrow the rest if I ever wanted to see them twenty-one bars. Well, I told the King that I would have to think about this for two more days, and I begged him to please take that fucking machine away but he wouldn't.

So I sent for Uncle Olly to tell him what happened, and what did he think? Uncle Olly said now that maybe this King had something for true, because nobody, not even he—again!—could tell that money was not real, and could he please see that treasure map? So I gave it to him and Uncle Olly studied it close and said that he would have to take that map back to he laboratory and test the ink to find out when it was drawn, and if in fact it was 1776 like the King said, then he was telling the truth for sure for sure, and if that was the case Uncle Olly said he would provide the remaining five thousand dollars to make the angel happy. Uncle Olly also said that he would look into that machine and make some science on him to find out how it was he talked so much, and I began a novena that same night I was so happy, and I slept for the first time in almost two weeks!

Well, exactly what happened that you would expect. Uncle Olly spent the next two days and two nights watching at that machine, and he forgot all about the map. So when the time came Uncle Olly and me went with the King to the bank to take out the fifteen thousand dollars, but we told him we would hand it over only when he took us to the exact place where the treasure was buried—and that he must burn it right there in front of we own eyes—and only then could he take out the treasure. The King said that was very fine, just as it should be, but he didn't ride in no motorcar, only in pirogue. So Uncle Olly asked him how long would he take to reach by Chaguarameras in pirogue, and he said depending on how much he beat the little baboos with a stick, maybe four or five days. Well! I got so upset when I heard about this beating business that I said to let's forget about this treasure and everything else right now, because I won't stand for none of that. So the

King said for us to come with the money in two weeks time that by then he would surely have reached Chaguarameras, and I said fine but he must leave the stick with me.

So in two weeks Uncle Olly and me went to Chaguarameras, but we didn't find no King. And Johnny, I tell you I was ready to cry when I saw what the soldiers had done to that estate, and when I found On-the-Eggs! who was working for the Americans now as one of the yardboys, my heart broke for true. To think how that man was the overseer of my whole estate, and he had charge over forty or fifty workers, and over all the shipping of the cocoa and copra, and now he was nothing more than a gardener swinging the cutlass! So I told On-the-Eggs! the story of the treasure and described the King good, and he said straight away that we could find him in a place called the "Officer's Club" with the soldiers and all the prostitutes. On-the-Eggs! took us to this place, and sure enough right there was the King now with all the whores playing up to him, and a crowd of soldiers standing around only to listen to the King talk. But when he saw me he jumped up quick quick to say that here was "Her Royal Benefactress of the Domain of Chaguarameras, and the cestuis que fu"—or something so that the King said means in Latin "half-of-an-owner," which of course I could never know nothing about since I only speak a little church-Latin—"the que fu of the long-lost treasure of Cha-cachacari!" So everybody commenced to clapping they hands now, and the King asked me first of all if I brought that money for the sacrifice, and I said yes, but he wouldn't see it not until we reached by the treasure. The King said that was very fine, just as it should be, and he told me how he had arranged for a big ceremony tonight for the digging of the treasure as it was only fitting. The Sergeant of the Army there had promised him a band of musicians to lead the procession, and a whole platoon of soldiers with guns to stand guard over the digging and to protect the treasure through the night. In the morning, the King said, we would divide the treasure and take out the twenty-one bars each.

So Uncle Olly and me left him there with the soldiers and the prostitutes, and we went with On-the-Eggs! to he house to wait for this
big celebration of the digging tonight. On-the-Eggs! wanted to know
all about this King, who seemed to him very very floozy, and why did
we want to trust him with all that amount of money like that? Well
Uncle Olly didn't even bother to waste he breath to answer. He
stopped the car right there in the middle of the street, and he took
On-the-Eggs! to open up the trunk and show him that machine! So
when we reached to the little house—that was me and Barto's old
house that I had given them to live in after the Americans took the
estate and everything finished—when we reached the house and
Indra saw me she started to bawl and beat she breast and said that she
could never believe she would see me in Chaguarameras never again!
I told her all about everything, and she said just like On-the-Eggs!
that we must watch out good for that King, because she knew him
from the Officer's Club where she worked and she didn't trust him a-
tall, and we must be very careful to hand him over all that amount of
money. I said one good thing was the platoon of soldiers with guns,
because not only could they protect the treasure, but they would
make sure that King didn't do no bub-ball neither. And straight away
I took out my little pearlhandled pistol from between my tot-tots to
show them I meant business too. Well! Everybody's eyes jumped out
they heads to see this thing, and of course they all begged me to
relate the story.

The Story of General Monagas's Pearlhandled Pistol
and The Tiger That Liked to Eat Cheese

YOU SEE, ever since I was a little girl I was raised on the cattle ranch
in Venezuela in Estado Monagas, and that was twelve hours riding on
a horse away from Caracas. But Johnny, let me tell you that was a
ranch, you hear? With hundreds of acres and packed full full with cattle, that we used to make fifty pounds of cheese every day! The name
of the ranch was Baranjas, which means to say "all jumbled up

together," because that was just how the cows were looking. So every holiday my father's uncle—he was a great man by the name of General Francisco Monagas—he would come to visit with us at the ranch. Now this General was the famous soldier because he had liberated the slaves in Venezuela, and he was twice president too, that you will find he statue there riding on the horse in the middle of the plaza in Caracas.

But the story of the pistol now. You see, one time when General Monagas came to visit a big big tiger came inside the house, and he walked straight through the middle of all of us sitting there conversing and telling stories, walking boldface like if he'd been in that house plenty of times before and he knew exactly where he was going, straight through the dining room into the kitchen to eat all the cheese. So the General jumped up quick and he ran behind this tiger, because he was a soldier so of course he had the gun at he side always ready, and he shot the tiger so—bam! bam!—twice like that, but the tiger didn't fall down. He stood up right there watching at the General and chewing the cheese, and only after he finished eating up all the fifty pounds did he turn around and walk through the house again, just the way he came, out the door and back inside the jungle.

Well, everybody said how that was something for true, and straight away we all started to argue about who was the dead person who'd come back as the ghost of that tiger, and what was the message he was trying to give us, because everybody knew good enough General Monagas would never miss the shot, so how come that tiger didn't fall down dead? But after a few days we all forgot about this big tiger—except the one cowboy that ate some of the cheese and said he'd changed into a leopard, and we found him the next morning sleeping naked up in a tree and painted head-to-toe in black-and-yellow stripes—and it was a long time later that one of the servants was shining the silver and she found inside of my Christening cup the two bullets, but of course, nobody didn't make that connection of those two bullets and the tiger.

But the next time General Monagas came to the ranch the very same thing happened. The big tiger came inside the house to stalk the cheese, the General shot him two times, and after that they found the bullets inside my Christening cup. So the next time General Monagas and the tiger came to visit, as soon as the shots went off and the tiger went home, everybody ran quick to look inside my Christening cup, and sure enough there were the bullets right there at the bottom! Now General Monagas said he knew for sure for sure that this tiger was the ghost of General Geraldo Domingo—who was of course my godfather—and therefore there was only one way to kill him dead for good and give the oldman a little peace.

So the next time General Monagas came to visit he presented me with this pistol that he'd had made for me special. But Johnny, you should have seen this thing! A little pistol you know, made to fit perfect inside my little hand, but the metal was all covered with silver and the handle only with mother-of-pearl! So this time when the tiger came the General took me up in he arms—because I was just a little girl of seven or eight years then—and he took me and put me to stand just there in front of the tiger. Well, the tiger turned around and he let loose two deep growls—gerrerr! gerrerr!—like if he was contemplating now which one he wanted to eat first, this little girl or the cheese. But soon enough he made he decision for the beautiful little girl, and as quick as that tiger could jump on top me I fired so—bam!—one shot straight between the eyes, and sure enough there was this big tiger lying dead as doornails right there at my feet! So we made a big fete that night and they took out the skin to make a blanket for me—and that tiger was so big he hung down to touch the ground at both sides of the bed—but when they looked inside my Christening cup this time they found it full full with blood that they said must belong to that tiger, and before the fete could finish General Monagas got so borracho they had to take the cup away from him not to drink it down!

WELL! AFTER that story now Indra and On-the-Eggs! and Uncle Olly begged me to tell more, so I obliged them and went on to relate the stories of how On-the-Eggs! got he name, and Toy Mushu, and the story of how Amadao disappeared for five days before we found him beneath the bed eating ants, and how Reggie got erysipelas and he legs swelled up big and fat like two balloons, and Dr. Salizar cured him with seven frogs that he passed up and down the child's legs until they turned red red red. And then he hung those frogs out on the clothesline to let them dry so each of us could keep one for a remembrance of this story—and Johnny, I still have mine hidden at the bottom of my bureau over there because I don't like to see no frogs!—and all the old stories they begged me to give them that in the end we got so distracted, we almost forgot about the treasure.

So when we returned to the King now he and the soldiers were good and borracho, with one set of commess going on. The King had taken off all those dirty dungarees, and he was dressed up now in what he called the "ceremonial gown." But this gown was only a dirty old sheet that he'd wrapped heself in to match he headdress, and Johnny, let me tell you this King was really looking like a chuff-chuff now! So the drunken soldiers commenced to beating drums and blowing bugles every which way, and marching all about the place in a big confusion, and every five seconds somebody would bawl "fire! fire!" and boodoom! all the guns would explode—because you know how the Yankees love to shoot guns!—and the King was leading this procession now from he pirogue, and trying he best not to tumble out on the ground. At last we reached to the place where the King said the treasure was, and he asked Uncle Olly for the "sacrificial funds"—and after he bowed he head a few times and danced around the place a little bit like some kind of obeah man, talking one set of nonsense about the gods of Chacachacari and such—he doused the money with pitchoil and touched he cigar to it, and that was that! Now the platoon of soldiers commenced to digging, and sure enough in no time a-tall out came the box. And sure enough when the King threw open the lid, there was the gold bars shining! Pure gold like gold, you know? Shining!

But then I saw something to take me back in one. Just there on top the pile of bricks was a single brown leaf. Right away I looked up to see if there was any tree to drop that leaf, and sure enough right overhead was a big ficus tree. But when I looked at the leaf in the box good I realized that it was a round seagrape leaf, not a narrow ficus one, and there was no seagrape tree in sight. So now I began to think!

And as fate would have it—or fortune, whichever one you choose to believe—Indra had given to me to eat that same afternoon some of the green jelly that you find in the bones of meat. She had been saving up this thing for a long time from the Officer's Club where she worked as a cook in the kitchen, because people said this jelly was very good for the lungs. But the thing about this jelly—and here is where the part about good fortune comes in—the good thing about this green jelly is that when you eat some it makes you push one set of farts, and stink stink stink!

Just like yesterday when Joe—the little Haitian boy you daddy has helping him in the garden—when Joe came running inside here bawling, "I find it, Granny! I find it!" So I asked what he found, and he told me, "The next rat." Well! I had to laugh at this thing yes, because here am I in my room only suffocating for three days now with this smell, and thinking it was me stinking so—that maybe my liver or some other organ died inside before the rest of me, and the smell was coming out through the pores of my skin—and running in the shower every five minutes to try and scrub out the stink, but all this time it was only another dead rat beneath the house. Sweet heart of Jesus!

Anyway, I was telling you about this green jelly that comes from the bones of meat. You see, in those old days people had plenty manners, and if a lady pushed a fart courtesy obliged everybody to turn around quick quick and look the other way so as not to make the lady feel ashamed. So now I realized that all I had to do was wait for the next good one to come, and when everybody turned around, to quick pick up one of the gold bricks, quick lift up the dress, and quick shove the brick between my legs like nothing had even happened. And that was just what I did! And I walked with it between the legs just so, all the way back to the Officer's Club where they carried the treasure. Of course, it was a little bit difficult walking and holding up this brick between my legs at the same time—and every now and then it would scrape a little bit against my pussy, and I had to pretend I was scratching my bamsee to fix it in a good place—but you see, in those days we used to wear plenty big skirts for me to disguise myself, and nobody wouldn't think nothing except maybe I was walking a little bit funny because I didn't wipe proper the last time, and I was suffering from a little bit of bitty-bambam.

So when we reached back to the Officer's Club now I told Uncle Olly about the leaf, and I took out the brick from beneath my dress. I said for him to go with that brick back to he laboratory straight away to test it to find out if it was gold or what. On-the-Eggs! said how he would watch over the treasure, and for me to go and wait for Uncle Olly with Indra back at the house, because the King and those soldiers and prostitutes would soon start off with one set of bacchanal just now as was they custom, and that was no place for a gentlelady like me!

Well I hadn't been with Indra long when On-the-Eggs! came running to say the King was borracho now for true, and like he'd gone crazy. He said the King was only boasting about how in Chacachacari they had more gold than they knew what to do with it, and he was so tired of looking at gold gold gold all the time it made him feel sick, and therefore he would sell a pure gold bar to anybody that gave him a thousand dollars cash-money. On-the-Eggs! said how he'd gone vie-kee-vie now for true, and we had better do something quick before he sold all the bars. So I gave On-the-Eggs! General Monagas's pistol and told him to get back to the Officer's Club fast as he could go, and don't worry about what was going on inside, only to stand by the door and make sure none of the soldiers and in particular the King didn't leave, until I could think out a plan. On-the-Eggs! said that wouldn't be no problem, because with all the money and gold flying about the place all those girls had gone wild, with every one latched onto a soldier and she ain't going to let him go before she could get she hands on some of that cash flying too.

So Indra and me started to discuss this thing now to try to decide what we would do. I said that it was no use to wait for Uncle Olly to come back from he laboratory because by then all the bars would be gone, in case that leaf did drop from some seagrape right behind me that I couldn't see the tree in the dark. Indra said yes, and that leaf could have blown from some distant tree, but anyway how were we to get back all of these gold bars?

Johnny, just then the idea struck me! So I asked Indra, because she had lived in that part of Corpus Christi all she life, if she'd ever heard of a plant that grew by the sea only in Chaguarameras, which we used to call in Spanish "trampa mosca de Venus." She said yes, she had, so I asked her why did she think they called it that, and she said of course about the mosquitos. I said yes, but why Venus? Indra answered me because that was the star that lived between Mercury and Earth, but I said not so a-tall!

You see, Venus was how they called one of those goddesses that belonged to the Greeks—the goddess of desire for sex—and that was why the real name for pussy was "la montaña de Venus." But Indra wanted to know why as always I had to mix up one story with the next to confuse everybody's head, because what the fuck did all this business about pussies have to do with eating flies? I told Indra to hold down she horses. You see, the old time legend went that the blood of this plant had magic sexual powers, and if a woman tasted even one drop, when the man went inside she pussy would clamp shut straight away—bam!—and he would never get out again, not until the sun rose the following morning. That is to say, not until the sun came up, could he go down! Indra told me she liked that idea good enough, but she didn't put no stock in oldwife's tales, and if I really believed that plant could help any pussy to hold on so wonderful? I asked Indra why did she think Barto's heart gave out so young?

So Indra and me ran to the seaside and collected up plenty of those plants, and we squeezed out the blood on all the food and cerveza, and even the channa and the plantain chips, and in no time a-tall we had the King and that entire American Army immobilized! Now me and Indra climbed the stairs to go in every one of those rooms and collect back all the bricks. But when we reached to the King's room now he didn't have no bricks left—but right there was all the money—so I counted it up good to make sure it was forty-one thousand taking out the one brick that Uncle Olly had. But Johnny, by this time I was so vex and exasperated with this King I was spitting fire! Now I went back down to the kitchen to pick out two of the biggest flowers, and I begged the whorelady permission to open up she legs a moment, and I put a flower to bite down hard on each one of those King's cojones the whole night long!

So On-the-Eggs! and Indra and me picked up all the bricks and the money and we carried them home to wait for Uncle Olly, and soon enough he arrived to say we might as well pitch all those bricks in the sea. He said that they were only bathed in a thin thin blanket of gold that even if we scraped off all the forty-two, we might not even be able to make an earring. Uncle Olly said that inside the bricks was only solid brass-metal, and that didn't have no value a-tall.

So what to do? Not a thing! Just drop down dead asleep for a good few hours until sunrise, because in truth we were all exhausted. Next morning we returned to the Base to give back that forty-one thousand to the soldiers that the King had robbed them of—because of course we couldn't keep that money that didn't belong to us—and we made sure they paid the girls after they long night of labor too. So Uncle Olly and me bid good-bye to Indra and On-the-Eggs! and we said that we have really had a good adventure there, even though we lost all that amount of money, and Uncle Olly and me climbed back in the car to drive back home again to St. Maggy.

BUT THIS story was not yet finished as you might believe. You see, Uncle Olly and me were still very tired, and not even paying much attention to the driving, when we saw a woman walking at the side of the road that looked like if she was suffering from a good case of bitty-bambam. Because every step she took she waffled from side to side swinging out the fat legs—that I decided if was not the bitties, then maybe she big thighs had rubbed up too much together to give her chafe—which is very painful and no joke because I know of a woman in Pastiche who died from that very thing! So I was thinking to tell Uncle Olly to stop for this poor woman as I felt so bad, but then again if she did have the bitties—or if she was too proud to use the bush and she was toting a load—then we didn't want her in the backseat a-tall. So I didn't say nothing to Uncle Olly, but when we reached by this woman we discovered, just as you have already suspected, that she was a he, and he was still dressed in the ceremonial gown. He'd given up the pirogue and the baboos to hold the palm leaf over he head, but sure enough he was the same old King! So I was perplexed now—and thinking maybe those flowers did bite off he cojones in truth—because why else would he be walking so peculiar like that? Then all in a sudden it dawned upon me what that ceremonial gown was all about, and why this King was walking so funny just like me. You see, in the middle of all that confusion last night to take out the treasure, the King had switched the good money for Uncle Olly's fluke money, and he hid it quick beneath the dress. It was Uncle Olly's fluke money then that the King had burned up for that sacrifice!

So I shouted out quick for Uncle Olly to stop the car, and in no time a-tall I had General Monagas's pearlhandled pistol shoved up against the King's cojones! I told him if he didn't hand it over straight away, I would blow them so fucking far apart that one would land by St. James and the next by Sangre Grande. Well! I have never met a man yet—not even a little fatty King—that didn't value he cojones above everything else in the world. And of course as soon as he reached between he legs to hand it over he could walk or skip or dance or whatever he wanted, but what he did instead was to grab onto those cojones like if they were gold, and he ran for the bush as fast as he little fatty feet could carry him!

Well then, now at last we have reached we happy ending. You see, the prostitutes finished happy because they discovered the secret of that plant, and it has made Chaguarameras the most popular place in the whole of Corpus Christi to this very day. Indra and On-the-Eggs! ended up happy because the Sergeant was so pleased to get back he thousand dollars that he finally permitted On-the-Eggs! to join the American Army. And if you look up in you history book you will see how On-the-Eggs! became a famous American soldier, many times decorated, and that says something good for the Yankees! Of course, Uncle Olly got back he five thousand dollars, but he also got he machine to which he dedicated the science of the rest of he life. And even though he never did decipher the language, he machine brought him very much happiness in the end. And as you know youself, Uncle Reggie, and Rodolfo, and Barnabas, and Uncle Simon have all reached Canada. And just when I was about to run out of money that old Lawyer for the Crown appeared with twenty-eight more thousand dollars for Chaguarameras, and so it happened that Uncle Josè, and Uncle Paco, and you daddy reached Canada too. And they are all eight of them very famous doctors today—even Uncle Amadao, who is the famous doctor of chickens with that big chicken-hospital in Arima—so I think that even Barto got he wish.

As for me now, I have my story. You see Johnny, what I didn't know then, but I know now, is that I was born to have children instead of money. Papa God gave me money, and he took it away just as quick, but he always makes sure I have plenty of children around me to hear my stories. And that is the other thing Papa God gave me, that maybe you have a little bit of it youself? This love for telling stories. Because Johnny, it is something to give you pleasure and good company all you life, and it can bring you very much happiness in the end.

Magic is when the impossible is made manifest. In Sparrow Town, peacock's tongues and marshmallows are equally rare delicacies; women and men lead practically separate lives, and the most certain bewitchment people encounter comes to them via the cinema screen. Someone who can create a poignant dream of solace for one night, even for only half of the community, is a sorcerer indeed.

Pot O' Rice Horowitz's House of Solace

IAN MCDONALD

Pot O' Rice Horowitz was a ideal grocer. He was accustom to have a snap of rum under the pitch-pine counter for customers, twelve cents for the snap. He didn't bother about liquor law license and that kind of Government botheration. He serve up the snaps in green eye glass and that was that. And he had well-stock shelf, you could never go there and say Pot O' Rice was out of cooking oil or lard or the good old saltfish or opium candy. And he didn't put too much fine fine white sand in the white flour or fix up his scales to show three pound when it only have two and seven-tenth all the time. Horowitz's Grocery Emporium had reputation for honesty and fair dealing. You couldn't make nasty jokes about that.

Too besides Pot O' Rice have a daughter he could lend customers for the night, to take to pictures at the Roxy in pit and bounce a little arse afterward. The daughter look old to be his daughter, because Pot O' Rice was not a old-looking test, only his eye look a bit old and hard, but nobody bothering about that to tell the truth. Pot O' Rice say is his daughter, well matter fix. Book up two pit at Roxy and let's get going. It is John Wayne shooting up Sante Fe, and afterward the daughter prepared to pull down she blood-red panty, and you could fix up a little business with she one time.

So you must expect the people in Sparrow Town accept Pot O' Rice as a good thing in their midst. He was a real mystery. No one know where he come from. One day he arrive fresh as a fart in Sparrow Town and set up a sweet drink stall and begin to disperse Pepsi and 7-Up and Puma power and Cokes-of-course. Then in quick time he seem to build up a big capital and Horowitz's Grocery Emporium was going up on the main street, like an American skyscraper only it only have one story high. Everybody talking about the Emporium.

"Oh Gawd! I never see grocery so. You see Ramlall saltfish shop behind Goatman Cemetry, that was the biggest thing outside George-town and now it beginning to look like a bad-shape piss-pot. Pot O' Rice, he selling peacock tongue and marshmallow when he open up!"

"Eh heh! When that man come to town money stick on he hand like laglie. Now look at that sweet big building, chile! A Governor come to town in truth."

A lot of other people begin to talk about him like he was a Fats Waller and the Kabaka combine, from the time he begin to make his mark. It was like he was a hero in their midst.

People talk a lot about the name. Horowitz puzzle them up for so. He get call Pot O' Rice by a coolie Indian passing by one day, a big professional beggar with gold ring like chupidness on every finger, and the name stick. But Horowitz puzzle them up. Anyhow it was a big name, and the people like to put their tongue around it like it was a lollipop or a piece of coconut cake.

One day Pot O' Rice put on a smooth silk blue suit and took his arse down the road in a white man taxi, down to Georgetown, proud capital of the old Guyana. Pot O' Rice customer feel for sure that he was going to stock up salt beef and flour and biscuit and all kind of ham and sweet and thing for the Emporium. But all the time he was only going to buy mahogany wood furniture and red red curtain in Kirpalani's to start up a whorehouse going, full up with brazen big-bust gold tooth belching hard-face woman! It was a hell of a thing!

This business didn't get find out right away you know. To tell the truth people in Sparrow Town feel it was only Pot O' Rice putting up a funeral parlor and making nice mahogany coffin for the dead so he could make a whole heap more money and surprise the world with his rich kingdom. And you know how it is. The people didn't mind a funeral parlor going up in their midst atall. Death is always with us you know. They was proud in fact. Pride and satisfaction light up the old people faces in Sparrow Town. You can imagine that! Sparrow Town poor people getting to enter the heavenly abode in style. Pot O' Rice going to fix them up with lacquer coffin and black ribbon and big ceremony to beat the band. Some of the old boys down the road near the dry river bridge when they get together to have an old talk about the quality of rum and the old-time cricket matches and how calypso really should play and how women really sweet in their young days, some of these same crab-foot smoke-stain old cabos even get together one day and drink a rum toast to Pot O' Rice for providing them with a big hope of glory in Sparrow Town funeral life. They get together and drink rum and celebrate like hell and get drunk as arse and fall down bap in four ditches. And all because they going to heaven in mahogany style. Foolish drunk old men! Life is a hell of a thing. The next thing you know they would want to mount the golden steps with their balls tie up in black ribbon and their heads tall with crowns.

So all this talk and glory going on and Pot O' Rice silent as hell and putting up his big new building just near the Emporium. And all the time it was a whorehouse! Scandal in the town. The building going up and everyone watching as if it was Neil Armstrong going up in space. Nice old ladies coming to watch what going on and glad to see Pot O' Rice providing so well for their deaths in Sparrow Town. Old men coming to praise God even in front the new building. Pot O' Rice still selling rice and saltfish and penny candle from his Emporium and every now and then coming to the door and smiling at all the big attraction in the road. You know how many people dipping a bow to him and praising his saltfish extra special! Nearly everyone please. Pot O' Rice please. The old ladies please. The old cabos drinking rum and old-talking by the dry river please. Only the young men not so please. They living slack as hell, nothing to do all day except carve flute and exercise their muscle and talk about fixing up women. And they seeing Pot O' Rice making a lot of money and look now he coming up with something else again, but no joy in that because the young bucks feeling the fire in their groin surely not thinking of death and mounting the golden steps. And the girls in Sparrow Town not so please either. Because you know how it is. The girls thinking of fineries and fashion show and film star and the bright lights and how to arrange their bust line big enough to attract the boys. So of course they not bothering about death atall, and Pot O' Rice new-building didn't make a note with them.

Well, one day the place ready for occupation, paint up all in white and gold and heavy green cord hanging up the curtain in the windows. The workmen finish with the place and Pot O' Rice was a proud man. The sky was shining blue and everything fix up nice.

Then big sensation. Pot O' Rice get ready to install the whores. Everybody looking to see the first white coffins come to the door and what happen? A big gold-color bus drive up like a chariot, full up with wabeen. At first it is a big shock to the waiting citizens of Sparrow Town. They seeing all these fat and thin wabeen dress up in stylish dress material straight from shop in Water Street and fix up with gold earring like the stars in the sky and they wondering what the hell happening. Everybody seeing wabeen descending on high hell like Princess Margaret or Dame Hilda Bynoe or somebody at a big parade. Except the wabeen laughing and waving and kissing hand and waving bottom as they descend. Pot O' Rice in all his glory by now! The wabeen really parading bottom as if it was watermelon at a fair. Well, the old people shock and the young people surprise and whisper going around that all is not what it had seem to be once upon a time. Still, everyone ready and willing to make a serious face and suggest that Pot O' Rice doing fine to get so many well-dress attendant for the funeral parlor. The old women standing around like old fowls not so sure about this explanation, but in general everyone begin to believe that something like that is the true story. They begin to say it is the modern way, that this is the latest business from America, that Pot O' Rice is smartness self to fix up the Sparrow Town parlor like it was in Chicago or the old New York. Their head nodding up and down and they saying yes that is how it is, the world changing fast, look at all those student behaving bad at the University, you must expect this modern business, Sparrow Town got to change with the times.

A couple days pass. Pot O' Rice still putting the finishing touches to the funeral parlor. You could hear hammering in the building and a house painter call Mohammed come to paint design on the walls of the parlor. Cool designs, man. Peacocks and palaces and bright moons and a test under a set of green trees with his feet cock up and playing the old flute dreamy-eye as hell. People have to wonder what funeral got to do with this, but nobody talking now, they only puzzling their heads and waiting to see what is what. A couple of the boys standing up outside praising Mohammed's design. "Oh God, man, that is good. That is art, boy. That is the old art." And Mohammed please as hell you could bet because he have a big desire to paint imprison in the heart like a sharp knife blade, and it only because it is Sparrow Town and he have a wife and six kids already and he is a sober man supporting them that he can't let the desire go like a hot piss and deluge the whole world with all the fire and the hot beauty and the rage of all the paintings lock up in the soul inside him and can't get out.

Mohammed paint a sign too, in gold letters all surround with wreath and stars and moon and thing. "Horowitz's House of Solace." It look good. It really look fine. Mohammed really excel heself. Discreet as hell but brave too, you know how. It bound to make an impression. "Horowitz's House of Solace." The citizens of Sparrow Town glad to have a brain who could think of a sweet name like that. "Horowitz's House of Solace." Oh God, man! Solace was bound to be the right word. It really sweep Sparrow Town like a storm. Everybody saying what a exact royal word. Because of that word all the old people not so frighten to die anymore. In fact, to tell the truth, a few old people get a little pleasure in their hearts and begin to get thinking about how sweet death going to be in Sparrow Town now they definitely have Pot O' Rice Horowitz's House of Solace just up the road. It true no man in he guts really like to dead don't mind how brown things might be. But if the setting is right, man, then at least the old people heavy like a stone with despair feeling a little music drowning out the terrible black eternal summons.

Well, now Pot O' Rice begin to put the idea of the whorehouse in people's mind. He begin to get the word going very judicious and discreet. A man come in the Emporium to buy a half pound of salt and Pot O' Rice find a way to tell him about the fleshly comforts of the House of Solace. "Not only my daughter in town you know man," he saying with a little little smile.

One or two young men with a bit of change in their pocket he tell straight out. "Funeral parlor balls, man! I opening next week with a big freeness. Free tail for so." So the word begin to spread fast around Sparrow Town. The young men laughing for joy. The old men not so sure but they beginning to get a little of the old rage in the groin, you know how. The young women pretending they don't know even what a whorehouse is and holding their face stiff as ice. Oh God! The old women vex as hell. No funeral parlor for them! A whorehouse in the middle of Sparrow Town! Mind you, they setting a little boy because they mostly like to suck scandal like a sweet, like a paradise plum, and this is the biggest scandal yet. But anyhow the old women vex as hell, their face sour like Essequibo lime, and already they deciding not to buy flour and salt and oil and curry powder from the old Emporium where they always bought before. Yes, man, they know about boycott. They read newspaper and they hear BBC World Service and they know what to do, so boycott in the old women mind like Pot O' Rice was a nasty thing like Rhodesia or the old Vietnam War.

On the other side Pot O' Rice giving everybody the argument that the House bound to benefit Sparrow Town economically. You know how that is the big word in these modern days. Economic development reigns supreme. People can't stop hearing the Kabaka say how economic development is the aim. And the UN full up with serious-face diplomat saying the same thing. They rich and fat and dress up nice you know but they groaning how the people downtrodden and poor and starving and how the thing must be economic development to save the world. They really meaning save their own sweet skin, but you know how it is, they saying save the world because that really sound better. And the old President Nixon and the old Mao, though they fighting and butting up like hell, every day talking about economic development. So Pot O' Rice keeping up with the times as usual, and he only giving them the serious talk about how the House bound to attract people from near and far, money pouring in like water, Sparrow Town getting big like Georgetown. Pot O' Rice saying how tourist must came to Sparrow Town in the days to come. He make a big thing about how Sparrow Town going build up like a big industrial center. And all the time all what is happening is Pot O' Rice bold as hell opening up a whorehouse! But you know how it is. All the men eye shining bright and they nodding their head up and down seriously, seriously and saying "That is the truth, man, economic development bound to come," as if the last thing in the world they thinking about is the sweet little piece of arse they going to be able to line up in the future!

The women in Sparrow Town not saying a word. Their face sour as lime, but they not saying a word. But they laying their plans like generals and only waiting until opening day dawn. Big trouble coming like fire in the forest!

So man, opening day arrive! Freeness for so! Pot O' Rice in all his glory opening Sparrow Town's House of Solace. That day could make history. If they going write a big book about Guyana history, even about the whole West Indies, I sure they must put in about the time the House of Solace open in Sparrow Town.

Flags flying on the House from early morning. Pot O' Rice walking about in town all day dress up in black pants and silk shirt and smart tie and shining shoe. The brazen-face woman sitting on the windowsill all day long smiling big golden-teeth smile and drinking cold Banks out the bottle. Sparrow Town tense as hell. Family quarrel going on loud as bulls behind every door. Man saying how it is their civic duty to attend the big opening. "Economic development, economic development!" The women behaving bad and making a lot of noise and threat. The young girl faces stiff like ice. Big drama in Sparrow Town!

When night falling and the moon coming out like a silver fruit the fun really begin to begin. Music start up in the House like a golden fire. Lights blazing too in all kind of color. The sweet smell of cooking coming cut on the air like a blessing. The men of Sparrow Town start to walk over for the fete. They walking like their leg and back stiff in all their Church clothes fine as kings. They walking and looking straight ahead with stiff necks and going in the door quick as they can out of sight. Pot O' Rice at the door smiling a thousand smile and shaking every man hand with his two hand. Man, Pot O' Rice look like the Kabaka receiving guest!

"Dancing open and the girls ready! Free drinks on the House tonight! Eat later, one and all!"

The brazen-face woman standing up in a slinky red dress with a lot of slit up the leg like the World of Suzie Wong and fluttering up their eye and offering shots of rum among other things. They not looking like funeral parlor attendant atall to tell the truth. Pot O' Rice daughter looking sour and out of place because now everybody examining the new talent.

The dancing start up and the men of Sparrow Town soon in the mood. Not only the young tests with their fancy steps you know. The old men who done see so many sad suns go down in their time, they going to town too, holding Pot O' Rice whores a bit far away at first but that not to say the blood not beginning to rise a little, you know how.

Nobody ever see such a fete! The old XM and Russian Bear and El Dorado flowing like Potaro River Valley water. Hardly any time pass and everybody dancing. Everybody drinking and the excitement getting hot. Pot O' Rice walking about everywhere full of smile and shake-hand. He taking a little dance here and a little dance there and a small shot here and a small shot there and in general playing it cool like he was Rex Harrison. Every two minute he taking a trip to the kitchen to make a check if the cooking going well. And Pot O' Rice begin to play a little trick. He have a master light switch and he going over all the time and giving it a little flick and bam the whole place in darkness! Confusion and jubilation! Everyone get the idea fast and a lot of feeling up begin. The whores screaming shrill as whistles and all the men of Sparrow Town having a royal time! Noise really beginning in the place. Noise like Carnival in Trinidad. Joy like the world fill with glory. Sweetness like everybody forget his own dirty problems. A old man call Flash Gordon fall down drunk and get up again twenty time in a hour. A young test call Jeffrey so happy he begin to sing "God save the Queen," nobody know why. Everybody feeling so sweet and happy and the drinks flowing and the hot music playing and the whores beginning to look really good and all the food still to come.

But you had to expect that the sweetness must end soon because you know how life is. What happen is that the women of Sparrow Town decide they can't take the offense any more. The noise and the revelry and the bareface laughing in the House so loud it sticking in the guts more and more every hour.

Action stations! Some had already paint up sign saying "Down with Pot O' Rice" and "Go Home Imperialist Whores" because you know how picketing and protest march is another big thing nowadays and don't think the citizens of Sparrow Town not up-to-date because they up-to-date all right from reading the *Graphic* and the *Evening Post* very regular. So they make up a few more sign quick and, man, the big march start on the House as if it was the American Embassy. The middle of the night and the street full up with women, old and young! The march have to go down in history.

Pot O' Rice just that minute call for quiet because he want to make a toast and open the House very official, you know how. He have champagne and all to pour out in sharp Bookers Store glassware. Oh God! You know the next thing that happen is a lot of women only battering up on the big door and really behaving wild-arse and bad like a host of Jezebels come to town! The middle of the night too, and not one soul asleep in Sparrow Town! The middle of the night in respectable Sparrow Town and everyone in the action one way or another, except one old lady who suddenly believe the end of the world come and she faint away, so no action for she. Pot O' Rice have a grave face. The door can't stand up atall. The door burst open so quick and sudden three old men don't have time even to take out their hands from certain embarrassing situations, you know how.

Confusion general! Montgomery of Alamein and Jomo Kenyatta combine together couldn't keep peace in that place, man. Men falling down to get away. Women fighting up and down, whores against housewives you could say. Women beating men. Rum spilling and bottles breaking. Screaming like it was Sonny Liston fighting the old Cassius and everyone going wild. Bacchanal and Congo Civil War combine! History in the making in Sparrow Town. Pot O' Rice trying to keep cool like Rex Harrison, but he not feeling so good. He shouting "Peace and Brotherhood!" loud loud all over the place to no avail and "Food Serve!" and turning up the music loud, but nothing doing. He only getting blow like everybody else and his dignity hurt like the people pee in a Parliament. The fight extending upstairs and furniture beginning to break up all about. Flash Gordon falling down much more times now on account of the fact his wife beating him on the head with a bread-board.

The women of Sparrow Town running wild. A respectable woman name Laura Emerson, fine as a piece of string, making it she aim in life to rip down all Pot O' Rice nice red curtain. She running about ripping cloth like madness. And licks sharing all about. A old woman name Rachel Lucky running behind Pot O' Rice with a placard mark "Disgrace in Sparrow Town." No passive resistance for them atall. Man, Mahatma Gandhi could never have live. Rex Harrison or no Rex Harrison, Pot O' Rice gone.

I have to tell you it only end when Pot O' Rice heself summon the police from quite by Mahaica. It look like the whole G.D.F. platoon have to come to quell the bad behavior. Man, it could have been revolt in the old Rupununi. It a wonder tear gas didn't have to use. Anyhow, everyone get their behind take in custody, and the old House of Solace looking like Cheddie hold a riot in it when the cold dawn come to Sparrow Town.

So Pot O' Rice have to admit defeat. The whores pick up and go back down Main Street in Georgetown, proud capital of the old Guyana. And all the men only saying how economic development have to wait for a little bit, Sparrow Town not ready for it yet.

Every man jack in Sparrow Town get haul up in court. They bring a big magistrate from Georgetown and he hand out fine like fire. It bound to be another red letter day in the history of Sparrow Town. The citizens looking doleful and embarrass but they take their licks good—especially because Pot O' Rice paying every one of the fines in town. The big magistrate get a chance to say a lot of nice big words about public order and how the decency of the community have to be upheld and thing like that. The only thing was while he speaking like a lord a fat old woman let out a sweet loud fart direct in the room. The old woman looking all about as if she surprise, and you can imagine how everybody laughing like they going to pass out. The big magistrate vex as hell, but what he could do? The old lady make a mistake. Anyhow, he fix up the citizens with fine and get in his big limousine and go on his way thinking in his head all the time about his standing in the community and how another duty well done and how all going smooth on the way to the top. And the citizens of Sparrow Town go out in the fresh air and feel the good hot sun and the bright day and they is all free men again.

Well, one week after it all over, after all the bacchanal and confusion done, I have to tell you everything back to normal in Sparrow Town. It surprising as hell but it a fact. Everything quiet, quiet. People walking in the street saying small hellos like nothing ever happen. The old men drinking their rums end old-talking by the dry river once more. The young men slacking and liming and carving flute and playing cricket again. The old women groaning and cooking and minding house like nothing happen. The young women same again and they not mentioning a word about the recent competition in town.

Too besides Pot O' Rice Horowitz doing normal business. The Emporium open and everybody buying their supplies like before. Pot O' Rice not looking embarrass atall. He passing the time of day with the old women and his face shining with smiles for all the citizens. Business good for him. In fact the Emporium more popular than ever. He still have his daughter ready for action any old time. You know how it is. What done, done. Cool breeze. That is life, boy. The drama was like Cleopatra and Goldfinger combine together, but it over now and it could be a dream to think about what happen in Sparrow Town when Pot O' Rice Horowitz decide to open a whorehouse.

down inside the chute

The branches of memory are buttressed by roots. Tradition has it that duppies (spirits) reside in the cotton tree roots. Older people with longer memories might be more precise—the spirits of our ancestors are supposed to inhabit those roots, and under the right circumstances they will talk to us from the base of the cotton tree. Those whispers of invisible truths can be a good thing or a frightening thing, but always a powerful, transformative experience. The late master calypsonian Lord Kitchener had a song about walking through a graveyard at night, tripping on a bamboo root, and falling "down inside a chute," where the spirits of the dead buried in the earth tried to get at him.

Your buried ghosts have a way of tripping you up.

I would not have included a story of my own in this anthology, except that the publisher urged me to do so and a number of other experienced anthologists felt that given the relatively small pool of Caribbean authors who make a point of writing fantastical fiction, it would be a mistake not to include some of my own work.

The seed story of "The Glass Bottle Trick" may be a familiar one to many. My take on it is a hybrid story set in a region of the world that has survived through the hybridization of many cultures. Eggs are seeds, perfectly white on the outside. Who knows what complexions their insides might reveal when they crack open to germinate and bear fruit?

The Glass Bottle Trick

NALO HOPKINSON

T HE AIR WAS full of storms, but they refused to break. In the wicker rocking chair on the front veranda, Beatrice flexed her bare feet against the wooden slat floor, rocking slowly back and forth. Another sweltering rainy season afternoon. The arid heat felt as though all the oxygen had boiled out of the parched air to hang as looming rainclouds, waiting.

Oh, but she loved it like this. The hotter the day, the slower she would move, basking. She stretched her arms and legs out to better feel the luxuriant warmth, then guiltily sat up straight again. Samuel would scold if he ever saw her slouching like that. Stuffy Sammy. She smiled fondly, admiring the lacy patterns the sunlight threw on the floor as it filtered through the white gingerbread fretwork that trimmed the roof of their house.

"Anything more today, Mistress Powell? I finish doing the dishes." Gloria had come out of the house and was standing in front of her, wiping her chapped hands on her apron.

Beatrice felt the shyness come over her as it always did when she thought of giving the older woman orders. Gloria was older than

Beatrice's mother. "Ah . . . no, I think that's everything, Gloria. . . ."

Gloria quirked an eyebrow, crinkling her face like running a fork through molasses. "Then I go take the rest of the afternoon off. You and Mister Samuel should be alone tonight. Is time you tell him."

Beatrice gave an abortive, shamefaced "huh" of a laugh. Gloria had known from the start, she'd had so many babies of her own. She'd been mad to run to Samuel with the news from since. But Beatrice had already decided to tell Samuel. Well, almost decided. She felt irritated, like a child whose tricks have been found out. She swallowed the feeling. "I think you right, Gloria," she said, fighting for some dignity before the older woman. "Maybe . . . maybe I cook him a special meal, feed him up nice, then tell him."

"Well I say is time and past time you make him know. A picknie is a blessing to a family."

"For true," Beatrice agreed, making her voice sound as certain as she could.

"Later then, Mistress Powell." Giving herself the afternoon off, not even a by-your-leave. Gloria headed off to the maid's room at the back of the house to change into her street clothes. A few minutes later, she let herself out the garden gate.

"That seems like a tough book for a young lady of such tender years."

"Excuse me?" Beatrice threw a defensive cutting glare at the older man. He'd caught her off guard, though she'd seen his eyes following her ever since she entered the bookstore. "You have something to say to me?" She curled the Gray's Anatomy *possessively into the crook of her arm, price sticker hidden against her body. Two more months of saving before she could afford it.*

He looked shyly at her. "Sorry if I offended, Miss," he said. "My name is Samuel."

Would be handsome, if he'd chill out a bit. Beatrice's wariness thawed a little. Middle of the sun-hot day, and he wearing black wool jacket and pants. His crisp white cotton shirt was buttoned right up, held in place by a tasteful, unimaginative tie. So proper, Jesus. He wasn't that much older than she.

"Is just . . . you're so pretty, and it's the only thing I could think of to say to get you to speak to me."

Beatrice softened more at that, smiled for him, and played with the collar of her blouse. He didn't seem too bad, if you could look beyond the stocious behaviour.

Beatrice doubtfully patted the slight swelling of her belly. Four months. She was shy to give Samuel her news, but she was starting to show. Silly to put it off, yes? Today she was going to make her husband very happy, break that thin shell of mourning that still insulated him from her. He never said so, but Beatrice knew that he still thought of the wife he'd lost, and tragically, the one before that. She wished she could make him warm up to life again.

Sunlight was flickering through the leaves of the guava tree in the front yard. Beatrice inhaled the sweet smell of the sun-warmed fruit. The tree's branches hung heavy with the pale yellow globes, smooth and round as eggs. The sun reflected off the two blue bottles suspended in the tree, sending cobalt light dancing through the leaves.

When Beatrice first came to Sammy's house, she'd been puzzled by the two bottles that were jammed onto branches of the guava tree.

"Is just my superstitiousness, darling," he'd told her. "You never heard the old people say that if someone dies, you must put a bottle in a tree to hold their spirit, otherwise it will come back as a duppie and haunt you? A blue bottle. To keep the duppie cool, so it won't come at you in hot anger for being dead."

Beatrice had heard something of the sort, but it was strange to think of her Sammy as a superstitious man. He was too controlled and logical for that. *Well, grief make somebody act in strange ways.* Maybe the bottles gave him some comfort, made him feel that he'd kept some essence of his poor wives near him.

"That Samuel is nice. Respectable, hard-working. Not like all them other ragamuffins you always going out with." Mummy picked up the butcher knife and began expertly slicing the goat meat into cubes for the curry.

Beatrice watched the red lumps of flesh part under the knife. Crimson liquid leaked onto the cutting board. She sighed, "But, Mummy, Samuel so boring! Michael and Clifton know how to have fun. All Samuel want to do is go for country drives. Always taking me away from other people."

"You should be studying your books, not having fun," her mother replied crossly.

Beatrice pleaded, "You well know I could do both, Mummy." Her mother just grunted.

Is only truth Beatrice was talking. Plenty men were always courting her, they flocked to her like birds, eager to take her dancing or out for a drink. But somehow she kept her marks up, even though it often meant studying right through the night, her head pounding and belly queasy from hangover while some man snored in the bed beside her. Mummy would kill her if she didn't get straight As for medical school. "You going have to look after yourself, Beatrice. Man not going do it for you. Them get their little piece of sweetness and then them bruk away."

"Two patty and a King Cola, please." The guy who'd given the order had a broad chest that tapered to a slim waist. Good face to look at, too. Beatrice smiled sweetly at him, made shift to gently brush his palm with her fingertips as she handed him the change.

A bird screeched from the guava tree; a tiny kiskedee, crying angrily, "Dit, dit, qu'est-ce qu'il dit!" A small snake was coiled around one of the upper branches, just withdrawing its head from the bird's nest. Its jaws were distended with the egg it had stolen. It swallowed the egg whole, throat bulging hugely with its meal. The bird hovered around the snake's head, giving its pitiful wail of, "Say, say, what's he saying!"

"Get away!" Beatrice shouted at the snake. It looked in the direction of the sound, but didn't back off. The gulping motion of its body as it forced the egg further down its own throat made Beatrice shudder. Then, oblivious to the fluttering of the parent bird, it arched its head over the nest again. Beatrice pushed herself to her feet and ran into the yard. "Hsst! Shoo! Come away from there!" But the snake took a second egg.

Sammy kept a long pole with a hook at one end leaned against the guava tree for pulling down the fruit. Beatrice grabbed up the pole, started jooking it at the branches as close to the bird and nest as she dared. "Leave them, you brute! Leave!" The pole connected with some of the boughs. The two bottles in the tree fell to the ground and shattered with a crash. A hot breeze sprang up. The snake slithered away quickly, two eggs bulging in its throat. The bird flew off, sobbing to itself.

Nothing she could do now. When Samuel came home, he would hunt down the nasty snake for her and kill it. She leaned the pole back against the tree.

The light breeze should have brought some coolness, but really it only made the day warmer. Two little dust devils danced briefly around Beatrice. They swirled across the yard, swung up into the air, and dashed themselves to powder against the shuttered window of the third bedroom.

Beatrice got her sandals from the veranda. Sammy wouldn't like it if she stepped on broken glass. She picked up the broom that was leaned against the house and began to sweep up the shards of bottle. She hoped Samuel wouldn't be too angry with her. He wasn't a man to cross, could be as stern as a father if he had a mind to.

That was mostly what she remembered about Daddy, his temper— quick to show and just as quick to go. So was he; had left his family before Beatrice turned five. The one cherished memory she had of him was of being swung back and forth through the air, her two small hands clasped in one big hand of his, her feet held tight in another. Safe. And as he swung her through the air, her Daddy had been chanting words from an old-time story:

> Yung-Kyung-Pyung, what a pretty basket!
> Margaret Powell Alone, what a pretty basket!
> Eggie-law, what a pretty basket!

Then he had held her tight to his chest, forcing the air from her lungs in a breathless giggle. The dressing down Mummy had given him for that game! "You want to drop the child and crack her head open on the hard ground? Ee? Why you can't be more responsible?"

"Responsible?" he'd snapped. "Is who working like dog sunup to sundown to put food in oonuh belly?" He'd set Beatrice down, her feet hitting the ground with a jar. She'd started to cry, but he'd just pushed her toward her mother and stormed out of the room. One more volley in the constant battle between them. After he'd left them Mummy had opened the little food shop in town to make ends meet. In the evenings, Beatrice would rub lotion into her mother's chapped, work-wrinkled hands. "See how that man make us come down in the world?" Mummy would grumble. "Look at what I come to."

Privately, Beatrice thought that maybe all Daddy had needed was a little patience. Mummy was too harsh, much as she loved her. To please her, she had studied hard all through high school: physics, chemistry, biology, describing the results of her lab experiments in her copy book in her cramped, resigned handwriting. Her mother greeted every "A" with a noncommittal grunt and anything less with a lecture. Beatrice would smile airily, seal the hurt away, pretend the approval meant nothing to her. She still worked hard, but she kept some time for play of her own. Rounders, netball, and later, boys. All those boys, wanting a chance for a little sweetness with a light-skin browning like her. Beatrice had discovered her appeal quickly.

"Leggo beast . . ." Loose woman. *The hissed words came from a knot of girls that slouched past Beatrice as she sat on the library steps, waiting for Clifton to come and pick her up. She willed her ears shut, smothered the sting of the words. But she knew some of them. Marguerita, Deborah. They used to be friends of hers. Though she sat up proudly, she found her fingers tugging self-consciously at the hem of her short white skirt. She put the big physics textbook in her lap, where it gave her thighs a little more coverage.*

The farting vroom of Clifton's motorcycle interrupted her thoughts. Grinning, he slewed the bike to a dramatic halt in front of her. "Study time done now, darling. Time to play."

He looked good this evening, as he always did. Tight white shirt, jeans that showed off the bulges of his thighs. The crinkle of the thin gold chain at his neck set off his dark brown skin. Beatrice stood; tucked the physics text under her arm; smoothed the skirt over her hips. Clifton's eyes followed the movement of her hands. See, it didn't take much to make people treat you nice. She smiled at him.

Samuel would still show up hopefully every so often to ask her to accompany him on a drive through the country. He was so much older than all her other suitors. And dry? Country drives; Lord! She went out with him a few times; he was so persistent and she couldn't figure out how to tell him no. He didn't seem to get her hints that really she should be studying. Truth to tell though, she started to find his quiet, undemanding presence soothing. His eggshell-white BMW took the graveled country roads so quietly that she could hear the kiskadee birds in the mango trees, chanting their query: "Dit, dit, qu'est-ce qu'il dit?"

One day, Samuel brought her a gift.

"These are for you and your family," he said shyly, handing her a wrinkled paper bag. "I know your mother likes them." Inside were three plump eggplants from his kitchen garden, raised by his own hands. Beatrice took the humble gift out of the bag. The skins of the eggplants had a taut, blue sheen to them. Later she would realize that that was when she'd begun to love Samuel. He was stable, solid, responsible. He would make Mummy and her happy.

Beatrice gave in more to Samuel's diffident wooing. He was cultured and well-spoken. He had been abroad, talked of exotic sports: ice hockey; downhill skiing. He took her to fancy restaurants she'd only heard of, that her other young, unestablished boyfriends would never have been able to afford, and would probably only have embarrassed her if they had taken her. Samuel had polish. But he was humble too, like the way he grew his own vegetables, or the self-deprecating tone in which he spoke of himself. He was always punctual, always courteous to her and her mother. Beatrice could count on him for little things, like picking her up after class, or driving her mother to the hairdresser's. With the other men, she always had to be on guard: pouting until they took her somewhere else for dinner, not another free meal in her mother's restaurant; wheedling them into using the condoms. She always had to hold something of herself shut away. With Samuel, Beatrice relaxed into trust.

"Beatrice, come! Come quick, nuh!"

Beatrice ran in from the backyard at the sound of her mother's voice. Had something happened to Mummy?

Her mother was sitting at the kitchen table, knife still poised to crack an egg into the bowl for the pound cake she was making to take to the shop. She was staring in openmouthed delight at Samuel, who was fretfully twisting the long stems on a bouquet of blood-red roses. "Lord, Beatrice; Samuel say he want to marry you!"

Beatrice looked to Sammy for verification. "Samuel," she asked unbelievingly, "what you saying? Is true?"

He nodded yes. "True, Beatrice."

Something gave way in Beatrice's chest, gently as a long-held breath. Her heart had been trapped in glass, and he'd freed it.

They'd been married two months later. Mummy was retired now; Samuel had bought her a little house in the suburbs, and he paid for the maid to come in three times a week. In the excitement of planning for the wedding, Beatrice had let her studying slip. To her dismay she finished her final year of university with barely a "C" average.

"Never mind, sweetness," Samuel told her. "I didn't like the idea of you studying, anyway. Is for children. You're a big woman now." Mummy had agreed with him too, said she didn't need all that now. She tried to argue with them, but Samuel was very clear about his wishes, and she'd stopped, not wanting anything to cause friction between them just yet. Despite his genteel manner, Samuel had just a bit of a temper. No point in crossing him, it took so little to make him happy, and he was her love, the one man she'd found in whom she could have faith.

Too besides, she was learning how to be the lady of the house, try-ing to use the right mix of authority and jocularity with Gloria the maid and Cleitis, the yardboy who came twice a month to do the mow-ing and the weeding. Odd to be giving orders to people when she was used to being the one taking orders, in Mummy's shop. It made her feel uncomfortable to tell people to do her work for her. Mummy said she should get used to it, it was her right now.

The sky rumbled with thunder. Still no rain. The warmth of the day was nice, but you could have too much of a good thing. Beatrice opened her mouth, gasping a little, trying to pull more air into her lungs. She was a little short of breath nowadays as the baby pressed on her diaphragm. She knew she could go inside for relief from the heat, but Samuel kept the air-conditioning on high, so cold that they could keep the butter in its dish on the kitchen counter. It never went rancid. Even insects refused to come inside. Sometimes Beatrice felt as though the house was really somewhere else, not the tropics. She had been used to waging constant war against ants and cockroaches, but not in Samuel's house. The cold in it made Beatrice shiver, dried her eyes out until they felt like boiled eggs sitting in their sockets. She went outside as often as possible, even though Samuel didn't like her to spend too much time in the sun. He said he feared that cancer would mar her soft skin, that he didn't want to lose another wife. But Beatrice knew he just didn't want her to get too brown. When the sun touched her, it brought out the sepia and cinnamon in her blood, overpowered the milk and honey, and he could no longer pretend she was white. He loved her skin pale. "Look how you gleam in the moonlight," he'd say to her when he made gentle, almost supplicating love to her at night in the four-poster bed. His hand would slide over her flesh, cup her breasts with an air of reverence. The look in his eyes was so close to worship that it sometimes frightened her. To be loved so much! He would whisper in her ear, "Beauty. Pale Beauty, to my Beast," then blow a cool breath over the delicate membranes of her ear, making her shiver in delight. For her part, she loved to look at him, his molasses-dark skin, his broad chest, the way the planes of flat muscle slid across it. She imagined tectonic plates shifting in the earth. She loved the bluish-black cast the moonlight lent him. Once, gazing up at him as he loomed above her, body working against and in hers, she had seen the moonlight playing glints of deepest blue in his trim beard.

"Black Beauty," she had joked softly, reaching to pull his face closer for a kiss. At the words, he had lurched up off her to sit on the edge of the bed, pulling a sheet over him to hide his nakedness. Beatrice watched him, confused, feeling their blended sweat cooling along her body.

"Never call me that, please, Beatrice," he said softly. "You don't have to draw attention to my color. I'm not a handsome man, and I know it. Black and ugly as my mother made me."

"But Samuel . . . !"

"No."

Shadows lay between them on the bed. He wouldn't touch her again that night.

Beatrice sometimes wondered why Samuel hadn't married a white woman. He could have met someone while he was studying abroad. She thought she knew the reason, though. She had seen the way that Samuel behaved around white people. He smiled too broadly, he simpered, he made silly jokes. It pained her to see it, and she could tell from the desperate look in his eyes that it hurt him too. For all his love of creamy white skin, Samuel probably couldn't bring himself to approach a white woman the way he'd courted her.

The broken glass was in a neat pile under the guava tree. Time to make Samuel's dinner now. She went up the veranda stairs to the front door, stopping to wipe her sandals on the coir mat just outside the door. Samuel hated dust. As she opened the door, she felt another gust of warm wind at her back, blowing past her into the cool house. Quickly, she stepped inside and closed the door, so that the interior would stay as cool as Sammy liked it. The insulated door shut behind her with a hollow sound. It was airtight. None of the windows in the house could be opened. She had asked Samuel, "Why you want to live in a box like this, sweetheart? The fresh air good for you."

"I don't like the heat, Beatrice. I don't like baking like meat in the sun. The sealed windows keep the conditioned air in." She hadn't argued.

She walked through the elegant, formal living room to the kitchen. She found the heavy imported furnishings cold and stuffy, but Samuel liked them.

In the kitchen she set water to boil and hunted a bit—where did Gloria keep it?—until she found the Dutch pot. She put it on the burner to toast the fragrant coriander seeds that would flavor the curry. She put on water to boil, stood staring at the steam rising from the pots. Dinner was going to be special tonight. Curried eggs, Samuel's favorite. The eggs in their cardboard case made Beatrice remember a trick she'd learned in physics class for getting an egg unbroken into a narrow-mouthed bottle. You had to boil the egg hard and peel it, then stand a lit candle in the bottle. If you put the narrow end of the egg into the mouth of the bottle, it made a seal, and when the candle had burnt up all the air in the bottle, the vacuum it created would suck the egg in, whole. Beatrice had been the only one in her class patient enough to make the trick work. Patience was all her husband needed. Poor, mysterious Samuel had lost two wives in this isolated country home. He'd been rattling about in the airless house like the egg in the bottle. He kept to himself. The closest neighbors were miles away, and he didn't even know their names.

She was going to change all that, though. Invite her mother to stay for a while, maybe have a dinner party for the distant neighbors. Before her pregnancy made her too lethargic to do much.

A baby would complete their family. Samuel would be pleased, wouldn't he? She remembered him joking that no woman should have to give birth to his ugly black babies, but she would show him how beautiful their children would be, little brown bodies new as the earth after the rain. She would show him how to love himself in them.

It was hot in the kitchen. Perhaps the heat from the stove? Beatrice went out into the living room, wandered through the guest bedroom, the master bedroom, both bathrooms. The whole house was warmer than she'd ever felt it. Then she realized she could hear sounds coming from the outside, the cicadas singing loudly for rain. There was no whisper of cool air through the vents in the house. The air conditioner wasn't running.

Beatrice began to feel worried. Samuel liked it cold. She had planned tonight to be a special night for the two of them, but he wouldn't react well if everything wasn't to his liking. He'd raised his voice at her a few times. Once or twice he had stopped in the middle of an argument, one hand pulled back as if to strike, to take deep breaths, battling for self-control. His dark face would flush almost blue-black as he fought his rage down. Those times she'd stayed out of his way until he was calm again.

What could be wrong with the air conditioner? Maybe it had just come unplugged? Beatrice wasn't even sure where the controls were. Gloria and Samuel took care of everything around the house. She made another circuit through her home, looking for the main controls. Nothing. Puzzled, she went back into the living room. It was becoming thick and close as a womb inside their closed-up home.

There was only one room left to search. The locked third bedroom. Samuel had told her that both his wives had died in there, first one, then the other. He had given her the keys to every room in the house, but requested that she never open that particular door.

"I feel like it's bad luck, love. I know I'm just being superstitious, but I hope I can trust you to honor my wishes in this." She had, not wanting to cause him any anguish. But where else could the control panel be? It was getting so hot!

As she reached into her pocket for the keys she always carried with her, she realized she was still holding a raw egg in her hand. She'd forgotten to put it into the pot when the heat in the house had made her curious. She managed a little smile. The hormones flushing her body were making her so absentminded! Samuel would tease her, until she told him why. Everything would be all right.

Beatrice put the egg into her other hand, got the keys out of her pocket, opened the door.

A wall of icy, dead air hit her body. It was freezing cold in the room. Her exhaled breath floated away from her in a long, misty curl. Frowning, she took a step inside and her eyes saw before her brain could understand, and when it did, the egg fell from her hands to smash open on the floor at her feet. Two women's bodies lay side by side on the double bed. Frozen mouths gaped open; frozen, gutted bellies too. A fine sheen of ice crystals glazed their skin, which like hers was barely brown, but laved in gelid, rime-covered blood that had solidified ruby red. Beatrice whimpered.

"But Miss," Beatrice asked her teacher, "how the egg going to come back out the bottle again?"

"How do you think, Beatrice? There's only one way; you have to break the bottle."

This was how Samuel punished the ones who had tried to bring his babies into the world, his beautiful black babies. For each woman had had the muscled sac of her womb removed and placed on her belly, hacked open to reveal the purplish mass of her placenta. Beatrice knew that if she were to dissect the thawing tissue, she'd find a tiny fetus in each one. The dead women had been pregnant too.

A movement at her feet caught her eyes. She tore her gaze away from the bodies long enough to glance down. Writhing in the fast congealing yolk was a pin-feathered embryo. A rooster must have been at Mister Herbert's hens. She put her hands on her belly to still the sympathetic twitching of her womb. Her eyes were drawn back to the horror on the beds. Another whimper escaped her lips.

A sound like a sigh whispered in through the door she'd left open. A current of hot air seared past her cheek, making a plume of fog as it entered the room. The fog split into two, settled over the heads of each woman, began to take on definition. Each misty column had a face, contorted in rage. The faces were those of the bodies on the bed. One of the duppie women leaned over her own corpse. She lapped like a cat at the blood thawing on its breast. She became a little more solid for having drunk of her own life blood. The other duppie stooped to do the same. The two duppie women each had a belly slightly swollen with the pregnancies for which Samuel had killed them. Beatrice had broken the bottles that had confined the duppie wives, their bodies held in stasis because their spirits were trapped. She'd freed them. She'd let them into the house. Now there was nothing to cool their fury. The heat of it was warming the room up quickly.

The duppie wives held their bellies and glared at her, anger flaring hot behind their eyes. Beatrice backed away from the beds. "I didn't know," she said to the wives. "Don't vex with me. I didn't know what it is Samuel do to you."

Was that understanding on their faces, or were they beyond compassion?

"I making baby for him too. Have mercy on the baby, at least?"

Beatrice heard the *snik* of the front door opening. Samuel was home. He would have seen the broken bottles, would feel the warmth of the house. Beatrice felt that initial calm of the prey that realizes it has no choice but to turn and face the beast that is pursuing it. She wondered if Samuel would be able to read the truth hidden in her body, like the egg in the bottle.

"Is not me you should be vex with," she pleaded with the duppie wives. She took a deep breath and spoke the words that broke her heart. "Is . . . is Samuel who do this."

She could hear Samuel moving around in the house, the angry rumbling of his voice like the thunder before the storm. The words were muffled, but she could hear the anger in his tone. She called out, "What you saying, Samuel?"

She stepped out of the meat locker and quietly pulled the door in, but left it open slightly so the duppie wives could come out when they were ready. Then with a welcoming smile, she went to greet her husband. She would stall him as long as she could from entering the third bedroom. Most of the blood in the wives' bodies would be clotted, but maybe it was only important that it be *warm*. She hoped that enough of it would thaw soon for the duppies to drink until they were fully real.

When they had fed, would they come and save her, or would they take revenge on her, their usurper, as well as on Samuel?

Eggie-Law, what a pretty basket.

A luxurious home, a close-knit family, a lush walled garden frequented by beautiful butterflies, and all the time in the world—all the ingredients of a tropical paradise.

Buried Statues

ANTONIO BENÍTEZ-ROJO

Translated from the Spanish by Lee H. Williams Jr.

T HAT SUMMER—I could never forget—after Don
Jorge's classes had been dismissed and at Honorata's pleading, we used
to hunt butterflies in the gardens of our mansion in Havana's exclusive
Vedado Heights. Aurelio and I would go to great lengths to humor
Honorata because she was not only the youngest of the three, having
just celebrated her fifteenth birthday last March, but was also lame
from birth. We usually teased her by pretending not to want to go just
for the fun of watching her pout and toss her braided tresses about,
although if the truth were known, both of us enjoyed as much as she
did drawing lots to see who could take the hunting horn from the
deserted dovecote. Our nets held ready, we would then wander among
the marble statues along the flagstone path of the Japanese garden,
with its unexpected turns through the wild, tall grass that grew right
up to the house.

The grass was our greatest danger. For some years it had overrun the
iron fence at the southeastern edge of our estate on the bank of the
Almendares River, which during the rainy season threatened to flood
the property and put the vegetation in a frenzy of proliferation. It had

completely taken over that part of the estate under Aunt Esther's care, and in spite of all of her and Honorata's efforts, it now covered the large windows of the library and the French shutters on the wall of the music room. As this botanic siege affected house security, which was Mama's responsibility, our meals usually ended in intractable arguments. At times Mama, who became very nervous when she was not intoxicated, would bring her hand to her head, in her characteristic signal of a headache, and burst suddenly into tears, threatening between sobs to desert the house and yield her part of it to the enemy if Aunt Esther did not clean the overgrowth immediately. Mama believed that the pullulating vegetation was likely a secret weapon of the evil people who lived beyond the boundaries of our enclosed property.

"If you would pray less and work more . . ," Mama would say as she cleaned off the table.

"And if you would lay off the bottle . . ," Aunt Esther would retort.

Fortunately, Don Jorge never took sides in these disputes. He would fold his napkin, his face long and gray, and would retire from the table, thus avoiding embroiling himself in the family discord. Not that Don Jorge was a stranger to us. He was, after all, Aurelio's father, having married the sister who came between Mama and Aunt Esther, but whose name no one mentioned anymore. And although we did not call Don Jorge "uncle," we treated him with a familiar respect.

It was different with Aurelio. When nobody was looking, he and I would hold hands as if we were engaged. And precisely that summer he would have to choose between Honorata and me, for time was running out, and we were no longer children.

We all loved Aurelio for the way he carried himself, for his flashing black eyes, and above all for that special way he had of laughing. At the table the largest portions were for him, and on those occasions when Mama's alcoholic breath could be noticed above the smells of dinner, you could bet that when Aurelio held out the plate she would seize his hand and serve him very slowly. Of course, Aunt Esther did not waste any time either. With the same dedication as when she told her rosary, she would kick her shoe off under the table and search for Aurelio's leg.

Thus went our meals. And, naturally, Aurelio let himself be loved. He lived with Don Jorge in the rooms of the old servants' quarters because it was so stipulated by the Code. Otherwise, both Mama and Aunt Esther would have given him rooms on any of the floors of the mansion to please him. And Honorata and I would have been delighted to have him nearer to us during those stormy nights, punctuated with flashing lights, as the house lay under siege.

We called the document that spelled out each of our duties and established our responsibilities and punishments, simply, the Code. It had been sworn and subscribed to during Grandfather's lifetime by his three daughters and their husbands. In it were gathered the patriarchal commandments, and although it had to be adapted to our newer circumstances, it became the rallying point of our resistance. Since we guided ourselves by it, I will briefly describe it.

It recognized Don Jorge as a permanent and usufructuary member of the Family Council. He was charged with the provision of food, with military intelligence, with the administration of the family funds, with education and cultural activities (he had been an under Secretary of Education during the times of Laredo Bru), with electrical repairs and masonry, and with cultivating the land along the northeastern wall by the Enríquez house, which had been converted into a polytechnic school at the end of 1965. Aunt Esther was left with the responsibility of attending to the flower gardens, including the park; caring for the breeding animals; political agitation; repairs on the water system and the plumbing; the organization of religious acts; and washing, ironing, and mending clothes.

Mama was assigned the cleaning of the floors and the furniture, the preparation of tactics for defense, carpentry repairs, the painting of the roofs and the walls, the practice of medicine, as well as the preparation of the meals and other related tasks. However, this last commitment occupied most of her time.

As for us, the cousins, we helped with the morning chores and listened to Don Jorge's lessons in the afternoon. Whatever time was left we dedicated to recreation. We, like the rest, were forbidden to venture beyond the limits of the estate, for that meant instant death. Moral death, that is. The death that waited on the other side of the iron fence, along that evil path onto which half the family had strayed in the nine years that the siege had lasted.

So, as matters stood, that summer we hunted butterflies. They would come across the river, flying over the tall grass, pausing on the flowers or on the marble shoulders of the garden statues. Honorata used to say that they made the air happy, that they perfumed it—poor little Honorata had such an imagination. But they upset me, for they came from the land beyond, and, like Mama, I was of the opinion that they were secret weapons that we did not yet understand. For this reason, though I liked to hunt them, I felt a hidden fear. At times they would startle me, and I would flee through the grass, anxious that they might seize me by the hair and by the skirt, as in the engraving that hung in Aurelio's room, and that they would carry me over the iron fence and beyond the river.

We caught the butterflies in nets made from old mosquito netting, and then put them in empty jelly jars that Mama gave us. Then, at dusk, we would gather in the study room for the big beauty contest, which could last for hours, for we dined late. Once we had decided which was the most colorful, we would take it from its jar, clean it, and paste it in an album that Don Jorge had given us.

Following a suggestion that I had made to prolong the sport, we would pull the wings off the others and organize butterfly foot races, betting illicit pinches and caresses. Finally, tired of our games, we would throw the mutilated insects into the toilet bowl, and Honorata, trembling, her eyes misty with tears, would pull the chain, releasing the sound of falling water, sweeping their bodies away in a whirlpool.

After we had dined, and after Aunt Esther's allegations had caused Mama to retire to the kitchen with the irrevocable decision to abandon the house as soon as she had finished washing the dishes, we would gather together in the music room, by the only candelabrum, and listen to Aunt Esther play her religious hymns on the piano. Don Jorge had taught us something of the violin, which we kept strung; but because we had no way to tune it, the piano itself being out of tune, we preferred not to take it from its box. On other occasions, when Aunt Esther was indisposed or when Mama had reproached her for being behind in her duties, we would read aloud at Don Jorge's suggestion, and, as he felt a great admiration for German culture, we could pass hours muttering stanzas by Goethe, Holderlin, Novalis, or Heine.

Very rarely, only on stormy nights when the house seemed on the point of being swept away, or on some other extraordinary occasion, would we examine the collection of butterflies in the album, feeling the mystery of their wings reach deep into us—those wings charged with the world beyond our spiked iron fence, beyond the walls topped with the sharp glass shards of bottles. Fascinated, we would sit there together in silence by the candles, under a shadow that concealed the moisture on the walls, our eyes shifting and our hands tense, knowing that we each felt the same, that we found ourselves in the depth of a dream as turbid as the river along our boundaries, while overhead the warped ceiling, cracking further, would powder our hair, our intimate gestures, with flaking calcium. And so we kept collecting them.

My greatest satisfaction during this time was to imagine that at the end of summer Aurelio would finally be mine. "A disguised priest will marry you through the fence," Don Jorge said circumspectly one day when Aunt Esther and Honorata were walking beyond earshot. From that moment on I did not stop thinking of it. It even made bearable the interminable morning session. Mama's deterioration proceeded apace. If she cooked, she hardly had time to do the dishes, and it was I who mopped the floor and shook the dust from the shabby furniture and battered chairs.

It may, perhaps, be a dangerous generalization, but in one way or another Aurelio sustained us all—his affection helped us to resist. Of course, Mama and Aunt Esther had hopes other than marriage. How else was one to explain their wild, gastronomical enthusiasms, their exceptional care for his occasional, light colds or even rarer headaches, their prodigious efforts to see him strong, stylishly dressed, content? Even Don Jorge, usually so discreet, at time acted like a brooding hen.

And one wouldn't believe the way Honorata fussed over him, the poor little thing always so optimistic, so unrealistic, totally unaware of her lameness. The fact is that Aurelio was our hope, our sweet taste of illusion, and it was he who kept us calm in our rusty fetters, us, so harassed from the outside.

"What a beautiful butterfly!" exclaimed Honorata one evening at twilight, only a summer ago. Aurelio and I were walking ahead on our way home, and he was making a passageway for me through the weeds with the handle of his net. We turned around to see Honorata's freckled face flying over the jungle of weeds as if she were being pulled by her tresses. Farther above, near the top of the royal poinciana tree that grew where the path turned down toward the statues, a gilded butterfly fluttered.

Aurelio stopped. He motioned for us to take up positions in the undergrowth. Advancing slowly, he slipped through the weeds with his net held high. The butterfly descended, opening its large defiant wings, almost coming within Aurelio's reach, then suddenly glided beyond the royal poinciana down to the gallery of marble statues. Aurelio followed, and both disappeared.

When Aurelio returned night had fallen, and we had already chosen the beauty queen for the evening and were getting her ready to surprise him. But he came in serious and sweaty, declaring that the gilded butterfly had escaped just as he had been at the point, by climbing the fence, of catching it. In spite of our insistence, he refused to remain for the games.

I began to worry. I envisioned Aurelio there on top of the wrought iron fence, his net hanging over the river, just one step from leaping over. I remember warning Honorata that the butterfly had been a decoy, and that we had to intensify our guard.

The next day was unforgettable. Since dawn the outsiders had been very worked up. They shot off cannonades. White exhaust trails of their gray airplanes laced the cloudless blue of the sky, and far below, their helicopters rippled the river's waters and the vegetation along its banks. No doubt they were celebrating something, perhaps a new victory, while we remained solitary and ignorant of the cause of their jubilation. It was not because we had no radios in the house, but because for some years we had not paid the bill for electricity. And the batteries of Aunt Esther's Zenith had become sticky and smelled of the Chinese ointment that Mama treasured in the back of her medicine cabinet. Nor did the telephone work, nor did we read newspapers, nor did we open the letters that we received from faithless friends and traitorous relatives from the world outside. It is true that Don Jorge traded through the fence. If he had not done so, we would not have been able to subsist. But he did it at night, and we were not permitted to witness the transactions, nor were we permitted to ask questions about them, although once, when he had a high fever and Honorata was taking care of him, he let it be known that our cause was not totally lost, and that well-known international organizations were preparing to assist those with the courage to resist.

In late afternoon of that memorable day, after the patriotic applause from the Polytechnic Institute had subsided, and the martial songs—which during the day had driven Mama crazy in spite of her ear plugs—ceased to be heard from over our glass-studded wall, we took down the hunting horn from the panoply and went to hunt butterflies. We walked slowly, Aurelio with a frown. Since early morning he had been gathering cabbage near the wall, and listening at close quarters without the necessary protection from the uproar of the songs and the fervid speeches that droned on past midday. Aurelio seemed disturbed. He rejected the results of the drawing and abruptly appointed Honorata to assign the hunting areas and to carry the hunting horn. We separated silently, without the usual jokes. In the past we had always respected established procedures.

For some time I had been wandering along the trail that followed the iron fence, waiting for the twilight, my jar full of fluttering, yellow wings, when suddenly I felt something tangling my hair. At first I thought it was the mesh of my own net, but when I raised my left hand my fingers rubbed something with more body, like a piece of silk that flew away after striking my wrist. I quickly turned around, and I saw hovering in the air before my eyes the gilded butterfly, its large wings opening and closing almost at the height of my neck. Alone and with my back to the fence, I could hardly contain the panic I felt. I seized the handle of my net and swung it furiously at the hovering thing, but it avoided my blow by gliding aside to the right. Moving slowly back along the fence, I tried to calm myself and not to think of Aurelio's engraving. Little by little I raised my arms, watching it carefully, and took aim, but this time the net became entangled in an iron post, and once again I missed. At this moment I dropped the handle of the net, and it fell in the foliage along the path. My heart was racing. The butterfly flew around me in a circle and attacked my throat. I hardly had time to shout and to hurl myself on the grass. A burning sensation caused me to raise my hand to my breast, and it was covered with blood. I had thrown myself on the tip hoop of the net, and it had wounded me. I waited some minutes, and then turned on my back, panting. It had disappeared. The tall grass that grew around me hid me, like the statue of Venus that had fallen from its pedestal and that Honorata had discovered in the back of the park. I stretched out motionless like it, looking fixedly at the twilight sky, and suddenly there were Aurelio's eyes, and I watching them quietly sweep over my nearly hidden body and stop at my breast, and then his chest coming among the stalks, his whole body struggling to force me down, and finally the long and painful kiss that made the grass tremble. Afterward, an inexplicable awakening: Aurelio on top of my body, still kissing my mouth, in spite of my biting his lips and scratching his forehead with my fingernails.

As we returned to the house, I was too disillusioned to speak.

Honorata had seen it all from her vantage point in the branches of the poinciana tree.

Before entering the house, we agreed to keep it a secret. I don't know if it was because of Mama's and Aunt Esther's glances across the steaming soup, or the nocturnal sighs from Honorata as she thrashed between her sheets, but when the new day dawned I realized that I no longer loved Aurelio as before, that I needed neither him nor that disgusting thing, and I swore not to do it again until our wedding night.

That next morning stretched on as never before, leaving me exhausted. At lunch I gave my portion of cabbage to Honorata (we were always so hungry), and I looked coldly at Aurelio when he explained to Mama that a cat from the Polytechnic Institute had bitten his hand and scratched his face before disappearing over the wall. Then we had our Logic class. I paid scant attention to Don Jorge, in spite of such words as *ferio, festino, baroco,* and many others.

"I am very tired. My shoulder hurts," I said to Honorata after the lesson, when she suggested that we hunt butterflies.

"Come on, don't be a bad sport," she insisted.

"No."

"Isn't it that you are afraid?" asked Aurelio.

"No, I am not afraid."

"Are you sure?"

"I am sure. I am not going to do it anymore."

"Hunt butterflies?"

"Hunt butterflies and the other. I am not going to do it anymore."

"Well, if you don't come along with us, I shall tell everything to Mama," screamed Honorata unexpectedly, her cheeks flushed.

"I have no objections," Aurelio said, laughing, as he seized me by the arm. And turning to Honorata without waiting for me to reply, he said: "Bring the nets and the jars. We will wait for you at the dovecote."

I felt confused and offended, but when I saw Honorata depart, limping pitifully, the truth suddenly dawned on me, and I understood everything that was happening. I let Aurelio put his arm around my waist, and we left the house.

We walked in silence, submerged in the tall grass, and I realized that I also felt pity for Aurelio, for I was strongest of the three, and perhaps of the whole household. It was curious, I was so young, not yet seventeen, and yet I was stronger than Mama with her progressive alcoholism, than Aunt Esther, who was always hanging onto her rosary. And, I realized suddenly, stronger than Aurelio. Aurelio was the weakest of all, even weaker than Don Jorge, than Honorata. And now he was smiling from the corner of his eye, rudely squeezing my waist, as if he had conquered me, without realizing, poor Aurelio, that only I could save him—him and the rest of the house.

"Shall we stop here?" he asked, pausing. "I believe it is the same place as yesterday," he said, winking at me.

I assented and lay down on the grass. I waited as he raised my skirt and began kissing my thighs—I, cold and quiet like the goddess, letting him do it to appease Honorata, so that she would not tattletale to the house and arouse those unsatisfied, envious females into open warfare.

"Move over a little to the right, I can't see very well," shouted Honorata from her vantage point astride a branch in the poinciana tree.

Aurelio paid no attention to her and unbuttoned my blouse.

It became dark and we returned, Honorata carrying the nets and the empty jars.

"Do you love me?" he asked as he removed a dry leaf that had become entangled in my hair.

"Yes, but I don't want to get married. Perhaps next summer."

"And will you continue doing it?"

"All right," I replied a little astonished, "provided no one learns about it."

"In that case, it's all the same to me, although the grass scratches and makes me itch."

That night Aurelio announced at the dinner table that he would not marry that year, that he would postpone his decision until the following summer. Mama and Aunt Esther both sighed sighs of relief. Don Jorge scarcely lifted his eyebrows.

Two weeks went by, and Aurelio continued with the illusion that he possessed me. I would lie down in the grass with my arms under my head, like a statue, and would let him caress me without suffering the outrage. As the days went by I perfected a rigid pose, which excited his desires and made him depend on me.

One evening we were walking along the riverbank while Honorata was hunting among the statues. The rainy season had begun, and the flowers, wet during the midday downpour, stuck to our clothing. We spoke of trivial matters—Aurelio was telling me that Aunt Esther had visited him at night in her nightgown. At that moment we saw the butterfly. It flew at the front of a swarm of ordinary butterflies. When it recognized us, it flew a few zig-zags and lit on a pike of the iron fence. It moved its wings up and down without flying, pretending to be tired. Aurelio, becoming tense, released my waist to climb up the fence. But this time victory was mine. Without saying a word, I lay down, my skirt up above my hips, and the situation was brought under control.

We were waiting for the man because Don Jorge had told us after our History lesson that he would come around 9 P.M. that night. He had supplied us with provisions over the years, and he insisted that he be called the Mohican. As he was an experienced and courageous soldier, according to Don Jorge (although this seemed difficult to believe, since they had taken his house away from him), we would accept him as a guest after feigning a debate. He could help Aunt Esther exterminate the invading grass, and after that he could cultivate the piece of property to the southeast that was bounded by the river.

"I believe he is coming," Honorata said, pressing her face against the wrought iron bars of the main gate. There was no moon, and we were using the candelabrum.

We drew closer to the chains that guarded the access while Aunt Esther prayed a hurried rosary. The foliage was pulled back, and a hand was revealed in the pale light of the candles. Then a wrinkled, expressionless face appeared.

"Password!" demanded Don Jorge.

"Gillete and Adams," replied the man in a subdued voice.

"That is correct. You may enter."

"But how?"

"Climb over the bars; the lock is rusted."

Suddenly a whisper surprised us all. There could be no doubt that on the other side of the great gate the man was talking with someone. We looked at each other in alarm, and it was Mama who broke the silence.

"With whom are you talking?" she asked, coming out of her stupor.

"The truth is . . . I am not alone."

"They have followed you!" cried Aunt Esther in an anguished tone.

"No, it is not that. . . . The truth is, I came with . . . someone."

"In the name of God, with whom?"

"A young lady . . . almost a child."

"I am his daughter," interrupted a voice of exceptional clarity.

We deliberated for some time. Mama and I were opposed to it, but there were three votes in favor, and one abstention—Don Jorge. Finally, they were allowed to cross over to our side.

She said her name was Cecilia, and she walked very proudly along the darkened path. She was the same age as Honorata, but much prettier, and without anatomical defects. Her eyes were blue, and her hair a rather unusual golden color. She wore it straight, parted in the middle, with the tips turned upward, reflecting the light of the candelabrum.

When we reached the house she said that she was very sleepy, as she was accustomed to going to bed early, and seizing a candle, she entered directly into the old room, at the end of the corridor, that had belonged to Grandfather; she locked the door from the inside as if she were familiar with it. The man, who now I know was not her father, after saying goodnight with a weary appearance and clutching his chest, went off with Don Jorge and Aurelio to the servants' quarters, coughing every step of the way. We never found out what his real name was. She refused to reveal his name the next day when Don Jorge, who always rose early, found him by his bed, dead and without identification.

We buried the Mohican in the afternoon near the well down by the Polytechnic Institute in the shade of a mango tree. Don Jorge pronounced the sermon, calling the deceased "our unknown soldier." And Cecilia produced from behind her back a bunch of flowers, which she put between his hands. After that, Aurelio began to shovel in the earth, and I helped him erect the cross that Don Jorge had made. And all of us returned to the house except Aunt Esther, who remained to pray.

Along the way I observed that Cecilia walked in a very curious manner. She reminded me of the ballet dancers that I had seen as a child at the Pro Arte concerts. She seemed very interested in the flowers and would stop to pick them and carry them to her face. Aurelio supported Mama, who staggered pathetically as they walked, but he never took his eyes off Cecilia, and he smiled stupidly every time she looked at him.

At dinner Cecilia did not eat a bite. She pushed her plate from her in disgust, and then offered it to Honorata, who, in turn, to show her gratitude, praised her hairdo. I finally decided to speak to her.

"What pretty dye you use on your hair. Where did you get it?"

"Dye? It isn't dyed. It's natural."

"That's impossible. No one has hair that color!"

"I do," she said smiling. "I'm glad you like it."

"Will you let me have a closer look at it?" I asked. The truth is, I didn't believe her.

"Yes, but don't touch it."

I picked up a candle and went to her chair; leaning over the back of it, I looked intently at her head. The color was even. It did not appear dyed. Yet there was something artificial among those gilded strands of hair. They looked as if they were made of golden silk. It suddenly occurred to me that it might be a wig. Impulsively, I gave it a jerk with both hands. I don't know if it was her howl that caused me to fall to the floor, or the fear I felt on seeing her jump about in that curious manner. The fact is, I sat stunned at Mama's feet, watching her run bumping into the furniture in the dining room, turn down the hall, and lock herself into Grandfather's room, all the time holding her head as if it were about to fall off. And Aurelio and Aunt Esther, feigning disbelief, pressed against the door to listen to her bleating. Mama brandished a knife without knowing what was going on at all, and to top it all, Honorata stood on a chair applauding. Fortunately, Don Jorge remained calm.

After Mama's babbling and Aunt Esther's tiresome response, I retired with dignity, and, refusing the candle Aurelio handed me, groped my way up the dark stairs with my head held high.

Honorata came into my room, while I pretended to be asleep to avoid discussion. Through half-opened eyes I saw her place the plate with the candle on the dresser. I rolled over on my side to make room for her. Her shadow, dancing along the wall, reminded me of the section on games and pastimes in the *Book of Knowledge,* whose twenty volumes Don Jorge had sold some years previously. Honorata's shadow limped exaggeratedly. She went from one side to the other untying her braids, opening the drawer where she kept the sheets. Then she approached the bed, looking taller, and leaning over me, touched my hand.

I pretended to yawn and turned over on my back. "What do you want?" I asked in a bad humor.

"Have you taken a look at your hands?"

"No."

"You should."

"There is nothing wrong with my hands," I said, without looking at them.

"They are stained."

"They must be dirty," I said. "Since I pulled that creature by the hair, and shoved Mama . . ."

"They are not dirty, but they are gilded," Honorata shouted impetuously.

I looked at my hands and it was true; a golden powder covered my palms and the underside of my fingers. I rinsed my hands in the washbowl and blew out the candle. When Honorata grew tired of her farfetched conjectures, I was finally able to close my eyes. I got up late the next morning, feeling groggy and confused.

I did not find Cecilia at breakfast because she had gone out with Aunt Esther to see what they could do with the weeds. Mama had already gotten drunk, and Honorata stayed with me to help with the cleaning. Afterward, we would make lunch. We had already finished downstairs and were cleaning Aunt Esther's room; I was dusting and Honorata was sweeping, when it occurred to me to look out the window. I put down the feather duster and looked out over our property: to the left and to the front, the iron fence separated us from the river, its spikes overgrown with weeds; closer, beyond the orange poincianas, I saw the heads of the statues, greenish, like the heads of drowned women, and the gray boards of the Japanese dovecote; to the right were the vegetable garden, the well, and Aurelio, squatting on the ground to gather mangoes near the small cross; farther on, the wall, the roof tiles of the Polytechnic Institute, and a waving flag. "Who will tell the Enríquezes?" I thought. And then I saw her. She flew very low in the direction of the wall. At times she would become lost among the flowers and then would reappear farther along, shining like a gilded dolphin. Then she changed direction and went in a beeline toward Aurelio. And, suddenly, she was Cecilia, Cecilia who came out from the bed of oleander bushes, running over the red earth, her hair fluttering in the air, almost floating over her head; Cecilia, who was now talking with Aurelio, kissing him before leading him by the hand along the path that crossed the park.

I asked Honorata to make lunch, and I stretched out in Aunt Esther's bed. Everything was spinning around in my head, and I felt my heart throbbing. After a while someone tried insistently to open the door, but I was crying, and I shouted that I felt sick and for them to leave me in peace.

When I awoke, night had fallen, and I knew something had happened. I leaped from the bed and ran down the stairs barefooted. I entered the hallway alarmed and muttering to myself that even yet there was the chance it was not too late.

They were all in the living room around Honorata. Don Jorge was crying softly on the edge of the sofa. Aunt Esther, kneeling by the lamp, leaned toward Mama, who was gesticulating in her rocking chair without being able to straighten up. Unnoticed, I leaned against the frame of the door, almost in the light, listening to Honorata, watching her act out her report in the center of the rug, and feeling myself become weaker by the second. She went into great detail, explaining how she had seen them just at twilight on the river road on the other side of the iron fence. Then, suddenly, there was the explosion, and the sound of Aunt Esther's prayer—as Mama became delirious.

I put my hands over my ears. I lowered my head, feeling the urge to vomit. Then, through my fingers, I heard a scream. Someone fell over the candles, and we were left in darkness.

Camille Hernandez-Ramdwar's powerful story "Soma" is of a desperate battle to literally fit in, to conform.

Soma

CAMILLE HERNANDEZ-RAMDWAR

October

I USED TO LIVE in a world of certainties, particular-
ities, crucial understandings of boundary, of seams and borders, but
lately all that has been changing, is changed, I woke up this morning
and my feet gave away my thoughts. It wasn't just the size that was
alarming, it was the color. In some areas they had become almost purple, as if gigantic bruises had been inflicted upon them, but painless-
ness let me know I was not injured.

The other day it was my hair. I went out of my house as usual, to
occupy myself in the Capitalist Cog Central building, my locks neatly
tied back in a bun. But by midday, the elastic holding my hair was
sprung, my hair seemed to have a life of its own, billowing and waving
and beckoning and threatening as if a hundred blowdryers were attacking it at once. I couldn't hide my shame. I knew the Heads were laughing at me, silently of course, but the Mouths bore no such tact and
incessantly commented on my misfortune. "She's giving herself away,"
they said, some snickering, others losing control of lips and tongue,
their enlarged orifices seeming to devour their own faces. I've never
interacted intimately with a Mouth, I never could. They have too

much to say, are always sure of their opinions, even when any Head or Ear or S/Org can plainly see they are erroneous. I could never trust a Mouth. I'd be afraid that if I lay down with one at night, I might wake up in their belly. Carnivorous cannibals—no matter how much they floss and brush one can always see the bloodstains leeched into their enamel.

My greatest fear, though, has always been that the inmost secret of my self will be revealed when I least expect it, exposing me for what I guess I truly am. Fortunately for me, this part of myself has only emerged behind closed doors. Only personal intimates have been witness to it. Like all S/Orgs, it is the shame we carry that should not be. We are sexed and sexualized from birth, and so what if our blossoming voluptuous nanis or hefty, intricately veined woods expand and announce themselves from beneath our clothes? These vulvas slithering from between our legs, large wet-lipped hibisci blooming for all to see, or massive penises commanding attention like celestial trumpets? Some of my best friends are overt S/Orgs, Vulvas to be exact. They say they hate the stares, the comments, the insinuations. But I know some Vulvas like to flaunt it, paint their parts even redder, apply lip gloss, just to accentuate that which becomes their all. Me, I'm still fraid the Vulvaness I know I am will leap out at unexpected and crucial moments, perhaps when I am passing as a Foot, as Hair, as Hands. I have remarkable hands—so skilled, so flexible and intricate, I am in demand when my Handness is obtuse.

My predicament is that I cannot single out only one part and lay claim to it. I'm multiply complex and uneasily identified. I wish I could be singular, to settle into one world, reap the benefits of that world and not worry that, at any moment, some other unknown part of me will suddenly appear, and re-define me again

January

ALL DAY, all day, trying vainly to conceal it. I'm getting worried, losing sleep. A Hand I know told me about some Vulva club, like a support or coming-out group—I think I'll see if they can be of any assistance. I wonder if it's limited to Vulva S/Orgs alone—I don't think I'd feel comfortable in a mixed S/Org group—some of those male S/Orgs carry on like peacocks, or wield their wood as weapons, a menacing stance, toughness set in by the definition of Self as male genitalia, of having lost jobs, family, respect once their S/Orgness manifests. Large and grotesque as a Vulva S/Org's parts can become, I've never felt intimidated by that. I mean, a vulva as a weapon? It's a contradiction.

Today at Capitalist Cog I saw that another Head got promoted. Small wonder. I know my father went through years of watching Heads pass him by—until he found out about some pills that would cause hydrocephalus. He came to work a week later with a *really* swelled head. But the bosses were skeptical—they sent him to be examined and it was declared his Headness was unauthentic. Major demotion. My father was never sure what he was after that—unlike those peacocks, he tried to deny his S/Orgness in every way, like many of us, ashamed of the stigmatism. He settled for being a Hand.

It used to bother me that he was unable to accept both parts of himself. But then I guess he isn't all that different from me. In fact it's not us. It's that we are allowed only one part to express our whole. What is visible becomes the sole indicator of who we are.

Still I wonder if it would have been easier for him as a male to accept his S/Orgness. Surely he would have been demoted even more than he was, ridiculed, assumed to be unintelligent and oversexed—but would he have felt afraid, physically vulnerable, x-tra naked in an obscene way?

February

STILL LOOKING for the Vulva group. I'm running out of time. I just got more responsibility as Clerical Station Manager XX and fear I will be demoted if Vulvaness manifests. Luckily I waver between Feet and Hands most days. I've learned to accommodate. It's harder for those of us who switch—two or three times the number of shoes, clothes, hats, gloves, just to accommodate. But thankfully, Feet and Hands are relatively acceptable, palatable, non-threatening. The drones, perhaps, of this world.

Joanie—the friend who is Eye, Hand, and S/Org—told me she heard about people who Chop It Off. That there's a clinic across the mountains where they eradicate S/Orgness for a hefty fee. I wonder how many people have done this? I hope it won't come to that for me. Where would I get that kind of money anyway? I wonder how—or even if—they protect the confidentiality of their clients? I wonder if it is permanent?

My feet hurt—all day they seemed swollen. I guess a switch is inevitable, but one never knows. Multiplicity becomes so unpredictable. If I were just Feet, it would be so much easier. If I were just one thing—any one thing, not many—it would be easier.

Joanie would cuss if she heard me say this. Says that multi-ness is what makes us special, beautiful, wiser—after all, how many singlenesses can say they have walked in another's Feet (or Hands, Hair, S/Orgs)?

March

ON THE transport today—saw a group of young male Heads and Mouths chasing and attacking a group of younger female S/Orgs. Little girls they were, already burdened by their body type, their soma, the supposed essence of everything they are and will ever be. One Head grabbed a girl in pigtailed braids by the jacket, pulled her down hard on the concrete. I saw the look of terror in her eyes. Nobody did anything. The people on the transport averted their faces, their eyes. A Mouth in the gang shouted, "Dirty filthy Sex Orgs!" I wanted to slap him, murder him. I hated him. I hated myself, this thing that threatens to engulf me every day. Why couldn't I just turn my head like everyone else? The other girls ran, too afraid to help their friend. The transport pulled away—I never saw what happened to her. What if I had a child like that one day? How would I protect her?

May

JOANIE'S going away. Says she's had enough of this crap—looking to be some place where she doesn't have to hide parts of herself. Says she's going Home, where her parents and grandparents and mine too came from. According to her, you can walk the streets there and not get called names; get jobs and not be looked over at promotion time; get housing in any district. Your children can grow up safe. S/Orgness is celebrated, is overt and acceptable and exalted. Says I should come, get out of this crazy place, be among "our own kind." A land of S/Orgs? I think. What kind of place can that be? Aren't they just randomly copulating all day? How does anyone get any work done? I can't imagine a country where the government, the police and hospitals, the schools, are run by S/Orgs. Wouldn't all that genitalia just get in the way, wrapping itself around everyone and everything like creeping vines, strangling and rooting everyone to the spot? Home? I couldn't live in such a place.

I overhear the other workers at Capitalist Cog discussing Home in these terms—S/Orgs serving, scraping, sexing, succulently served up on a smorgasbord of S/Orgosity, those "S/Org Getaway Packages" for assorted Heads and Mouths and others who come with their wallets open, curiosity seekers, perverts, pedophiles, rapists. "Those S/Orgs sure know how to have a good time!" the Hands and Ears and Heads and Mouths wink and salivate to each other. I feel ashamed. I avert my eyes, immerse myself in my work. Pray that I will not be found out.

August

I'M ON LEAVE from Capitalist Cog. The worst has happened—there's no going back now. I hide in my house, curtains drawn, vainly trying to disguise my new identity. I know some people just wear baggy baggy clothes for as long as possible, but I think I'm past that point. The dread of unexpected exposure paralyzes me. I have to do something. I can't bear to look at myself. I know if I do, the anger will overtake me and thoughts of slicing and dicing will run through my head. Why was I given this fate?

September

MY LEAVE is almost up. It's now or never. I've got the brochures. The clinic is only a fifteen-hour journey by transport. Somehow I have managed to scrape together the money, even though it meant selling off a few of my meager possessions. They say it'll all be over in a few hours, then bed rest and I can be back at work in two weeks. No one will know. I will avenge my father. No Head can sneer at me, surreptitiously try to grab a handful of tender flesh as he passes by. No Mouth will ever tell me I'm good for only one thing. To hell with them all.

September

CLOSED ALL the mirrors in the house—turned them to the wall. That is not where I am to be becoming. . . .

Dreamed the slithering vines.

September

THE CLINIC called—they want me there in one week.

September

TODAY I GOT a message from Joanie. She says it's all good Home. I want to believe her, but she doesn't know what kind of choice I have to make. She says if I come, she can set me up—work and house. I have my appointment in one week. How can I go Home? The clinic is expecting me, and the new Me that will become. I'm not Joanie. I can't see the goodness in this S/Org thing. I can't see it at all. I have my appointment in one week. Doesn't she know this? Why should she come and tell me all this now? As if it will really change anything. I can't go Home. I already allotted my money. I have to be strong. Can't fall trap to the fantasies of Home. Home is where you leave. Not where you go to. She says come soon. Do I have the time for that foolishness now? I have a life to lead, I have important things to do. What can I accomplish in a place where S/Orgness abounds? A dirty little place. A dirty little secret. They will cut it out of me. They will cut out my past, cut Home right out of me. Can't Joanie see that this is the only way? She says come soon. Soon is now, now is Not Me. Not Me anymore. I gone. I gone and I leaving all the Joanies and dem behind.

dream

A CARIBBEAN PERSON who says, "My mother dream me," means, "My mother visited me in a dream." Dream messages can come from the living or the dead and are of vital importance. Dreams can be nightmares or fantasies, hopes or wishes. The final two stories of this anthology invoke the logic of dream in which the rules can be broken, the truth transformed.

"Tell all the truth but tell it slant," says Emily Dickinson. The tradition of the man-of-words has long roots in the Caribbean. Speechifying—as in the masked Midnight Robber's convoluted tale at Carnival, or in the preacher's Sunday sermon—has been raised to an art form in which words do not so much carry meaning as they indicate, evoke, and redouble meaning. A woman once told me that reading written Creole became easier for her when she stopped trying to identify the meaning of each individual word and instead read the text "sideways."

Kamau Brathwaite, griot extraordinaire, brings his own particular mix of rhythm, history, image, nation, language, and poetic sensibility to a layered, poignant tale with its own truths. Read it slant.

My Funny Valentine

KAMAU BRATHWAITE

●HE NIGHT after my second eye is re. move by the han
(g)mans noose. me & my two one wife is in the miggle of this
room in like a whirlpool or serpent of electric wires & she
right font catch-up in a loop as she cross the room & she rea
lly already tangle-up like in a lassoo unloose rounn she fine
St. Valentine body esp all up at de top rounn she breasts & sh
oulders & i don't know how it get here/how she gett like dis
& i ask. in ask. in about it as she try. in to come cross the
room like to ford & stellin for help when this other guy whose face i don't see just as i don't see she face neither agai
(n) after she get-cross to where I like lying-down in a deck
or dock or prostate chair of the dream

& i can bare. ly move to help her to help her & try as i try
i can't ever raise my hann so i cd hold-on to the top a de w-
all to help her to help her while this guy like some kind of
a English = like kind & kind-a concern & po. lice like Jeremy

Irons in most a e flim tho this isn't no Jerry but real like some
a dem broni livin off the flat a we ilann & e like he comim >
towards she to help she even tho e inn see how she comin to
me/me she husbann tryin to get up outta this chair of tirade

& e quiet & .sistin & offerin help / even tho she so close to
me so close to mwe now i can see the soft sea weave a she ski
(n) & feel the half-halt heat that she breathe that she breathe. in & a watchin she turn how she turnin she black back to
mwe now . this brown well-build universe mine . be-

ginnin to like let dis guy help she out a she virus while i
have was to watch how he tellin she how to tek-off she blouse
- a kind a soff off-white & flimsy sea-islann stirrup in cool
Trinidaddy crush-cotton that she buy in-at CaveShepherd store
w/dese young rounn white muttons all down she full front—

sayin all this like quiet & tact/full—show. in proper respec for his kind-a cute immigration & i watchin these women a
mine from where I am prostrate . um. bottom she shirt like s-
ome meek scarifrice of a blackbelly sheep of Barabados. all
she four eye(s) down to the buttomholes toggellin each one a
dem one after one wid she tum from de top & side a she number
one finger . pushin dem thru de hole after hole wid she tum &
slidin & pressin dem down thu de hole like she playin piano
mbira or thimble or onion . till all de gorgeous flash a she
back peel-out & x/plose from de dress till she owl x/pose to
de view in she black brassiare wid-it black plastic hook at >
de back & she plump & dark plum-colour skin all skin-out & fa
cin dis guy wid all she big rounn or. ganics & powder & all
allmost all outta she bellows & close close close to e face
wid she power

as he had was to benn slightly down like towar
ds she affront . bend. in e knee to be closer
& closer & like more careful & kisses. so e cd
work like the lassoo awound her & up those brown wonderful beasts - the slight shruggle of
soldiers - & then care. full & slow. ly up ove
(r) she grassbottle neck & the sweet wire hair
(s) of this once was my dearly belovèds -

she keep. in she heads down not sayin a word to this sword in
my soul & i watchin all a this wheelin & turn. in & try. in <
to get off the chair so i cd like stann-up & do what is *mwe*
shd be doin this wifes & Valentine mornin . but a still week
week in de tangle & dream & she stannin-up here a while where
it happen a little while after it happen & lover till she free from the wire that tingle & tripple she foot & the Jeremy
I. rons guy like e

it & gone

& the brown demon eyes of the once was my di. & my di. amond
darlin nvr once anymore like breaking towards me . nor nvr sh
(e) lookin towards me . she back to me back to me back to me
still in the black brassiere lookin down at she breasts that
she had had to dance & x/pouse to the worll . & i remind/er
re/minder before i wake up how i make one lass chance to get-
up to get-up . but try as i try. i cyaaan get de sun. rise up
from mi head so i cd grapple-on to dis top a de wall . is so
so gnashlish & sutil & incontinent .

When first the eldritch girls and then the boys too begin to be revealed, people are afraid they are a sign from the devil. But Ma Pouksie has dreamed it, what the truth really is. . . .

I chose to end this anthology on a rising note of power and rebirth with marina ama omowale maxwell's praise song of celebration, identity, and vision, dedicated to writer Andrew Salkey.

Devil Beads

MARINA AMA OMOWALE MAXWELL

Dedicated to Andrew "Che" Salkey

SHE WOKE UP that morning to find rainbow beads threaded in her hair. Not joined on but intricately threaded right into her own hair. What should she make of it? Her voice dropped when she asked who had done it. No one in the family knew or could even bead hair.

The family stood around her, walked around her—all keeping a little distance from her. Nobody wanted to touch them, the devil beads, though they were so beautiful. All down the back of her hairline and on her forehead these lovely beads . . . every color of the rainbow, winking on black, fringed her head. She didn't want to touch them either. But they touched her. They playfully fell on her forehead, at her third eye, around her ears and down the nape of her neck.

The next week it happened to another girl in the town. Then another—all young girls at first, young black and quiet. Always the quiet ones. And a certain gaiety came with the beads. Beads they couldn't remove either. Didn't know what to do with . . .

The beads will not be devil beads . . . but blessings said the old woman who sold bush and herbs in the marketplace near Palm Tree.

Blessings from ancient ancestors . . . and she had dreamed an Andrew . . . did they know an Andrew, someone also named Che of the Healing Hands . . . ? said the old woman who they say grew wings in the night. . . . No, no one knew, except an old uncle who had heard of him, a poetman and storyteller from Jamaica, now dead these years, loved, well-loved . . . the young ones began to try to find out more about him. . . .

They will appear glinting in the hair of chosen spirit women, and later men who are capable of growing, tendrils capable of growing . . . like Andrew Che did, "beautiful right under the skin where people are beautiful—and not capable of arranging it either . . ." as someone said to him once. Beads of the Rainbow for rainbow people, like African beads but more. Diaspora beads since they came to the heads too of Indian and Chinese, African and dougla, all the mixed peoples of the rainbow Caribbean. But how they know it was really a gift . . . and not from the devil? They only had what Ma Pouksie say really. . . .

But they kept on coming. To those Ma say who would learn to shine in the dark . . . the Shining Ones coming again . . . from their Sirius home worshiped by the Dogon tribe long time ago. . . . Mysteries of beads, beads of their bones, brilliant with splashes of all colors, big ones and little ones, graded to the strand, tiny ones on the length and they got larger and larger at the ends. A,a,a, the old ones said, time curving round again, something new coming . . .

Each girl, now a spirit woman, began to wear them with pride and as chosen. Took off the shame headties first put on by parents who dragged them to church to be exorcised, doused them in the Toco waves to wash away their sins. But Father priest of the white religions couldn't take the beads out. His fingers get shocked when he touches them. No hand can touch them but the owners themselves who began in fear which changed to a deep wild joy and then to a caress of love.

They began to gather together at the well and fountain on the edge of the town near Mission beach where huge trees spread their gigantic green wings over the blasted dry sands. A gaggle of girls, quiet but full of a forest-blessed joy, a sea joy, a waterfall joy, rich as the Mother turtles who came up horseshoeing their way in the moonlight from their nest of eggs back to the deep waters of night. Girls and boys with eyes like green leaves. Five then ten then fifteen. At twenty-three the whole miracle stopped.

THEN IT began again . . . resonating. It was heard in the next Caribbean island, then another and then another . . . spreading like tremulous vibrations in a mystic resonance. Always the knowledge stopped at twenty-three . . . sign and number of Sirius, the Dogstar, of the illuminati of the chamber and pole mitan. The loas talking Ma said. The French priests said masses.

Right up the swinging black diaspora archipelago of islands, the spirit people began to appear. Some say they came from Atlantis but Sara mother and Falco sister objected strongly and say they born right here. The rainbow messengers were gathering for some Calling . . . the Third Octave of time, houngan said . . . the movements and trodding on toward the Eighth Octave. But who knew what? Who knew about all that? The youths don't know anything about that. . . .

Music, distant music, tenor and soprano pans, cymbals. Faint horns, stringed drums, sitars, tambourines, soft shekkere chac-chacs, tassas, dholaks, and castanets are heard tremulously on the wind wherever they gather . . . always at water, at the wells, the waterfalls, the rivers, and the sea. They need to speak no word, these messengers, only walk through the villages and the towns and the green countrysides. That would begin changing heads and this is where it had to start, houngan said.

Not even the Catolique priests could stop them nor the politicians nor the big business men with their hit men. No one could stone them, like they did Mikey. No one could arrest them like so many others or blow them up like Walter or shoot them down like at the Fort or cut off their lara hands like in the stadium. This was a reggeh someting, a new movement in space. . . .

The houngans, olorans, santeros, amangwahs, babaloas, mambos, pundits, and the muslim priests, santerias all, touched their feet and blesse them, blesse them as messages. . . .

Even many who bowed down to white idols and statues began to waver and to look out for the rainbow beads swing in the wind. Everybodyee, except the orisha and the poojah and satsang people, shocked to know that their gods and goddesses still alive and minding them, still attend them and calling out to them in these dark and turning years. But the palais people know this is the third octave, after the massacre slavery and indenture days and the olmec, tolmec heads days of blood before them. Is a third thing, now . . . and anything could happen. . . .

No cult or following can be formed. The spirit girls and boys attend in the yards and the compounds, at cremations and at phagwah, at divali and the mandirs, at rapso and the steelband temples, at carnival, at the mourning grounds.

The police tried to lock them up once but next day they found the cells open and the beds and chairs rolled away into the next room. The exorcists who went to the Mount to get clearance to do what they called ethnic cleansing found their rooms singed with fire and sprinkled with corn and salt. A hit man who tried to rape and murder one young beaded girl was found hanging over a precipice at Blanchishears.

Some say they can hear the music. Some don't. Some think they do. But all begin to Listen. . . .

The bead bearers do not speak any message but are a message themselves, setting the ritual. The kaiso singers and the chantwelles, the ears and the voices of the land, begin to see them as horizons and to recognize and welcome them with praise songs. Children of tomorrow, children of yesterday, timeless, spaceless like the sea. . . .

All races of the diaspora, all creeds of the baroque Caribbean, shaping and re-shaping itself always, like mud temples in the rains. . . .

The beads begin to appear it is heard across Antillianite, and Antilidad too, across the whole creolite mestizo rainbow Caribbean making a new cantilever of bridges . . . making the Calling. Began in a little

Atlantis seaside fishing village in Toco where Seya the seachile with green hands had come, beached by the turtle mothers, drawn by the Sequi santero babalawo priest from the darknight waters of Sans Souci bay . . . and then spread their fire up the curving islands, full of black loas beating in every pore, went down the Main, across Bogota and Sutatenza to Panama and Santiago, Citadel and Ponce and arced back to the favelas of Brazil . . . wherever our blood had wet the earth . . . wherever the sound of drums and of sitars are heard late at night, wherever bright and rainbow flags fly from their slender bowing bamboo poles, announcing prayers. . . .

Contributors' Notes

OPAL PALMER ADISA, born in Jamaica, is a literary critic, poet, prose writer, and storyteller. She has published *It Begins With Tears; Tamarind and Mango Women,* which won the PEN Oakland/Josephine Miles Award; *Traveling Women; Bake-Face and Other Guava Stories;* and *Pina, The Many-Eyed Fruit.* Her poems, essays, articles, and reviews have appeared in numerous journals and anthologies in the United States, London, Canada, and Jamaica. Adisa has taught at San Francisco State University and the University of California, Berkeley. She has a Ph.D. in Ethnic Studies Literature. Presently she is Associate Professor and Chair of Ethnic Studies at California College of Arts and Crafts. She lives in Oakland, California, where she is raising her three Ja-Merican children, Shola, Jawara, and Teju.

LILLIAN ALLEN, a leading Canadian poet and international exponent of dub poetry, is also a writer of plays and short fiction. She has received many citations and awards for her writings, recordings, and performances, including two Canadian Juno awards (music) and the Toronto Arts Foundation award for her leadership and vision and for having a significant impact on the arts in Toronto. She gives lectures and readings around the world and lives in Toronto, where she teaches creative writing at the Ontario College of Art and Design. Her latest publication is a collection of poetry, *Psychic Unrest,* published by Insomniac Press, Toronto, in 1999.

ROBERT ANTONI was born in the United States in 1958, and he carries three passports: U.S., Trinidad and Tobago, and the Bahamas. His fictional world is the island of Corpus Christi, and to recreate it he draws upon his two hundred years of family history in Trinidad and Tobago and his upbringing in the Bahamas. His first novel, *Divina Trace,* received the Commonwealth Writers' Prize for Best First Book, a National Endowment for the Arts award, and James Michener and Orowitz fellowships. His second novel is *Blessed Is the Fruit.* His new book is *My Grandmother's Erotic Folktales.*

ANTONIO BENÍTEZ-ROJO is the Thomas B. Walton Jr. Memorial Professor at Amherst College. In Cuba he was head of the Center for Caribbean Studies and the Publishing Department of Casa de las Américas. He is the recipient of the Casa de las Américas Prize and the Union of Cuban Artists and Writers Prize. His short fiction has been translated into seven languages and has been included in over fifty anthologies, among them *The Oxford Book of Latin American Short Stories, The Picador Book of Latin American Short Stories,* and *The Oxford Book of Caribbean Short Stories.* He has published numerous scholarly articles. Several of his books have been translated into English: *A View from the Mangrove; The Repeating Island: The Caribbean and the Postmodern Perspective; Sea of Lentils;* and *The Magic Dog and Other Stories,* which includes "Heaven and Earth," a 1985 Pushcart Prize winner.

KAMAU BRATHWAITE, poet, historian, literary critic, and dreamstory writer, was brought up in Barbados, Cambridge (England), and Ghana. He is the founder/secretary of the Caribbean Artists Movement (CAM) and editor/publisher of *Savacou & Savacou Cooperative,* the journal of the Caribbean Artists Movement. He served some thirty years as teacher at the University of the West Indies at Mona, Jamaica, and is now a professor of comparative literature, specializing in aspects of Caribbean culture and aesthetics, at New York University. His recent books include *Conversations with Nathaniel Mackey* and *MR: Magical Realism in Caribbean Orature and Literature,* which won the Casa de las Américas Prize for anglophone Caribbean literature in 1998. "My Funny Valentine" is from Brathwaite's forthcoming *DreamStories 2.*

TOBIAS S. BUCKELL was born in the Caribbean and grew up spending time in Grenada and the British and U.S. Virgin Islands. He moved with his parents to the United States after Hurricane Marilyn swept through the Virgin Islands, destroying the boat on which they lived. His parents now live just out of town near Amish farmland in Ohio. This contrast is one of the many reasons why Tobias feels comfortable writing about strange things happening to seemingly normal people. Tobias is currently finishing up his degree at Bluffton College in Ohio. He declared his intention to be a writer his freshman year of high school and has been working at it ever since. He is a graduate of the Clarion Science Fiction and Fantasy Writers' workshop, has had fiction published in *Science Fiction Age,* and won 1999's fourth quarter of the Writers of the Future Contest.

MARCIA DOUGLAS was born in England and raised in Jamaica. She is currently a professor of creative writing at North Carolina State University in Raleigh. She received an M.F.A. in Creative Writing from Ohio State University and was awarded a doctorate in English by the State University of New York, Binghamton. Her first volume of poetry, *Electricity Comes to Cocoa Bottom,* was recently published in England by Peepal Tree Press, where it received the recommendation of the Poetry Book Society of the British Arts Council. Her novel *Madam Fate* was published by Soho Press in New York in 1999.

WILSON HARRIS, born in Guyana in 1921, now lives in the UK. He has twice been a Guggenheim Fellow and is recipient of the Guyana Prize for Fiction. He is the author of numerous books of fiction, poetry, and essays, including *Palace of the Peacock; Tradition, the Writer and Society; Critical Essays; The Sleepers of Roraima (a Carib Trilogy);* and *Jonestown.* In 1999 he received a doctorate from Macerata, Italy.

Of "Yurokon," Wilson Harris says:

"The Caribs were accused by the Spanish Conquistadores of gross cannibalism in the sixteenth century when, after Columbus, they invaded the Caribbean and the Central and South Americas.

"Their accusation—scholars now assert—sprang from a profound animus against the Caribs, who resisted them tooth and nail.

"From immemorial times the Caribs ate a morsel of flesh plucked from their enemies in order to gain some insight into their enemies' inner plans of assault. Thus they dreamed of seeing into the enemy, of digesting his innermost plans. Beneath the morsel they chose a bone, which they fashioned into a flute.

"Here is the primitive birth of music.

"This bone of the birth of music is a transfigurative anatomy of Self and Other which, in some ways, resembles the Catholic Mass when the congregation consumes presumably a morsel from the body and blood of Christ. The Mass transfigures itself into bread and wine as symbols of food, which gain thereby a sacramental rhythm.

"What little we know of the origins of arts—such as music—is that they seem to appear within terror, or degradation, or crisis, and to bring a transfiguring threshold into deepened and heightened being. Such illuminations of the rhythm of origins have lost their meaning in a world where art has become a technicality.

"'Yurokon' is the Bush Baby of Carib myth. I have sought by way of musical imageries and associations to suggest the impact of such primordial myth, which differs from purely material logic. If anything it may offer a quantum understanding of the mystery of nature. Nature has many faces and to inscribe ourselves in one of these as an absolute is a deception of creativity. Thus it is, for instance, that in the 'broken

voices of water and fire . . . water and fire are cold and wood and leaf
are hot.'"

CAMILLE HERNANDEZ-RAMDWAR is a writer, teacher, and student
of Trinidadian/Ukrainian heritage. Her work focuses on identities,
particularly multiracial and diasporic ones, and can be found in *Mercury Retrograde, . . . but where are you really from?* and *Miscegenation Blues*,
among others. She teaches at the University of Toronto and York University in Canada, although her mind and spirit frequently wander the
streets of St. James, the beach at Macqueripe, and the Northern Range.

NALO HOPKINSON has published the novels *Brown Girl in the Ring* and
Midnight Robber, both from Warner Books. She is currently working on
a third novel, *Griffonne.* She has received the Locus Award, the Ontario
Arts Council Foundation Award, and the John W. Campbell Award.
She has had short stories published in journals and anthologies and has
been a juror for the Crawford Award for First Fantasy Novels and the
James Tiptree Jr. Award for speculative fiction that explores gender and
gender roles.

ISMITH KHAN is the author of the fiction titles *The Jumbie Bird, The
Obeah Man, The Crucifixion,* and *A Day in the Country and Other Stories.*

JAMAICA KINCAID was born in Antigua and now lives in Vermont.
Many of her short stories have appeared in *The New Yorker,* and she is
the author of numerous books, including *Annie John, A Small Place,
Lucy, At the Bottom of the River, Autobiography of My Mother, Generations
of Women: In Their Own Words, My Garden Book,* and *My Brother.*

MARINA AMA OMOWALE MAXWELL is a Trinidadian writer, television
producer/director, lecturer, playwright, singer, poet, and a Ph.D. can-
didate. She is the author of two novels, ten plays, and two books of
poetry. She is the founder of the Writers' Union of Trinidad and
Tobago. Her most recent novel is the magic realist *Chopstix in Mauby.*

IAN MCDONALD was born in Trinidad but makes his home in Guyana. Poet and author of the novel *The Humming-bird Tree* and of the poetry collections *Mercy Ward, Essequibo,* and *Jaffo the Calypsonian,* he is a Fellow of the Royal Society of Literature and the editor of the literary journal *Kyk-Over-Al.*

ROGER MCTAIR is an award-winning writer, director, poet, and short story writer. His short stories have been published in *Critical Strategies* and the *Faber Book of Caribbean Short Stories* and have been aired on CBC and BBC radio. He was a national finalist in *Descant Magazine's* novella competition in 1988. He also coedited the 1997 Caribbean Canadian issue of *Descant Magazine.* He is currently completing a script for a feature film and a collection of short stories for publication.

PAMELA MORDECAI is a poet, veteran anthologist *(Jamaica Woman, From Our Yard, Her True-True Name, Sunsong Tide Rising),* and writer of textbooks and academic works. Although she has written fiction "ever since . . . ," her published creative work has been mostly poetry/poetic drama for adults and poetry and stories for children. She is the author of the poetry works *Jamaica Woman, Journey Poem, Ezra's Goldfish and Other Poems,* and *De Man.* Her first published short story, "Limber Like Me," was a runner-up in the 1998 short story competition of the journal *Prism International.* "Once on the Shores of the Stream Senegambia" is her first venture into speculative fiction.

GEOFFREY PHILP is the author of four poetry collections: *Exodus and Other Poems, Hurricane Center, Florida Bound,* and *Xango Music.* He has also written a book of short stories, *Uncle Obadiah and the Alien,* and a novel, *Benjamin, My Son.* A recipient of many awards for his work, including an Individual Artist Fellowship from the Florida Arts Council, James Michener fellowships at the University of Miami, and an artist-in-residence at the Seaside Institute, he is currently working on a new collection of short stories, *Sister Faye and the Dreadlocked Vampire.* "The River," which appears in *Uncle Obadiah and the Alien,* won the

Canute Brodhurst Prize from the journal *The Caribbean Writer.* Philp's poems and short stories have also appeared in *The Mississippi Review, Gulf Stream, The Apalachee Quarterly, Journal of Caribbean Studies, Florida in Poetry,* and most recently, *The Oxford Book of Caribbean Short Stories.* He is an associate professor of English at Miami-Dade Community College.

CLAUDE-MICHEL PRÉVOST says of himself: "Writer. Screenwriter. 1st mentor: Elisabeth Vonarburg. Idol: Doris Lessing. Radar: wired.com. Decks: Osho Zen and New Orleans Voodoo Tarots. Shameless plug: Got a kick-ass manuscript, 'Men without Shadow': a Catholic priest, a Voodoo shaman, a mermaid, and a reptilian."

OLIVE SENIOR was born and spent most of her life in Jamaica and now lives in Toronto, Canada. She is the author of eight books, including three collections of short stories, two of poetry and nonfiction works on Caribbean culture. Her first short story collection, *Summer Lightning,* won the Commonwealth Writers Prize. She was most recently Writer-in-Residence at the University of Alberta, Canada, and Internet Poet-in-Residence on the "Common . . . Places" website launched by the Commonwealth Institute in London, England. She reads her work and conducts writing workshops internationally and is on the faculty of The Humber School for Writers, Humber College, Toronto.

H. NIGEL THOMAS is professor of American literature at Université Laval in Quebec, Canada. He grew up on the Caribbean island of Saint Vincent. His novel *Spirits in the Dark* was shortlisted for the 1994 QSPELL Hugh MacClennan Fiction Award. He is also the author of *From Folklore to Fiction: A Study of Folk Heroes and Rituals in the Black American Novel; How Loud Can the Village Cock Crow?;* and *Moving Through Darkness,* a collection of poems.

Acknowledgments

"Widows' Walk" by Opal Palmer Adisa. Previously published in *Bake-Face and Other Guava Stories*, Kelsey St. Press, 1986.

"In the Beginning" by Lillian Allen. Copyright Lillian Allen, 2000.

"My Grandmother's Tale of the Buried Treasure and How She Defeated the King of Chacachacari and the Entire American Army with Her Venus-Flytraps" by Robert Antoni. Previously appeared in *My Grandmother's Erotic Folktales*, Faber and Faber, 2000.

"Buried Statues" by Antonio Benítez-Rojo. Previously published in Spanish in the author's collection *Tute de Reyes*, Casa de las Américas, 1967. Reprinted from *The Oxford Book of Latin American Short Stories*, Oxford University Press, 1997. Translated into English by Lee H. Williams Jr. English translation reprinted with the permission of Ediciones del Norte, Hanover, New Hampshire.

"My Funny Valentine" by Kamau Brathwaite. Copyright Kamau Brathwaite, 2000.

"Spurn Babylon" by Tobias S. Buckell. Copyright Tobias S. Buckell, 2000.

"What the Periwinkle Remember" by Marcia Douglas. Excerpted from the novel *Madam Fate*, Soho Press, 1999.

"Yurokon" by Wilson Harris. Previously published in *The Sleepers of Roraima (a Carib Trilogy)*, Faber and Faber, 1970.

"Soma" by Camille Hernandez-Ramdwar. Copyright Camille Hernandez-Ramdwar, 2000.

"Glass Bottle Trick" by Nalo Hopkinson. Copyright Nalo Hopkinson, 2000.

"Shadows Move in the Brittannia Bar" by Ismith Khan. Previously published in *The Oxford Book of Caribbean Short Stories*, Oxford University Press, 1999.

"My Mother" by Jamaica Kincaid. Previously published in *At the Bottom of the River*, Plume, 1992.

"Devil Beads" by marina ama omowale maxwell. Copyright marina ama omowale maxwell, 2000.

"Pot O' Rice Horowitz's House of Solace" by Ian McDonald. Previously published in *The Caribbean Writer*, vol. 5, University of the Virgin Islands, 1991.

"Just a Lark (or the Crypt of Matthew Ashdown)" by Roger McTair. Copyright Roger McTair, 2000.

"Once on the Shores of the Stream Senegambia" by Pamela Mordecai. Copyright Pamela Mordecai, 2000.

"Uncle Obadiah and the Alien" by Geoffrey Philp. Previously published in *The Mississippi Review*, vol. 24, no. 3, 1996.

"Tears for Érsulie Frèda: Men without Shadow" by Claude-Michel Prévost. Copyright Claude-Michel Prévost, 2000.

"Mad Fish" by Olive Senior. Previously published in *Turn of the Story: Canadian Short Fiction on the Eve of the Millennium*, House of Anansi Press, 1999.

"The Village Cock" by H. Nigel Thomas. Previously titled "How Loud Can the Village Cock Crow?" and published in the collection of the same name, Afo Enterprises, 1996.